RAINBOW FALLS

~ A Mystery Novel ~

Keith Charles Koski

Ferconio Publishing
Portland, Oregon
2015

Ferconio Publishing
Portland, Oregon
www.SandraCopyeditor.com

Editor's Note and About the Author by Sandra Ferconio
Cover by Christopher Derrick / Unauthorized Media

Ebook ISBN: 978-0-6925713-4-7
Print ISBN: 978-0-9977247-1-4

"Every secret of a writer's soul,
every experience of his life,
every quality of his mind,
is written large in his works."

—Virginia Woolf

In memory of KCK,
who always carefully and thoughtfully tended his flock...
And dedicated to all the caregivers and flock-tenders
that grace our lives.

—Sandra Ferconio

TABLE OF CONTENTS

Editor's Note

This book was written by Keith Charles Koski around the year 1990. The manuscript was probably in the making, in the open file folders of his consciousness, for many years prior. Keith penned the manuscript for this book in the year following his departure as an executive with the Bic Corporation. After a year of working exclusively as an author and with the first draft of the manuscript complete, he pursued publication. But business called, so the manuscript did not get published at that time.

In 1997, the manuscript was updated and converted into a working file. From 1997 throughout the rest of his life, Keith continued to tinker and toil on his beloved manuscript. Reading was always his passion, and writing his elusive calling.

Rainbow Falls is an aggregation of all the characters he knew in his life—the war heroes and bushmen who fished and hunted with him as a child and young man; the fellow fishing guides, native Indians, and lodge owners and guests he came to know guiding in the Northwest Territories during summer breaks from university; and the business associates, executives, and advertising geniuses he hired and engaged during the fifteen years that he worked his way from a salesman in the prairies of Saskatchewan, Canada, to vice president of North America with the Bic Corporation. This book also reflects the larger-than-life nature of the author. Keith's perceptions, beliefs, life stories, and lessons he learned are sprinkled throughout this book.

During the publishing process of this manuscript, great care was taken to retain the original concept, theme, story structure, character development, and authentic voice of the author. Geographic and cultural biases characteristic of life in a small town in northern Ontario in the 1980s have also been retained for authenticity. This is his book, as he wrote it.

I owe a special thanks to Cathleen Small, freelance copyeditor and instructor at UC Berkeley Extension, for her patience, guidance, and extraordinary attention to detail. Her editorial assistance, wise counsel and friendly encouragement were essential to transforming the author's well-written manuscript into a smartly polished novel. Her delightful wit often brought a smile to my face, and her passion for preserving the author's authentic voice comfort to my heart. Thank you, Cathleen.

Sandra Ferconio, editor
October 15, 2015

CHAPTER 1

Jackpine Keating stared at the piece of paper in front of him while drubbing it with his pen, as if he were trying to force reluctant words out of the pen. As chief of police of Rainbow Falls (population 1,475) the volume of paperwork was not overwhelming, but the little he had to do was the bane of his existence. It was the only flaw in an otherwise perfect job. He could always pick up the phone and call, but Jackpine believed that for something serious, a letter was more impactful. After a few more taps of his stupid pen against the pad finally resolved the blockage, he decided to at least commit the salutation to paper. "Dear Boone," was too formal and "Hi Boone," too casual. He perfected it on the third try, beginning his letter with "Boone." He was able to continue. "You haven't been up to see us all summer, and it's getting late in the season." In fact, by early October tourist season and fishing season were pretty well finished. The town would enjoy a little resurgence in hunting season and then be dormant until spring when the cycle repeated itself. "Fishing is still good, and there's a lot of partridge this year." He was conscious of putting the *g* on fishin'. He had dropped all meaningless *g*'s from his oral vocabulary many years ago. "Now that I have some help, I have a lot of time for fishing and hunting." Reviewing the letter, Jackpine felt it was a little better. At least he had written something, but it sounded too frivolous to make a man like Alistair Boone drop everything in his busy schedule and come fifteen hundred miles from New York to Rainbow Falls. Jackpine needed the sage advice of his friend Boone.

A few more punishing slams of pen against paper brought a stronger closing. "It's important you come." Now completed, he added, "Regards, Jackpine."

Fifteen years of police work had honed his instincts to the point where he knew when all was not what it appeared to be. Perhaps if his police career had been spent somewhere other than a small, remote town in the wilderness of northwestern Ontario, he would have developed more deductive skills and systematic approaches to accompany his gut instincts—but that was not the case.

Until recently, Jackpine's staff had consisted of a secretary, receptionist, dispatcher, purchasing agent, and coffee maker: all embodied in the person of the capable Mrs. Inez Mahoney. Jackpine had doubled his support staff when he enlisted Big Paul Desroches as the town's first full-time constable. Neither of them was ever really busy. Very little happened in Rainbow Falls, and most of what did happen fell within the ample boundaries of Jackpine's interpretation of the law.

The most frequent potential crime was the tendency of some of the citizenry to overindulge in the bars at the Rainbow Falls Hotel or the Legion. Jackpine's modus operandi was usually to follow, or in some cases to drive, the overimbiber home. A cab was a viable alternative; but since the nearest taxi was forty-five miles away in Blackwater, it was hardly practical. Jackpine did not want drunks trying to walk home in twenty degree below zero weather—in the summer he was more tolerant.

Occasionally there were brawls in the bar at the hotel requiring Jackpine or Paul. There was seldom trouble in the Legion. Most members were World War II veterans and too long of tooth to be rambunctious. There had been a series of problems with a rowdy crew from Polarex (a mining exploration company) camped near town, but they would soon be closing up shop for the winter.

Jackpine was called upon to settle domestic disputes now and then. He investigated the odd theft and occasionally had to deal with a shoplifter. He would get involved with kids' pranks if they entailed vandalism. Although not in his job description, most people turned to Jackpine to arbitrate civil disagreements, with both parties usually agreeing that Jackpine's opinion would be binding.

There was a one-cell jail in the police station, but Jackpine only used it when necessary. He had to remove files, office supplies, guns, and the watercooler before he could incarcerate anyone. He also had to arrange for the Rainbow Falls Hotel to deliver meals to an inmate, which presented two problems. The first was fiscal; meals were charged to his operating budget, which was stretched with the hiring of Paul Desroches. The second was logistics; the hotel usually could not spare anyone for delivery, so Paul, Inez, or Jackpine would have to go and pick up the meal.

Crime did not rear its ugly head very often in Rainbow Falls. The people knew Jackpine's rules, and for the most part they respected the rules as much as they respected the man behind them. They knew that behind the easygoing demeanor and the liberal but practical laws, Jackpine Keating was a man of strong convictions, and at forty-two years of age, he was still as fast as the rapids above the Falls and as strong as the North Wind in January.

Jackpine had sealed the letter to his friend when a second thought on the urgency of the situation prompted him to remove the letter from the envelope and proceed instead to the fax machine. As Jackpine was transmitting the letter, Big Paul Desroches lumbered into the office.

Paul Desroches should have been six foot seven inches and 250 pounds, but God, continuing to experiment with the species, had compressed his 250 pounds into a five-foot-ten-inch frame. Everything about Paul Desroches was big. His body was anchored with huge feet for which no width had been established by the shoe trade. If mutants like Paul ever went from the genetic-experimental lab to standard-production models, they might formalize the sizing as a 16EEEE. His legs were like pistons on a steam locomotive. The forty-five-inch waist only looked small because it supported a big barrel chest and a mammoth set of shoulders. Paul's body got bigger as it went up. There was no neck; his shoulders met a huge head the size of a state-fair pumpkin. His globe was covered with a mat of tight curly brown hair. It was such a Herculean task to shear this vast expanse that Elmer at the Rainbow Falls Barber Salon had charged Paul as an adult since he was six, and as a rite of manhood, on Paul's twelfth birthday, he began to charge double the adult price. Now, at age twenty-five, it was only Paul's status as town "constabull" (the locals had inevitably abridged constable) that had silenced Elmer's demand to raise the price to three times. It had reached near event status; there was usually an audience on hand to witness the monthly shearing of Big Paul Desroches.

His brown eyes were not as big proportionately as the rest of his head. They sparkled amiably, but not intensely, hinting modest-to-average cerebral powers. His nose was short, but as broad as a punch-drunk boxer's who had been in the ring a decade longer than prudence dictated. Below the nose was a wide jack-o'-lantern mouth that was usually smiling. The big head leaned forward as if the supporting frame was weary from the heavy load. In the winter, when Paul wore the police-issue buffalo coat, he looked considerably similar to the animals from whose carcasses the hides were taken.

Paul eased his frame into the oversized chair at his desk and turned slightly toward Jackpine. Being neckless, his head did not pivot well. "Good morning, Chief, Mrs. Mahoney; got six for $420," Paul boomed in his normal speaking voice. This shorthand was clearly understood by Jackpine. To solve his budget woes and to be able to afford Paul, he had invested in a radar device and a car with an oversized engine. Paul approached this mundane police work with relish. Paul had nabbed six speeders and garnered

$420 for the town coffers. He proceeded to make the entries in the log before turning over the cash and checks to Mrs. Mahoney.

Rainbow Falls was situated on a secondary highway, missing the more extensive traffic on Highways 11 and 17, the two primary routes through northwestern Ontario north of Lake Superior. Some traffic was generated because the road through Rainbow Falls connected the two major arteries. There was a posted forty-five kilometers per hour (roughly thirty miles per hour) speed zone through town, which heretofore had never been respected. Jackpine had accomplished two objectives: radar was keeping streets safe, and revenue was flowing.

"No runners, though," said Paul sadly. The day was not complete unless a motorist refused to stop for Paul's outstretched paw, allowing Paul a merry chase. Jackpine had given Paul the hot car and sent him on a driving course offered by the Ontario Provincial Police. Paul's standard operating procedure called for him to radio the OPP when he had a runner, but Paul never followed the procedure. He chased them down. The highway near the bridge where Paul parked was marred with burnt rubber and strewn with loose gravel from Paul's enthusiastic pedal-to-the-metal chases. No one had ever escaped. Paul had a fast car, a tank full of gas, and a hell-bent-for-leather dedication to pursuit. The voices of discretion and safety were muted by the blaring sirens. The faster they fled, the higher the fine.

Jackpine normally listened to an in-depth report of Paul's crime-busting fundraisers, but today his thoughts were elsewhere. He was thinking of the death of Desmond Lesmontaignes. Desmond was a good kid. Jackpine had known him all his life. He was planning to become a mechanic like his brother Nelson. He had just returned from Blackbear Point Lodge where he had been employed as a fishing guide all summer. Most lodges closed in September, but the new owner at Blackbear had kept a skeleton staff to serve the few enthusiasts willing to fish in cold weather.

5

Desmond's body had been found lodged against one of the pylons of a bridge over Muskrat River. His overturned canoe was found downstream. The OPP (this was their jurisdiction) surmised that he had been out fishing when his canoe overturned. They were having an autopsy performed, but Jackpine knew there would not be anything conclusive other than a verification of death by drowning. They would also confirm sobriety. Jackpine knew Desmond didn't drink.

The OPP were not taking Jackpine's questions seriously. Why would a kid who has been fishing twelve hours a day, seven days a week, all summer want to go fishing when he got home? Why would Desmond fish in the Muskrat River when he knew fifty better places? These questions bothered Jackpine. He was convinced that he was missing something. He had also argued that Desmond was an Ojibway Indian who had grown up on the banks of a river and been in canoes all his life. People like Desmond Lesmontaignes did not fall out of canoes.

There had been three other deaths in the past few weeks. Jackpine had questioned each of them. The OPP was satisfied that all were accidents. Boone was certainly not a detective, but Jackpine looked forward to enlisting the support of the razor-sharp mind of the analytical Alistair Boone.

* * * * * *

Alistair Boone charged down the hall. On the way by the fax machine his left hand reached out and tore the latest collection of fifteen or twenty faxes from the tray. One step later, his right hand grabbed the raincoat preferred by his secretary. A fast "Thanks, Linda, back by three or three-thirty at the latest, tell Nigel I'll call at five, that's ten o'clock London time. Get his home number, bye." Boone stabbed the elevator button. He gave it a few more pokes to hurry it up. As Boone swept out onto 57th Street, Pork Chop reached quickly to open the back door of the blue Lincoln stretch limo and managed to open it just before Alistair leaped into the seat.

"Grand Central, Poke. I'll be twenty-five minutes. Park at the Hyatt, and I'll meet you there." How his driver had gotten his nickname, Boone had never really been able to determine. Boone had shortened the name in half to "Poke," which was synonymous with pork in the vernacular of Pork Chop Miller.

Boone knew that a fresh shipment of Olympia oysters had arrived at the Oyster Bar at Grand Central, and he thought he would partake of a few dozen of the delectable crustaceans before lunch. He had to meet an investment banker to sign some papers. They had agreed to meet at the Oyster Bar. He thought two dozen wouldn't impair his appetite for lunch, since they were small. The oysters and his Bombay and tonic arrived at the same time. A touch of lemon, a little dollop of fresh horseradish, and it was time for gastronomical ecstasy. The banker declined both a drink and the oysters. Boone signed the documents, and the banker left. After the last oyster and the last sip of his Bombay, Boone stood up, put the cash for the check and the tip on the table, and hurried out to rendezvous with Pork Chop. He hadn't waited for the check. As a man who had enjoyed the same haunts for many years, he always knew within a dollar or two what the check would be.

He was on time to meet Adam Klein at HSF for dim sum; in fact, Adam was just paying a cabbie when he arrived. Boone had been wondering how Adam was going to react to the news. He and Adam had been doing business for years. Boone's ideas had enhanced Adam's reputation as a marketing and sales promotion guru, and Boone had made a lot of money over the years selling ideas, concepts, and products through Adam Klein. Adam was a senior vice president in charge of sales promotion for a major advertising agency. In the early 1980s, agencies found traditional growth opportunities stifled. With many companies controlling costs by paring ad budgets, it was no longer possible to go into an

7

account with the big idea and get the ad budget doubled to really blast the message.

Agencies coped with the changes. They began buying each other and expanded into businesses that, although related to advertising, were considered beneath them. Fields of endeavor, such as public relations and sales promotion, became attractive for the traditional advertising agency; the definition of a full-service agency suddenly took on a much wider meaning.

Alistair Boone and Boone Promotions had done very well maneuvering the ship through the rocky shoals of these turbulent times. Boone Promotions had stayed small, around $10 million in sales per year. Although he had four salespeople (promotion specialists, they were called) and an office staff of five, the driving force in creativity and in the energy applied to execution was Alistair Boone himself. He had been meeting for the last three weeks with all of his longtime clients to tell them his news. Adam had been out of town; this was the last meeting on Boone's list.

As soon as they were seated at their table, two Tsingtao beers appeared with frosty glasses and the waiter said, "Dim Sum, of course, Mr. Boone, correct?"

"Correct," replied Boone as they waited for the onslaught of little appetizer dishes that would constitute the meal. Boone and Adam both enjoyed the Hong Kong tea-room-style service. Adam's office was nearby, and he came here often. Boone's office was farther, but he wandered far afield for culinary excellence. A large selection of small tidbits were presented and each diner chose which and how many of each. The normal procedure was to stack the empty dishes on the table, and at the end of the feast the waiter would calculate the check by counting the number of empty dishes. Boone's appetite precluded the normal accounting method. Empty dishes were whisked away a few times during the repast to be tallied elsewhere.

They chatted over an assortment of dumplings, some crab claws, some sticky rice, and a few Tsingtaos. "You know Boone, they should put a sign in each of your thirty or forty favorite restaurants saying, 'Our restaurant is frequented by Alistair Boone.' That endorsement should double any restaurant's business," Adam pronounced while endeavoring to get the last succulent bit of meat from the crab claw. Most of Adam's favorite restaurants, this one included, had been introduced to him by Boone.

"That's kind of you, Adam. Unfortunately, my waistline indicates my propensity for good food. But if a restaurant doubled its business it would be too crowded, number one, and number two, the quality would probably go down, so I wouldn't frequent it anymore. Plus, I might not habituate these environs much longer."

"Sure, Boone, you're going to leave New York—and pigs can fly!"

"Adam, I'm serious. I've sold Boone Promotions—lock, stock, and calculator—to a company based in England, Whitby & Strothers, PLC. They're big in sales promotion in the UK and they want a foothold in America."

"Do they get Alistair Boone with Boone Promotions?" Adam queried.

"No, they wanted me. Without me in it, the price came down; but it's still a very generous offer," Boone stated.

"But there is no Boone Promotions; there is only Alistair Boone. You are the company. They are either pompous asses or very naive. Boone, it's you my man. You think up the idea for a giveaway at a fast-food chain, you sell millions of 'em at $0.10 each, and it's you who arranges to get them made in Taiwan for $0.03. No one comes close to your reliability. It's you and none of your so-called organization."

Adam was shocked at what he was hearing. Warhorses like Boone didn't bail out, especially in their prime.

"Adam, do me one favor. Don't approach these guys with a closed mind. I want you to give them a fair shot. They seem to know their stuff. Plus some of these young guys working for me are good, real good. They're bright, creative, and full of energy. They wouldn't be with me if they weren't."

"OK, Boone, I will give them a chance. But I'm flabbergasted. What are you going to do? You're not getting out of the business?"

"One at a time. First, I don't know what I'm going to do. But I live at such a fast pace, I can't keep it up forever…and I can't seem to function any slower. I've been trying to slow down, and it doesn't work. The doctors tell me I better slow down or I'll have big trouble in a few years." Boone paused to inhale a few dumplings. This conversation was slowing down his dim summing. "Plus, I'm out of shape, and it's getting worse, not better. And secondly, I'm out of the business. Part of the deal is that I don't compete. I'm out for ten years, which is a lifetime in this game."

Adam looked up at Boone. He remembered the bright, cocky, young world-buster who first called on him years ago. He remembered wondering what a Yale MBA (half established as a sports agent) was doing hocking pens, Frisbees, sweepstakes, and such things. He remembered the answer, too: the excitement of living deal to deal…of creating business through your own ideas. And he saw the bright, young, athletic-looking big guy become the old fat guy. The tailored English suit didn't hide the big belly anymore, and the wrinkles were a sign of twenty years of sixteen-hour days, and eating, drinking, and smoking Monte Cristo cigars to excess.

After lunch Boone returned to his office. He still hadn't looked at the faxes he had collected earlier. He spent a few hours on the telephone, tying up the last loose ends. He felt better knowing that all his major clients would give these new owners a fair shot. At five o'clock he phoned Nigel Fitzwater, his British attorney, and confirmed that the money had been deposited into his account. It was a done deal.

He skimmed through the faxes, details on orders and shipments of products mostly. Then he got to the fax from his old buddy Jackpine. So Jackpine had some dilemma. You had to know Jackpine to determine that from the fax. He would go. Why not? For the first time in his adult life, his schedule was not dictated by business concerns.

Boone called Jackpine and told him he was coming. As usual, Jackpine wanted Boone to stay at his place. As usual, Boone deferred and asked Jackpine to book room eighteen at the Rainbow Falls Hotel. Boone did not like to leave such things to chance. Since he went to the Falls on a regular basis, he had inspected all of the rooms, finding number eighteen to be the best. It was also the best room for Inez Mahoney to come to and go from without being seen. He had last seen Inez in June; he had taken her on a Caribbean cruise. He could not get the enchanting Inez off his mind. His weekly calls to her had become daily calls over the last few months.

Jackpine had sounded troubled. He could help Jackpine, see Inez, and maybe decide what he was going to do to occupy himself. He had his secretary book a nine o'clock flight from La Guardia to Toronto and the morning flight to Thunder Bay. Boone raced out of the office. He would have to hurry to get home and pack and get to La Guardia. He didn't mind. He was always in a hurry.

Boone arrived at La Guardia ninety minutes before his scheduled departure. He hadn't been to Toronto in a while. He remembered the scheduled flight time had been an hour and a few minutes. Now it was scheduled at an hour and a half. Either the city of Toronto had been moved, which he doubted, since an event of that proportion would have caught his eye in the *Times*, or the airlines, under scrutiny for late arrivals, had conveniently stretched the scheduled time to allow for snafus caused by heavy traffic and their own employees' lack of dedication and motivation to adhere to schedules. He knew it was the latter, because since this latest "innovation," one airline after another had launched print campaigns bragging unabashedly about their on-time percentages.

In fact, when Boone had noticed this trend evolving, he had designed an attractive mailing piece that, upon opening, a flag popped out of saying "When Time Counts—Count on Us." Inside the box was a watch with the airline's logo. The watch for the top one hundred corporate clients was a Rolex, five thousand Seikos for tier-two corporate clients, and five hundred thousand no-name watches for other clients.

The first two airlines he had pitched with the idea had rejected it. One had said, "Good idea, Boone, but our promotional budget is exhausted." The other had said, "Doesn't fit within our corporate marketing philosophy at this time" (which meant they were still having problems being on time and didn't want to emphasize the issue). The third presentation was to the airline that he had really wanted to sell to in the first place. The first two were "cannon fodder" to hone his pitch— not that he would have refused the order.

On the first two calls, he had noticed that the Rolexes had held the buyers' attention. Whether dealing with a CEO, a vice president of marketing, or a vice president of sales promotion, to Alistair Boone they were the buyer and he was the seller. By the third call, Alistair was ready. Instead of handmade mock-ups, he had made five of the real mailers. They would only be $0.40 each when he made five hundred thousand, but these five had cost $6,200. By now, in his presentation, the Rolexes were not $3,000, they were free. He would charge a little more for the cheap ones and give the Rolex watches free.

Alistair knew he wasn't dealing with babes in the woods. The airline marketing department knew they would be paying for the watches somewhere, but marketing was built on the illusion of free, and it had as much magic with the wise practitioners of the trade, surprisingly, as it had with the public in general. Boone had closed the sale, and within eight weeks the finished mailing pieces had been sent.

The secret to the deal had been the five hundred thousand no-name watches. Every detail had been priced competitively, but by sourcing the watches in Taiwan himself, he was able to net a profit of $1 per watch. Even better, most of the $500,000 had been made by the trading company in Grand Cayman that sourced the watches. Of course, the trading company was owned by one Alistair Boone. He was even able to show the airline the invoice from the trading company to prove that he wasn't taking an exorbitant "up charge" on the watches.

Alistair Boone moved at a fast pace, and he noticed everything going on around him as he moved through his world. Boone was mindful of change; in his business, change meant opportunity. All of his clients knew that Alistair made a lot of money selling programs to them, but none of them begrudged the money because Boone's ideas increased sales and enhanced their reputations and careers.

Alistair was going to miss his businesses. But after twenty years, the ideas weren't coming as quickly, and most of the buyers in the LBO era there focused on building the bottom line for the quarter, instead of investment spending on promotion and advertising to stimulate long-term growth.

With these thoughts in mind, he walked past his gate, all the way to the end of the terminal. As alert as Boone was, he was also paradoxically absent-minded, forever walking past his destination or droving past his freeway exit. He daydreamed through Broadway plays, where he couldn't remember a thing that had occurred on stage. Alistair never stopped to smell the roses. But he stopped by the roses to wonder why they were planted there, who chose those certain colors, and what options did they consider for the money that the roses cost.

He returned to his gate and boarded the plane with three minutes to spare.

During the flight Boone pretended to read the *Wall Street Journal* to keep the man in the next seat at conversational bay. He reflected on the dismantling of his mini-empire. He had sold his graphic-design firm and his marketing-research operation to the general manager of each company. He had helped them arrange financing with investment bankers. It had been easy. Both companies were growing profitably, and Boone's selling price had been more than fair. The managers were competent professionals in their fields. Boone's philosophy had been to recruit top managers, develop the goals and strategies with them, and then get out of the way and let the managers manage. He had met with them after each quarter to review the results. It had paid off; the businesses prospered.

The manager of his incentive travel company had not been willing to accept the financial burden of ownership, so Boone had sold the company to a competitor. He had negotiated a top-dollar selling price. He had sold the mail-order office-supply business to a group of outside investors. Boone was sure the general manager had been skimming money from the business, but he had been unable to prove it. As a payback, Boone had not offered the business for sale to the manager with the same sweetheart deal that he had given the others.

Boone Promotions had been the last to go. Selling the company had been the hardest thing Boone had ever done. Harder than walking into the empty house the day his wife left him. Their relationship had deteriorated to the point where divorce was inevitable, but it was the sense of failure that burdened Boone.

Acceptance of failure was a talent Boone had not developed, never having practiced it.

The other businesses had been acquired. Boone Promotions had been built by Alistair Boone, step by step, deal by deal. He had never relinquished control. As the company grew, Boone continued to be involved in every aspect of the operation. He had tried to back off from the sixteen-hour days and the relentless fast pace, but he had been unable to. Even his modest social life was interwoven with Boone Promotions. Except for Inez, Jackpine, and Janice Keating, all of his friends were either customers or suppliers to Boone Promotions.

Boone wasn't sure what he was going to do after his sojourn to Rainbow Falls, but he wanted to be alive and doing it in twenty years.

CHAPTER 2

Boone overnighted in Toronto and caught a late-morning, direct flight to Thunder Bay. Normally, he preferred the aisle seat for the extra legroom. Airplane seating arrangements were not designed to accommodate the Alistair Boones of the world, but on this flight he had requested a window seat on the right-hand side of the plane. The views of Lake Huron, Lake Superior, and the rugged Canadian Shield were spectacular—the pristine boreal forest charged into the immense blue glory of Superior, the ocean lake. Coming into Thunder Bay, he thought the Air Canada pilot had decided to land on the Sleeping Giant Mountain, but the pilot cruised over the top of the Giant's head and into the Thunder Bay airport.

The car rental company did not have a full-size car available without advance reservation. It took Boone fifteen minutes of hard work to convince the overpowered clerk that a Lincoln Town Car was available. After gaining the concession, it took only five minutes longer to secure the Town Car at the rate of a midsize car. On his way out of Thunder Bay, he stopped at a few souvenir stores. He wanted to find something new and interesting for Janice Keating to sell in her store, Northland Crafts. New ideas did not come often to the souvenir trade, and Boone was unable to find anything appropriate.

He stopped at a sporting goods store to buy a fishing rod. Boone had rods at home for almost every species and size of fish, but rod cases meant checked bags, and Alistair Boone was always a man in a hurry, with no time to waste waiting for luggage.

It was almost three hours after leaving Thunder Bay that he saw the sign proclaiming "Rainbow Falls pop.1,475." The next sign was a weather-tested collage announcing the presence of Lions, Kiwanis, and a branch of the Royal Canadian Legion, followed by a billboard for "Rainbow Falls Hotel" with bullet points outlining the reasons why a traveler should be compelled to check in: "Color TV, Home Cooking, $18 and up." Boone was familiar with the establishment, always staying there on his trips to the Falls. He started to think of what the sign should say to really attract customers. He was snapped out of his reverie by the appearance of a new sign. Things never changed much in Rainbow Falls, so Boone was quick to notice something different. The big sign said "Speed Limit 45 kph." with "Radar Enforced" underneath. The Canadian government had decided, in the 1970s, to test the resilience of the people by adapting the unfamiliar metric lexicon. Now, in the 1990s, only Americans were confused. Boone chuckled. Jackpine had told him he now had radar, a fast police car, and Constable Paul Desroches. Boone saw the sign as vintage Jackpine, giving speeders a more than adequate warning to satisfy his own sense of fair play. Fairness and integrity were such to Jackpine that Boone had once told him that his gravestone should read "Here lies Oscar John Keating…He Played Fair."

Boone remembered the sign that had been erected in 1973 much to the embarrassment and consternation of the modest Jackpine. It read "Rainbow Falls Home of JACKPINE KEATING," complete with a huge die-cut picture of Jackpine in his New York Rangers uniform. Jackpine had never considered being a defenseman for the New York Rangers to be an accomplishment of such Homeric proportion. He thought it was a good way to put away a nest egg for the future, which it turned out to be, and a way to see some of the continent before he settled down in the Falls.

The nest egg that Jackpine had been able to accumulate he attributed to Boone. They had met on a double date during Jackpine's year in the minor leagues in New Haven, while Boone was at Yale. They had become fast friends, even though their upbringings were Poles apart. Jackpine had served as his own agent in negotiating with Rangers management until he met Boone. He realized he was a neophyte in these negotiations, but he trusted his own common sense more than he had trusted any of the glib urbane agents that had tried to sign him. Rather than the customary percentage of salary, Boone worked for free pizza and fishing trips. The pizza had to be Pepe's, and the fishing had to be in the Falls. Jackpine had delivered many times on both demands. Jackpine had been about to sign a two-year contract, which Boone had converted to a three-year contract at fifty percent more money per season. Before he graduated from the MBA program at Yale, Boone used his work negotiating Jackpine's contract to springboard himself into becoming a bona fide sports agent, securing five NHL players, three MLB players, and two NFL players into his stable. The new recruits had, of course, paid percentages of salary. Jackpine was grateful to Boone, and Boone was thankful for the opportunity Jackpine had presented him.

Although it was lucrative, Boone had not enjoyed being a sports agent. He felt parasitic earning a living from the sweat of another man's brow, and he did not subscribe to the established practice of negotiating contracts via the media. Soon after Jackpine's retirement, Boone had left the sports-agent business to form Boone Promotions, which became the nucleus of his future endeavors.

Jackpine's frequent requests to remove the sign had fallen on deaf ears. The town fathers were going to immortalize their native son and that was that. In February of 1980, seven long years after it was up, the sign mysteriously burned to the ground late one cold, dark night. Chief of Police Keating investigated and found no evidence of foul play. The Chief had been on duty that night and had not seen any evildoers in the vicinity. Perhaps, he had told the town council, which convened the next day to discuss the travesty, it was an act of God (a merciful God). By the time the billboard burnt, Jackpine had himself become a town father, and he was thus able to nip the idea of erecting a new monument in the proverbial bud. Only Janice Keating suspected that her husband had torched the sign.

Boone carefully observed the speed limit as he drove over the bridge and into the heart of downtown Rainbow Falls. He thought the other side of the bridge would be good cover for a cop, and sure enough as he glanced right he saw a police car with a mastodon-like head in it.

Boone stopped for a few minutes to view the craggy majesty of the Falls. The surging white water cascaded one hundred fifty feet, hurrying to get to Lake Superior. "Almost as high as Niagara Falls," locals proclaimed to anyone who would listen. At a width of three hundred feet, there were no claims of parity with the two thousand six hundred feet of Niagara's mighty Horseshoe Falls.

Rainbow Falls was rough, wild, and untamed, like all of the land the Blackwater River traversed. The surging raw power was harnessed, but not domesticated, by the electricity-generating turbines of Ontario Hydro. The often present rainbow was visible, but dim. Boone's eyes followed the course of the mystical protective arc. It seemed to Boone to end right about where Inez Mahoney's house was located. Boone parked in front of the police station and charged into the office. Seeing no sign of Jackpine and knowing Paul Desroches was on patrol, he bolted over to Mrs. Mahoney, almost knocking her over, and gave her a big kiss on the lips. "Inez, darling, you look better every time I see you!" Indeed it was true. He saw Inez Mahoney once or twice a year in the Falls and twice each winter on short vacations together. She seemed more attractive to Boone each time he saw her.

Inez Mahoney was a serious, no-nonsense, practical person, but when she laughed her whole face erupted in joy, and her big sea-green eyes sparkled. Her teeth were a little too large for her mouth, her rather thin lips accentuating them further, but the prominence of her teeth only enhanced the beauty of her smile (to Alistair Drayton Boone).

"Boone, honey! I've been so excited since Jackpine told me you were coming. We have to be quick. Jackpine was just on the radio; he's going to be here any minute. What time tonight?" Inez Mahoney's sense of propriety made them keep their romance a secret. "It's fine for you if everyone knows about us, but I have to live in this town," she always said. She had been widowed for fifteen years, and Boone was divorced, but she did not want to appear a trollop in the eyes of her peers.

Boone just had time to say, "About eleven thirty," when the door opened and Jackpine strolled in.

"Hey, ol' buddy. I wasn't expectin' you so soon!"

"Well, King of Rainbow Falls, you're looking good, Jackpine!"

They shook hands and sat down, chatting amiably while Jackpine sifted through a few messages on his desk. Finding nothing of importance, Jackpine stood up. "Let's head over to the house; I've got some 50 Ale on ice waitin' for us. We'll stop and get some two-inch, prime T-bones." Jackpine was not usually so specific, but he knew his friend. It could not just be beer; it had to be Labatt's 50 Ale, and on ice, not in the fridge. Not just any steak would do. Boone would badger poor Otto, the butcher, into finding prime cuts that Boone would personally supervise and critique as Otto carved the two inches. There was not much demand for prime aged beef in Rainbow Falls. Otto had been warned by Jackpine that Boone was coming, so he had some inventory on hand.

Jackpine thought it was much ado about nothing; a steak was a steak, and a beer was a beer. "You're pickin' out the steaks, you're pickin' out the veggies, and you're gonna cook supper. Otherwise you'll be criticizin' my technique."

"Not criticizing, Jackpine, merely offering suggestions to guide you to culinary vistas that your palate has yet to view. And don't forget condiments in order to turn the meal into an experience. Your larder only proffers ketchup, A-1 sauce, and a paltry selection of mediocre pickles."

"There's probably still some of the junk you bought last trip in the fridge, unless Janice has eaten it."

"It's a wonder that poor martyr has retained a shred of epicurean adventure after twenty years with Mr. Meat and Potatoes." It was a sign of their long and enduring friendship that Boone's taunting solicited a wide grin from Jackpine.

On the way out, Boone winked at Inez and mouthed, "Eleven thirty."

* * * * * *

They finished their late lunch, or early dinner, by four o'clock. Janice was at her store, Northland Crafts, and would not be home until seven. Jackpine had eaten everything on his plate, but he had not enjoyed the salad. That damn Boone had put anchovies in the salad, and he had tried to avoid the disgusting, salty little creatures.

"Something is on your mind besides fishing. What is it, Jackpine?" Jackpine was accustomed to Boone's abruptness.

"Let's go and try to catch some walleye, and we'll talk." Locals called the fish pickerel, but Jackpine used Boone's name for the species. Boone was just as accustomed to Jackpine's reticence. The Keatings lived beside a lake on the edge of town. That was not unusual in this area. Anyone who flew over northwestern Ontario would see a gigantic lake with millions of islands, instead of the reverse. Boone knew there were fish in the lake, but for some reason these outdoorsmen always had to take you to a better place. It always involved long rides over gut-wrenching gravel roads that could only qualify as roads under the most liberal definitions of the word. Boone knew he was in for trouble when

Jackpine headed for the four-wheel-drive Bronco instead of his car. Boone tried to drink a beer on the way, but it was so rough that foam kept jumping out of the bottle onto his hands and pants. Mercifully, the ride was over in fifteen minutes.

The lake was named Wabakimi. It looked to Boone like a hundred other lakes in the area, distinguishable only by its tongue-twisting Ojibway name. Boone had always wondered why they had never admitted the error of their ways and wiped the slate clean of these names, renaming them with good, old-fashioned, easy-to-remember, English names. Boone could never comprehend Jackpine's ability to keep all of these names in his head, and even more profound, with most of the lakes being mazes of islands and channels, how Jackpine could navigate with ease, even in the fog, and never seem to get lost. Jackpine swore he had never gotten lost but did admit to being temporarily misplaced a few times—once for twenty-four hours.

Jackpine, of course, had a boat and motor at the lake. Jackpine and Janice lived very modestly considering their ample bank account. They really only indulged in two kinds of luxuries. The first was travel. They always spent a month each winter at an exotic resort. Boone would sometimes join them for a few days and play golf with Jackpine. Boone was a devoted golfer, and Jackpine only played on his winter vacation. Boone had always somewhat resented that after a few days' practice, Jackpine's athletic prowess enabled him to shoot in the high seventies or low eighties, always beating Boone.

The other luxury that Jackpine enjoyed was boats and motors. On virtually every lake that could be driven to, and many that had to be flown into, there was a boat and motor belonging to Jackpine. Lakes that were accessible in summer by hiking had boats or canoes hauled in by snowmachine in the winter. They ran the gamut from his pride and joy, the twenty-eight-foot cruiser harbored in Blackwater for use on Lake Superior, to beat-up, old twelve-foot aluminums with clunky, old, but reliable Evinrudes and Johnsons. The cruiser was kept in a secure boathouse, but none of the others were locked in any way. Each of these boats and canoes had a sign nearby that stated: "Property of Chief of Police Keating. DO NOT USE without owner's permission." Permission was always granted to the local citizenry with four provisos: treat it like it was your own, use your own gas, clean it after use, and put it back where you found it. Not following one of these rules meant you did not borrow a boat in the future. Borrowing one without permission was not worth, on the remote chance you were caught, enduring the wrath of Jackpine Keating. He could be a good friend, but he was a very bad enemy.

After a short ride, Jackpine tossed out the anchor. He selected yellow jigs with frisky minnows for both of them. The walleye action was fast and furious. They each kept one under the limit, hoping for a big one. All were the same size, just under two pounds. The fish suddenly quit biting, and the impatient Boone wanted to try a new spot. "This here's as good as any place," replied Jackpine. Boone then wanted to change baits, but Jackpine insisted that yellow jigs and minnows were best.

"Somethin' peculiar has been goin' on, and I'm not rightly sure what." Jackpine wanted Boone's opinion on the crime wave that he thought had hit the Falls, and he wanted Boone's suggestions on ways to help save the town's major industry, Rainbow Falls Lumber, from sinking into insolvency. He wasn't sure Boone could help with either problem, but Alistair Boone was the most astute person Jackpine knew. He decided to start with the crimes—imagined or real.

Boone took his mind off apprehending a trophy walleye. He lit a Monte Cristo cigar and sat back in the boat to enjoy the crisp autumn air and the sunset, prepared to listen to Jackpine, anticipating a preamble before his friend got to the point.

"As you know, Boone, fishin' lodges are a big part of the economy around here, especially for the Reserve." Jackpine was referring to the Lac des Iles Indian Reservation fifteen miles west of town, normally called "des Iles" (pronounced "days eel") or just "the Reserve." Most of the guides at the many lodges were recruited from the population of Lac des Iles. "They close up between Labor Day and the end of September, dependin' on bookings. Some stay open for huntin', some don't. Anyway, the Falls is usually hoppin' in September when they have their summer's pay in their pockets. I expect trouble, but this year I got it with a capital T."

"Explain on," prodded Boone, hoping Jackpine was nearing his point.

"First it was a young native, name o' Jimmy Boucher, he killed himself in a car wreck up on Spruce Hill Road. He was pissed up; car went over a cliff." Spruce Hill was the name of a gold mine; it had been a major employer in the Falls, but it closed when the vein petered out. The only lasting legacy was the use-at-your-own-risk road stretching for twenty-six miles from the highway north to the abandoned mine.

"Excuse me for offending your sensibilities, Jackpine, but a shit-faced Indian wrecking a car is not unheard of around here. Is it?"

"No," Jackpine sighed, "unfortunately it isn't." The battle with alcohol was one that he and Chief Lawrence Musgrove of the Lac des Iles band had fought for many years, winning some battles, but losing many. "If young Boucher had died out on the Reserve, or on his way to or from town, or even if he got the wild-ass notion to go to Thunder Bay or even Blackwater, I could understand it. But he wasn't goin' west to the Reserve, or south to Blackwater or Thunder Bay. Spruce Hill is north of town. There's not one reason on God's green earth why that kid would be twenty miles up Spruce Hill Road in the middle of the night!"

"'Was he alone?'"

"No. Had a girl with him. I didn't know her. She wasn't from des Iles. They were both killed.

"Maybe they were going up there to screw around."

"There's a million places for that on the Reserve. No, there's not a reason I can think of."

"Peculiar, but probably nothing sinister," said Boone.

"Not in itself, maybe, but there's more. Few days later young Desmond Lesmontaignes was drowned. Now, Boucher was on his way to being a bum, but Desmond was a real good kid. His older brother, Nelson, really made something of himself—works as a diesel mechanic on construction. He's out in Alberta. Young Desmond wanted to follow in his footsteps. Would've too. They're gifted mechanically, all of them Lesmontaignes. Now, supposedly he's fishin' on the Muskrat River, falls out of his canoe and drowns."

"That can happen, can't it?"

"Yeah, but Desmond was almost born in a canoe; he was more comfortable in a canoe than most men are on land. I fished with the kid once. Second, there's a million better places to fish than that stretch of the Muskrat River this time of year. Desmond knew that as well as I do. Third, the kid was guiding all summer. The last thing a guy wants to do after a summer guiding is go fishing. Kid was a hustler. A bum like Boucher would take every day off he could and would avoid overtime, but Desmond worked twelve to fifteen hours a day, seven days a week, since June…. He's not goin' fishin', that's for sure."

"Did he drown? Were there marks on the body?"

"Sure, he drowned, and he was all beat up. That part of the Muskrat River is nasty; seems he got washed through four miles of white-water rapids. But that nitwit O'Toole won't even listen to me." He was referring to Sergeant William—not Bill, as he would be quick to correct you—O'Toole, who was in charge of the

Ontario Provincial Police detachment at Blackwater with jurisdiction for Lac des Iles.

"So, you don't think it was an accident," confirmed Boone. He realized that Jackpine knew the people, he knew the land, and fifteen years as a cop had honed his instincts. "But why would anyone kill these kids? What's the motive? Somebody around here got a Custer complex?" Boone smiled.

"C'mon, Boone, I'm serious.... Next one was a white guy, old White Horse Parker. White Horse was an old widower, probably a little crazy." Boone surmised from what Jackpine was saying that this guy was completely nuts. Small-town people could be very protective of their own. Behavior that would indicate lunacy to an outsider would be passed off as idiosyncratic by his peers. "He cooked at lodges in the summer and drew pogey all winter." (Pogey was the vernacular for collecting unemployment insurance benefits.) "You gotta figger he's happy! Busted his ass all summer; now he gets to live on easy street all winter. He's home for three days, his daughter drives in from Blackwater to see him, and there he is hangin' from the rafters in his basement with his tongue stuck out. Deader than a doornail."

Boone had always wondered what a doornail was. No one had ever been able to tell him. How could an inanimate object, never having lived, experience such a death? Not wanting to confuse the issue, Boone said, "Old guy, missed his wife, a little crazy—those things happen."

"Mrs. Parker's been dead over ten years. She 'as meaner than a spring bear—I don't think White Horse missed her much. He was a little wacky, I'll give you that, but no wackier than he was the day he shot the horse. It just don't add up, Boone."

"What's this about the horse? There're no horses in the middle of the bush!"

"There were some, years ago before my time, used horses in the bush camps to drag pulpwood to the river; those days they still drove pulp down the river. It was late fall, moose season. Some of the horses got out of the corral, I guess. The walkin' boss for the paper company heard shots. He walked over to take a look at the moose. He saw a dead white Clydesdale. An' there's ol' White Horse Parker, course he was young then, standin' there with a big shit-eatin' grin on his face, sayin', 'Got me an albino cow moose, will you look at that!' Story was all over town by nightfall. People 'round here don't forget things. He was White Horse Parker from that day forward. I wouldn't-a known his real name if I hadn't seen the death certificate."

Jackpine understood lifelong nicknames. He had been a tall, gangly kid. A Jackpine was a skinny, scraggly, unbecoming tree that grows in muskeg. His uncle had begun calling him Jackpine and the name stuck. And when your name is Oscar, you don't fight any kind of nickname very hard.

"Maybe White Horse got tired of carrying the burden of one little fuck-up forty years ago," Boone chuckled.

"Kind of funny, if you weren't the guy who had to go and cut him down!" Boone blushed with the reprimand.

"I'm sorry, Jackpine, I shouldn't laugh. Maybe you're right, maybe somebody killed him. Could be coincidence though, ten years' worth of tragedies all happening in a month?"

"Maybe, Boone, maybe. I'll give you one more coincidence. Jimmy, Desmond, and White Horse all worked the lodges. This summer they all worked at Blackbear Point Lodge!"

"So you think there's some kind of chicanery going on at the lodge, and someone slinked into town, killed four people, and slinked back to the lodge."

"You think I'm nuts too! That's what Janice tells me. She says I should go to New York and see you for a few days. She told me to go to Mickey Mantle's Restaurant and hang around with some old jock friends, and relive my golden days with the Broadway

Blueshirts. But somethin' stinks here, Boone...and I'm gonna' find out what!" Jackpine's voice rose.

Boone's demeanor changed instantly. His buddy was really wired over this. "Well, Jackpine, I'll go up to the lodge and fish for a few days. I'll see if anything sinister is going on. Does anyone know I'm in town yet?"

"Boone, you erupt into this town, you've been here four or five hours, and you've lectured Otto again on how to cut meat and about buying quality. You told him that his German sausage was the 'wurst' in town and pissed him off. He wouldn't-a caught your joke if I didn't explain. You lectured Tony at the grocery store on merchandising the produce section and ordered him to stock Belgian endive. When I stopped for gas, you gave Phil at the Esso a plan to double his business by giving away encyclopedias." Jackpine pretended to be smoking a Monte Cristo and using it as a pointer, imitating Boone, "Just think about it, Phil, you will lend a helping hand in education, twice as many kids will go to college, and you'll make twice as much money. Think about it, Phil! Probably get better pricing from Esso too; you'd be buying full truckloads of gas instead of paltry half-trucks. And your mechanic...look at him, Phil, he's loafing, nothing to do! He's costing you money, Phil; he is an asset, an unused asset! You need a plan to make the sweat roll off his brow and money roll into both your pockets! Work him ten hours a day, Phil! He'll be happier! No one likes sitting on their ass watching a clock tick, Phil. The business is out there waiting for you, Phil! Promote. Promote. Promote!" Jackpine slammed a fist into his hand, Boone-like. "Free oil change with a tune-up, free fifteen-point inspection. You gotta give to get in this world! Use your head, Phil; that's not a turnip sitting on your shoulders. Be a salesman, Phil, not an order taker!" Jackpine ran out of gas. Imitating Boone for a two-minute tirade was exhausting; he couldn't imagine being Boone for a day. That was, give or take, what Boone had told Phil in the few minutes it had taken to fill Jackpine's tank.

"You forgot signage, Jackpine. Get the idea in front of the people. The word FREE in big letters. Nice and simple, easy to comprehend. To..." Jackpine interrupted. You couldn't bait Boone. Boone would talk all night about Phil's Esso—or any other business, for that matter. He wanted to finish what he had been saying to Phil before Jackpine had dragged him away from the mesmerized petroleum pumper.

"No, Boone. You don't drift into town incognito. I'm sure everyone knows now that Alistair Boone is in town. When you leave this town every business has some kind of promotion running, and the *Gazette* loves you. They double their ad pages for a few weeks until everything quiets down and gets back to normal. People from the lodge come to town all the time. There could be trouble if I'm right and they learn my best friend is up at their place."

"So, they're still open?"

"Yeah, I guess. Still some people up there, so I guess they wouldn't refuse a booking."

"I'll go in disguise. We'll pretend I'm going off canoeing by myself for a few days. Get Punkinhead Paul to meet me and drive me to Thunder Bay. We'll hide my canoe and a different person will appear at the lodge, someone the opposite of Alistair Boone."

"Don't call Paul 'Punkinhead.' He's sensitive!"

"Of course he is. He should be. Got a head like a fucking buffalo! Never seen anything like it."

"Can you carry this off, Boone?" asked Jackpine, concerned.

"Sure, I'll be a bona fide American sportsman. Last minute chance for R & R. Coming to experience the tonic of the Canadian wilderness and catch a trophy northern pike. I'll color my hair, drop the trademark Monte Cristo, get a pair of glasses—Harvey Meek from Shadow Creek—I'll think up a proper alias. I'll be back in a few days, and I'll either confirm that something is rotten in the state of Denmark or that it was all just coincidence." The sun had gone down, and it was getting cold. "Let's get home before I freeze my ass off!"

CHAPTER 3

Inez Mahoney sat at her desk, sipping a cup of hot coffee. She was having trouble concentrating on her work. Fortunately, she did not have very much work to do. Boone had assured her that there was no reason for her to be concerned about his sojourn to Blackbear Point Lodge, but she remained deeply troubled. Jackpine may have had problems enlisting converts to his sinister theory, but Inez Mahoney was not among the skeptics. She had seen the new owner of the lodge, Danny Golias, a few times, and her instincts told her he was a dangerous, evil man. That Golias had recruited those two reprobates, Bear Sawchuk and Flip Lafontaine, to work at the lodge only fueled the fires of her concern. Neither one of them had done a day's work in his life. Pushing drugs and bootlegging liquor did not qualify as work in the eyes of Inez Mahoney. Boone and Jackpine had cooked up this harebrained scheme between them, and she was unable to discourage Boone.

Here she was, almost forty and head over heels in love like a giddy schoolgirl for the first time in her life. She had thought she loved Pat, her first and only husband. She had gotten pregnant, and they were married three days before her eighteenth birthday. It had been fifteen years since Pat died. He had been a truck driver for Kenogami Paper: paid by the trip for hauling pulpwood from the bush to feed the hungry paper mill in Blackwater. The real highballing daredevils made four trips a day, and Pat was a charter member of that fraternity. He crashed head on with a fraternity brother, both of them cheating on a curve, both killed instantly. The romance had evaporated from their marriage long before the accident. As they stepped from high school graduation through the portals of the future, their love had stayed behind, hidden forever in the hallowed halls of Blackwater High. Having finally found true love, she could not bear the thought of losing Boone.

Her daughter, Jennifer, had graduated from University with a Bachelor of Nursing degree in June. She was now working at a hospital in Winnipeg, contemplating marriage. Soon, Inez would be a grandmother-in-waiting. The thought made her seem much older than she felt.

Paul Desroches sat at his desk pecking away at a police report. Concentration furrowed his brow as he did battle with his mortal enemy, the word processor, and its fiendish ally, the English language.

Paul had apprehended two twelve-year-olds "makin' ravens" at the town dump last evening. They had a fishing rod baited with a wiener to catch seagulls. When they got one they spray-painted it black, cut the fishing line, and let it go. The gull would try to rejoin the flock. The other gulls, predictably, attacked the "raven" in their midst, driving it away, much to the glee of the two boys. Paul had also thought it was hilarious. He told Inez the funny story and was surprised when she reprimanded him for not caring about the abused gull. Inez thought that if the poor gull lived through the beating, it would develop a severe personality disorder, its psyche remaining scarred long after the paint had washed off. Paul had endured another tirade when he replied, "I bet those black gulls are screwed up. They'd be the ones that fly around shittin' on people's heads." Paul had, in fact, been the target for such fecal air raids numerous times. Living among a large seagull population and having a huge head, like Paul Desroches, getting shit upon was a statistical inevitability.

It was a chastised Paul Desroches who was now glumly finishing the report. The abuse of gulls was a serious offense, but Paul had decided not to mention it in the report, letting the boys off with a severe tongue-lashing. Under questioning, the boys had admitted stealing the two cans of spray paint and the wieners.

Paul had assigned them twenty hours each of sweeping floors at the hardware store as penance for the paint; the wieners, being of less value, had earned them ten hours of toil at the grocery store.

Paul finished the report and the coffee then prepared to leave. He had to rendezvous with Mr. Boone and was glad to get away from Mrs. Mahoney. He knew she would give him hell again if he stuck around. He did not really know what "flippant and sadistic" meant, but it had sounded like she was cursing at him.

Boone met Jackpine at the boat launch on the river a mile south of town. Boone was enjoying the elaborate subterfuge. He placed his bag and his fishing tackle in the canoe, and Jackpine steadied it as he got in. He was wearing a vest that Jackpine had given him over a heavy wool shirt. There were three Monte Cristo cigars in his shirt pocket. If he was going to give them up for a few days, he planned to puff on one all the way to Thunder Bay.

He said good-bye to Jackpine and paddled out to catch the current. He drifted down the river for two miles, where the highway crossed the river. He had just gotten the canoe hidden in the underbrush when Paul Desroches pulled up. Boone scampered up the hill and got into the cruiser. Paul got out as Boone got in, "Morning, Mr. Boone."

"Where you going, Paul?"

"Chief says you're a city fella, wouldn't know how to hide a canoe. Sure 'nuff, I can see the canoe from here!" he proclaimed with satisfaction. He seldom tasted triumph in his dealings with Alistair Boone. "I'll be right back." When the job was completed, the canoe was invisible. Paul lumbered up the embankment to the car.

Boone puffed contentedly on a fresh Monte Cristo. He considered this whole plot nothing more than an exercise to allay Jackpine's suspicions. Nevertheless, once involved in the game, he planned to play his hand with Tom Sawyer-like enthusiasm. His secretary in New York had called the lodge. They were dropping two guests off in Thunder Bay and would pick up "Jack Patterson" for a two-day trip. Mr. Patterson would have to pay for four days, their minimum stay. Normally they flew out of Minneapolis but they had a drop-off in Thunder Bay. This was his lucky day, they said. It would prove to be far from the truth.

Paul pulled out a cigarette and lit it. "I didn't know you smoked, Paul."

"I don't. Least not anywhere around the Chief or Mrs. Mahoney. Most guys go to work with their peers. With me, it's like goin' into work with your mother and father. They both harp at me when I smoke, so I wouldn't dare smoke around them. Sorry, I'm goin' so slow, Mr. Boone, but the Chief told me last thing he wants is my big ass in a OPP radar trap."

"Wouldn't they let you go, Paul? You know, honor among thieves, that kind of thing."

Paul bristled at the inference but ignored it. "There's some bad blood between us and the OPP. They're pissed off at our radar patrol. They were always in charge of the highway, but no one ever slowed down goin' through town. Chief said we have the right to protect the welfare of our citizens. It's our duty. They fought back and forth. Finally, the Chief just went ahead and started the radar program; nothin' the OPP could do about it, 'cept bitch. Now O'Toole, he runs the OPP, has really got a hard-on against me and the Chief, and Rainbow Falls for that matter."

"William, not Bill, O'Toole." Boone knew that O'Toole headed the detachment. Rainbow Falls was the whole world to Paul, so in Paul's eyes, O'Toole ran the OPP.

"So! You've heard of him."

"Yup." Boone knew Jackpine was a little corny; his primary goal was protection of the people. But Jackpine was also practical and calculating—using the radar to add a needed man to the force without increasing taxes, probably even a profit center. "So, how's your radar working out?"

"Started out gangbusters, busier than a bush-camp whore on payday. Now it's slow. Tourist season is pretty well over. I need truckers, but they're all wise to me. I need some thousand-dollar days, but I don't think I'll get them." Paul was worried. He had the best job in the world, and he desperately wanted to pay his own way.

"Well, Paul," Boone had assumed his professional air, and was about to lecture Paul Desroches on fundraising via radar, a topic that until three minutes ago, Boone had never focused his mind upon. "First, the speed-limit sign is too big; make it as small as the law allows."

"That's the Chief," interrupted Paul. "We must be fair!" declared Paul in his Jackpine voice.

Boone laughed. "Yeah, that's Jackpine, all right. OK. We won't offend his sensibilities. Here's what you do. Take Jackpine's cruiser; park it down by the bridge where you normally sit. People see the car. They think they're through the trap, and then they speed up because the coast is clear. You're waiting at the other end of town—whammo!" Boone put his cigar in the ashtray to have his hands free for the obligatory punching of his right fist into his open left hand. "You'll have a few thousand-dollar days before they get wise to you."

Big Paul Desroches beamed. It was a good idea! He wondered why he hadn't thought of it.

"Chief tell you we had another run-in with O'Toole last week?"

"No, he didn't mention it."

"Makes sense I guess. Chief gets pissed off just thinkin' about it."

They were silent for a few minutes. Boone was enjoying the scenery, and Paul was concentrating on staying within the speed limit.

"Well?" said Boone finally.

"Deep subject," countered Paul.

"Are you going to tell me about the confrontation with old William, not Bill?"

"Started like so much of our trouble 'round here with Bear Sawchuk and Flip Lafontaine," began Paul. "They were down from Blackbear Point Lodge, where they're supposedly workin'."

Boone had heard of these two ne'er-do-wells on previous trips to the Falls. Peter "Bear" Sawchuk's mind was lodged in the backwaters of intellectual mediocrity. But he was both intellectually and physically superior to inseparable pal Phillip "Flip" Lafontaine. Thus, he was the undisputed leader of this less-than-dynamic duo. The dimwitted, sadistic pair was suspected, if not always guilty, of virtually every crime in Rainbow Falls and its environs. Bear was a big, fat man with long, unruly dirty blond hair. His eyes were small and vacant—set so far apart that to look at him in the eye you would have to select one or the other. It was physically impossible to focus on both of them at once. Not that many bothered to look him in the eye. In his eye you could often read anger, sometimes confusion, but always a vacant expression of bovine simplicity.

Flip Lafontaine was short and wiry, with long greasy black hair. Profuse with body and facial hair, he only shaved when the mood struck him which was once or twice a week. His eyes were fiery and expressive with a wild, demonic craziness. Both men's arms were heavily tattooed.

Bear and Flip were the bane of Jackpine Keating's existence. He had managed to put them away for two years on a drug-trafficking charge. Jackpine had also nailed them for selling liquor to minors and secured a four-month sentence for each of them. Three times Jackpine had garnered assault convictions with short prison sentences. Overnighters in the Rainbow Falls jail and surrounding crowbar hotels for drunk and disorderly were so common that Jackpine had lost count.

Two summers ago, Janice Keating had called Boone and

asked him to come up for a few days, hoping that Boone would be able to calm Jackpine down. Sawchuk and Lafontaine had raped, sodomized, and beaten a fourteen-year-old Indian girl. The girl had refused to testify, fearing for the lives of herself and her family. Jackpine had pleaded with the girl and her parents, to no avail. Janice had worried that Jackpine would kill both Sawchuk and Lafontaine. When Boone arrived, he had been horrified to discover how close Jackpine had been to doing it. "Those bastards belong in prison, and if our legal system won't do it, then I will give them the death sentence." Boone and Janice had pleaded for two days before Jackpine backed off his threat. Boone was still worried, and so was Janice, that some future incident would trigger Jackpine's latent fury. Bear and Flip drifted away from time to time, but they always ended up returning to Rainbow Falls.

"Bear and Flip were in the bar at the hotel," continued Paul. "They were up to their old tricks, threatening people and makin' them buy them drinks. Chief and I got a call, and we went over. Chief hauls the two of them outside. He told them to leave town and never come back. He says to them, 'If I ever see you two assholes in town, I'm going to get Paul here'—he points at me with his flashlight—'to squeeze you 'til the shit runs down your legs!' Then he yells at Bear, 'Do you understand?'"

"What did Bear do?"

"It's what he didn't do that got him in trouble. He didn't say 'yes sir,' like the Chief wanted, so the Chief whacked him on the side of the head with his flashlight."

This seemed out of character to Boone. Jackpine was devoted to law and order, but these two seemed to bring out the worst in him, thought Boone. "What did Bear do?"

"He fell down," Paul answered. "And then Flip says, 'You can't do that! That's police brutality!' Chief says to him, 'Fuckin' right it is, and here's some for you!' and then he whacks Flip with his flashlight."

"So, how does O'Toole get involved?"

"Next mornin' Chief and I were havin' coffee. In walks O'Toole and this little piss-ass lawyer, Steve Appleton, and Bear and Flip. They had big white bandages 'round their heads. Looked like a pair of camel jockeys. O'Toole starts yellin' at the Chief, tells him he ain't no feudal lord, that he has no right to beat up innocent people, and where does he come off orderin' people out of town. Then the lawyer pipes up that this time they weren't pressin' assault charges, but next time they would."

"What did Jackpine do?"

"He turned red, like he was going to explode. But he never said a word. Not one word. Surprised the hell outta me. After they ranted and raved for a while, they stormed out and slammed the door. Jackpine, still smokin' mad, says to me cool as a cucumber, 'Paul, next time you see those two bastards in this town, you come and get me right away.'"

The car was quiet for the rest of the trip. Boone mulled over this disturbing news. He was deeply troubled over Jackpine—sinister murder plots and assaulting people. He would get this lodge delusion cleared up, and then he would have a long talk with Janice about Jackpine.

When they reached the city, Boone started to look for a combination barber shop and beauty salon. When he saw one that didn't appear very busy, he had Paul pull over. He thanked Paul and told him he could head back to the Falls. Boone had his hair cut short, much shorter than he had ever worn it. He went next door to the beauty salon and had his hair colored. His short gray hair became short brown hair, a shade closer to its original color. Looking in the mirror he thought he looked younger, but the haircut made his face look too big. A cab took him to a marina outside of the city. As he arrived, he saw a vintage Single Otter airplane disgorging a pair of anglers. Boone became Jack Patterson, as he dropped his heads-up swagger for a heads-down shuffle toward the dock.

They flew over the lodge before landing on the lake and tailing back. In keeping with its name, Blackbear Point Lodge was situated midway on a point of land stretching a few hundred yards into the lake. Perhaps the rest of the name was chosen for its authentic north-woods ring. Boone did not know, but today the point was bearless. Except, Boone knew, for the two-legged Sawchuk variety (of "bear") lurking below, who was at least as wild as his namesake and considerably more unpredictable and dangerous. The thinly treed point met the land abruptly, facing a big, heavily forested hill. There was a big log-cabin-style structure that had to be the main lodge, with numerous smaller buildings nearby. On the lake there was a well-maintained permanent dock, where the planes and boats dropped off and picked up guests. In the protected back bay on the other side of the dock, there was a ramshackle floating dock supported by empty forty-five-gallon drums, where the boats and motors were kept. Fifty yards further down the shore, on the bayside, were the big fuel-storage tanks storing gasoline for the outboards and diesel fuel for the power generator, well out of view of the guests.

Boone took a few minutes to stroll around and further familiarize himself with the camp. Behind the main lodge there were eight log cabins, much smaller but of similar design. These were the guest quarters. Boone walked over to the back bay, the working area of the lodge. These buildings were cheaply constructed and well weathered, ghetto-like in comparison to the main lodge. Near the dock was a building for storing motors and equipment. Another building housed freezers for the fish, with a screened-in porch with wooden tables and sinks for fish cleaning. Scattered along the shoreline were six small, decrepit shacks where the guides lived.

On his way back to the main lodge, Boone noticed what

looked like a prefabricated bungalow. It was totally incongruous in appearance and in location; it was a good fifty yards from the lodge toward the hill. It also looked very new, like it had been constructed this year. It looked like the model home in a very low-income housing development.

From the minute they landed, Alistair Boone (or rather Jack Patterson) was enjoying himself immensely. After a quick lunch, he was escorted down to the front dock by a waitress. Golias was nowhere to be seen. The standard arrangement was two guests and one guide per boat. Since Boone was alone, they had arranged for the other solo in camp to come in from the lake to team up. His fishing partner was a balding fellow from Peoria, whose name Boone could not be bothered to remember. The guy had booked his trip six months prior, choosing October because the potential for very cold weather meant discount rates. Boone thought if the guy had six months to convince a friend to accompany him and still came alone, it meant he had very few, if any, friends. Boone confirmed his suspicions after a few moments of inane conversation. The guy was wearing a hat that said "Bass Master" so Boone named him "Bass Master," and his partner seemed proud to carry the moniker.

True to the Code of the North the fishing hole was a forty-five minute ass-pounding ride, but it turned out to be worthwhile. The guide had them jigging with yellow Mr. Twisters, and they caught two-pound walleye continuously for two hours. Boone could have stayed there all afternoon, but Bass Master began to whine; he wanted a trophy and had lost interest in two-pounders. The guide knew of a spot where the fishing was less prolific but more rewarding in terms of size.

The sun was warm, and the spray from the lake was cold. Both Boone and Bass Master were chilled after the half-hour drive to the new hole. Bass Master told Boone during the trip that his fantasy was to be on the professional fishing circuit, comparing tournament fishing competition to "heaven on earth," "celestial bliss." This patter was totally anathematic to Boone's way of thinking. Boone thought a person fished for peace and tranquility, the harmony of being in the outdoors, at one with nature. The fish themselves were secondary. Fishing was a state of mind. Boone fished hard (like he lived) changing spots and changing lures while stalking his sometimes elusive quarry, but retaining an inner peace while doing it. He enjoyed the cerebral exercise of locating fish traditionally. He considered the use of electronic fish finders to be cheating. Boone played the game of business like he played golf—by the scorecard. But fishing was his escape from that life, a way to charge the batteries for tomorrow's battles. Many of his fondest memories of days spent fishing happened also to be days when the fish were not biting. Bass Master's dream would have elicited a verbose denial from Alistair Boone, but Jack Patterson said, "Yeah. Sure would be a great way to make a living."

In the new hole, both Boone and Bass Master nailed walleyes over six pounds. Bass Master had struggled valiantly with a whopper, but in his exuberance had given the behemoth a little slack line, and the fish had spit the hook. Bass Master was crestfallen, losing a fish that the guide confirmed was a ten-pounder. None of them had seen the fish. Following the Code of the North, the guide had added three or four pounds to what he really thought. Losing a ten-pounder would be a much better memory and a much better reason to return to Blackbear Point Lodge than a six-pounder. In these days of catch and release, any guide worth his salt also had a scale that weighed heavy.

The generous northern sun was beating down on the bay; protected from the wind, it was not hot, but it was comfortable. A beautiful day, great fishing, boring company—two out of three ain't bad, thought a contented Alistair Boone.

"You look happy as a clam," offered Bass Master.

"I surely am. How couldn't you be, on a day like today!" said

Boone. He wondered why a mollusk buried in the stinking, rotting mud of a tidal basin, waiting to be wrenched from his habitat, washed in cold water, and eaten alive had any reason to be happy. On the way back to the lodge, they stopped in a shallow, weedy bay to take a few casts for northern pike. Boone continued with his eight-pound test line, but added a steel leader baited with a five-of-diamonds spoon. Bass Master switched from the fifteen-pound test he had been using for walleye to an equally unsporting twenty-five-pound line for the pike. Small ones were hitting fast and furious. A big one hit Boone's lure but snapped the line on the strike. Bass Master admonished him for using a light line, and Jack Patterson accepted the criticism meekly, while Alistair Boone mentally roared in rebuttal. The guide told them to reel in; they were supposed to be back by five. In the summer, with the long days, ardent fishermen would hire the guide to go out in the evening. This time of year, it was too dark and cold to contemplate such plans. But since dinner was not served until seven, Boone asked the guide to stay out for a while.

The only things to do in a fishing lodge in the evening were to read, play cards and/or drink. The natives were not allowed to drink. Their particular guide was illiterate, didn't play cards, and insisted on returning. When Boone coaxed him and gave him twenty dollars on top of his normal stipend, the guide reluctantly agreed. Bass Master appreciated his partner's largess. The small northerns also agreed to work overtime, continuing their feeding frenzy. Bass Master finally hooked a big one. His reel was screaming as the freshwater barracuda protested its fate. Bass Master had the denizen of the deep well hooked, and even though he gave it slack line, it could not disgorge the hook or hope to break the heavy line. The twenty-pounder could barely fit in the net. Michael, the guide, managed to hoist it into the boat, where it flapped rebelliously. Rather than being satisfied with a photo, Bass Master decided the fish must sacrifice its life to become a wall ornament. The kill order given, Michael dispatched the fish efficiently with a piece of hardwood kept aboard for such assignments.

Back at the lodge, Boone went to his cabin to freshen up. It was a cold evening, and someone had started a welcome fire in the small stove. On his way to dinner, Boone saw lights on in the bungalow and people in the window. Everyone staying here should be at dinner, Boone thought. Walking by the kitchen, he looked through the window and saw the four guides who were here to service the eight guests. The pilot was there, and the other two scraggly looking creatures had to be Bear Sawchuk and Flip Lafontaine. They were all eating.

Walking into the dining room, he did a quick head count: two waitress and eight heads (the seven other guests and one head belonging to Danny Golias). That added up. Who were the people in the bungalow who did not even join them for dinner? Boone did not know the answer, but the question bothered him.

Most of the space of the main lodge was devoted to the dining room/great room. There were dining tables to accommodate forty guests. One wall, facing the lake, was all windows from floor to ceiling. There were couches and comfortable-looking chairs in front of the windows. The end wall was dominated by a huge stone fireplace, which now had a large birch fire roaring. A bearskin rug lay in front of the fire. Across the room was a small combination office and store, and the kitchen. Behind the kitchen were small bedrooms for the kitchen staff. Behind the office was the owner's quarters.

Across from the lakeside windows was a show wall. In the center was a large map of the lake. Scattered about on the rest of the wall were mounted specimens of walleye, northern pike, smallmouth bass, speckled trout, rainbow trout, lake trout, whitefish, and perch. Some animals had also given their lives for this display. A moth-eaten old bull moose looked like he had been a decoration for much longer than he had roamed the swampy muskeg. A beaver was chewing a stick in what the stuffer had thought was a lifelike pose, beavers being known for their propensity to chew sticks. A glass-eyed wolverine watched the beaver. The deer was framed in a sad repose, and the caribou looked like it needed a shave.

In the corner stood a bear. It had been forced into an unnatural hind-leg stance, looking more ferocious with bared fangs than it ever had in life. It looked like it had become afflicted with rabies moments before its innards were replaced with stuffing and its eyeballs ripped out to make room for marbles. The pair of ruffed grouse, on the other hand, looked natural and as happy as they had been when roaming these hills, led by the dictates of their pea-like brains.

Boone got a drink and joined Bass Master, his back to the party of six at the next table. Danny Golias, drink in one hand, cigarette in the other, came over to greet Boone. Fishing lodge owners, in Boone's extensive observation of the breed, came in two varieties: Type 1 and Type 2. A Type 1 was an entrepreneur, often a bush pilot but not always. Born and raised in one of the small towns or cities of the North, he had either built the lodge or bought a distressed property and was making his living running the operation. He was often a pilot, because the difference between making and losing money was controlling overhead. Hiring a pilot and a plane were the biggest expense in the lodge business. Owning and flying your own plane was the best way to control cost. This type of owner always knew the lake or lakes well. He knew where the fish were at different times of the season, in all kinds of weather, and what bait they would most likely go for. He knew the best places for a guest to see moose, bears, eagles, ospreys, otters, and beavers. He knew old Indian legends about the surrounding area, some authentic, some basically authentic but embellished, and some totally fabricated. Usually, the latter were the most entertaining. He would circulate from table to table during cocktails and dinner, telling stories, listening sympathetically to tales of woe about the big ones that got away, and regaling listeners with "You should-a been here last week" stories. The best time to ever visit any lodge (yes, the Code of the North again) was "last week."

This type of owner always maintained three or four outpost camps on virgin lakes, which guests could fly into for a day for an extra fee. These were high-margin extras and selling these outpost trips were always part of his patter. These owners certainly had different personalities, but this description fit all of the many Type 1 owners that Boone had encountered over the years.

The Type 2 owner that Boone had come to know was a successful man in his fifties or sixties who had retired from his business or medical practice. He had visited northern lodges a few times a year for twenty years and had finally acted on his dream and bought his favorite lodge at an inflated price from a Type 1 owner. A Type 2 owner offered better meals, newer boats and motors, and more amenities but lost money. He did not circulate among the guests as frequently, and he did not sell outpost trips as hard. If he did tell old Indian legends, he lacked the authenticity to carry them off, and rather than telling guests the best places to fish, he kept those spots for himself.

Three things would happen to a Type 2. First, he continued the pattern and was only modestly wealthy; he would lose his shirt in a few years and sell out to a Type 1 at a distressed price. Second, he continued the pattern and was wealthy enough to lose money while playing with his toy until he tired of it, usually in a few years. He then sold at a low price to a Type 1, or if he was lucky to another Type 2 at a high price. Third, he continued the pattern and started losing money and then, applying the common sense and drive that made him successful in business, he was transformed into a Type 1.

Of all lodges, Boone preferred those owned by a Type 2 of the third type. He found this to be the best combination of fishing, equipment, food, lodging, and ambience. Occasionally, corp-orations owned lodges, but they usually hired a Type 1 to be manager.

Nothing in Boone's classification system prepared him for his brief encounter with Danny Golias. He looked like Boone's mental picture of a time-share condo salesman who, in his spare time, sold used cars with the odometer turned back. His dark hair (a rich chestnut shade not included in God's original equipment selection) was meticulously parted and imprisoned in styling gel. His face was white, a shade as common in Manhattan in February as it was rare here. His eyes were dark and menacing. They were shifty: Boone thought of the seagull he had seen on the dock earlier, taking in all the sights without moving its head. The phony, forced smile did not match the eyes. He wore a lime-green polo shirt, white dungarees, and Italian loafers with no socks. Boone wasn't sure where this fashion was appropriate, but it certainly was not fishing-lodge chic. One wrist sported a gold Rolex, the other a heavy gold chain-link bracelet. His neck was adorned with a series of gold chains looking like a Mr. T starter set.

From the brief conversation Golias had with Boone and Bass Master, it was obvious Golias knew nothing about fishing. Trophy fish were the best sales promotion a lodge could enjoy, but Golias expressed no interest whatsoever in Bass Master's saga of catching the lunker northern. Boone knew there was some logical explanation for a man like Danny Golias buying a fishing lodge, but it concerned Boone that he could not develop any reasonable scenario. Boone's instincts on reading people were very sharp, and he had prospered in business by trusting those instincts. Boone felt a loathing for Danny Golias, and his throat went dry, for he also sensed fear and danger.

Boone should have had a big appetite after an afternoon on the lake, but his churning stomach would not settle down and let him enjoy the evening repast. Before dessert, he excused himself from Bass Master's company. He wanted to go down while all the outdoor lights were still on and look around the buildings on the back bay. He bought a six-pack of Coke. Sodas were exorbitantly priced in fly-in lodges, and Boone had hoped the offering of a six-pack to Michael might help to induce some conversation. He had been unable to solicit any more than yes or no answers from the taciturn guide all afternoon.

Michael was alone in the fish-cleaning shack when Boone got there. There were only four guides left at camp this late in the year, and Michael was the only one who stayed out late on the lake. "Last guide in has to clean up and go dump the fish guts," said Michael, obviously unhappy with the predicament that Boone had put him in.

"Here's some Cokes. I'll give you a hand cleaning up," offered Boone. Michael grunted. "That's Ojibway for thanks for the Cokes and thank you for helping me, isn't it?" asked Boone. Michael smiled. Boone saw one reason why the guide did not smile often. His rotting teeth looked like a mouthful of rusty rivets. Boone began hosing down the rest of the shack, while Michael finished filleting the last few walleyes. Like most experienced guides, he deftly operated with surgeon-like skills on the fish. "Last year I was up here, my guide was Jimmy Boucher. Is he still here? I wanted to say hello."

"No, he went home. Got out of this nuthouse. Lucky guy." Boone realized Michael had not heard how unlucky Jimmy Boucher had become.

"Why is this place a nuthouse?" The Coke he was drinking had loosened his tongue, thought Boone.

"Planes fly around with no guests. Wake us up at night." Odd, thought Boone. With the price of gas up here, pilots did not take joyrides. They only flew when a guest was paying the freight. No reason to fly at night that Boone could think of. "And a house full'a Mexicans all summer. Never go fishin'. Just sit up in the house." Resident Latin Americans with no purpose for being here. Boone was becoming more worried.

"Every lodge lets guides go home for a few days when they're not workin'. Not this crazy place." Boone knew that was true. If the lodge was not fully booked, the owner could save on salaries by letting some guides go home. The plane was going to the Falls regularly for supplies, so it was easy to shuttle the guides in and out. The owner ran the risk of the guide not showing up for the return, but there was a fairly large pool of experienced guides to draw from at Lac des Iles. Golias kept the guides here for the entire season, and then two of them died when they got back home.

"They lock up the freezers. Who is going to steal fish with a lake full of them? I have to go all the way up to the lodge and find Bear to get the key, so I can freeze your fish." He made the lodge sound like a ten-mile walk. This made no sense to Boone either. He was beginning to draw some conclusions, but they were so outlandish that he dismissed them from his train of thought.

"What is Bear's job?" Boone asked.

"This nuthouse hires people to sit on their ass. Him and Flip are carpenters. They put up that new house. That was in June. Now they sit around all day and plan how to make life miserable for guides." Boone had finished helping Michael wipe down the tables with Pine-Sol. He said he would see Michael in the morning and headed back up to the lodge. He wanted a large whiskey to try to settle his frazzled nerves.

The guests were standing around talking. Golias was sitting down reading a magazine and having a cigarette. Boone envied the man enjoying a smoke. He craved a Monte Cristo. He had not paid much attention to the other guests, and now looking at them, he almost choked on his drink. Curse the luck, he thought, what were the chances of this? He was turning to leave, when Marty Hess saw him. "Why, Alistair Boone! What the hell are you doing here, Boone?" Marty worked for an oil company in Baltimore and had been doing programs with Boone Promotions for many years. "You're looking young for an old retired son of a bitch."

Boone saw Golias's head snap up; his cold hard eyes bored into Boone like lasers. There was no longer the pretense of the false grin. Trying to recoup, Boone walked over to Marty Hess and put his arm around his shoulder. Culling him from his cohorts, he quietly explained his alias. He said he would explain later. Boone finished his drink quickly. As he was leaving the lodge, Martin yelled out, "Night, Jack. Sorry about mistaking you for someone else." Boone felt the transparent attempt worsening his situation.

It was not that uncommon to bump into an acquaintance at a remote wilderness lodge. Guests were almost exclusively Americans. Even though situated in Canada, all prices quoted and all cash transactions were in American dollars. Lodges catered to the well-to-do and to sellers hosting buyers on expense accounts. Boone had occasionally run into people he knew and had struck up many new business connections in rooms just like this one. On the way to his cabin, Boone had the chilling feeling that his life was in jeopardy. He had never been so scared, but later he would find his fear gauge was calibrated to a much higher level. He considered going back to Marty, but it would be hard enough to explain the alias, let alone some sinister vague plot that he had no evidence to support. What would he tell Marty—an owner who didn't look like an owner, an icy stare, planes flying at night with no reason, a new cabin full of Latinos, fish fillets under lock and key, guides not getting time off, and two goons in the kitchen? Marty probably already thought Boone was crazy for bailing out of his businesses. This would confirm it. Besides, thought Boone, what the hell could Marty Hess do to help him?

Boone went to bed. His body fought sleep until fatigue triumphed. At two a.m. he woke up as planned, as if he had an alarm clock in his head. This is a talent many frequent travelers developed out of necessity after missing important meetings and flights, waiting for wake-up calls that never came.

He dressed quietly in the dark. Leaving his cabin, he walked through the trees down to the shore of the back bay. The lodge was completely dark, except for a light shining in the fish-cleaning shack. Boone hunched over and walked quietly along the shore. He moved up to the back of the building containing the freezers and sat down with his back to the building, right beside the screened-in fish-cleaning porch. He heard two voices and determined they belonged to Bear Sawchuk and Flip Lafontaine. He thought he would listen for a few minutes to the friendly banter before screwing up his courage to look in.

"Best job we ever had, ain't it, Bear, eh?"

"You can say that again. And in a couple of weeks, we'll have a hundred grand each. We'll find our island in the Carrabeen and live there forever."

"You figger forever with that much money, eh?"

"Forever...and then some, Flip. We're just gonna sit there on the beach; we'll be snortin' coke, and we'll have garbage bags full of smokin' dope, too."

"And lots of broads, too!" exclaimed Flip. They had obviously worked on this fantasy for some time. Boone could tell that Flip did not want to have parts omitted.

"Yup. Maybe a dozen of 'em. All natives with big tits. Fetchin' us rum and coke all day long. Our job will be drinkin' 'em."

"They'll be bare-ass naked all the time, right, Bear?"

"Yeah, but sometimes they might wear grass skirts."

"And what happens Bear when one of 'em accidentally spills a drink? What happens then?"

"Well it won't cost much. Rum is a dollar a gallon. But we'll have to slap her around some to set an example. Might have to get you to give it to her up the ass, Flip, right there on the beach.

Flip snickered. "You can't give 'er the Duke of Earl. Might kill her, right, Bear?" Flip did not think that Bear's Duke of Earl was any bigger than his own penis, but you did not say that to Bear Sawchuk if you knew what was good for you. "And there's no cops there, right, Bear?"

"No, you and me, we'll be the only law."

"And we'll eat pineapples."

"Yeah, Flip. We'll have them natives climb way up them palm trees and throw them pineapples down."

"And for holidays we'll just get in our boat and drive to Spain and see bullfights."

"Yup. Spain is just around the corner in Mexico. We'll watch them swordfight them bulls. You might puke, Flip. You didn't have the stomach to hang old White Horse."

"That's 'cause he was my friend, Bear, you know that. A guy don't feel right hangin' his friend, I won't give a fuck for no bull!"

"For a hundred grand, gimme a rope and I'll hang anybody. That was fun, me an' you pullin' on ol' White Horse's legs. Ol' fucker, he didn't wanna get hung."

"You sure Spain is close?" Flip tried to change the topic. He had twinges of remorse from hanging a nice old man just because he had seen too much.

"Course it is. Gotta be in Mexico, 'cause they speak Mexican. How far can it be? Maybe as far as from here to Thunder Bay. No farther."

Boone was trembling. He wondered who had helped these demented, sodomitic half-wits paint their picture. They obviously believed their delusions and discussed them all the time.

"Mr. Golias thought we was smart, knowing who Alistair Boone is; big pal of Keating he is."

"Don't never forget no fucker comin' to town, smoking $20

cigars, 'specially with a faggot name like 'Alice-ter.' We'll show that big bag of wind what a big shot he is. Make fish food outta the fucker. We gotta drown the guide, too. Mr. Golias says he'll get shitfaced some night and tell everyone we drowned Boone."

"Won't matter to us, Bear. We'll be long gone."

"Mr. Golias says to drown him, so we'll drown him. Besides he'll be easy. Just hold his head under the water. It's the other one worries me. He might be tough. Mr. Golias says not to mark them up, but maybe we should whack him with the paddle a few times— soften him up some first."

"Poor fuckin' Keating; he'll be heartbroke, hearin' his pal drowned." Flip laughed demonically.

"I'll shoot that bastard Keating before we leave town, if I get half a chance…just half a chance!" claimed Bear.

"I'd like to see Boone's fishing partner right now. Mr. Golias spiked his supper with somethin'. He says that asshole is gonna be pukin' and shittin' all night." The hilarity of Bass Master's anguish made them both erupt in gales of laughter.

"So now Boone will be alone. Mr. Golias told Michael to take him up north to Loon Bay; rest of the boats will be miles away. We gotta go up to Loon Bay tonight and wait for them."

"It's not fair, Bear. We'll freeze our asses off!"

"Nah. There's a trapper's cabin up there we'll use. Build us a warm fire. I swiped a jug of vodka from the lodge, and Mr. Golias said we can have some of this snort to take up. He just warned us not to be wired tomorrow. Did you put water in Michael's second gas tank?"

"Yeah, I did it. No one saw me."

"Good, 'round Loon Bay he'll switch over to his second tank, and his motor will conk out. Me and you—we ride to the rescue. We drive over and say 'need a hand?' and when we get close, I whack fuckin' Boone with the paddle. You get the fuckin' savage, Flip, and for chrissake watch out for his knife. Them fuckin' wagon burners are quick to pull a knife. Put '"em both in the lake, turn their boat over, 'n come home. Drowning accident. Shit happens."

"Couple more weeks 'n we're off to Carrabeen. This is our last fish shipment. Next shipment won't be so much work."

"Yeah, not long, but I'm havin' fun here too. You go up and get us some grub, and get some Tang for the vodka." Boone heard the screen door open and close as Flip left.

Boone, petrified with fear, forced his unwilling body to cooperate. He got to his knees and peeked through the screened window. Bear was working with his back to Boone. The day's catch had been wrapped in brown paper by the guides. There was a big bag of white powder on the table. Bear used a small scoop to fill a ziplock bag with the white powder. He opened a pack of fillets and spread them out. He placed the bag on a fillet and covered it with another fillet, making in effect a cocaine sandwich. He wrapped the sandwich in fresh brown paper and marked it with what Boone assumed was a *W* to signify walleye. He then unwrapped what had once been an eight-pound pike. To this one he added four of the ziplock bags, repeating the process, marking it with *NP*.

Boone sat quietly down again. He thought it would be safer to wait until Bear left before he moved. Jackpine was right about the death of White Horse Parker and probably about Desmond Lesmontaignes and Jimmy Boucher. Boone understood the late-night flights, bringing cocaine from somewhere. He understood why the Latinos were here and why the freezer room was locked. He knew why they had not let guides go back and forth, in case they had seen something, which obviously White Horse, and probably Desmond and Jimmy, had. More than anything, he understood Jackpine's attitude toward the demented duo of Bear and Flip.

It was surely a foolproof method of smuggling. The Caribbean area was under much closer surveillance than it had been in the past. Who would ever expect fishermen returning from the wilds of northern Canada of being cocaine mules. They obviously had some system to get the drugs back after the innocent mules had carried the cocaine sandwiches through US Customs in Minneapolis.

Boone heard Bear lock the door to the freezer room. The screen door slammed shut. A few moments later he heard footsteps on the back-bay dock, and then an outboard motor roared into life. Boone's first thought was to take a boat and go somewhere and hide. He would either freeze, starve, or worse. (Flip and Bear would find him.) He could have a massive heart attack and die right there. Since that did not occur when he heard the plan of his death, he thought it would not happen now. There was only one choice. He had read, in the brochure in the cabin, that the lodge offered a trip for adventuresome guests down the Blackwater River to Rainbow Falls. It was sixty miles with stretches of severe whitewater and high waterfalls. According to the brochure, the lodge maintained boats and motors beneath the rapids and falls, so you could portage to the next boat. Boone thought that Bear and Flip must have used this system to slip in and out of town incognito. He would have to navigate the treacherous Blackwater River in a run for his life.

Boone crept down to the dock. He could not risk the sound of an outboard. There were two canoes at the dock. He slipped into one canoe, untied the rope, and began paddling south out into the black night. The wind was blowing from the north, so it was easy paddling. The consistent wind direction helped him keep his bearings on a southern course. It was three a.m. when he started. He estimated the distance to the river to be about five miles. They would not notice his absence until six thirty, when someone came to wake him to prepare for the day of fishing. He should be on the river by then. He had to be, or he was a dead man. The thought propelled Boone to a more aggressive stroke.

He was no expert in a canoe, but Jackpine had taught him the basics. He was using a J- stroke, which enabled him to keep the canoe on a straight course without switching from side to side. By six, he was well into the long, narrow bay that would become the Blackwater River. The sound of the roaring water had helped him to navigate the last few miles in the darkness. The last thing he wanted was to get swept into the current of the mighty river in the dark. He pulled into shore. He had not realized how cold it was. Boone built a fire from the dry driftwood strewn along the shoreline and waited for the sun to come up before beginning the next leg of his journey.

CHAPTER 4

In the mountainous terrain, a gray half-light gradually emerged before the sun first poked over the nearest hill. As soon as Boone was able to make out the far shoreline of the narrow bay he prepared to leave. When they discovered his absence, they would not pursue him immediately. Boone thought they would waste fifteen or twenty minutes searching for him before they noticed the canoe gone. Golias and his Latino guests were not outdoorsmen. Golias would have to send someone to get Bear and Flip from Loon Bay. Boone calculated that he would have about a two-hour head start down the river. If everything went well, he could be in Rainbow Falls by nightfall.

The first few hours of the trip were idyllic. Boone was paddling, and the fast flowing water was working for him. He had not encountered any white-water rapids. Boone was thinking how much he would enjoy this trip, if it were not for the pair of demented killers that would soon be in pursuit. The rugged virgin river surged with the power of the wilderness, cutting through pristine coniferous forests. As he rounded each bend, Boone's eyes swept the new panoramic vista.

Boone considered his situation. The enemy was armed and they knew the river well. They would be able to navigate this stretch of river in minutes with a motorboat at full throttle. He was unarmed and had no knowledge of the river. Advantage, enemy! The only plus Boone had was intellect. Bear Sawchuk was the smarter of the two. Conservatively, Boone felt he was twice as clever as Bear. All things considered, Boone would have gladly bartered thirty IQ points for a rifle.

He had a few options. He could continue on his course and hope that Bear and Flip would not catch up with him. It was tempting, but he would be casting his fate to chance and not controlling his own destiny. How long would it take them to recover from his head start? He could guess, but he really did not know the answer. He could hide somewhere along the river and wait for them to pass. Then he could follow them down the river. He would have some measure of control. The safest option was to leave the river and hike overland to Rainbow Falls. It would be a strenuous trek through rugged country, with no trail to follow. He would run the risk of getting lost and freezing to death or starving, but he would avoid a pair of thugs with his untimely demise on the forefront of their feeble minds. He decided to stay on the river until the first set of impenetrable rapids. He would cross the portage and release the waiting boat into the current, to make Bear and Flip think he was still on the river. Then he would begin the overland journey to Rainbow Falls.

The current was faster than it had been. Boone went through a few sets of rapids. There was some white water and a few boulders to avoid, but even a novice like Boone was able to steer clear of potential dangers. Boone thought he would be able to hear the big rapids or falls that would indicate the time to make for shore and portage. The roaring din of the rapids had lulled him like sweet songs of sirens. The noise level had grown so gradually that Boone didn't realize that the deafening thunder was foretelling trouble. Suddenly, there were sheer cliffs on both sides of the river. The river funneled from a width of fifty yards to a compressed raging torrent only twenty yards across. The angry river protested in a resounding booming din. The white torrent of thrashing water afforded no escape. Boone hunched lower in the canoe and was swept into the gut of raging water. In a matter of seconds, he was through the narrow gut and into a somewhat slower current. He sensed more dangerous water ahead; he had just seen the opening act of this natural drama. He would paddle to shore before he hit the next obstacle.

His paddle was gone! He had held onto the canoe for dear life, and his paddle had disappeared. He flipped out of the canoe. The icy water momentarily took his breath away. Boone was a strong swimmer. He had been on the swim team in college and still swam frequently for exercise. But this was not a heated pool. He swam furiously toward the shore. He should have angled his way to the shore, using the current instead of fighting it. He was losing the fight and being swept downstream. Boone saw the waterfall; he quit fighting and accepted the inevitable. He would save whatever strength was left for the bottom of the falls, if he was alive.

As he began to go over, he was surprised how calm he was and how it seemed to be happening in slow motion. It was about sixty feet to the bottom; anywhere except the wilderness, a falls of this magnitude would have a name and a tourist viewing area. But here he was, Alistair Drayton Boone, about to die in a no-name waterfall. He never felt the sensation of falling. His body was being battered as he was rolling along the river bottom beneath the falls. He swallowed water and began to lose consciousness when he felt the river release him. Kicking feebly, he bobbed to the surface. He tried to breathe but couldn't. He started to vomit and then swallowed more water. A few desperate kicks brought him near the shore. He climbed onto the slippery rocks using the last of his strength. He lay on his side, vomiting water and coughing. Finally, some precious air found its way to his lungs. He shivered violently, and then he felt like sleeping. He forced himself to his unsteady feet. If he passed out here beside the river, they would find him.

As he stood, he saw small fragments of his canoe circling in the backwaters. The canoe had been smashed into hundreds of pieces. Boone stumbled unsteadily into the woods, trying not to leave any broken branches to signal his whereabouts. When he was out of sight of the river, he sat down on an old log. He was freezing, but he knew he could not risk a fire.

He thought he should take an inventory of his possessions. There were a dozen pockets on the vest that Jackpine had given him. He emptied all of them and found a stick with a fishing line wrapped around it; a small tin with hooks and a few lures; four candy bars (which he ate two of, hoping the fuel would generate some body heat); a compass; some heavy string; a Swiss Army knife; two Bic lighters that had gotten wet but worked when Boone flicked them; Muskol insect repellant (mercifully, it was too late in the season for the hordes of hungry mosquitoes that ruin many a wilderness experience for the uninitiated); a small bottle of airplane gas (Jackpine's 'old Indian trick for lighting fires in the rain); a small flashlight; and small containers of salt and pepper.

The next package that Boone examined contained a folded plastic rain poncho. Boone put it on, hoping it would help him warm up. He also found a ziplock bag containing flour and another with tea bags. Jackpine, always prepared, had given him a survival kit. Stranded in the wilderness, this collection could be the difference between living and dying. The next package contained a device Boone had never seen before. He thought it was quite clever; it unfolded into an aluminum pot. After unfolding it, he read the little message telling him that once the pot had been constructed it could not be recompacted.

The last bag contained a map. It showed where each one of the portages was along the river. He had taken a shortcut instead of the first portage. There were six more portages designated. The longest was two miles; the shortest was a few hundred yards. Each trail was marked by a slashed tree. A landmark was indicated to tell you when to begin to look for the marked tree. At the end of each portage, there was supposed to be a boat and motor. According to the map, the first boat was about two hundred yards downstream from the base of the falls.

Boone reprimanded himself for not discovering the map earlier. Boone had always been very impulsive, a potentially dangerous flaw in the game of business and life, where prudence is usually rewarded. Boone would continually jump into situations before the smoke cleared. To compensate, Boone had an ability to make fast, accurate analyses of situations, followed quickly by decisive action. Most of his more cautious peers thought Boone was just lucky, and perhaps to some extent he was, but he was also clever and resourceful. He was also blessed with high energy levels and the capacity for hard work, believing in the old adage that the harder he worked, the luckier he got.

Boone replaced everything in the pockets of the vest except the pot and wearily got to his feet. He knew from the map that the boat was on the other side of the river, so he picked his way downstream looking for the best place to attempt to ford. He picked a spot, and although the current was strong, there did not seem to be any violent whirlpools. This time he swam with the river and ended up on the other side, about a hundred yards downstream. He saw where the trail came down the mountain, and his eyes followed the trail to its destination where he saw the boat—two boats actually, a pair of battered-looking sixteen-foot Lunds. Boone turned the boat over and found an outboard motor. He dragged the boat to the water and went back for the motor.

The motor started on the sixth pull. He was about to leave when he thought that he should do something about the other boat to slow down his pursuers. He decided to take the second boat with him. As he was dragging it down to the water, he saw a hole appear in the boat. Then suddenly there was a hole in the tree beside him. He looked up toward the trail and saw Bear Sawchuk about eighty yards up the mountain, sighting for another shot. He hadn't heard the shots because of the roar of the river. Where was the other one? Boone wondered, remarkably cool in this predicament. Then he saw Flip burst out of the woods at the end of the trail, running towards him, rifle in his hands.

Boone hauled the second boat the last few feet and pushed it into the river. He jumped into his boat, almost capsizing it. He gunned the motor in reverse; water was coming in over the back of the boat. Then full-throttle forward as a hole appeared in his boat just beneath his hand. He slumped over, heading down river, and within twenty seconds he had rounded a bend in the river and knew he was safe—at least for the time being. His heart left his mouth and returned to its domicile in his chest cavity. He noticed the second boat being held in place by a wind-befallen tree. He rescued the boat and tied it to his craft. He ventured downstream.

Boone had thought all the fear he was able to muster had been exhausted in his plunge over the falls. Somewhere in his system there had been a reserve supply of raw fear. When he had seen Flip Lafontaine stop running and raise his rifle, with a demonic grin on his face to throw some hot lead in Boone's direction, cold fear had clutched his throat. As he devoted his attention to navigating the river, Boone realized one final consequence of his naked terror. Sometime during the mad dash to the boat his anal sphincter had succumbed. This would be one part of the story he would omit, if he lived to tell about it. There would be no mention of shitting himself.

Boone vowed to never hunt deer again. He knew now how a deer felt during hunting season. Deer got smart quickly, after the trauma of opening day, if they survived it. Boone set his jaw, knowing that he too had just become much smarter in pursuit of survival.

The river was navigable for fifteen miles. Boone was making good time with the outboard motor. The next portage was past a cliff faced with red rock. Boone continued downstream until he saw the cliff. Then he saw the slashed tree. Landing the boats near the tree, he saw the beginning of the trail. Boone was freezing; his fingers were numb and blue. He walked the mile-long portage quickly and felt a bit warmer when he'd finished the walk.

At the end of the portage he found two more boats. He took both boats and proceeded about five miles downstream. Boone thought he had about an hour and a half of daylight left. He decided to make camp at a point where a stream flowed into the river. He knew he would be safe for the night. There was no way for Flip and Bear to cover that much distance by foot. They would have walked back up the portage above the falls and taken their boat back to the lodge. Golias would have them or some other thugs flown to town at daybreak, and they would head upstream to set up an ambush.

There was nothing to be done about it now. Boone was starving, freezing, and nearing complete exhaustion. He made a roaring fire, then washed his clothes, and had a bath in the frigid river. He didn't think they would send a plane after him at night and try to shoot him beside his fire from the air. To be on the safe side, he had chosen to camp where the river was slow moving and quiet. He thought he would hear a plane coming and have time to get away from the fire. While his clothes were drying, Boone (wearing only his poncho) set out to forage for dinner.

He took his boat back upstream a ways, where he had noticed a shallow bay on one side of the river. He had calculated correctly that he would find wild rice in the bay. After harvesting some rice, he moved out of the bay, slowly watching the bottom for a drop off. He anchored his boat at the edge of the drop and attached a yellow jig to his fishing line. As he tossed the jig into the water, he hoped that there were small walleye there. For the first time in his life, he didn't want a twenty-pound northern pike attacking his jig. He let the lure down to the bottom, pulling it up a few inches, and lightly jigged. He lost the first fish by setting the hook too aggressively. Patience was difficult to muster when you were starving and dinner was swimming around twenty feet below you. Boone refined his technique and within ten minutes he had three walleye, each about one and a half pounds, flopping in the bottom of the boat.

Back at camp, Boone took a look for some mushrooms. Jackpine had shown him a few years ago which mushrooms were edible, and he found a batch near camp. He also picked a hatful of blueberries for dessert. The blueberries were frost damaged but still plentiful late in the season; that was a good sign for Boone. In addition to loving wild blueberries, he also knew that well-fed bears were not nearly as cantankerous as hungry ones.

As Boone began to fillet his catch, he thought about eating walleye sushi but fought the urge and continued on with his feast preparation. He put the fish heads, bones, and water in his pot. As his stock was boiling, he carved a makeshift spoon out of a small piece of driftwood. He then fished the bones and heads out of his stock. He ate the walleye cheeks for an appetizer and threw the bones and heads into the river. He did not want to leave the heads around to attract bears. He added the walleye fillets, wild rice, and mushrooms to the stock and devoured his dessert blueberries as dinner cooked. Boone could not remember eating anything as delicious as the fish stew. He finished all of it, washed out his pot, built up the fire, and curled up beside it for a few hours of sleep.

Boone awoke at three in the morning feeling refreshed and ready to go. He built up the fire to generate light and studied his map. It would take them at least an hour to fly from the lodge to town and then backtrack up the river to set up an ambush. They would leave at first light, so Boone calculated that he had three and a half hours. It was a clear night with a half-moon. If he traveled carefully, he thought he could navigate the river. It was about twelve miles to the next portage. If he found the portage, he could walk two miles due east through the forest and hit the Spruce Hill Road. Then if he walked a few miles up the road to the mine, he could call Jackpine from the watchman's office. He was sure Golias and his crew would expect him to stay on the river all the way to Rainbow Falls. Sure enough—he thought grimly—to bet his life on it.

He found the portage at dawn, took a reading on his compass, and headed due east. It was a hard walk through thick bush, but at least, Boone thought, there would be no way he could be spotted from the air. By seven a.m., he came out of the woods at the gravel road, and although exhausted, he broke into a trot heading north to the mine. He heard a vehicle coming north on the road. He stopped, planning to flag it down when it came into view. Instead, the instinct of the hunted prompted him to run and dive into the ditch beside the road. He hunkered down in the high grass as a pickup truck came into view. He saw Dan Golias looking out the passenger-side window and Flip Lafontaine at the wheel. Two Latinos were in the back of the truck, dressed more for a promenade down 42nd Street than a drive up a gravel road in the north woods. He stayed where he was and twenty minutes later the truck came back down the road minus Flip Lafontaine.

Since the mine had closed, the only one on duty at the mine was a watchman who lived in a small cabin near the entrance to the mine. Boone did not know that Flip was planning on killing the watchman nor that Flip would be waiting for him at the mine. Golias and his crew were getting sloppy. The ruse of running the lodge as a front for cocaine smuggling was getting harder to maintain. Golias hoped he would be long gone when they discovered, if they ever did, that the watchman's body was in the water at the bottom of shaft number one. It would be another in a growing list of perfect crimes, providing (of course) that they were able to kill Alistair Boone.

They had covered both of Boone's options for escape. Bear was no doubt waiting somewhere near the river. Golias was sharper than Boone had given him credit for. Golias had developed the rat-like cunning of a man who lived on the wrong side of the law.

Boone had no choice now but to try to walk to Rainbow Falls. It was ten or fifteen miles. He started south, staying in the ditch. It was muddy and slow going. Boone finally went back up to the road. He would never make it to town staying in the ditch; it was too difficult walking in the mud. He heard a vehicle coming and was ready to dive into the ditch when it came into view. It was an old orange pickup truck. Instinct took over again; instead of hitting the ditch, he went to the middle of the road and waved his arms.

The truck stopped. A grizzled face poked through the open window. "Yeah."

"Please, can you take me into town? It's an emergency!" Boone pleaded.

"Son of a bitch, get in. Name's Slim Hiller"

"I have to get to the police station."

"Had an accident, eh?"

"I have just barely survived a series of catastrophic events," said Boone, returning to form.

"Talk fuckin' English," said Slim, not a man to beat around the bush.

"OK, I'm in trouble up to my fuckin' eyeballs and I've got to see Jackpine Keating right away!"

"Not mixed up with them Mexican assholes, are ye?"

"What?"

"I was at the airport this mornin', just gettin' off work. I drive the grader there, keep the runway level, eh. Saw a plane from Blackbear, Flip and Bear, that asshole from Toronto who runs the lodge, and a bunch of Mexicans all with rifles. Jackpine fines me two-hunert bucks, and lets these goddamn Mexicans run around with rifles."

Boone knew firsthand about Golias and his gang, but his natural curiosity made him ask, "Why did Jackpine fine you?"

"We were in the bar Saturday afternoon. Havin' a few beers and bullshittin'. I tell the guys there's two white egrets up at Lost

Lake. Never seen them before, and I lived here all my life. Had to look it up in a book; sure enough, they're white egrets. Don't come this far north. Who can figger it? Gotta be you Americans pollutin' the air and fuckin' up the climate. Y'are American?"

"Yes, I am." Boone felt as if he was confessing but didn't want to address the issue of global warming with his savior.

"Anyway, everyone gets to laughin', telling me I'm nuts. Tell me it's a pair o' seagulls. Can you believe it? Me not knowin' a fuckin' seagull. Pretty birds, these egrets, real graceful. Kinda' like a crane, but smaller. Ya ever seen an egret?"

"Yes, I have. I agree. Beautiful birds. There's millions of them in Florida. Nice to see them extending their range," Boone replied.

"I bet them fuckers fifty bucks right there!" said Slim, continuing his story. "I left the bar right then. Didn't even finish my beer. I was pissed off!"

"Interesting, so you decided to go and get a picture of the egrets and prove your point.

"Picture, my ass! Who's got a fuckin' camera? I went up to Lost Lake. Sure enough, there's the egrets. I shot 'em both. Went back to the bar and threw them goddamn egrets on the table. Ya shoulda seen the looks on their faces!" Slim laughed.

"Too bad about the egrets," Boone said.

"Don't you start on me! Jackpine comes into the bar, and he lit into me. Sure made me out to be an asshole. Read me the riot act, he did. I thought he was gonna kick my ass. Fined me a hunert an egret. Never seen no bird worth a hunert bucks. Y'ud a thought I shot a fuckin' whoopin' crane. Never seen one of them."

Good thing, thought Boone, or there would be one less whooping crane.

"Learned my lesson, I did." Well, Boone thought, there's Jackpine bringing another lost soul into the fold of law and order.

"You learned that next time a picture would be cheaper."

"No. Next time I'll bet them fuckers two-hunert bucks, not fifty. Yes sir, I learned my lesson."

Boone just rolled his eyes. They were pulling up in front of the police station. Boone thanked Slim and walked into the station. Jackpine jumped up from his chair to greet him.

Boone filled in Jackpine with what he had seen and heard in the fish-cleaning house and with the details of his harrowing escape. Jackpine grabbed his hat, "Let's go to the hotel and get you cleaned up. Then we're going to the OPP. Jesus, Boone, you smell like you shit yourself."

Boone hadn't told him *all* of the details. Being so scared that you shit your pants did not fit in with Boone's self-image. As they were leaving, Jackpine turned back to answer the phone, as Inez Mahoney walked into the office after returning from lunch.

"Boone!" she yelled, as she rushed into his arms. "Darling, I was so worried. Are you OK?" She hugged Boone, suddenly not caring if the cat was out of the bag about their relationship. Boone felt a flood of relief. After years of intimacy, it was always so hard to treat her like a stranger in Rainbow Falls.

"I'm fine, honey. There's some bad people up at that lodge and Jackpine and I are going to straighten things out."

"You sure smell bad, Boone!"

"Let's go, Boone." Jackpine bailed him out before he had to answer.

In the car Jackpine laughed, "So you finally decided to come clean about you and Inez, about time!"

"You knew? How long have you known?"

"For years, the way you two looked at each other. Paul's girlfriend, Bertha, the clerk at the hotel, has seen Inez sneaking into your room on more than one occasion. And the capper, Inez Mahoney taking up golf and spending a week a year at Hilton Head, probably more clues if I thought about it.

"It was Inez who wanted to keep it a secret. She didn't want everyone in town to think she was *that* type of woman."

"She's one fine woman. You and her make a great couple. Ever think of marryin'?"

"We've talked, Jackpine. There are obstacles. Living in Manhattan, for one. But now that I've sold my business, I'm thinking of leaving the city, maybe keep an apartment there and live somewhere else. Maybe here."

Jackpine didn't know if he was serious. Neither did Boone, for that matter.

"Anyway, back to the business at hand. I'll radio Paul and send him up to Spruce Hill."

Jackpine discovered that Flip was back in town. Paul had seen him in the back of a pickup truck with Golias and two Latinos in the cab. So, they picked Flip up, and they must know by now that Boone was in town, thought Jackpine.

"Paul, go on up to Spruce Hill and check it out. Talk to Reg Frenette and ask him what Flip was doin' up there earlier, over."

"Right away, Chief, over and out."

Paul pulled out of his spot reluctantly. Boone's advice was paying dividends. He knew he would only have a few more days before the word was out among the truckers, and he was trying to maximize earnings. When he got to the mine, he was surprised that Reg didn't come out of the cabin to greet him. They were sort of friends. Paul drove up to see him now and then on slow days to have a cup of coffee and talk. In the cabin he found a note that read "I had to go to Thunder Bay. Some important business to tend to" and signed Reg Frenette. It looked like Reg's writing, but it didn't make sense to Paul. For one thing, Paul couldn't imagine Reg having any business in Thunder Bay. For another, he would have told someone he was going. Paul looked around the cabin. He saw Reg's suit hanging up. If he did have business, he probably would have taken his suit. Reg took his job seriously. He would not leave the mine unattended. He looked around some more but didn't notice anything. He decided to head back to town and report to Jackpine.

* * * * * *

Jackpine slammed the door of O'Toole's office as he and Boone departed. Boone had never seen Jackpine so angry. He could have played a lot longer in the NHL if he could summon up that kind of intensity and anger at will, thought Boone. O'Toole hadn't taken the charges very seriously. He said Golias had called yesterday and reported a man named Patterson missing from the lodge and that he thought he'd headed down river. He acted as if Boone had fabricated the story. Jackpine had told him to check the boats for bullet holes, to ask why a group of Latinos were living at the lodge, to check the fish in the freezer for cocaine, or at least come to Rainbow Falls and question Lafontaine. O'Toole had said he was busy, but he would fly to the lodge tomorrow and conduct a full investigation.

Boone waited ten minutes during the drive home, letting Jackpine cool down a bit, before he started. "Has he always had a deep tan like that, Jackpine?"

"No, come to think of it, he hasn't. Must have been out in the sun a lot. Maybe the sun fried his brain."

"Does he travel down south? That's a Florida or California tan he's sporting. Did you notice the envelope in the out basket addressed to McFadden Travel in Thunder Bay?"

"No, I was so fuckin' mad I didn't notice anything except the dickhead's blank stare."

"You noticed his eyes? Jackpine. His eyes told me he was lying. Perhaps the cop should have had these instincts, but Boone had spent his career and made his fortune by knowing when people lied and when they didn't.

"Now, Boone! He's a stupid son of a bitch but I've never seen a crooked OPP in all my years."

"Crooked is your word, Jackpine. I just said he was lying." Boone paused. "Tell me everything you know about O'Toole."

"Not much, really. Grew up down east, Toronto or near there. His old man was a big shot in the Mounties. One of his brothers is a Mountie, doin' pretty good I hear. Other brother owns a car dealership in Toronto. O'Toole tried to get into the Mounties years ago: either didn't get in or fucked up and got kicked out. I don't know which. Even with all his old man's pull, he didn't make it. Anyway, he joined the OPP, I guess twenty years, pushin' twenty-five maybe. Guess he hoped he would stay down east, but he's been up north here his whole career. Kenora, Nakina, Schreiber...maybe a few more places; I've heard him mention those. Was married when he came up north, his wife bailed out in Nakina. Can't say as I blame her. Nakina is a far cry from Toronto, and her married to an asshole. O'Toole's one of those types who needs a uniform, know what I mean? 'Bout all I know. 'Cept he's getting stupider by the day."

"Stupid, but not crooked?"

"I've never even heard of a crook in the OPP. Most of 'em are good people."

Boone knew there were stupid people in all walks of life, at all levels, up to and including the corner office. You didn't often find a stupid CEO. Darwinian selection through the ranks worked well, but every now and then it happened. Boone knew that O'Toole probably made sergeant more on seniority than ability, but he didn't strike him as being stupid. Crooked yes, stupid no.

"Is he a sailor, Jackpine?"

"No, not that I know of. Why?"

"There were five books on his shelf. Four law enforcement–related and one on sailing the Caribbean."

"Maybe someone gave it to him," Jackpine offered.

"Maybe," said Boone. "So what happens next, Chief?"

"I don't know, Boone. Maybe I'll haul in Flip and Bear and make them confess. They're in for a rough time anyway, if I see them back in town."

"You know your confessions wouldn't hold up if you beat the shit out of them. I hate to admit it, but I would enjoy watching it." Boone had always been vindictive in business. When someone screwed Boone in a deal, he never forgot it. He would wait patiently, for years if necessary, until the opportunity presented itself. He would get them back, as many times as he deemed necessary, to settle the score. The score was measured in money, not lives. For the first time in his memory, he wanted to extract physical vengeance from the hides of Flip Lafontaine and Bear Sawchuk, up to and including murdering the worthless bastards. The extremity of his emotion worried Boone, but it didn't change things. "Besides, if you arrest those two you might spook Golias."

"We could go up there. Find the coke and bust them all."

"I got the impression they were working off the tail end of a shipment. Another one has to be coming, because Bear and Flip said they would be there a few weeks before they headed out to find their Shangri-La. I think we have time to get organized."

"OK," agreed Jackpine. "You're right about one thing. It's a foolproof way to smuggle drugs. But the airline or at least some of the employees have to be in on it. Somebody in Minneapolis is switching the fish with the dope for some clean fillets. The season is virtually over though; they must have another plan to smuggle the next shipment. He's got that big boat down on Lake Superior. Supposed to be for lake trout fishin', but guys have been saying they've never seen it out on the lake. You know, it's less than a hundred miles across the lake to Copper Harbor, Michigan."

"Maybe you're right. We know the drugs are coming in by floatplane from up north. But how do they get from South America to the subarctic?"

"I haven't got a clue, Boone."

"Fair enough. Tell me what you know about Danny Golias."

"Not much. He bought the lodge last winter. He used that weasel Steve Appleton to do the deal. It was March, just after Appleton moved to the Falls and put up his shingle. Golias was, or is, a car dealer in Toronto—used cars. Doesn't appear to be married. 'Bout all I know, except he don't belong running a fishing lodge."

"OK, here's what we should do. Check out the murders again. If Bear and Flip hung White Horse Parker, they probably were involved in the others. Check out the Reserve with your pal the Indian chief. See if you can make Bear and Flip on the Reserve the night of the murders. Then check out the boat. See if it's really been idle all summer. Use your computer to do a check on Golias. See if he's got a record."

"Gotcha, Boone."

"If you see those Latinos in town, bust them for littering or something. Get a look at their IDs and check them out too."

"OK."

"Where do most folks go to buy a used car?"

"Blackwater, maybe Thunder Bay."

"Not Toronto?"

"Course not, it's too far. Why?"

"Just wondered," Boone moved on, "I'll have the charter airline that the lodge uses checked out, try and find who owns it. I'll go to Toronto and find a way to get info on shipping schedules in Hudson Bay. Dope must be coming by ship. What's the port up there?"

"Churchill, Manitoba. Mainly grain handling. Summer only, naturally."

"Good. I'll check out Golias from the business side while I'm there. First, I'm going to find out where O'Toole got his tan."

"How the hell will you do that?"

"I don't know. But I'll start out tomorrow at McFadden Travel in Thunder Bay."

"Maybe you can check out Steve Appleton in Toronto. Guys like him don't move to places like Rainbow Falls."

"OK, Jackpine. There's more people than Golias and those two half-wits mixed up in this. We'll see what we can find out."

CHAPTER 5

Jackpine dropped Boone off at the hotel for a much-needed nap and drove to Northland Crafts to see Janice. As he entered the lot, he saw a tour bus pulling out. The presence of Northland Crafts and the premium-quality, reasonably priced meals presented by the Shultzes at the Falls View Restaurant—combined, of course, with the awesome majesty of the cascading falls—were sufficient to lure the tour buses from the Trans-Canada Highway into side trips to Rainbow Falls. The money that stayed behind when the buses bid farewell was a welcome windfall to the struggling town.

As Jackpine walked in, he saw Janice remerchandising her shelves and restoring the trademark neatness that had been decimated by the ravaging of forty elderly browsers. Janice looked up and smiled when she saw her stalwart pal, lover, and confidant. Many people had wondered how long she would last in the Falls when Jackpine first brought home his obviously worldly, urbane, sophisticated bride. Janice Keating was not what she appeared. The nurse at Yale-New Haven Hospital that Jackpine had fallen in love with was a small-town girl from the rolling foothills of the Berkshires in northwest Connecticut. This practical, no-nonsense New England Yankee came from a town (if you removed the expensive prep school and a few country estates of rich New Yorkers) that was remarkably similar to Rainbow Falls. Janice Keating had felt at home the minute she arrived in Rainbow Falls

Janice, at forty-one, had aged like a fine wine, becoming more attractive with the years. She had been attractive in her twenties, but her sharp features had been too hawk-like to be considered beautiful. Time had beneficially softened her sharp lines, but she retained the lovely smile she was born with. When gray hairs first appeared, she rushed to the hairdresser because her light-brown hair with blond highlights was much more becoming than her dirty-brown natural hue. Her few extra pounds only accentuated her shapely figure, and her lively blue eyes shone through the glasses she wore.

Her smile melted Jackpine's seething anger at O'Toole. He knew it would; perhaps that was why he had stopped in. Janice was excited. She had done over $1,000 in business with the bus. Two high-ticket sales of moose-hide mukluks at $180 per pair had nudged the tally over $1,000. With a good October, Janice would accomplish her goal of $100,000 for the year.

She sold most of the odds and ends expected in a resort store, but she avoided any souvenirs she thought were particularly tacky. Her specialties were leather goods and wood carvings crafted by natives, primarily from Lac des Iles, but also from a couple of other area reserves. Because she was a good and fair person, a solid source of employment, and the wife of Jackpine Keating, the natives tolerated her antitrapping posture.

Janice hated the thought of animals dying slow deaths in leg traps, their only crime being the valuable coats they wore. Sales in Northland Crafts could be much higher with a broader selection of hide-based merchandise, but there was no merchandise crafted in whole or in part from wolverine, wolf, fox, beaver, marten, mink, or otter (especially the cute playful otter) sold in her store. There never would be. Moose hide was different to Janice Keating. The moose were being slaughtered anyway as a source of food, and they were shot, not trapped. She was not aware that in order to supply hides and snowshoe guts for Northland Crafts more moose were being killed than could possibly be eaten. Of course, none of the Indians would let that particular cat out of the bag to this crazy white woman. The mukluks, slippers, belts, gloves, vests, jackets, and purses kept coming. The supply was sometimes tight due to lack of initiative by some of the craftspeople, but never from a lack of raw material.

Most of the goods were produced in the winter, and Janice's strict, no-nonsense quality control ensured premium quality on the shelves. Northland Crafts had developed a solid reputation and was a must stop for any visitor to Rainbow Falls.

She also offered prints of paintings by Norval Morrisseau, the renowned Ojibway artist. The artwork was displayed to enhance the decor and ambience. A customer had bought a print once. The next day Janice doubled the price of all the remaining prints. She enjoyed looking at them—so simple, yet so complex—and did not want customers tampering with her private collection.

This policy bothered one Alistair Drayton Boone. Starting the store had been his idea. Janice had wanted to return to work but did not relish the idea of commuting to Blackwater Hospital to resume her nursing career. "So, you want something to do now that the kids are older, you want to be your own boss, and you want time off in the winter for vacation. How 'bout all that plus some much-needed employment on the Reserve?" It had taken Boone some time to convince her. The idea of providing employment for natives was what finally swayed her. Now she couldn't imagine not having Northland Crafts.

Although she had grown to like Boone immensely, his exuberance and dominating personality had repelled her at first. Jackpine had helped her to see the big heart hidden beneath the bombastic ego. She still resented his ongoing advice.

Her resentment was good-natured, but she dug her heels in and ran the operation the way she wanted to—not the way Boone envisioned. Boone's original idea was a retail outlet combined with a mail-order business. She enjoyed the store, but she had no interest in mail order (much to Boone's dismay). Three years ago, she had taken Boone's advice on some low-end souvenir crafts: rocks hand-painted with a Falls scene, small birch-bark canoes, rocks affixed to pieces of varnished driftwood, little doll-size beaded mukluks, and other such items. These types of souvenirs were now a big part of her business, and her craftspeople were bringing her new ideas along the same lines.

Boone also constantly told her that she was paying the natives too much for the work. She shrugged that off. Above all she wanted to treat people fairly, and it wasn't as if she and Jackpine needed the money. Her other sources of supply for core items were an annual trade show and a wholesaler in Thunder Bay. Now, the local citizenry was getting involved. The Ladies Auxiliary at the United Church had come to her with the idea of making wild blueberry, raspberry, and cranberry jams and jellies. Janice put the jams on display with sampler jars of each variety. The line was doing so well that the Boy Scouts, Girl Scouts, and Jackpine's boys hockey team were picking berries as fundraisers. The ladies' jam-making sessions were becoming the social center of the Falls society. Different recipes were tested and Hattie Bailey's grandmother's recipes were the official bona fide requirement for Northland Preserves. A dozen recipes were tested to determine the best. The judge's decision was final. Janice probably would have used Boone as the judge (had he been around), so she employed the next best choice as judge—Paul Desroches. Paul did not accept any accolades for the important assignment; he insisted on remaining incognito for fear of offending the eleven losers. It was a difficult decision. All of the recipes were very good. Paul had to eat two loaves of toast and a dozen English muffins before he could determine the winner.

Jackpine helped himself to crackers and the remnants of the sample jars, while Janice finished straightening her shelves. "See you've sold out again," he chuckled as he tossed a blueberry-jam-laden cracker into his mouth.

"Isn't that something? Couple of old girls were fighting over the last jar. I thought I was going to have to call you in an official capacity to mediate," Janice laughed.

"How did you resolve it?"

"I had a jar for us in my purse. I let them buy it. You'll be having store-bought at home."

"Curse my luck."

"Should have a fresh batch of cranberry jelly tomorrow, but we're out of luck today."

"You know, Janice, you're creating another dilemma. The folks at the church don't know how to spend their newfound wealth."

"I know," she laughed. "There's even talk of getting our own minister back."

Rainbow Falls was a town like so many other small towns everywhere, fighting to survive. Having a resident minister was a symbol of the health and continuation of the town's existence. After the mine had closed, they could no longer support a minister. Their sermons were delivered on Sunday afternoon (which negatively affected attendance) by the preacher from Blackwater; he would drive up after tending to his own flock. During blizzards in the winter, church was cancelled because the star of the show could not make the drive. The Roman Catholic Church, the only other church in town, faced the same ignominy.

"Well, let's not rush into anything until we find out what's goin' to happen at the mill," cautioned Jackpine. The tom-toms of rumor were pounding ominously with news of the imminent closing of Rainbow Falls Lumber.

Rainbow Falls had had ups and downs before but had always managed to survive. The town was founded in the late 1800s with the building of the Canadian National Railroad: the second of two rail services to be implemented across Canada. A spur line was built from Blackwater, on Lake Superior, to Rainbow Falls. Coal was shipped by boat up Lake Superior to the harbor at Blackwater and transferred up the spur line. Rainbow Falls was a railroad town, supplying coal, abundant water, and a point for crew changes.

Rainbow Falls had become a thriving two-industry boomtown in the 1920s, with the development of a gold mine near town. When the diesel replaced the locomotive, the railroad no longer needed coal or water. The diesel was much faster—crews could travel longer distances between changes. Rainbow Falls ceased to be a railroad town but continued to prosper as a gold-mining town. The town made the transition without missing a beat. Some of the old-timers lamented that the railroad got in your blood, but the younger generation shoveled ore as readily as the old-timers had once shoveled coal.

The gold mine continued to increase production, and jobs continued to be available. Then, in the mid-1950s, Kenogami Paper had decided that some of their better quality timber reserves could deliver higher returns on investment being converted to lumber rather than being mushed in their pulp mill in Blackwater. Fates of small towns (and the hopes and dreams of the people) were decided in the boardrooms of Toronto and New York. The survival of small towns was seldom, if ever, one of the issues discussed. Fate had smiled on Rainbow Falls with the opening of the Rainbow Falls Lumber Company.

The two-industry town had prospered until 1972, when the gold vein petered out. Inevitably, the gold mine had ceased production. Only Reg Frenette, the watchman, kept his job. It was a miracle of bureaucracy that he remained on the payroll for almost twenty years watching the abandoned mine. The first dark omen was the closing of Rainbow Falls High School in 1973. Students began commuting forty-five miles each way by bus to Blackwater. The second omen, affecting morale and image, was the folding of the Rainbow Falls Warriors men's hockey team. The Falls had always had a competitive team, and beating bigger towns, especially Blackwater, was a source of pride to the town. The gold mine lured good players to town with jobs and preferential treatment. The lumber company could not shoulder that burden alone.

The one-industry town had expanded and contracted with the ups and downs of the lumber market. There was a period of apprehension in the early 1980s when Kenogami Paper decided they must change their corporate direction and focus on core business. They decided that Rainbow Falls Lumber Company was not a part of this newly defined core and they put the company up for sale. Some company named CMI bought the lumber mill and it was business as usual—albeit without the sense of security of being part of a well-known entity like Kenogami.

The Falls they all took for granted was a marvel of Mother Nature's engineering prowess. A substantial tourist business had developed from this concept, but it was not enough to compensate for the catastrophic closing of the mill. There was a glimmer of hope created by the appearance of the Polarex Mining Exploration crew, but Jackpine had come to realize that these bums would not find anything of value (except maybe a wallet in the Rainbow Falls Hotel Bar).

Jackpine switched topics, not wanting to add the demise of the town to his already troubled frame of mind. He told Janice that Boone and Inez had brought their romance out from under the shroud of secrecy. "Inez, of all people, should know there's no such thing as a secret in this town," said Janice. Jackpine and Janice decided to celebrate the occasion by having Boone and Inez over for dinner. Inez and Janice had planned to go to bingo, so they decided they would all go. Jackpine invited Paul and Bertha as well.

Bertha Olesen watched Mr. Boone walk into the lobby— usually dapper and exuberant, today he looked like death warmed over. He wanted a wake-up call at five thirty, just before Bertha left for the day. She was also told that she was due at the Keatings' at six for dinner.

This should have been a happy occasion for Bertha. Going out for an evening with the Keatings, Mr. Boone, and Mrs. Mahoney was very prestigious and would no doubt raise her status in town a few notches, but prestige was not an issue with the modest Bertha Olesen. She was concerned about what she would say and how she would act in such distinguished company. There was a far more serious concern, and she felt a sense of impending doom in her love life.

Bertha was normally cheerful and pleasant. Her short blond curls did not complement her large, round face, but she was almost pretty when she smiled. She was not very pretty with the anguished countenance she now affected. She looked in the lobby mirror. She would not have time to go home and change. Her ample frame was concealed under a baggy sweater and loose-fitting plaid skirt, at least as well as 180 pounds on a five-foot-seven frame could be concealed.

Her love for Paul Desroches was obvious to even the most casual observer. Now that Paul had a steady job, most expected the wedding bells to ring out soon. As one cynic noted, "It's not like either one of 'em's got much competition." Of the few eligible bachelors in town, it was only Big Paul Desroches who could allay Bertha's self-consciousness about her size. She actually created the illusion of being dainty when she was on the arm of Big Paul. Their personalities meshed, as Jackpine noted: "They go together like blueberry pie and ice cream." Jackpine, the matchmaker, was trying to prod Paul along to bring the romance to the inevitable commitment. There remained only one stumbling block to the engagement. Paul had insisted that Bertha promise him never to become large enough to require two chairs at bingo. Bertha did not want to make a promise to Paul that she was not sure she could keep.

Every second Thursday night, coinciding with payday at Rainbow Falls Lumber, bingo was played at the Legion Hall. It was always well attended. Men went on occasion, but many women attended religiously. When admission was paid, you were given a folding chair that you returned at the end of the gambling session. This saved the legionnaires from having to set out the chairs and collect them later. In effect, there was no admission charge but instead a two-dollar fee to rent a chair. The truly corpulent players were obligated to rent two chairs for four dollars—one chair for each mammoth buttock. The experienced obese players would tie the two chairs together with scarves before gingerly resting one cheek on each chair. The scarves kept the chairs from separating in the heat of the action, preventing the hall-echoing thud of a huge butt hitting the floor.

There were seven ladies in town resigned to their fates of being a two-chairs-at-bingo woman. Word spread through town like wildfire when a new recruit was enlisted to serve the rotund brigade. The transition from pleasantly plump to obese was fast and irrevocable. Marilyn Kennedy had been the last to blossom to these ranks. She defied nature, steadfastly refusing to rent more than one chair. One night, in the throes of euphoric victory, just as the war cry "BINGO!" was erupting from her bountiful bosom the folding chair collapsed under the strain. A chubby big-boned girl fell to the floor and a two-chairs-at-bingo woman got up. Thus, the seventh member of the club was initiated. Now a seasoned veteran, Marilyn brought scarves with her to fasten two chairs.

The husbands were not spared. Mike Kennedy heard the gibes over the sound of the whining saws at the mill. "Ol' Mike gits a hard-on an' he's gotta roll'er in flour an' look for the wet spot." Coming out of Blackwater Tent and Awning one day, he overheard someone say, "Looks like Mike is buying his wife a dress." Paul had heard these lines and a hundred others. His male ego was more fragile than his intimidating physical stature would indicate. It was important to Paul that his wife not be a two-chairs-at-bingo. Any weight gain by his beloved would present no problem as long as she was able to perch on a single chair every second Thursday night.

When Bertha sat watching TV in the evening, devouring microwave popcorn, she would wash it down with a six-pack of diet soda. That seemed to be the limit of her self-discipline. Bertha had refused to go to bingo for the past year. She had feigned repugnance for the game. Now she was in love with a handsome man. Seeing Paul in his uniform made her heart flutter, and she was manipulated into going to bingo. What if old Earl at the door made her rent two chairs? Her life would be ruined.

* * * * * *

Dinner at the Keatings seemed an eternity to Bertha Olesen. She decided that if she passed this test tonight, she would give Paul his promise and marry the big hunk as soon as she could. During dinner, Jackpine said something odd to her: "You look as nervous as the biggest turkey in the flock on the day before Thanksgiving." Then he said "don't worry" and winked at her.

The newly refreshed Alistair Drayton Boone knew not of the drama that was unfolding, but he had heard of Paul's requested promise. Bertha was the first to run Earl's gauntlet. He accepted two dollars from Paul and gave Bertha a chair. To Big Paul Desroches he said, "That'll be four dollars, Paul, you're two-chairs-at-bingo, son." Paul looked as if he had been shot. His face blanched as his unsteady hands fished for another two dollars. Boone noticed Earl wink at Jackpine. That sly, old fox, thought Boone, he put Earl up to this—that manipulative matchmaker. A thought crossed Boone's mind. He remembered Jackpine singing the praises of Inez Mahoney. No, he couldn't have, thought Boone, I am a manipulator, not a manipulatee.

By the third game, Paul had overcome his discomfort; his old ebullient self returned. By the fourth game, Paul and the relieved Bertha were committing the cardinal sin at bingo—holding hands and making goo-goo eyes. They were not listening to the numbers being called. They did not seem to notice Boone leaning over them and tending to their cards.

CHAPTER 6

Boone was on his way to Thunder Bay by nine a.m. He had spent the night with Inez at her house for a change. Inez had won a bingo game and was pleased with herself. She went regularly but never won. She attributed her change in luck to a karma enhanced by the presence of Boone. Boone modestly accepted credit. Bertha had also won. Boone, who sat beside Bertha, had filled in her numbers while she was mesmerized by Big Paul. Boone did not win. He wanted to. It was not for the money. He wanted to yell "BINGO!" but never got the opportunity. He had been looking forward to a night in the sweet embrace of the lovely Inez Mahoney. It was not to be. Boone had fallen asleep the minute his head hit the pillow, and he had slept soundly until Inez woke him up on her way to work. Luckily, the opportunity would present itself again. He was beginning to think he should spend every night of his life with his arms around Inez Mahoney.

Boone skipped breakfast. At ten o'clock he stopped to buy a smoked lake trout. The same old Indian had been selling trout from the same location for countless years. Boone was a regular customer whenever he was in the area. The fish were one price regardless of size. A big fish was cheaper per pound, but the small ones tasted better. It was, to Boone, a sophisticated pricing program enveloped in ultimate simplicity. Boone bought two small ones. He stripped the skin and bones from the trout to accommodate snackability. He bought a cold club soda and perfected the beverage with a quartered lime he had taken from Inez's fridge. He set the cruise control and nibbled on the succulent trout.

When he got to Thunder Bay, he stopped for gas. He washed the oily reminders of his repast from his hands, licking his fingers first for a last taste of nature's bounty. He found McFadden Travel.

It was a small agency, so the chances were good they would know O'Toole. Boone sat a few minutes in the car to plan strategy. He couldn't burst into the office with full-Boone power—that would be too intimidating. He also talked to himself, trying to sound Canadian. He practiced clipping his words, focusing on pronouncing *r*'s, "New York" and not "Noo Yawk." He decided not to add "eh" to sentences; he never really knew when to add an "eh" and when not to.

"Can I help you?" There was only one girl on duty, and she didn't look busy. Twenty-five or so, thought Boone, an employee—not a McFadden.

"Yes, I have a week off work and I thought—on a whim, really—that I should go down south…Florida, maybe. But do you think it's too hot down there this time of year?" October was his favorite time of year in Florida, but he thought a discussion about weather would be a good way to get the conversational ball rolling.

"Yes, it's hot. But everything is air-conditioned. And the ocean is cool and refreshing."

"Where do you think I should go?"

"Well, Orlando is nice: Disney World and Sea World or Sanibel Island or Fort Lauderdale or Tampa Bay. Do you want to see attractions, fish, golf, or just lay on a beach? Or what?"

"I think something on the ocean. It's so hard to decide. Tell me, do you have any clients that go to Florida a lot? If somebody from here went to a place frequently, it must be nice."

"We have a client who has been there four times already this summer."

"Probably a doctor or lawyer. Too rich for my blood."

"No, actually, he's an OPP. A sergeant, I think."

Bingo! thought Boone. Fucking O'Toole, trying to be incognito, but having to wear his uniform even to impress a travel agent. "That might be good. Where does he go? Same place all the time?"

"Yes, he goes to Fort Lauderdale. Sometimes he flies to Miami though, depending on flights and fares."

"That's where I'll go. That sounds nice. Where does he stay?"

"I'm not sure. He doesn't book a hotel through us. Wait, let me look at our phone bill. I had to call him there a few weeks ago to change his flight." She looked at a file. "Here it is, Turnberry Isle Yacht Club."

"OK, book me a flight to Fort Lauderdale. Return, leave the return date open. But I'll find a hotel down there; a yacht club sounds too hoity-toity." Boone had heard of Turnberry Isle, lovely place. Condos and boat slips there were extravagant, even by Boone's standards. "On second thought, let me think about it for a while. It's a lot of money to spend on a whim. I'll be back later." Boone thanked the girl and left. It would have been easier to book the ticket there, but he didn't want to take the chance of O'Toole finding out he was checking up on him—not a great risk, just an unnecessary one.

Boone drove to the airport and parked his rental car. He only planned to be gone two days at most and didn't want the hassle of turning the car in and re-renting it. He booked a flight with a connection through Toronto.

* * * * * *

Jackpine was at the office early. When Inez came in, Jackpine spent a few minutes reinforcing the positive traits of Alistair Drayton Boone, even though it hardly seemed necessary. A few minutes later, a moonstruck Paul Desroches drifted into the office. He announced his engagement to Bertha Olesen and was heartily congratulated by Jackpine and Inez. Inez gave Paul a demi-hug. Her arms, fully extended, only reached the rib cage on his mammoth frame. Big Paul was beaming. The eighth member of the two-chairs-at-bingo club had officially withdrawn his request for a promise of relative slimness from his betrothed, asking instead for a promise of undying love. Bertha had readily accepted the commitment. Paul promised the same, regardless of how much dear Bertha might someday tip the Toledos. Jackpine agreed to serve as best man for his diligent deputy.

After giving Inez and Paul their assignments for the day, Jackpine left for Lac des Iles. Chief Lawrence Musgrove, of the Lac des Iles Ojibway band, welcomed Jackpine. Chief Musgrove had known Jackpine all his life. They played hockey with and against each other as kids. Although chief was an elected position, the office became almost a birthright for Lawrence Musgrove. He always ran unopposed in elections, as his father had before him. Lawrence was active in the fight for Indian rights and land claims. Jackpine's view was that the claims should be equitably settled between the natives and the provincial and federal governments. He was not totally cognizant of the arguments on either side of the issue, but he believed action should be taken toward settlement instead of the continual waffling by the governments.

The chief respected Jackpine. Jackpine Keating's law was fair and just. More importantly, to Lawrence Musgrove, natives and whites were treated equally.

"What brings you out here, Jackpine? Not trouble, I hope?"

"Not really, but if any of your young fellas plan to spend their summer wages on a car, you better tell them to keep the speed down. Big Paul Desroches gonna ketch 'em in his radar."

"Yeah," Lawrence chuckled. "I've heard some bitchin'. Mostly trucks he gets, though. Always seem to see a truck in his trap when I go by. Guys out here call him 'Truckhunter' Desroches."

"Better than Constabull. I'll tell Paul. He'll get a kick out of bein' called Truckhunter." Jackpine changed topics.

"I'm still upset about Desmond Lesmontaignes and Jimmy Boucher. I can't see Desmond drowning and Jimmy bein' up Spruce Hill Road. Who was the girl with Jimmy?"

"She wasn't from here. I told the OPP that Desmond wouldn't drown himself. They say they're investigatin'. They must be investigatin' 'round their coffee pot because they haven't bin out here much."

"Well, Lawrence, I wouldn't know how to investigate, myself. No witnesses. Nothin' to go on."

"Guess so. Too bad, anyway. Good young fella that Desmond." By omission, Jackpine knew that Lawrence did not think highly of Jimmy Boucher. Neither did Jackpine. "Young Esther Martin is pretty broken up. She was runnin' around with Desmond."

"I didn't know. Can you do me a favor, Lawrence? Come with me to talk to Esther." Jackpine knew that if he went around the Reserve alone, asking questions, no one would talk to a cop.

"You don't have your cruiser, do you?"

"No, I've got my Bronco." The cruiser was not available, even if he wanted it. Truckhunter had commandeered it as a decoy for his radar trap. Jackpine was not in uniform. He was wearing a checkered wool shirt and blue jeans. Everyone on the Reserve knew him, but he didn't want to look like he was there on police business. For one thing, it was not his jurisdiction.

They drove out to the Martin house. Esther answered the door. She looked about sixteen: a pretty girl, dressed in old blue jeans, sneakers, and a sweater. She opened the door, not saying anything. Napoleon Martin was sitting at the kitchen table. His fiddle was on the table. He had just finished playing along with an old Andy de Jarlis record. Nap was well known locally for his prowess on the fiddle. He played by ear, not being able to read music. Andy de Jarlis had been dead for years and Napoleon knew all of his tunes by heart; he had just finished practicing.

Like many Indians, Nap was a man of few words. In seven carefully chosen words, he greeted his guests, explained his wife's absence, and offered hospitality. "Lawrence, Jackpine, old woman's pickin' cranberries. Coffee?" They sat down while Esther put the fiddle away and got a mug of coffee for each of them. She opened a small can of Carnation milk for the distinguished company. Sugar cubes were already on the table. Esther still had not said a word. Jackpine asked Nap permission to ask his granddaughter a few questions. Nap nodded approval.

"I understand Desmond Lesmontaignes was your boyfriend."

Esther nodded.

"He got home from Blackbear Point Lodge and died that same night. Did you see him?"

She nodded.

"Did he say anything about the lodge?"

Esther looked down at the floor. "He said somethin' was goin' on there. He was goin' to the Falls next mornin' to tell Paul Desroches. Then he drowned."

"Did he say anything else?"

She shook her head no.

"Do you know who Bear Sawchuk and Flip Lafontaine are?"

She nodded.

"Did you see them the night Desmond drowned?"

"Yeah. They were out here. Me and Desmond saw them. He said they were 'sposed to be at the lodge. Wondered what they were doing here."

They thanked the Martins and left. Lawrence and Jackpine drove around the Reserve, knocking on doors and talking to people for three hours. Two other people confirmed the presence of Bear and Flip on the Reserve the night that Desmond died. No one had seen them with Desmond, but three people had seen them the night Jimmy Boucher died. Jimmy had been drunk and was driving around raising hell, keeping a high profile. Two of the three witnesses claimed they saw Bear and Flip in the car with Jimmy Boucher and the young girl.

Jackpine dropped Lawrence off at the chief's office. He drove back to Rainbow Falls and went to see the personnel manager, who was also in charge of security at Rainbow Falls Lumber.

There had been two complaints of gas missing from worker's cars. Jackpine assumed some kids siphoned the gas for use in their own cars. They checked the records. The dates of the complaints coincided with the nights of the murders. Both workers were on the third shift: midnight until eight a.m. Both had left their keys in their unlocked cars (a fairly common practice in Rainbow Falls, especially at the lumber mill). Jackpine now knew how Bear and Flip had come and gone without being seen. The mill was beside the river. They had come down the river from the lodge, parked their boat, and stolen a car. Before dawn they would have returned the car and headed up river.

Jackpine left the mill and drove to Blackwater. He went into the Royal Bank and asked to see the manager. The managers changed every couple of years. Jackpine was not sure whether he knew this one or not.

"Chief Keating, nice to see you! C'mon in." Jackpine thought they must have met, if the guy knew him. They all looked the same to Jackpine.

"Is this police business or personal, Chief?" Jackpine noticed the business cards on the desk—Robin Cook.

"Curiosity more than anything, Mr. Cook. I understand you hold the note on Blackbear Point Lodge."

"Hey, boy news travels fast in these one-horse towns." Cook beamed, not realizing he was being offensive. If Blackwater was a one-horse town, Jackpine wondered how he would classify the Falls: a one-pony town, perhaps. Toronto, thought Jackpine, paying his dues with a stint in the boondocks. "We just finalized the sale a few days ago. Mr. Golias is selling out. I guess he decided the lodge business was not his cup of tea, wants to return to the civilized world. A retired doctor from Michigan has bought the business."

Pompous little prick in a cheap suit, looking down his nose on honest working folk, when they come in for a loan, thought

Jackpine, making them grovel and lose self-respect for a car loan. He tried to be polite when he spoke. "How was business there this summer?"

"I don't know for sure. I guess bookings were down somewhat, but the payments were always current."

"What was Mr. Golias's collateral for the loan?" He had outstepped his bounds, and he knew it. He stared at Cook with his don't-you-dare-fuck-with-me stare. It usually worked.

"There was a substantial cash down payment. Of course, I took into account the inherent value of the property, and it was cosigned by CMI."

Why would the owners of Rainbow Falls Lumber have signed a note for a Toronto used-car dealer to buy a wilderness lodge? It did not make sense to Jackpine. "When is the sale effective?"

"Mr. Golias is leaving October 30th. Mr. McDonald and I will finalize the transfer with the new owner November 1st."

Jackpine thought of asking the selling price, but he knew that even Cook would balk at that question. He thanked Cook and left. Jackpine had missed lunch, so he stopped at the Voyageur Restaurant at the Esso on the Trans-Canada Highway. Two cheeseburgers, fries, coleslaw, and a large Coke curbed his hunger. Inez and Paul were waiting for him at the station when he returned.

Jackpine asked Inez how she had made out checking on Golias. Efficient and thorough as always, Inez handed him a typed report. Your past could not be hidden from the long arm of the law in the computer age. The rap sheet looked like a novel. He armed himself with a cup of coffee before sitting down to read. Czdeno, aka Danny Golias, was born in Hungary and came to Canada with his family in 1956. He was raised in the Cabbagetown section of Toronto, a ghetto-like melting pot that was transformed into inner-city chic in the last twenty years. Conviction for car theft at sixteen, suspended sentence, breaking and entering at seventeen, and armed robbery at eighteen. Served two years in the Kingston Penitentiary. At twenty-one, arrested for beating his wife. She dropped the charges. Two arrests for failure to pay child support. Then he seemed to end his career as a petty criminal, maturing and developing into a con man. Sold penny stocks, charged with fraud and acquitted. Selling nonexistent vending routes, witnesses suddenly refused to testify. Investigated for fraud in selling diamonds and aluminum siding, no charges laid. He had not suddenly gotten honest, thought Jackpine; he was honing his skills and getting smarter. At twenty-nine he beat his second wife badly, not charged. The inference in the police report was that she was intimidated into dropping the charges.

In the late 1970s, Golias was convicted for swindling senior citizens out of their life savings in an investment scam. The wife beating disgusted Jackpine; the last crime infuriated him. Golias had paid a fine and did two and a half years. Then, for the last ten years, it seemed Golias was in the used-car business. Two charges of selling stolen cars were dropped. A few fines paid for selling cars with false odometer readings. Suspected of dealing cocaine, arrested, and released without charges.

After finishing the report, Jackpine knew what he had already suspected. Danny Golias was capable of ordering Bear and Flip to commit murder—without losing any sleep over it.

Jackpine sent Paul on radar patrol. Toivo Huhtela, at the airport, was to call Paul if a floatplane from the lodge came in. The airport was located on the shore of Dead Horse Lake. There was a landing strip and a marina for floatplanes on the lake.

When the railroad was being built, two workers had been hauling supplies across the lake with a team of horses. The ice had not been thick enough to hold the weight. The workers and the horses had drowned. Jackpine had told Boone the story. Boone had made a social comment about the value of two immigrant workers versus a team of horses at that time in history.

Had it happened today, perhaps it would have been named "Dead Man Lake" or maybe "Why Didn't You Stupid Bastards Test the Ice Lake." But Dead Horse Lake had a ring to it, and it provided more fodder in the long list of stories to regale the tourists. The story had been accepted as gospel, but for all Jackpine knew, the saga could have been invented and gained veracity over the years.

* * * * * *

If given the opportunity, Paul was to arrest the Latinos for littering or something and check their IDs. Paul pulled out his notebook and flipped it open to give his report. He had seen enough cop shows to master the maneuver. "Toy Huhtela called at 11:04 a.m., reporting that the Blackbear Point Cessna had landed. Steve Appleton met the plane. Dan Golias, the pilot, and two gentlemen of Mexican persuasion went into town with Appleton. At 11:48 a.m., the two Mexicans were dropped off. They proceeded to wait. They tossed candy-bar wrappers on the ground. These ones," Paul pulled the crinkled evidence out of his pocket. If Jackpine Keating told Paul to go jump in a lake, Paul would leave and return in a few minutes dripping wet, asking for another assignment. Paul was told to arrest them for littering or something. The something was far too vague. He had waited for the littering. "I proceeded to arrest the perpetrators for littering."

"What did they do?" asked Jackpine, smiling.

"This part isn't in the report. They yelled and screamed, they told me to...." In deference to Inez Mahoney, he spelled out "*f-u-c-k o-f-f.*" "I told them if they resisted arrest I would knock their heads together like a pair of coconuts. I lightly took hold of them, just to show I was serious." Jackpine could imagine how lightly Paul had grabbed them. "The perpetrators calmed down. I brought them here, checked their IDs, and printed them. I then drove them back to the airport. Both paid the fifty-dollar fine in cash. The sign at the viewing area of the Falls says fifty-dollar fine for littering, so I figured this would be the same. I mean a candy wrapper at the Falls or the airport."

"Yes, Paul. Go on." Jackpine did not need the dissertation on how he arrived at the amount of the fine.

"Mrs. Mahoney then proceeded to check them out." He flipped the notebook shut with authority. Inez handed Jackpine a piece of paper. "Both Colombian citizens. One has a green card and lives in Miami; the other's home is Cartagena, Colombia. Neither one had an arrest record, as far as Inez could determine."

* * * * * *

Boone woke up early and had breakfast in his suite at a Marriott in Fort Lauderdale. He phoned the sales manager at Turnberry Isle at nine. As the chairman of Pinnacle Incentive Travel, he wanted to stop by and tour the facility. He still had a few business cards from when he owned the company. He made the appointment for ten. He phoned Jackpine, and they discussed developments. Boone went to see the sales manager and suffered through a two-hour tour and sales pitch. He asked the right questions, anticipated the standard answers, and was finally able to escape the clutches of the professional (but aggressive) manager.

On his way out, he stopped at the reception desk. Boone's charm and persuasiveness were no match for the ramparts erected to protect the privacy of the rich and famous. He got nowhere asking about William O'Toole. Before leaving, he thought he would take a shot in the dark, using a tidbit he had picked up from Jackpine. "Would you please ring through to the CMI condo? They're friends, and I wanted to see if they happen to be here."

The clerk checked the records and placed a call—no answer. "Can you just give me the number? I'll try later."

"Just call the desk, sir. We'll be happy to put you through."

"Mr. O'Toole should be there today. Could you do me one favor? Just tell me if Mr. O'Toole is staying there now."

"Certainly, sir. No, it seems Mr. O'Toole was here two weeks ago for three days. He is not scheduled to return until the evening of October 30th."

"Thank you very much," said Boone. While on his tour, he had noticed a Crew Galley: a small bar and restaurant for the crews of the yachts at the facility. He arrived at noon and was happy to see it was fairly crowded. He ordered a hamburger and a Bud, striking up a conversation with the bartender and the sailors perched near him at the bar. He purported to be a guest at the hotel who found the place too formal and stuffy and had stopped in for a few beers and a game of pool with some real folks.

Shortly after finishing his burger, Boone was at the pool table. Winning a few, losing a few, and buying rounds of beer for the guys around the table. Boone was in vintage form: telling jokes and stories, and entertaining as the consummate good ol' boy. Boone let the conversation turn to boats. It was easy to do. Yachts were the common bond of his new pals. A sailor's prestige was reflected in the type of ship he crewed. The worst job was working for someone who could not really afford to be playing the game.

Tales abounded of legendary penny pinchers that the guys had worked for. Stories, too, of flamboyant, high-rolling land developers and builders—great to work for until the bubble bursts, leaving the crew without jobs and usually with a few rubber checks as souvenirs. There was talk of first-timers realizing their fantasy by buying a yacht. Combine the penny pincher with the first-timer, and you had the worst possible owner. Of course, most owners were financially stable, veteran sailors, but they did not make good copy.

In the good times, experienced sailors could pick the type of owner they worked for. But these were tough times in the leisure business, and even penny-pinching first-timers could hire a good crew. Boone kept the focus on penny-pinching first-timers. He hit pay dirt on the seventh round of beers. A friend of one of Boone's new pals had signed on with a Canadian who qualified on both criteria: bought a forty-two-foot fishing boat in Fort Lauderdale.

As a guest at Turnberry, the owner had used the Crew Galley as a recruiting ground. Bobby had signed on for a year as a one-man captain and crew. Bobby had experience charter fishing, and the owner's plan was to start a business somewhere in the Caribbean. Boone asked what the owner looked like. "Five eleven, short hair, receding hairline, a neat well-trimmed moustache...walked like he had a poker stuck up his ass." Sounds like O'Toole, Boone thought.

Boone said he fished a lot in the Caribbean and might give these guys some business. His pal called Bobby's place and got his girlfriend. Bobby had the boat on the gulf at Tampa, getting some work done. He would be back in a week. She wasn't sure where they were going to set up shop. She was going to fly down and sign on as the cook once they were established. They planned to sail October 31st, the day after Mr. O'Toole arrived in Fort Lauderdale. Boone thanked her and said he'd call back before the end of the month. Boone bought another round of beers while waiting for the cab. With all the beer, he was glad that he had not rented a car.

He noticed the *Monkey Business* moored at the dock (the scene of Senator Hart's undoing). When politicians got caught lying, cheating, breaking promises, or with their fingers in the till, they were slapped on their hands and re-elected. When they offended a sense of morality, they made history.

Boone called Poke Chop from the airport. His chauffeur and bodyguard had done a lot of driving and very little body guarding. Now, Boone felt he could use Poke Chop in that latter capacity. He presented the mission as potentially dangerous but totally voluntary. Poke Chop leaped at the opportunity. Boone got Linda back on the line. He was going to have Poke Chop meet him in Toronto; then he reconsidered. A giant black man with a ghetto-inspired uneasiness around uniformed officials trying to lie to a customs officer (who spent his life watching for lies)—it wouldn't work. He told Linda to have Poke Chop rendezvous with him at La Guardia. They would fly to Toronto together.

Boone went for a cup of coffee while waiting for his plane. The beer had given him a headache. As he thought of the last few days, a sudden anger seethed through him. He felt fury at Bear and Flip for trying to kill him in cold blood, fury at a legal system that let these guys walk the streets, fury at O'Toole (under oath to serve and protect) for selling out, fury at the drug runner Golias (peddling death, destruction, and ruining lives), and fury at society—what went wrong that make cocaine such an attraction to so many?

Danny Golias did not know something that Bear and Flip were already aware of—Jackpine Keating and Alistair Boone were a formidable pair of enemies.

* * * * * *

At breakfast in the hotel in Toronto, Boone gave Poke Chop his assignment. They agreed to meet back at the hotel later. Boone was at the Ministry of Tourism by nine a.m. He was prepared to exude a consummate aura of patience and understanding as he attempted to slash through the tangled undergrowth of bureaucratic procedures. Surprisingly, he got in to see a young staff officer within ten minutes. Once again, he assumed the role of chairman at Pinnacle Incentive Travel. Linda had been briefed to answer the phone with the travel company name rather than "Boone Corporation" for the day. The phone seldom rang these days. When it did, it was usually Boone checking in.

Boone explained his concept to "Junior Tourism" enthusiastically. He assumed his role of Boone the pitchman as readily as Henny Youngman might toss off an irreverent one-liner. He was launching a totally new travel incentive adventure for companies—a true wilderness experience. The rough itinerary was a day or two in Toronto enjoying the sights and sounds of the beautiful city, and then they would board the Polar Bear Express train to Moosonee on James Bay and experience nature for a day, doing some Indian kinds of things. Next, a fully equipped first-class cruise ship would pick them up. Exploring the majestic subarctic sea, they would cruise up to York Factory (the original settlement and headquarters of Hudson's Bay Company) and then on to Churchill to see polar bears. If polar bears weren't normally there that time of year, he would just arrange so some were. Then they'd fly back to Toronto. What did Junior Tourism think of the plan? Once pioneered, all the competition would jump on it. They would create an industry. It sounded so good to Boone that he decided he would really do it—if he had not retired.

It was the grandest plan the young fellow had heard in his entire career. A career that had begun a few months ago (upon his college graduation) was not the point.

"How can I help you, Mr. Boone?" Junior Tourism saw that if this really worked, it would jump-start his career. If it did not, he had never heard of it.

"There are a few details I have to work out. This is a wilderness extravaganza. We'll be looking for seals and whales and things. I can't have the cruise ship in a crowded shipping lane full of dirty oil tankers and mundane cargo ships. Would ruin the mood, and the mood is everything. I'll have to examine a maritime shipping schedule for Hudson Bay, to see if the trip is feasible. Imagine selling a pristine setting with a Russian grain boat beside you."

"I understand completely. I'll personally get copies of the shipping schedules and be in touch in two or three weeks."

Now came the hard part, thought Boone—to instill a sense of urgency. "I just got this idea." That was certainly true. "I'm presenting it to two major clients in New York tomorrow. I've already set up Alaskan cruises, but this idea is totally different. I'll have to answer this one question today, to at least mention this trip as a plausible alternative."

Junior Tourism understood. He leaped from his desk, startling Boone, and said, "Let me see what I can do. I'm going upstairs. You wait here, Mr. Boone."

Boone knew the kid was going upstairs, both literally and figuratively, to where the seasoned turtles toiled. To Boone's surprise, Junior was back in twenty minutes. "Maritime Shipping is federal. They have an office in Toronto." He handed Boone a piece of paper. "Go there and ask for Mrs. Matthews. She's expecting you and she'll have the information you need."

Boone thanked him sincerely and left. On his way to the Maritime Shipping office, he stopped and bought two-dozen donuts. Donuts were an inexpensive but effective aid in oiling the wheels of commerce. He asked to see Mrs. Matthews and took a chair, putting the donuts beneath it. If she looked like an aerobics instructor, he would leave them there. Mrs. Matthews, her big bosom jiggling and her ample butt swaying, came to greet him. Boone grabbed the donuts and walked over to meet her. She selected a Bavarian cream, before placing the box on a filing cabinet near the coffeepot and watercooler. He saw that word was travelling fast. There were already five people standing around the filing cabinet waiting their turn at selection. Boone watched Mrs. Matthews' big ass as he followed her. She should've been doing double duty at the salad bar and passing up the Bavarian creams. By the time they reached the office, the evidence of her transgression had disappeared—save for the trace of powdered sugar that she licked politely but thoroughly from her fingers before pointing Boone toward a chair.

Boone ran through his idea quickly and ended with aesthetic concerns of freighters and tankers. Mrs. Matthews said she would get the logbook, maintained in the office, and be right back. She returned with the book in a few minutes. She put the book down in front of Boone, left the room, and returned a few minutes later with coffees for Boone and herself and another donut—this time a honey-dipped.

The first section of the logbook was a list of research ships sailing in James Bay and Hudson Bay. A brief synopsis of their missions included studying weather and climate, fish, whales, Viking settlements, and Franklin's expeditions—almost any scientific or historic venture that someone thought worthwhile enough to fund. They seemed to be all Canadian or American ships, nothing out of the ordinary.

The next section listed cargo ships travelling to and from Churchill. Boone scanned the list and then began to read it carefully. The port of Churchill shipping season was short. Boone noticed that a ship of Panamanian registry had sailed from Colombia, arriving in Churchill on July 20th. It sailed with a cargo of wheat on July 24th, destined for Indonesia. Only one other ship was coming from Colombia. It was due to arrive at Churchill on October 25th. It was also picking up a shipment of wheat, probably destined for Russia, but sailing to Rotterdam. Boone thought he had solved the sourcing part of the scenario. The ships picked up the cocaine in Colombia. Somewhere on Hudson Bay the drugs were off-loaded onto a boat or floatplane. The ship would clear customs in Churchill. The drugs were taken to some point on or near James Bay. Golias then arranged to have the shipment picked up piecemeal under the guise of outpost fishing trips from Blackbear Point Lodge.

"Can I check the ownership on two of these vessels, Mrs. Matthews?" Boone was overstepping, well outside of the boundaries of his cover story. The donuts worked wonders.

"Certainly, Mr. Boone. Are you finished with the log?"

"Yes."

"Good. I'll put this back and get another book. We have a record of ownership in case of fire or a ship sinking, or God forbid, an oil spill." Boone could tell that a ship sinking and all hands aboard drowning was a minor inconvenience, but an oil spill was a tragedy. Boone sifted through the ownership records. Both boats were owned by a Panamanian shipping company. The shipping company was owned by a holding company in Grand Cayman. He wrote down the name of the company and went to find Mrs. Matthews to thank her. He found her the first place he looked, fishing in the box for the last donut. He thanked her and went to the pay phone outside the office.

Boone called his cooperative banker in Grand Cayman. The information on ownership was confidential. Understanding how things worked, Boone offered to pick up any incidental expenses involved in finding the answer. It would take some time. Boone agreed to call back early in the evening. He was a couple of miles from the hotel, but he was early for his meeting with Poke Chop, so Boone decided to walk. He enjoyed the clean, big downtown of Toronto. The city fathers had foresight. They had the sense to locate the ghettos in the suburbs. The Jane and Finch area was not to be found on any tourist maps. When he got to the hotel, he called and booked a flight to Thunder Bay for himself and Poke Chop.

Poke Chop was in the bar at the hotel, sipping a Diet Coke, when Boone arrived. They checked out of the hotel and stopped at a Swiss Chalet for a late lunch on their way to the airport. When they finished their chicken, Boone asked Poke Chop how he did.

"Y'all are a wizard, Bossman. Jest the way you figguhed." Boone had sent Poke Chop to Eastside Motors. That was the name of the used-car dealership that Boone had noticed on the license-plate holder on William, not Bill, O'Toole's Oldsmobile Delta 88. Poke Chop would be more credible at the kind of dealership Boone envisioned than he personally would have been. Poke Chop pulled out a business card. Boone read the name "Romeo Dubrovnik."

"Ah talked to a salesman name a Romeeeo Du somethin'. Ah didn't know people was really named Romeeeo. Ah said ah was lookin' for some wheels. He's a fast-talkin' mothuh that Romeeeo. Ah said ah wanted qualitee an' doan wanna pay no fortshun. He says ah come to the right place. He says they doan buy from no wholesaler. They doan buy no junk. He says they buy mose-a der cars from a big Chev Olds dealer. The dealer has too many trade-ins; they help him out. They gits only the bess used cars from the dealer."

"What was the name of the Chev dealer?"

"Was O'Toole Chev Olds."

"Did you find out who Romeo works for?"

"Romeeeo says his boss be outta town. Says it's mah lucky day. Says boss wants to make big profit. Romeeeo says he jest wants to move iron. Do anything ah want. Line a bull if ah ever heard one!"

"The name, Poke."

Poke Chop had it written down. "Mr. Danny Golias. Then ah tried what you said. Ah said ah wrecked mah car up near Thunner Bay an' took the bus to Toronto. Ah told him the cop at the accident, Mr. O'Toole, says ah should come here to buy a car. Romeeeo says he knows him. His brutheh is the Chev Olds dealer. Sent the cop heah for a deal on a car last winter. Diddin want no new car, wanted to save money and get a used one. He says Mr. Golias be good friends with the cop O'Toole now."

"Great job, Poke." Boone had calculated correctly that someone would open up to Poke Chop, not sensing any ulterior motive. Golias was an opportunist. He saw a bitter, unhappy, disillusioned man. He read the vulnerability in William, not Bill, O'Toole and took advantage. Did he have the plan to buy the lodge and smuggle dope (first) and then buy a cop? Or did he find a cop who commanded a big stretch of wilderness and then figure a way to use that to his advantage? The result was the same, but somehow Boone thought the sequence mattered. Golias must have locked up O'Toole first. A crooked cop was integral to the safety of the big operation. He couldn't just interview OPP officers who commanded detachments, looking for one who would take a bribe. The lodge and the rest of the scheme must have been developed after Golias bought O'Toole.

On the way to the airport, Boone began to feel guilty. He could not drag Poke into a life-threatening situation—no matter how much he wanted to come. Poke was hired as a driver (first) and a bodyguard (second). Poke served as a deterrent to potential muggers, convincing them with his intimidating physical presence to search for easier prey. Poke was concerned about his job security with Boone gone and probably thought this was a way to keep his job. Boone would look after Poke, financially. But to involve the guy with a wife-beating drug smuggler, two sadomasochistic killers, a bunch of Colombian thugs, and a crooked cop did not seem right. Boone's feelings of revenge had temporarily overcome his conscience.

At the airport, he told the protesting Poke Chop about the change in plans. The crestfallen chauffeur headed for the American Airlines terminal to catch a return flight to New York. Boone called his banker in Grand Cayman and got the name of the owner of the holding company. He had never heard of it, but he wrote the name down anyway. Boone charged toward the Air Canada gate. He was a little early, so there was no reason to rush, but old habits died hard.

CHAPTER 7

Boone had an aisle seat in first class. He was surprised to recognize the man in the next seat. "Lumber business must be pretty good," Boone said. It was Andrew McLeod: general manager of Rainbow Falls Lumber and member of the town council of Rainbow Falls.

"Hi, Alistair." Friends called him Boone, strangers called him Mr. Boone, and Alistair was in between. "Actually, it isn't very good at all. Jackpine Keating told me you were on this flight. There was a cancellation at the last minute, so I was able to upgrade to this first-class seat." He had gotten Poke Chop's seat. "I wanted the opportunity to speak with you."

Boone realized how forlorn Andrew looked. Always serious and somewhat dour, the added countenance of dejection had escaped Boone at first. They were interrupted by the stewardess. She does not feel like smiling, thought Boone, so she's forcing one and taking it a few degrees too far. It was something deeper than the prospect of overnighting in Regina. Maybe it was just too many miles, too many safety demonstrations, too many dreams faded with the realization that she was a waitress in the sky, Boone thought. But one problem at a time. Andrew ordered a Labatt Lite and Boone a gin and tonic. "Tell me about Rainbow Falls Lumber."

"It will have to be between us. I don't want to worry everyone in the Falls; not just yet, anyway."

"Deal," said Boone. Sometimes he wondered why people were always willing to share secrets and burdens with him. He wondered, too, why he never opened up to people the same way (maybe that was one of the reasons why Lisa had left him).

"Well, the economy is weak, and there's no building going on. Our business has been going downhill for a few years. I'm running at sixty percent capacity. The company is losing over a hundred thousand dollars a month. The owners have had enough."

"So, they're going to sell the business?"

"Nope. They've tried. No takers at any price. I've managed to have them stay with it for the summer. Now with the slow season coming, they want to close down permanently."

"Have they tried the government?" Both the provincial and federal governments in Canada seemed far more willing to become involved in the private sector than their American counterparts, especially in one-industry, rural towns.

"Even the government doesn't want any part of us," sighed Andrew McLeod.

"Tell me about the owner."

"CMI, Consolidated Manufacturing International. They own a lot of different companies."

And one fishing lodge and an OPP sergeant, thought Boone.

"They've owned it for eight years. We did a lot of business with Toth Brothers. They're builders in Toronto and part of CMI. I guess that's why CMI bought a lumber company in the first place. Now, in bad times, Toth Brothers can force desperate suppliers to sell to them at a loss and then take a long time to pay. So they don't buy lumber from their own company. I've been pleading my case all day, begging them not to close us down."

Andrew McLeod did not strike Boone as a man to whom begging came easy. "What happened?"

"Normally, I just deal with the managers. We're pretty small potatoes to CMI. But today they let me in to see Mr. Sandor Toth himself. Him and his younger brother own CMI."

"What did he do?"

"He laughed in my face. He doesn't care about me or the people or the town."

"The town will die without the lumber mill. People have worked there for generations."

"They've raped the company. They made us rely on Toth Brothers for business; then they pulled the rug out from under us. They sold most liquid assets and have not provided the cash for proper preventative maintenance. The company has always been highly leveraged, but they never put the money against the debt. They siphoned the cash off to some other CMI company. Now, they're going to close the mill and walk away from it."

"Have you considered buying it yourself?"

"I'm not a wealthy man, Alistair, but I did talk to some banks. They were not interested."

You're also not a risk taker, thought Boone. If McLeod himself thought the situation was beyond salvage, he could imagine the "power" presentation he had made to the banks.

"What's the reputation of the company in the industry?"

"Very good!" said McLeod emphatically. "We produce high quality consistently and offer great service to our customers."

"But business is terrible." Boone restated the obvious.

"Yes, I'm afraid so. The phones are quiet most of the day. I've had to reduce people on the order desks."

"How is your competition reacting to hard times?"

"Who knows? You hear one thing one day and another thing the next day. The guys on the order desk don't know if they're coming or going. I carry a huge inventory; then, when we do get an order it's always for something we don't have. Then we run around like chickens with our heads cut off trying to produce the order. We twiddle our thumbs all week and then pay overtime to get an order out."

Boone did not understand the lumber business, but he did understand business. "First thing you have to do is transfer the people on your order desks. You need to get some pros in there, some rainmakers. You're in a commodity business. You need people who know what's going on in your market. You have to know where the demand is and what each of your competitors is doing to fill the demand. Second, get rid of the huge inventory. If you have pros selling the product, they will understand the market well enough to accurately forecast what they will sell. You need a fast reaction time. Develop a just-in-time philosophy to slash inventory and improve service. Hell, you could put millions in the bank instead of in the lumberyard. You can't sit there and wait for business to come to you—not these days. You need movers and shakers to start scratching the pad. You guys got complacent relying on in-house business from Toth Brothers." Boone was becoming animated.

"That's true, but I wouldn't know where to begin to…"

"Nonsense! Just a question of finding the right people. Now, how does your cost compare with competition?"

"Favorable, I would guess. Our labor costs are substantially lower than the big mills out west, for one thing. But any advantage disappears when we run at half capacity. The fixed costs kill us."

"It's all the same problem. Drive the business, and the overhead per two-by-four comes tumbling down. Then you have to identify the closest markets." Boone was changing gears too quickly for the befuddled Andrew McLeod. "The closer the market, the greater the competitive advantage. If you try to compete too far away from your mill, there's nobody making money except for the railroad." Boone paused to take a sip of his drink. This company needs a catalyst, he thought.

"It's difficult times we live in, Andrew, very difficult times."

There was nothing very profound in the statement, but Boone's tone made it sound profound. Andrew McLeod paused to ponder the profundity.

Boone did some mental arithmetic. With sound management and slashing operating expenses, it should be possible to stop the bleeding and make the operation at least breakeven. When the economy improved, it would become profitable. He could buy the company cheap. Anything CMI got for a business they were going to close down would be gravy. The Toths sounded like a pair of scoundrels, but their backs were against the wall in this deal. The key would be the amount of debt and how it would be structured. Saving the town appealed to Boone's sense of chivalry; plus, if he could breakeven in the bad times, he could make a lot of money in the good times. Was it the white-knight appeal, the profit motive, or his love for Inez Mahoney that had him thinking this way? Inez's only objection to marriage would disappear if he lived in the Falls. Could he live there? Emotion had no place in a business deal—Boone knew that. But with ego and love running amuck, Boone said, "I might buy it, Andrew. I'd like to come in and see the books and tour the operation. I'd like to talk to the production manager, the finance manager, and the guy in charge of sales."

"Any time you want, Alistair. Thank you."

"Thanking me is premature. A lot of things would have to be worked out." Board Foot Boone, Lumber Baron Boone—Boone was liking the ring of it, as the plane landed in Thunder Bay. Andrew McLeod left the plane in considerably higher spirits—thanks in part to his potential savior and in part to Labatt Lite.

* * * * * *

Boone got up at eight, feeling content but hardly refreshed. To make love to Inez Mahoney was to experience heaven on earth. Boone was tired from his long journey and the three trips to heaven. He wanted to see Jackpine, but Jackpine was in Thunder Bay. As a member of the town council, Janice Keating was attending a meeting of rural municipalities. Jackpine had escorted her to the city and was going to run some errands while she was at the meeting. Boone had other work to do.

He pored over the atlas that he had just bought at the drugstore. Minneapolis was a potential market. It seemed to be around six hundred miles from the Falls. Boone was not sure of the efficiency, if any, of international rail connections and tariff rates. Looking at the map, he reasoned that the Twin Cities would have more viable options to source lumber in northern Minnesota, Wisconsin, and the Upper Peninsula of Michigan.

The best target seemed to be Winnipeg—a smaller market than Toronto or the Twin Cities, with a population of five hundred fifty thousand. Geographically, Rainbow Falls Lumber should be competitive. To the west of Winnipeg were the treeless expanses of the Great Plains. Boone had fished a few times north of Winnipeg and remembered forested land (primarily poplar and scrub pines more suited to pulp and paper production than lumber). Garnering strong penetration with lumberyards in Winnipeg would be a solid step toward solvency. Boone called and booked the noon flight to Winnipeg from Thunder Bay. He called the marina and chartered a small plane to take him to Thunder Bay.

Boone called Sidney Rosenfeld in New York. Sid was a partner in a major law firm. Boone had worked with Sid for twenty years. Sid gave Boone the personal service of an independent, along with the resources and the variety in fields of expertise that only the big firms could offer. Sid was expensive, but the quality of his work justified the exorbitant fee. The impetuous (sometimes reckless) wheeler-dealer Boone would have been sunk many times if he had used an ordinary lawyer.

Boone told him he was thinking of buying a lumber company. Sid was not surprised that Boone was wandering so far afield. Nothing Boone did ever surprised Sid. Boone wanted everything Sid could dig up on CMI. Sid's firm was affiliated with a law firm in Toronto. The information would be no problem, but it would take a few days to gather. Sid also agreed to find out what he could about Steve Appleton.

Boone called his investment banker and told him to coordinate the information gathering with Sid. The banker agreed to make initial contact with CMI to say that there was a client expressing interest in Rainbow Falls Lumber. When he knew more about the company, the banker would put up some trial balloons to investors for financing part of the deal. The bank also had an affiliate in Toronto that he would use to get the ball rolling. He also agreed to find out what he could about Sportsmen's Paradise Airline, the charter company out of Minneapolis that serviced Blackbear Point Lodge.

* * * * * *

Boone took a window seat to enjoy the scenery on the flight to Winnipeg. The first landmark Boone was able to identify was not very scenic—the effluent-spewing paper mill in Dryden. Slag heaps from mines and paper-mill effluent were the by-products of jobs in northern Ontario. The noxious odors emanating from giant smokestacks were the sweet smell of the bread and butter of the North. Some of the rivers were so polluted that Indians who defied warnings and continued to eat the mercury-laden walleye died long, slow deaths—their bodies twitching with contamination. Boone looked to the north: hundreds of thousands of square miles of vast unspoiled wilderness and thousands of lakes never traversed by a white man. Below was a huge roadless expanse with no towns—just a few remote Indian villages accessible only by air—a land far bigger than the state of Texas with a total population less than the city of Austin. Lake of the Woods was the last piece of artistry as the rugged mural of the Canadian Shield succumbed inevitably to the allure of the prairie. Miles upon miles of wheat fields stood empty, resting until spring. The landscape was carved geometrically with uniformly straight roads. Now and then there was a field of sunflowers still standing sentry. The city of Winnipeg erupted suddenly out of the plains.

Boone checked the yellow pages for the three most prominently featured lumberyards. He got directions from the helpful clerk at the rental-car booth and headed for his first call. It was premature to present himself as a would-be mill owner. He was an American involved with a consortium that (among other ventures) built resorts. They planned to build a wilderness retreat with five-star amenities, including a championship golf course and tennis courts, to complement the beach and fishing. They had not made a final site selection, but they were focusing their efforts on northwestern Ontario and northern Manitoba. He was conducting a preliminary site inspection. Since they would be buying a lot of lumber, he thought it made sense to start to develop a relationship with a local supplier. He did not have any concrete specifications or requirements at this early date. He was up here fishing, and half the reason for his visit (he would wink knowingly) was so Uncle Sam would pay for part of the trip. During general discussions, he would mention that he saw a lumber mill on his fishing trip, and out of curiosity, did they deal with Rainbow Falls Lumber?

The first two calls were inconsequential. By observation, they were about equal size. He spent twenty minutes with each sales manager. Both ran the biggest yards; neither one asked Boone many questions. They just pitched themselves and their lumberyards. Both repeated frequently that they had the lowest prices in town. Both warned him that other dealers were not to be trusted: others would quote low but fuck him first chance they got. Both knew of Rainbow Falls Lumber, but they were both too big to deal with chicken-shit little mills. They each dealt with the major players. Both gave him a final warning about the buggering habits of their competitors, and Boone unconsciously tightened his ass as he turned to leave.

On the third call, he found a sales manager he could talk to. After explaining his cover, Boone said, "I bet you have the lowest prices in town."

"I see I'm not your first call." Chip Carpenter smiled. "No, frankly my prices are not the lowest. But I will do three things. First..." He brought his hands to eye level and grabbed the index finger of his left hand without giving up eye contact with Boone. "I'll inspect your shipments personally before they leave the yard, to ensure you're getting top quality. Second..." He clutched his middle finger. "I'll work out a delivery schedule so you get what you need for the day's work. I won't ship early so it gets stolen. I won't ship late so you have an idle crew. I will ship what you need, when you need it." He grabbed his ring finger and added it to the collection of fingers. "Third, when something goes wrong your guy can call me here or at home. He won't get a runaround from a customer service clerk or the order desk. He'll call me and I'll solve the problem. Now, I won't sell lumber at a loss. I'll take a fair profit. But by doing the things I say, I will save you money over the long haul on the entire job. By the way, I would want the entire job. It won't pay for either one of us for you to bid out bits and pieces and try to save a few dollars." He released the three fingers from captivity.

Boone was used to leading any conversation. It was natural to him and it was also an acquired skill. Somehow, he was losing badly in this talk. Chip then asked him a dozen pointed questions about his venture. Boone was vague in his replies; he had no choice. This guy was too sharp for Boone to spin any elaborate scenario; he knew instinctively that he would be trapped by his own words. Before he could bridge any answer into changing the topic, Chip fired another question at him. Boone was on the run and he was not used to this position. After what seemed like the hundredth question, but may have only been the tenth, Chip paused, smiled, and said, "Mr. Boone, you have no intention of building a resort here or anywhere else. Why did you want to see me?"

Boone knew he could get some answers to his real questions. "First, Mr. Carpenter, this conversation is casual. I haven't done anything or made any offers, but as you may or may not know, Rainbow Falls Lumber is up for sale." This is public knowledge, thought Boone. "And I don't know a goddamn thing about lumber, but I'm thinking about buying it."

"You must have a lot of money, Mr. Boone."

"Call me Boone; my friends call me Boone. At the risk of sounding altruistic, it means everything to the town of Rainbow Falls. My best friend lives there—my fiancée." God, he was rushing to conclusions, Boone thought. "I would like to play some part, if I can, in saving the town. But I have to believe firmly that I can make money on my investment. If I can't, then I go broke and the town dies anyway. Plus, I have no desire to go broke—I've worked too hard for my money. It does seem, however, from the little I know, that I should be able to turn a profit. Do you do business with Rainbow, Chip?"

Now that he had come clean, Boone felt comfortable taking charge of the conversation.

"Yes, and I know Rainbow's for sale—has been for quite a while. Nobody is expanding today; everyone is trying to keep their own doors open, so there are no buyers. It's tough for a yard to keep going in this economy—must be just as hard for a mill. But, good operators can make money."

"How about you? Are you making money?"

"I'm paying the bills. But I've had to lay off some longtime employees: good men too. I've cut all discretionary spending. I'm not buying the new trucks I need, not fixing the roof. I put pails out when it rains instead of spending twenty grand to fix the roof. And I keep a low inventory and react fast when I get a big order."

Boone thought, this guy knows what he's doing. "Do you do much with Rainbow?" he asked.

"More now than I used to. I know they have a big inventory and they're hungry. And they're closer than British Columbia lumber mills."

"What's their biggest problem?"

"I don't know the answer to that. But from my perspective their real problem is they don't follow the market. The world is bigger than Rainbow Falls."

"How do you mean?"

"This is a commodity business: supply and demand. I spend an hour a day studying the lumber market: who needs what on the demand end, all across western Canada, but especially close to Winnipeg. I know every building project underway and most of the projects being thought about. Then, I talk to all the mills and brokers. I know what they're long on and short on. That knowledge can make the difference in a high-volume, low-margin business. A mill should know more about the market than a guy running a yard in Winnipeg. But in the case of Rainbow, they're always a step behind, reacting instead of anticipating and leading. They know less than I do, and I don't pretend to be some kind of guru."

No, but you know a lot more than a lot of people in this business, thought Boone. "You've been a big help. Thank you." Boone looked at his watch; it was two o'clock. "It's late, but have you had lunch yet?"

"No, I haven't."

"Do you have time to let me buy you lunch?"

"I wish I was too busy to go, but I'm not. Sure. What kind of food do you like?"

"All styles, but I like good food." Boone realized he was starving. Chip took him to an Italian restaurant but told him to have the T-bone steak instead of any Italian entree.

"The Italian food is mediocre, but their steaks are great."

The food lived up to the billing. Within a few minutes, the only things on Boone's plate were a T-shaped bone, picked clean, and a sprig of parsley. Boone lit a Monte Cristo and ordered a Sambuca with his coffee. Chip just ordered coffee.

"If I buy the mill, do you think you could run it?"

"I'm not very strong on the operations end, but I think I could learn. I could get to speed on the sales end very quickly. Yes, I could. But we're happy here. My wife is a teacher and has a good job. We would be reluctant to move. But I suppose we could talk about it."

"That's all I ask." Boone knew he could sign him. Andrew McLeod was strong on operations. Boone needed a take-charge guy and a crackerjack salesman; he was confident he had found both in Chip Carpenter. He came looking for information and did better than he had hoped. The key to success of the business was finding the right manager and paying him well with a big bonus incentive. Boone trusted his instincts to evaluate people. His instincts said Chip Carpenter was the man to run Rainbow Falls Lumber.

Boone dropped Chip off at the lumberyard and said he would be in touch. He headed for the airport, quite pleased with his day's work. He looked forward to getting back to the intoxicating Inez Mahoney—he was becoming addicted.

* * * * * *

Boone was in economy near the back of the plane. There was no first class on the flight. Boone had the aisle seat. Next to him sat an older man about seventy, Boone thought. He wore polyester slacks, suspenders, and a belt. This was a cautious man, thought Boone. A tan-colored shirt; an inexpensive, chocolate-brown sports jacket; a nondescript reddish-hued tie (that Boone suspected was a clip-on); a big nose; alert eyes; and a straw fedora with a brightly colored band rounded out the man's appearance. Boone hadn't seen a hat like that in thirty years. He didn't think they still made them. The man was wiry of build with gnarled brown hands, and fingernails that looked as hard as granite. These were hands that had done a lifetime of physical outdoor work. The woman beside him looked a few years younger: a healthy ruddy glow in her plump cheeks, small eyes hidden behind a pair of glasses (that she must have had for thirty years), a loose-fitting floral-patterned dress that covered her fleshy frame. Her shoulders were draped with a white wool sweater that either she had made herself or someone else had made and given to her. Going to Thunder Bay on family business, Boone thought—either something very good had happened or something very bad. Must be bad, thought Boone—a death would create a sense of urgency, making air travel necessary. The man clutched the armrests at the first sign of movement. "First time flying?" Boone asked.

"Yes, sir. The wife's idea. I wanted to take the bus. But no sir. Three-hour bus trip into Winnipeg and then ketch this fool contraption. Granddaughter's havin' a baby, and the wife has to be there."

"Well, relax. If they can put a man on the moon, they should be able to fly to Thunder Bay."

"That's bullshit."

"What is?"

"Never did put a man on the moon. Everyone believin' it. Not me. One of your Hollywood stories. Wearin' big helmets to breathe. There's nuttin' up there. There's nuttin' here and we breathe okay. Nuttin' is nuttin', and you can't tell me you need a big helmet to breathe nuttin'."

"So, you think it was an elaborate hoax. A put-on."

"Yessir, gov'mint did it. I proved it. Wife and I was watchin' on tellyvision when they was carryin' on. I went and looked outside. Little sliver of a moon that night. Any fool knows they woulda waited for a full moon. Lot bigger target ta aim at, to hit a full moon. You woulda thought more people woulda gone and checked the moon like I did."

"Does your wife agree with you?"

He lightly elbowed his wife. "Fella wants to know what you think a puttin' a man on the moon."

"I don't care one way or t'uther, long as we get to Thunder Bay in one piece."

Boone spent the rest of the flight trying to think of a logical explanation to convince the nonbeliever that man did indeed land on the moon. How could he explain that the moon was always the same size, that oxygen was essential to life? Maybe there was a lesson in the old man's logic. Not everything is what it appears. The guy wore a belt just in case his suspenders broke. Boone had met a true skeptic. This man would never lose a nickel to a con man like Golias.

* * * * * *

Paul Desroches and Bertha Olesen were walking hand in hand, chatting quietly as lovers do. They were oblivious to the world around them and had somehow ended up on the extreme south end of town on the road that ran beside the river. The autumn air was too brisk for anyone else to be out for a walk. They were enjoying the solitude; neither one of them was bothered by the cold. Bertha's nose and cheeks were red. Paul noticed the crimson accent in the glow of the streetlights and thought it added to her alluring beauty. Paul was not cold. The combination of the long walk and his steaming desire for the seductive Bertha resulted in beads of perspiration on his forehead.

The ring of the cell phone shattered the mood. "Paul, it's Rene, we have trouble here. Goddamn Polarex exploration outfit."

"On my way!" Paul hung up. "Sorry, honey. There's a fight in the bar at the hotel. I have to run." At first, Paul had used the word run as a figure of speech. It dawned on him suddenly that his police cruiser was in front of the hotel. He had met Bertha there after her shift as front-desk clerk, and they had started walking. Paul would literally have to run. He bid Bertha farewell and took off.

The phone, the flashlight, the billy club, his gun, his badge, and his whistle all flapped wildly as Big Paul Desroches rapidly accelerated to his version of full speed. Fortunately, Paul could think and run simultaneously. Mining exploration crews were common in this area. The Canadian Shield was a cornucopia of precious minerals, but most of them were securely hidden. Paul had heard that the geologist and the technicians had quit. Some idiot was still paying the crew to spend most of their time drinking and causing trouble in the Falls and Blackwater. They were a bad bunch, and Paul did not understand why anyone would hire them in the first place, let alone keep paying them when there was no work to be done.

Paul Desroches barged into the barroom. It was difficult for him to tell how many men were involved in the altercation. The local stalwarts that had been providing the opposition quickly took their chairs. None of them wanted any trouble with Jackpine Keating or Paul Desroches.

The Polarex crew was well aware of the folklore surrounding Jackpine. The fact that Jackpine was out of town was the very reason they had decided to do their hell-raising in Rainbow Falls.

As outsiders, they completely misread Paul Desroches. Paul's appearance compounded their misjudgment. His shirt had become completely untucked during the heroic run. The thirty pounds of fat on Paul's short frame hid two hundred and ten pounds of steel. Paul was sweating profusely; little rivers were pouring down his face. A wide smile dominated the lower half of his huge head. He indeed appeared to be a badly frightened man. Fear had not prompted the smile. Paul Desroches enjoyed a good brawl almost as much as a high-speed chase. To wear a uniform representing law and order made it even more special. He wore the smile of a child running toward the tree on Christmas morning.

The draft beer the crew had been swilling all evening sapped their analytical abilities, but it had the opposite effect on their swelling reservoirs of courage. One of the toughs grabbed Paul's hat and put it on. It came down over his ears. "The cop's out of town, so they sent fat boy here." He pointed to the hat. "I'm the cop now, so fuck off, fat boy!"

"Get outta here, tubby!" another one echoed.

Paul reached for his hat. The first fellow flipped it to a companion.

Jackpine had told Paul never to punch anyone under any circumstances. Jackpine feared that if Paul lost control and punched someone he would probably kill him. Paul Desroches obeyed orders. "You will all leave immediately, or I will arrest you!" The smile had turned to a grimace.

"You and who else, porky?"

As Paul was distracted, one of them kicked him squarely in the testicles. Another man drilled Paul with a hard right to the side of his head. The jackals circled and moved in. Neither the punch nor the kick had rocked Big Paul Desroches. Rene swore later that he saw smoke rising from Paul's ears. Paul did something a trained police officer should not do. Big Paul Desroches blew his stack.

He reached out and grabbed the two closest assailants. With his oak-tree arms he lifted them off the ground, one in each vise. He started banging them together. The other four were flailing away on Paul with kicks and punches that may as well have been mosquito bites. Paul continued banging the bodies together until there was no fight left in them. He grabbed the next two closest bodies and repeated the exercise—like he was playing the cymbals. When they were no longer wiggling, he dropped them to the floor. The last two had their false courage drained by this exhibition and fled for the door.

Big Paul was like an alligator: slow in the long run, but incredibly and deceptively fast for a short distance. There was no escape. Just before the exit, Paul caught the hat stealer by the right arm and the other by the back of the neck. He let go of the arm briefly to secure better purchase. Once he had them both by the neck, he said, "Never take my hat again!" That was the chant as he banged them together—"Never take my hat again." The bodies thudded. Paul threw them in a heap. He went to retrieve his hat from the floor. He asked Rene to hold the door open. Paul started to throw them out into the alley. Two managed to get to their feet and wobble out before Paul got to them.

Before Paul closed the door, he yelled, "I'll be out in ten minutes! Stick around if you want to go another round and spend the night in jail!" He tucked in his shirt and sat down at a table. "Large Coke, Rene, lots of ice," said Paul nonchalantly. He heard the doors of the pickup trucks slamming, signaling the departure of the Polarex crew.

* * * * * *

Boone was in his hotel by ten thirty p.m. Inez had lost some of her earlier devil-may-care spunk and insisted that she slink over to the hotel, rather than have him over. Within minutes they were in bed loving on each other. Either Inez was the world's best lay, or his love for her created that illusion. Soon, they were both spent and exhausted. She was lying on Boone, neither one of them moving.

Later, Inez asked Boone about Rainbow Falls Lumber. He started to tell her and then became animated talking about the lumber business. Soon Board Foot Boone, lumber-baron-to-be, was on his feet pacing back and forth. His hands flamboyantly emphasized points; his penis flapped as he walked.

Inez felt relieved that the capable Boone was involved in the salvation of the mill. The viability of the mill was essential to Rainbow Falls (the center of her universe). "What happened to the new Boone—the mellow, retired man?" Boone didn't answer. He took the question to be rhetorical. Inez smiled. "Come back to bed, you old warhorse."

Boone fell soundly asleep in the sanctuary of Inez's bosom. He awoke at seven thirty a.m. The note on the mirror read "You were sleeping so soundly, I didn't want to wake you. Until tonight.

Love you." Damn it, thought Boone, she escaped. He showered and went down to the hotel coffee shop for breakfast.

Andrew McLeod was with a group of people. He came over and joined Boone. "So, you're still interested?"

"Tentatively, yes. My people in New York will make contact. Let's keep my activity between us for the time being."

"Of course."

"Your guys will need a sharp pencil."

"I'm not sure what I can do to help, but I'll do everything I can." Andrew McLeod took his leave. Boone wanted bacon and fried eggs for breakfast. He wrestled valiantly with his cholesterol-conscious conscience; he lost on a split decision. Boone ordered Special K with skim milk and a bran muffin. He had real butter with the muffin instead of the edible oil compound, so it was not a complete victory for his conscience.

Boone went back to his room after breakfast to make a few calls. His conscience, having tasted success, would not leave him alone. Boone experienced pangs of guilt. If his investment banker was going to solicit outside funding for the project, Boone thought he should make it clear that one of his primary goals was to save jobs in Rainbow Falls. His motivation for this acquisition was not entirely profit.

After making the call, Boone was not sure how the banker had taken the disclosure of Boone's intent. Altruism was unfamiliar turf to the banker. The banker had brought the discussion back to the familiar financial footing, and Boone had reiterated a sound fiscal belief in the project. The banker had gotten a D&B and had made a few calls concerning Sportsmen's Paradise. The airline had been purchased in March by a company in Toronto. The company's other concerns were a used-car dealership and a fishing lodge. The principal owner was one Dan Golias. Effective October 31st, the airline was being sold to a small group of employees. The selling price was a few hundred thousand less than what Golias had paid for the business eight months prior.

It became clear to Boone how Golias had induced some of Sportsmen's Paradise's employees to become involved in the smuggling operation. They played a fairly low-risk but integral part in the operation. Once a guest's cocaine-laden, frozen fish fillets cleared customs, they would replace the package with a different one containing only fish: thaw the fillets, remove the cocaine, and refreeze the fish. The refrozen fillets would then replace the next innocent mule's cocaine-laden parcel. The fish would lose most of its flavor in the thawing and refreezing. When the lodge guest got home and ate some of the fish, he would notice it and tell his friends and family, "You can't believe how much better this fish tastes in the great outdoors cooked by an Indian guide at shore lunch." Nobody would be any the wiser.

The airline employees were rewarded for their efforts with a sweetheart deal to acquire the airline (their brief flirtation with a life of crime paying handsome dividends). The death and destruction that followed in their wake was out of sight, out of mind—not their problem.

Boone then called Sid. The Law Society of Ontario kept track of its members, and Sid procured a brief bio on Steve Appleton: graduated five years ago from Osgoode Hall at the University of Toronto, two years with a big law firm, one year of private practice, four and a half years in corporate working for a land developer, and now back to private practice in Rainbow Falls. Boone saw a familiar pattern. He graduated with the dreams and aspirations of a partnership in a major firm. Big firms hired many graduates and then worked them like slaves at low wages for a few years. Most drifted away in disillusionment or got fired and replaced with a new crop of eager beavers. Only the few truly gifted and/or truly well connected emerged from the spawning grounds into significant legal careers. A few of those would make partner someday. Steve

Appleton was one of the mediocre. He was pushed out of the big law firm and hung up his own shingle. He sat pompously in his office and starved. Now, completely disillusioned, he would take a job that would have been beneath his dignity a few years ago. A big land developer would have a few top-notch lawyers either on staff or on retainer. They would also have a pool of lawyers on staff for the mounds of routine mundane work. Long monotonous days, cramped quarters, pay far less than the going rate, no chance for advancement—Steve Appleton had been one of those hacks.

The familiar pattern was broken when Appleton moved to Rainbow Falls. Boone did not see how the town of Rainbow Falls would generate enough potential to keep even one lawyer busy. Folks did not make a practice of suing each other, houses were rarely bought or sold, and most of the businesses stayed in the same hands year after year. Keeping Flip Lafontaine and Bear Sawchuk out of jail did not seem to be full-time employment. And Steve Appleton certainly did not seem the type to enjoy the great outdoors.

* * * * * *

Boone went to the police station. Inez was alone. Boone helped himself to a cup of coffee and sat down. Boone thought Inez Mahoney was becoming more beautiful with each passing day. He was contemplating kissing her when Jackpine came in. Jackpine showed Boone the new walkie-talkies he had purchased in Thunder Bay. Boone wondered why a two-man police department needed six of them, but he did not ask. Jackpine was having too much fun demonstrating them. When he had finished playing with his new toys, Jackpine took Boone into his office. They spent an hour comparing notes on what they had learned in the past few days.

Near noon, Big Paul Desroches lumbered in looking glum. "I've bin up to Spruce Hill; still no sign of Reg Frenette."

"We think he's down at the bottom of shaft number two, Boone," said Jackpine.

"Can you do a search?"

"It's about eight hundred feet deep; a hundred feet or so is water. It's slowly fillin' up over the years. Near the bottom there are strong currents. I think they weighted his body and threw it down there. Could be swept into one of the tunnels with the current by now. There's no way we'd find a diver crazy enough to get lowered down there to look. I told O'Toole about it. He's got a missing persons out on him; he says there's nothin' more he can do. Says there's no evidence to support my theory."

"How did they make him write the note, Jackpine?"

"I spoke to Slim Hiller. He was a buddy of Reg. Reg didn't leave his post very often, but when he did, he wanted to cover his ass. He didn't want some big shot from the company drivin' up and not seein' the watchman. The letter wasn't dated. Slim says Reg used the same letter for years. He'd tack it on the door every time he left. Not that anyone ever checked up on him, but I guess he wanted to justify his absence, just in case. Lafontaine must have found the note and put it on the table."

Paul flipped open his notebook. "I was down in Blackwater early this mornin' checkin' out the boat. Number one, I inspected said boat. Nice boat, Chief. But it ain't a fishin' boat. No place at the back of the boat to fish from. I talked to the commercial fishermen before they went out; they've never seen the boat out. Seems they never even had a skipper lined up who knew how to fish the Lake." Other lakes were referred to by name. In that whole north shore area, the mighty Superior was "the Lake." "I verified that there was no big gas purchases all summer."

"OK, so it's clear that he bought the boat to run this next shipment across the Lake. Now we go find O'Toole's boss. We tell him the whole story. The OPP moves in and busts them all, and we live happily ever after," said Boone.

"I'm afraid it might not be that easy, Boone. Let's review what we have." Jackpine walked over to his flip chart and turned over a fresh page. "Now, first..." Jackpine assumed a professorial manner as he stood looking down on the earnest faces of his seated students: Inez, Paul, and Boone. "Desmond Lesmontaignes is dead. We suspect foul play, but officially a drowning accident. Second, Jimmy Boucher's car goes over a cliff on Spruce Hill Road—drunk, accident. Third, old White Horse Parker hangs himself. Fourth, we have Boone's testimony. You heard Bear and Flip confess to murderin' White Horse, you saw them stuffing what appeared to be cocaine into fish fillets, and they chased you down the river tryin' to kill you. In a court of law, it's your word against theirs." Jackpine's list on his flip chart now consisted of: 1) Desmond? 2) Jimmy? 3) White Horse? 4) Boone's testimony?

Jackpine continued, "Fifth, Golias, a slimy bastard, buys a fishin' lodge and a charter airline. He sells them both after the first season. Pretty common. A guy wants to escape the stress of big-city life. He finds out the bush is not what he'd bargained for. He bails out." Jackpine shrugged his shoulders. "Sixth, we have a bunch of Colombians living at the lodge. They don't mingle with the other guests. Really weird, but not illegal. Seventh, we have a police officer stayin' in fancy digs in Florida and buyin' a yacht. Maybe they find somethin', maybe they don't. But the drugs are long gone."

With the seemingly formal setting, Paul Desroches raised his hand for permission to speak. "I had coffee with my friend Ernest Marshall on the OPP this morning. Marshall says O'Toole is retirin'. Got twenty-five years in September. He's gonna be gone at the end of October."

"OK, so if an OPP investigation turns up anything it might affect O'Toole's pension. Big deal, he's got his own pension plan with Golias. Eighth, we know O'Toole bought, or was given, a car by Golias. Coincidence, but not illegal. Ninth, we have two grain boats on Hudson Bay that came from Colombia. Drug running? Just a theory at this stage. Tenth, we have Reg Frenette missing." Jackpine sat down. His last six points on the chart were: 5) Golias? 6) Colombians? 7) O'Toole's yacht. 8) O'Toole's car. 9) Grain boats? 10) Reg?

Boone was shocked. He thought the case was, to use Jackpine's expression, done like dinner. Jackpine added further wrinkles. "Let's say the OPP takes our word over a twenty-five-year veteran on the force. Doubtful, but let's say they do. They storm up to the lodge. The first shipment has been disbursed; the second has yet to arrive. They find nuthin'. Or worse, they fly up and board the grain boat in Hudson Bay; they find the drugs and bust the captain. Bear, Flip, Golias, and whoever is behind Golias all get away scot-free. If we go to the Mounties instead of the OPP, the same thing is likely to happen."

"What the hell are we going to do?" queried Boone.

"Seems only one thing to do. We figure out when the next shipment will be there. Paul and I go up there and arrest them. The cocaine is the evidence we need."

"Jackpine, it won't be that easy. You just walk up to a bunch of murderers and cutthroats, and put them under arrest!"

"Now, Boone, I know it won't be that easy. If it was easy, I'd go alone. That's why I'm taking Paul."

"I'm going with you guys!" Boone declared.

"No, this ain't your cup of tea, Boone!" said Jackpine forcefully.

"Damn it, Jackpine! Those Neanderthals tried to kill me. I was so scared on that river that I shit my pants!" Oops, thought Boone, not meaning to blurt that out. He reddened as he glanced at Inez Mahoney.

"Fair enough, Boone. If you insist, I'll make you a special constable." Jackpine rummaged in the drawer of his desk and found a badge. He had Boone raise his hand and solemnly swore him in.

Paul Desroches laughed, "Hey, Jackpine, now we got us a plainclothes detective."

Jackpine smiled, then the serious look returned to his face. "We'll have to calculate somehow when we think the shipment will arrive. It'll be at least a week or so. Meantime, I don't want any more murders in town or at Lac des Iles. This town is closed to Bear and Flip; no more pussyfootin'."

"I'm goin' back out on radar patrol," said Paul. "Gonna need a fresh approach pretty soon, Mr. Boone."

Jackpine looked at Inez. "Can you call that supply place and order a bulletproof jacket for Boone, same kind Paul and I have?"

"Forty-six tall," said Inez. She blushed, thinking she should not be so knowledgeable about Boone's requirement.

Boone had the privilege of having lunch with the radiant Inez Mahoney at the Canton Garden. Fortunately for Tom Lee, Inez held Boone's undivided attention. When he ate alone at the restaurant, Boone devoted his time to lecturing the recalcitrant, but patient, Tom Lee. A working title for the crash course to retrain Tom was "The Progressive Chinese Restaurant of the '90s."

After lunch, he drove over to Rainbow Falls Lumber. He started with a tour of the mill. McLeod seemed to be a competent operations man. The place was clean, for a sawmill. Work in progress was orderly and neat. The equipment looked old but well maintained and in good working order. The workers appeared competent. It was not a high-tech operation. Logs went in one end, saws attacked them, and lumber came out the other end.

After the tour, Boone sat down with Andrew McLeod and looked at the books. The overhead was high because they were running at fifty to sixty percent of capacity. The cost of a full complement of electricians, pipefitters, millwrights, mechanics, quality-control inspectors, and technicians was prohibitive with low production. Boone argued the merits of having only one shift at full capacity rather than three shifts at half speed. McLeod argued that if they laid off skilled help, the people would move and they could not readily replace them in the future. The argument seemed valid to Boone, but maybe future stability was a luxury they could not afford.

A walk around the yard convinced Boone they were choking on excessive inventories. The people on the order desk were chatting idly, waiting for phones to ring. They should be on the phone trying to drum up business, thought Boone. They would be trained in telemarketing or replaced if they could not cut it.

Boone conceived of four steps that he would take. He would hire Chip Carpenter. They needed to train salespeople and order-desk staff and give timely, reliable feedback to the floor, so that they were producing exactly what they were selling. He would recruit a very good cost accountant. In a low-margin commodity business, you needed to know every component of your cost. He would find the name of the most progressive, well-run lumber mill in the country, and he would hire their best engineer. If there were new ways to do things, that would be the fastest way to implement them. The fourth step was the risky one. When the staff was in place, he would wind the mill up to full capacity. He would have to become the low-cost producer and aggressively market his product. He would find a way to sell lumber—a lot of lumber.

Boone left the mill feeling uneasy. He did not have knowledge or background in this business. He knew this decision to buy the company was impulsive. In the past, decisions like this had put him on the brink of the abyss of fiscal disaster. Maybe we never did put a man on the moon, he thought. On the positive side, he was a fast-thinking, quick-reacting entrepreneur. Soon the dark clouds of impending doom had blown over his horizon of self-doubt, replaced by the clear skies and steady winds upon which he would sail into his next adventure—Board Foot Boone, Lumber Baron Boone.

CHAPTER 8

When Boone got back to the police station, it was late afternoon. Jackpine was just hanging up from talking to Chief Lawrence Musgrove. "This lumber deal is looking good, folks!" Boone exclaimed.

Jackpine looked up. "I thought you would help Andrew out with some advice. I never thought for a minute it would end up with you buyin' the whole shebang. Some things are just beyond my scope, I guess." Jackpine grabbed his hat. "I have Toy Huhtela watchin' the airport and Lawrence put a couple of scouts on the river—only two ways into town. A scout just called Lawrence; Bear and Flip have been spoted headin' toward town on the river."

"Jackpine, you can't just Wyatt Earp' these guys out of town."

"Goddamn right I can! No more innocent people are going to be hurt or killed by those two fuckin' assholes!" Jackpine looked to Inez. "I'm sorry Inez, 'scuse my French."

"That's OK; the adjective seems appropriate and the noun certainly fits."

"Golias probably sent them down to locate the boats Boone scattered. They probably figger since it's Friday night they might as well come to town and raise a little hell. Where the hell is my cruiser, Paul?"

"Sorry, Chief. It was my decoy on the west end. It's still there."

Jackpine stormed out of the office.

"Chief's riled. I wouldn't wanna be those two guys. Can you drive me over to get the Chief's cruiser, Mr. Boone?"

Jackpine drove his Bronco to the liquor store. He had assumed correctly it would be their first stop. They were just leaving with two cases of beer and a brown bag of liquor when Jackpine pulled up. "Where you boys headin'?" he asked politely.

Flip chirped, "We's gettin' us some panty remover an' we're gonna look fer some poontang."

"You boys better not be taking liquor out to the Reserve."

"Call the OPP and tell them. Not your turf out there. 'Sides, it's none of your fuckin' business where we go," snarled Bear Sawchuk.

Jackpine did not want a confrontation in front of the busiest place in town on a Friday evening. "That's true, boys. None of my business. I just need your help for two minutes. I have a suspect in the murder of Desmond Lesmontaignes. I know you boys were out there that night. Just want you to look at a few pictures over at the station; then you can go out and have a good time. OK?"

Flip looked puzzled. It was an expression he was good at. He had a lot of practice. Bear looked wary but relieved. "Some wagon burner knocks off some other wagon burner. Don't see why anyone gives a fuck. Yeah, we'll look at your pi'chers." They put their beer and whisky in the back of Bear's pickup truck and followed Jackpine to the station. They left their booze unattended, when they entered the station. Most folks in the Falls were honest. The few that weren't were not crazy enough to risk stealing Bear Sawchuk's most prized possessions.

Boone and Paul were back from getting Jackpine's cruiser. Boone felt secure in this milieu. Jackpine and Paul were a fine set of bookends. "You guys in town for some rifle practice? Neither one of you could hit a cow in the ass with a banjo," Boone chuckled.

Flip stared maniacally at Boone. "Next time…"

Bear cut him off. "Shut up. We don't know what the fuck you're talkin' about."

"Watch your tongue. There's a lady present," warned Jackpine.

"I don't give a fuck," Bear sneered.

Flip laughed at Bear's rapier-like wit.

Jackpine was surprisingly calm. "Paul, Inez, Boone, I'd like you to leave for a few minutes. I want to have a private chat with these gentlemen." His polite tone did not match the fire in his eyes. After they left, Jackpine locked the door and pulled the window shades down.

Bear looked apprehensive. Flip looked scared. "Now, boys, I'm gonna tell you a story. When I was a kid, I liked to hunt partridge a lot. I'd walk for miles with my twenty-two. I'd see one now and then, but not very often. I asked my dad how I could become a better hunter. He took me out to the Reserve to see old Francis Daley. Now old Francis, he was old then, been dead for years, of course, spent the time to teach me to hunt partridge. My dad let me stay away from school. He said, 'Learnin' to hunt partridge, it'll serve you better in life than what you woulda learned in three days in school.' And you know, guys, he was right. I'm probably the best partridge hunter in these parts. First thing old Francis says to me was, 'You think like a white man when you hunt.' I says to him, 'I should think like an Indian, hey?' He says to me, 'No, you're not huntin' Indians. You must think like a partridge. Then you always know where the partridge will be.' So, I learned what partridge eat, when they eat it, where they go at different times of day, what they like and don't like, and what they know and don't know. Now when I hunt, I become a partridge. I always know where they are. I just know, because I can think like a partridge."

"What the fuck's the point a' all this? Where's the fuckin' pi'chers? We gotta go." Bear started to get up.

"See the point is, boys, I've been doin' my best as chief of police to handle you guys. And I've failed. You see fellas; it's just like hunting partridge." The smooth conciliatory tone evaporated—replaced by ice. "Because you two are fuckin' animals, a human bein' can't relate to you two."

"I've hadda nuff of this bullshit."

Jackpine's billy club was as fast as lightning. There was a loud smack as he hit Bear in the forehead with it. "You're not movin' 'til I tell you to move, asshole," Jackpine yelled. Then he thwacked Flip in the forehead. "Just in case you were thinkin' of leavin'." They both rubbed their foreheads. Pain and anger filled their faces.

"Police brutality," whined Flip.

"No! No! No! *This* is brutality," Jackpine explained, as he leaned over and whacked each of them on the shin with his billy stick. "You see, that hurts a lot more."

They both yelped. The look of pain in their faces intensified, but the anger disappeared, replaced by fear.

Jackpine threw his badge on the desk. "You see, boys, we have to deal animal to animal." His voice was again calm. "You see, guys, I'm the meanest, toughest son of a bitch in this town, and I don't like you. You guys killed Desmond and Jimmy Boucher and White Horse and probably Reg Frenette. And you tried to kill my best friend. The chief of police can't do anything about it. But I can because I'm a fucking animal." He sneered at them, looking as wolf-like as he could muster. "Next time I see you guys in this town, I'm going to kill you. First, I'll beat you within an inch of your sorry lives. Then, I'm going to shoot you both in the belly. Next, I'm going to throw you into shaft number two at Spruce Hill. And I'll always wonder if you drowned or died of being gut shot. There will be no witnesses. I'll deny this conversation ever took place if you run to O'Toole. The chief of police doesn't lie, but I'm an animal just like you two. I'll lie, and I like to hurt other animals. Do you both understand?"

They both nodded, stricken with fear. Jackpine yelled, "Do you understand?"

Bear said, "Yeah."

"Yeah, what?" yelled Jackpine and whacked him again in the forehead.

"Yes, sir," said Bear.

"Yes, sir," echoed Flip.

"I'm glad we understand each other." Jackpine was calm and once more conciliatory. "Now, in case you were going to the Reserve, Chief Musgrove wants to speak with you." Jackpine phoned and got Lawrence and put him on the speakerphone. "Can you hear me, Jackpine, Bear, Flip?"

"Yeah," all three said.

"I'd like to see you guys here. I had a trial today. As chief I appointed myself judge, and since there was no one else here, I volunteered for jury too. I found you two guilty of killing Desmond Lesmontaignes."

"You can't do that," whined Bear.

"It wasn't your white-man's court—it was *my* court. And I did it. I've got men hunting you now, on *my* Reserve—that's *my* jurisdiction. When we catch you, I'm going to cut your pricks off. Then I'm going to boil your pricks. Then I'm going to make you eat them. Then when you're done eatin' your pricks, you can leave. So, come whenever you want. The pot's boiling on my stove." He hung up. Bear and Flip were as white as ghosts, and Flip was trembling.

"Chief forgot one thing. This conversation didn't happen either. Now, I'd like to see you boys go out there. Then, you can run into O'Toole's office squealing in soprano. He might bust Lawrence, but you two will never get your pricks back."

Jackpine escorted them, hobbling out to their truck.

"I won't forget this," said Bear Sawchuk from the relative safety of the cab of his truck.

"That's good, Bear. That's the whole idea. I want you assholes on the river headin' north right away. If you aren't, I'll come and get you! Have a nice trip."

Boone, Inez, and Paul followed Jackpine back into the station.

"Those two had the fear of God in them. What did you do?" asked Boone.

"Just a man-to-man chat or animal-to-animal," said Jackpine. He phoned Lawrence. "They're gone. I don't think you'll see them out there, but keep an eye open. Was that some ancient Ojibway torture you threatened them with?"

"No, I saw that in a ninja movie my son rented. Made me squirm just tellin' them."

"Me too. Call me when your guys see them headin' up river."

They were all having coffee when the phone rang. Inez fielded the call. "That was Olga Shultz." Olga and Heinz Shultz owned the Falls View Restaurant. It was located on the shoreline at the base of the Falls, offering (as the name implied) a spectacular view of Rainbow Falls. They came to the Falls six years ago and started the restaurant. It was a very good restaurant (as Boone would attest to), especially for a small, remote town. They catered almost exclusively to the tourist trade. Locals would visit for special occasions, but the menu selections were too exotic and the prices too steep for most of the citizenry. They enjoyed a growing reputation and did a solid business during tourist season. The bus tours made a special trip to view the Falls, shop at Northland Crafts, and dine in the rustic elegance of the Falls View.

The decor was authentic Bavarian country, although few patrons could verify the authenticity. That it was incongruous with the setting seemed to bother no one. The ambience added to the mystique.

Heinz purported to be a European-trained chef who had worked in some of Toronto's finest restaurants before coming to the Falls. Boone had questioned Heinz extensively about his background. Backed into a corner, Heinz told Boone that in reality he had been a barber in Toronto. Boone promised not to reveal his hair-clipping past. Heinz hoped Boone never asked him for a haircut.

Boone was always afforded preferential treatment in the restaurant. Partly for keeping Heinz's secret, but also because Boone was a steady customer when he was in town, and because Boone truly appreciated the quality of the food served by the proud, hardworking Shultzes.

Olga called to say a bus tour was there for dinner and asked Inez to warn Constable Desroches or Chief of Police Keating to prevent a murder during dinner. Boone was aghast at the casual treatment afforded this news by Paul, Jackpine, and especially dear Inez Mahoney. "Paul, why don't you head up after you finish your coffee." Jackpine looked at Boone and laughed.

"Whoa, Boone, let me tell you about these murders. They'll get the old gals from the bus nicely settled in the dinin' room. All of them will be lookin' out at the Falls. They will see a nice-looking young man, Robby McLeod, Andrew's young 'un, holdin' hands with his pretty girlfriend. He'll have a ziplock bag full of ketchup taped to his back. Two guys will screech up in a car. They'll all start yellin'. One of the guys will nail Robby in the back with one of those fake knives, where the blade disappears into the hilt. Robby will fall down, 'blood' all over him. The two guys **will** throw the body into the river, grab the screamin' girl, and drive away. The old ladies will go nuts. Heinz and Olga and the waitresses will try to calm them down. But nothing will work until we find Robby, usually downstream at the boat landing, and haul his ass into the restaurant for all of them to see."

Boone laughed and said it would be fun to see.

"Funny the first time. But they've done it six times. Last time, I read them the riot act. Besides, with the current in the river, it's dangerous. I'm surprised Robby would do it again."

A few minutes later Paul Desroches came back in. "We've got us a copycat killer. I got there just before the murder. It was young Koslowski gonna take the dive. Robby wasn't anywhere around."

The phone rang again, "Oscar," he knew it was Olga by the use of his hated first name. She was calling to thank him "ferry mush" for having Paul prevent the disruptive murder.

* * * * * *

Boone and Inez left together. They were going to have dinner later at the Falls View with Janice Keating. Jackpine and Paul would be working. It was the Columbus Day long weekend, which in Canada is Thanksgiving. It was a homecoming weekend for sons and daughters who had moved on to greener pastures. It was traditionally the time to close summer cottages for the winter on the area's many lakes. The hotels and motels in the Falls offered promotions, ensuring one last sell-out for the season. There were also dances planned for both Friday and Saturday nights.

Friday night's dance was sponsored by the RFBF (Rainbow Falls Building Fund). Having built the arena ten years ago, the group was still actively raising funds to pay the mortgage on the building. The building's official name was "the Arena," but since at ten years of age it was still substantially younger than the building built in 1928 that it replaced, it was unofficially called "the New Arena" and probably would be until it was replaced at some future date by "the Newer New Arena." The town fathers wanted to name it the Jackpine Keating Memorial Arena. Jackpine fought it hard. Memorial meant he was dead, and he did not plan to die. He insisted his name not be on the arena, threatening to withdraw the substantial contributions he had committed. The town fathers did not have a backup name; so "the Arena" it became. The name was appropriate in that it fit in so well with other area institutions and landmarks; such as the Falls, the River, the Park, the Airport, the Chinese Restaurant, the Highway, the Post Office, the Drug Store, and the Grocery Store.

Saturday's dance was sponsored by the chamber of commerce. Drawing visitors to town was in every member's best fiscal interest. It would be the last busy weekend of the season.

Jackpine knew from experience that the best way to prevent trouble was to keep a high profile. Both he and Paul would be very visible around the Falls all weekend. Jackpine liked to leave the patrolling of the downtown on foot to Paul Desroches. Jackpine (still famous from his hockey career) would have to pose for pictures, shake hands, sign autographs, and make small talk. He did not enjoy these activities, but he did them without objection. He was happy he did not have to do them very often anymore.

On the other hand, it was Paul Desroches' favorite part of police work, with the exception of high-speed chases and barroom brawls. The amiable Paul would swagger, if a man his size could ever be said to achieve a full swagger, up and down the street with a big smile on his face. The chamber of commerce could not wish for a better envoy. He was continually encouraging tourists to "enjoy our town" and insisting that they "have a nice day" or "have a nice evening," as the case dictated. Jackpine wished he wouldn't eat and drink as he walked, but that was the one request from Jackpine that fell on deaf ears. His right hand was always free for shaking hands; Paul was a compulsive hand shaker. He never ate and drank at the same time, so his left hand always held ammunition of one or the other. Most of the storekeepers thought the jovial, corpulent Paul was a billboard for their establishment, so whenever his left hand was free, one of them would stuff something into it—free of charge, of course. Depending on where he was on the street, you could expect Paul to be enjoying a slice of pizza, a hot dog, an ice-cream cone, popcorn, a roast beef sandwich, a blueberry slushy, a cola, a mineral water, or a cup of coffee. If he was munching a candy bar, he would have paid for it. He was quick to point out to tourists that whatever he happened to be eating tasted great, and he would point out where he had acquired the tempting tidbit.

The only establishment not offering snacks to Big Paul was the Canton Garden, the Chinese Restaurant to locals. Tom Lee didn't believe in this type of marketing, and Paul would not have accepted his largess. Paul was told as a youth that Chinese restaurants served cat, and although he didn't really believe it anymore, he didn't want to run the risk. "I like to eat pussy, but I don't eat cat," Paul would guffaw when someone suggested he dine in the Canton Garden.

One time, Tom complained to Jackpine about Paul's remarks. In the spring, redfin suckers, a revolting-looking scrap fish, would spawn in the streams. Kids would catch them by the hundreds (with hooks or pitchforks) and throw them up on shore to die. No one complained about this barbaric practice because they didn't want the lakes overrun with a large population of the prolific suckers. Tom Lee was seen every year filling garbage pails with suckers and taking them home. Locals would shudder with disgust when they imagined "them Chinamen eatin' suckers." These same locals would go to the Canton Garden and eat sweet-and-sour fish balls and crispy Hunan fish and think it was great: "Don't taste like any fish we got around here." Of course it doesn't, thought Jackpine, because none of you eat suckers at home. Jackpine's answer to the complaint about Paul was "Look, Tom, I'll make a deal. You don't bitch about Paul sayin' you serve cat, and I won't tell everyone in town you're feeding them suckers." Tom accepted the deal. It was one of the mysteries of life that Jackpine would never understand—no one else seemed to make the link between spring suckers and sweet-and-sour fish balls.

There was seldom trouble in the Roxy Theatre, but that did not keep the vigilant eye of the diligent Paul Desroches from the premises. When a movie that Paul liked was playing, he would patrol the Roxy three or four times in an evening (sometimes for as long as half an hour). He would stand at the back entrance with popcorn in hand. When something struck Paul funny, as many things did, every patron of the theatre would know they were safe in the arms of the law when they heard the hearty belly laugh coming from the back of the theatre.

* * * * * *

Boone left Inez's home at seven a.m. He broke down the wall of resistance and was allowed to spend the night again, but Inez could not completely abandon her sense of propriety. She told Boone to leave before everyone in town was awake to see him leaving. Boone walked out to his car with a spring in his step. The gait of a man in love—of a man who had spent the night with the object of his passion. Boone went back to the hotel to shower and change. He selected a pair of blue jeans, hiking boots, wool socks, a cotton T-shirt, and a heavy wool shirt. It was going to be a cool day, probably not getting higher than the low fifties. By eight, he was downstairs in the restaurant waiting for Jackpine to join him for breakfast. Jackpine came in, helped himself to a cup of coffee, and joined Boone.

"Did Bear and Flip leave town?"

"Yeah. Lawrence called shortly after you and Inez left. He said his guys saw them hightailin' it up the river. I guess I was able to reach out and communicate effectively with them."

They ate their breakfast and had a few more cups of coffee. Boone told Jackpine he wanted to take Inez on a picnic, maybe a little fishing and a shore lunch, and asked Jackpine to recommend a nice spot. As expected, Jackpine had numerous options. They discussed the merits of each, and Boone picked Big Beaver Lake. Jackpine gave Boone the keys to his pickup truck. It had a trailer hitch, so he could take one of Jackpine's boats.

Boone went to the grocery store to buy the supplies he needed. Then he stopped at Mrs. Riccio's home and bought a loaf of fresh bread. There was no bakery in town. Mrs. Riccio baked bread every day for the Falls View Restaurant and for many of the residents of the Falls. There was no sign evident, but everyone in town knew. Inez had volunteered to get the bread, but Boone wanted to. He loved the smell of Mrs. Riccio's kitchen. He always lingered there longer than he had to, chatting with Mrs. Riccio, inhaling the aromas of fresh-baked bread. He packed his supplies in his backpack and went to get Jackpine's truck and boat.

Inez came out of her house as soon as Boone parked. Boone thought she looked stunning. She was wearing a colorful Icelandic knit sweater. The blue in the sweater matched her eyes, making them dance. She was wearing very little, if any, makeup for her day in the woods, giving her a fresh, clean aura. Her tight blue jeans looked as if they were about to come alive.

Boone had a lump in his throat as he reached to grab her supplies. He kissed her heartily, neighbors be damned. He stuffed her supplies into the bulging backpack.

They drove out to Dead Horse Lake, chatting amicably. Boone had always been amazed by her wide conversational range. Inez headed the selection committee for books for the Rainbow Falls Public Library, and the diverse offerings available were a tribute to her myriad interests.

Boone was proud of himself at the Dead Horse Lake boat ramp because it only took four passes to back the boat trailer into the water. Boone headed north on the lake. When they were nearing the north shore, Boone looked for a small creek entering the lake surrounded by a stand of white birch. The trail to Big Beaver Lake was, according to Jackpine, on the west side of the creek. Boone found the creek and carefully beached the boat. Inez helped Boone get the backpack on his back. Boone grabbed the fishing rods, and Inez carried the small tackle box. They started up the trail. Jackpine had said it was only a mile—a very hard mile, all uphill. The first few hundred yards were steep and rocky. Only a few hardy birch were growing, managing to survive with their roots in small cracks in the lichen-covered rock. Boone, leading the way, kicked up a family of rabbits. They scattered in all directions; none of them ran more than twenty feet, where they stopped motionless, thinking they were sufficiently well hidden to thwart any attack by these interlopers. Boone and Inez stopped for a few minutes to watch the rabbits. Boone was happy to stop. His legs were already sore from the steep climb, but he didn't dare admit that he wanted a rest. The rabbits were cautious but not really afraid of Boone or Inez. They had never been hunted; probably the only other humans they ever saw were Jackpine or maybe a few fishermen en route to Big Beaver Lake. They would have run much farther if a fox or a wolf had been the one to surprise them.

They continued on their way. Boone looked over his shoulder and saw that the rabbit family had continued feeding on the lichens. They came to a flat area of muskeg. Boone wondered how they would cross the knee-deep black muck. Then he noticed that Jackpine had provided the solution. Two large pines had been felled over the swamp, parallel and about one foot apart. Jackpine had limbed the pines and nailed the branches (as slats) to the trees, providing a makeshift bridge over the worst area. They made their way across.

There was a transitional area after the muskeg where the ground was still damp and a stand of scraggly jack pines tried to survive. Then the trail went uphill again through a mature mixed forest. The tops of big spruce trees kept sunlight from the forest floor. There was very little undergrowth or carpeting of lush moss. Boone and Inez stopped for a rest. They sat in the moss. There was no breeze, it was cool, and very little sunlight penetrated. Boone asked Inez about the name of Big Beaver Lake—whether it was a big lake with a beaver or a small lake with a particularly large beaver. Inez laughed. Although she had never been there, she had heard Jackpine say the latter was the case. It was a small lake with a colony of beaver, and one of the beavers was apparently huge. Jackpine had seen the big beaver years ago, but the trapper who worked this area had trapped it one winter. The big beaver was now part of a coat somewhere, but he was immortalized with the honor of having the lake named after him. Perhaps the thought of everlasting fame made the trap hurt a little bit less, thought Boone sarcastically.

They continued on their way. The small creek appeared on their right, babbling happily downhill. The trail followed the creek. They were in a clearing beside the creek, and it was warmer. The sun felt good. They came upon a family of ruffed grouse (called partridge in these parts). The grouse ran instead of taking flight. Boone was surprised at how fast and agile they were. Within ten feet, their colors blended in with the background of the forest so well that they became invisible. Boone couldn't think like a partridge; he supposed Jackpine would have known exactly where they went. They were feeding on high-bush cranberries when Boone and Inez come upon them. Inez identified the berries; Boone was not able to. Boone ate a few of them, but they were bitter. "Cranberries need sugar," said Inez. "Let's pick some, and we'll have them in our tea with some sugar." Inez pulled a ziplock bag from the back pocket of her jeans, and they filled the bag with cranberries.

Nearing the lake, they came upon a big owl perched in a tree, looking down at them. They had awakened the owl from its day's sleep, but it did not seem too concerned. First, the owl decided that these two creatures were too big to attempt to kill and eat. Then, it decided that they didn't appear to be a threat—no reason to fly. But the owl prudently kept a big eye on them until they were gone and over the hill.

Their first view of the lake was a giant beaver dam. It had been there for countless years: generation after generation of beaver toiled at the maintenance of the dam, patching and fortifying. The small creek they were following began at the base of the dam.

They walked up past the dam and along the lakeshore. A beaver slapped its tail on the calm water, announcing their presence. The loud slaps echoed off the hilltops. The lake looked like a giant gravy bowl: about a mile long and half a mile wide at its widest point, tapering off at both ends. There were no year-round brooks flowing into the lake. It was spring fed. Boone knelt down, cupped his hands, and tasted the water. It was clean and fresh and, surprisingly to Boone, ice cold. Jackpine had said it would be cold, but it was colder than expected. The cold crystal-clear water was the reason, according to Jackpine, that the trout of Big Beaver were the best-tasting trout—firm fleshed with no muddy taste.

They found Jackpine's canoe: a green, sixteen-foot fiberglass. Under the canoe there were two paddles, a wire grate for a cooking fire, and two life jackets in a plastic garbage bag. They put the jackets on, put the canoe in the water, and then Boone steadied the canoe while Inez got in. Boone told her to face him and that he would paddle. But she refused; saying she could paddle with him, she knelt in the bow with her back facing Boone.

"I didn't know if you had ever been in a canoe before. It looks like you know what you're doing."

Inez laughed. "I'm certainly no expert, but I grew up around here, Boone, and canoeing was just something you did from time to time. It has been years, though."

Boone launched the canoe. An expert would have pushed it out without getting wet. Boone was leery of tipping the canoe upon launch, so reluctantly he waded out into the frigid water before getting in the canoe. Boone had planned to talk the demure Inez Mahoney into a skinny-dip at lunch, but he promptly shelved the plan. Halfway up the lake there was a small rocky point of land jutting out into the lake. It was only about twenty feet wide. There were three weathered pines standing sentry duty and a small sandy beach (actually more gravel than sand, but a beach all the same). Boone stopped at the point to off-load the backpack, just in case they tipped the canoe. He took the bottle of Pinot Grigio, which was still cool, and safely placed it in the water. He untied the rope from the bow of the canoe and threw one end over a branch of one of the pines. He hoisted the backpack about twelve feet in the air and tied the rope to the tree. He thought it would be high enough to prevent a bear from ruining their lunch.

They returned to the canoe and paddled out to a likely-looking spot to catch lunch. The lake was calm, surprising for midday; usually, there would be a wind at this time of day. Fish were jumping occasionally, so Boone rigged his fly rod with a fly that Jackpine had given him for this lake. Inez rigged a night crawler on a straight hook and set a bobber at about five feet above the bait. Boone suggested an alternate strategy, but she would have none of it. She didn't like casting, and she loved seeing the bobber sink. Inez watched her bobber float as Boone casted his fly.

Boone got the first strike. There were few things in life that Boone found more exhilarating than a two-and-a-half-pound wild trout hitting a fly. Boone played the fish well and landed it. Brightly speckled with a deep orange-red belly, it was a beautiful fish. Inez yelped when her bobber sank. The fish fought furiously as she brought it toward the canoe. "Too quickly," Boone admonished. Not heeding the advice, Inez reeled it in quickly to the net. It was a duplicate of Boone's fish. Boone looked up and saw a golden eagle circling lazily high above the lake. He alerted Inez, and she too looked up. The eagle came down closer to the lake but was still a hundred feet above the surface. The graceful eagle commanded the sky. The golden hunter turned in a tighter circle and then soared a second time following the same course. On the third circling maneuver, it suddenly dropped from the sky, plummeting headfirst toward the lake. A second before impact the wings spread and the eagle turned upright: its talons hitting the surface of the lake. The eagle struggled briefly and flapped its wings loudly—taking off with a trout flopping in the tight grip of its talons. It flew off with its trophy toward the big pines on the hill that overlooked the lake.

Boone enjoyed watching the eagle catch a fish even more than he enjoyed catching his own. Inez was rather matter of fact about it, turning to stare intently at her bobber, willing it to sink. The eagle's attack seemed to have spooked the trout that were feeding on flies. Inez landed one more trout, while Boone flogged the water with futility. He switched to his spinning rod with a night crawler for bait and hooked a trout on the first cast. It was smaller than the others: maybe one and a half pounds. They were both hungry and decided to head to shore for lunch.

They returned to the point. A bear was standing upright on its hind legs, front legs groping in the air, trying to reach the backpack. Boone grabbed both paddles, banged them together, and yelled. The bear stopped and looked at them and then slowly walked away toward the woods. The bear wouldn't be any further trouble. It would wait in the woods for a more opportune time.

Boone stacked some rocks to support the wire grill. He collected an armful of firewood and some birch bark. Inez began peeling potatoes, dicing onion, mincing garlic, and chopping celery while Boone started the fire. After he had a nice blaze going, he turned his attention to cleaning the trout. He gilled and gutted one of the trout, rubbed it inside and out with a lemon, salt and peppered it, and then wrapped it in foil. The other three he filleted, chopping the meat into bite-size pieces.

While they were waiting for the fire to die down into cooking coals, Boone opened the wine. It was nicely chilled. He poured drinks for Inez and himself into ceramic coffee mugs. Boone added the onions, garlic, celery, and butter to the pot he had bought in the grocery store and sautéed the ingredients in the pot over the cooking coals. He emptied the concoction onto a piece of foil and filled the pot with water to boil potatoes. While the potatoes were boiling, he placed the trout wrapped in foil onto the hot coals. He discarded most of the water from the pot, after the potatoes cooked. In Canada, milk was sold in plastic bags. He was happy to see that the bag wasn't broken. He added milk; a bottle of clam juice; the potatoes, onions, garlic, and celery; and then the bite-size pieces of trout to the pot. He moved the pot to the edge of the fire so that it would simmer without breaking into a furious boil. He added salt, pepper, bay leaves, and basil; then he watched the pot carefully. Later, he added some butter, a pint of cream, and stirred it briefly before declaring that the "Trout Chowder a la Boone" was ready. Inez sliced some fresh bread. She opened two Tupperware bowls: one contained Greek olives, the other homemade garlic dill pickles. She also cut Boone's block of Brie into wedges. Boone ladled the hot chowder into bowls and poured them each more wine.

The meal was delicious. The walk and the paddling combined with the fresh air gave them enormous appetites. Boone devoured three bowls of chowder, Inez two. Boone boiled water to make tea. Boone added some sugar; Inez squeezed the cranberries through a piece of pantyhose before adding them to the hot tea.

Boone wrung out his socks and then put his socks and boots near the fire to dry. They spread the blanket on the gravel beach and sat down to enjoy the cranberry tea.

Two otters swam by. The otters noticed Boone and Inez, but they paid no attention to the otters. The otters frolicked gracefully in the water, doing the backstroke, and then diving and surfacing. Otters seemed to be the only creatures of the north woods who had leisure time, and they took full advantage of it.

After their tea, Boone and Inez lied down—Boone on his back and Inez on her side with her head resting on Boone's chest. "Now that you're fed and watered and purring contently, I have a question for you." Boone paused. "I love you, Inez; I want to spend my life with you. Will you marry me?"

"Oh, don't, Boone." Inez was expecting this. The environs helped her frame her answer. "I love you, Alistair Boone. I count the minutes when I know we're going to be together. I'm not very good at explaining, but let me try. You and I are happy together: I'm never as happy alone as I am when I'm with you. I see you on your vacation time—either here at the Falls or at Hilton Head or in the Caribbean—when you're like those otters, just laid back and enjoying life. But those other times, Boone, I think you are like a beaver: single-minded, driven to your goal, work, work, work. I've seen flashes of that Boone; I'm not sure I fit in that part of your life and whether I could support you then like I would want to."

"Honey, that life was killing me. I've sold my business. I've left that life behind me," Boone protested. "That's when I need you the most, Inez. I know I appear jovial, but I get so wound up sometimes. It's like I'm going to burst."

"I couldn't live in New York, Boone. The Falls is part of me, and I'm part of the Falls."

"I can live here. I'm going to have to, if I become a lumber baron. I need to go to New York sometimes. I still have some business to tend to there, but I don't have to live there. I'm not sure I could stay here all winter, though."

"Let's talk some more. I have to think, Boone."

Boone, forever the optimist, was encouraged. She never said no. Just a few objections to overcome, he thought. They lay on the blanket for a while, watching the otters cavorting, then got up to pack up. Boone put all of the leftover food on a flat rock. "You have been an excellent host, Mr. Bear," he shouted. The bear reappeared, looking out from the woods.

They fished for another hour. Boone caught two trout on his fly rod; Inez caught one. They released two of them. One was mortally wounded (hooked through the gills), so Boone killed it, and as they paddled by the point, Boone threw the trout to the bear. The bear was licking the rock where the leftover food had once been. The bear enjoyed the unexpected bounty.

It was late afternoon before they got back into the bay near the beaver dam. A flock of Canadian geese flew in low. They wanted to land and enjoy the wild rice growing in the shallows near the bay. The first one to see the canoe sounded the alert. The geese left, protesting loudly about the presence of the canoe. They would find another place to spend the night. Unlike the wilderness rabbits and grouse, these well-traveled geese feared mankind more than any natural predator, having seen too many times the "booming sticks" that brought indiscriminate death.

The walk to the lake was much easier, mostly downhill. Before they got in the boat, Inez gave Boone a long hug and a big kiss. "Thank you, Boone," she said. Boone did not ask what he was being thanked for. Instead, he kissed her again.

CHAPTER 9

After breakfasting with Boone, Jackpine returned to his office. He thought Big Beaver Lake would be the perfect spot for Boone and Inez. Jackpine had often described for Inez his views on the perfect man for her, not that Inez Mahoney was shopping for a man. It was no accident that Jackpine's description always fit Alistair Boone like a deerskin glove. He had, of course, sung the praises of Inez Mahoney to Boone just as ardently (and Boone seemed convinced). Jackpine's success as a matchmaker was due, in a large part, to his rugged, straightforward man's man demeanor. Few suspected him capable of such subtleties.

Jackpine's reverie was interrupted by the entrance of a pensive Chief Lawrence Musgrove.

"Mornin', chief. Didn't expect you in town."

"Mornin', Chief," said Lawrence, heading for the coffee pot.

"Java's not up to usual standards. Inez isn't here."

"Probably better than mine. Looks fresh, anyways." Lawrence sipped some coffee. "Might be we got a problem. I been tryin' to keep everythin' quiet, but Nelson Lesmontaignes is home. He came in to see me this mornin'. Says he heard that me and you thought his brother was murdered. You bein' out askin' questions. Everyone talks. Especially Nap Martin. I'd trust Nap with my life, but not with a secret."

"I know. You want word to get around the Reserve—you telephone, telegraph, or tell Nap Martin. What'd you tell Nelson?"

"Told him you thought Bear Sawchuk and Flip Lafontaine killed Desmond." Lawrence Musgrove, when asked a direct question, was no more likely than Jackpine to go beating around any bushes.

"What did he say?"

"Not much. Said he was goin' huntin' for a few days."

"So, he's gonna hunt moose. Gonna go up Blackbear Point way. Might be there's two huntin' accidents. He mistakes Bear and Flip for two moose. Accidents happen. We can't let him go, Lawrence. He'd probably get himself shot. There's some rough customers up there besides those two," said Jackpine. The door opened. In walked Sergeant William, not Bill, O'Toole and Dan Golias. Lawyer Steve Appleton followed like a dog on a short leash.

"If it isn't the Lone Ranger and Tonto," sneered Golias.

"That's an ethnic slur against a chief of the Ojibway nation. Isn't it, Bill?" asked Jackpine.

"I warned you once, Keating, and now you've done it again!" shouted O'Toole, ignoring Jackpine's question. "You have assaulted Mr. Sawchuk and Mr. Lafontaine, and worse, you have threatened their lives!"

Jackpine sipped his coffee calmly. "I don't know what you mean." Boone had predicted this encounter. Boone's idea was to use the meeting to sow seeds of distrust and dissension in the ranks of the enemy. Boone had told Jackpine to lie. Jackpine had argued, but finally agreed that the ends justified the means in this situation. "Nothing of the sort happened, Billy."

"It's Sergeant O'Toole to you, Keating," snapped O'Toole.

"When you call me Chief of Police Keating, but Chief would be fine. Bear and Flip stopped in to see me last night." Jackpine sipped his coffee and continued, "They told me some cockamamie story. I think those boys are bushed." (Bushed was a local expression for the temporary craziness that happened to people who lived away from civilization for a long period of time.) "They said Mr. Golias was a drug runner. I never heard such nonsense. They said they planted cocaine into fish fillets and sent them to the States. They said somethin' even crazier. They said you were mixed up in the whole scheme, Billy. I told them to leave. Said I was too busy to sit and listen to fairy tales."

O'Toole and Golias looked as if the Ghost of Christmas Past was perched on Jackpine's shoulder. O'Toole stuttered, but no intelligible words came out. Golias regained his composure faster. Maybe you're right, Chief Keating. It's been a long summer. Maybe Mr. Sawchuk and Mr. Lafontaine are feeling the effects of too much time in the wilderness." He put on his used-car salesman's smile. "Let's go, gentlemen." Golias assessed it was time for a full retreat.

O'Toole's white face turned crimson red as he lashed a finger in the direction of Chief Musgrove. "And I suppose you never said you would boil their cocks and make them eat them!" he screamed.

"I do not have to listen to your racial slurs." Lawrence yelled back. O'Toole's bluster disappeared as quickly as it had arisen.

"But, but..." O'Toole sputtered.

"Enough, sergeant, I said let's go."

Golias and O'Toole turned and left. Steve Appleton, with eyes stretching to owl-like proportions, had not said a word. He turned and followed before his leash was tugged.

"If we had any doubts who's givin' the orders, we know now," said Jackpine. "We have sown seeds of distrust. Now we have to get a hold of Nelson Lesmontaignes and talk some sense into him."

"I thought you'd say that. I brought him into town with me. He's over at the hotel havin' coffee. I'll go get him." Lawrence walked toward the door.

In five minutes, he returned with Nelson Lesmontaignes. Nelson was in his mid-twenties, slight of build, and a serious, pensive-looking person. He was wearing a "CAT" baseball cap, sunglasses, a clean white sweatshirt, denim jacket and slacks, and cowboy boots. Nelson was a diesel mechanic and a very good one. In addition to formal training, he had instincts around motors. He almost always diagnosed a problem by the sound of an engine.

He was as serious in nature as his looks indicated, and he had a reputation as a hard worker and an honest man.

Jackpine got up and shook his hand. "Nice to see you, Nelson. I'm sorry about your brother."

"Thank you, Jackpine. I know you mean it. Nice to see you."

"Last I heard, you were buildin' a road up in northern Alberta."

"Yeah, I was. Road got built. Came home to see my family with what happened. I'll be goin' to BC in January, building another road. My brother didn't drown, Jackpine. Grandfather taught us both the bush and Indian ways. Lesmontaigneses don't fish where there's no fish, and we don't fall out of canoes."

"I don't think he drowned either. But I don't want you runnin' off half-cocked for revenge. You'll get shot or end up in jail, and I don't want to see either, Nelson."

"You got any other ideas, Jackpine?"

Jackpine trusted Nelson Lesmontaignes. He filled a coffee cup for Nelson and sat down and told him everything he knew about the death of his brother and the rest of the facts and assumptions concerning Blackbear Point Lodge. He ended by looking Nelson in the eye and saying, "Justice will be served, Nelson. I promise you that." The look on Jackpine's face and his tone of voice confirmed his sincerity.

"OK, I won't tell anybody anything, and you can count me in. What do you want me to do?" asked Nelson.

"Well, if Boone is right, our little talk with them is going to make them want to push their plan forward. They're not sure what we know and don't know. We think it'll be a week, maybe ten days. We'll take them when they have the cocaine at the lodge. We'll tell you what you can do when the time comes."

"OK, I'll be at my mother's house. There's no phone, but Lawrence can find me." Nelson rose to leave.

Jackpine said, "There's one more thing, Nelson." He described Golias's boat that was harbored down at Blackwater. "If for some reason we don't stop them at the lodge, is there something you could do to the boat so that it would go twenty or thirty miles out into the lake and then die?"

Nelson smiled. "Sure, easy, I could play with the cooling system for the engine. It would run fine for about an hour, then it would overheat—would seize up."

"Could they fix it?" asked Lawrence.

"With spare parts on board and a mechanic as good as me, maybe," said Nelson. "But I doubt it."

"How long would you need to do it?" asked Jackpine.

"Twenty minutes, maybe half an hour." Nelson left, leaving Jackpine and Lawrence.

Lawrence and Jackpine argued for a few minutes. Lawrence was insistent on accompanying Jackpine when he went to Blackbear Point. Jackpine was adamant in his refusal. He succumbed when he saw that there was no way to talk Lawrence out of going. Jackpine was reluctant to have his friend risk his life, but he knew at the same time that Lawrence would be a big asset if things got rough.

Lawrence left. He was on his way to a chiefs' conference in Thunder Bay.

Jackpine took his Bronco over to the Riverview Motel. He missed having his cruiser to cruise in. The river could be viewed from the motel, but only from small bathroom windows in four of the sixteen units and by people six foot four inches or taller. Such limited vistas were commonplace in the "sea views," "lake views," "mountain views," and "valley views" advertised everywhere.

Jackpine did not consider the minor duplicity at the Jensens' Riverview Motel to be a matter for the chief of police. Perhaps it was an issue for society at large, but not for Jackpine Keating. Nonetheless, Jackpine stopped in to see Mr. and Mrs. Jensen. There had been no further complaints in the past two months of guests getting their license plates switched. During the summer, there had been a rash of them. Unknown perpetrators were sneaking into the motel parking lot and quietly switching plates—an Illinois family would stop later in the day to buy gas, only to find that they were now from Minnesota. The OPP had to deal with the irate victims.

The common link turned out to be the Riverview Motel. Constable Ernest Marshall had asked for Jackpine's help. The Jensens liked to go to bed at ten thirty sharp, so at ten thirty they lit the "No Vacancy" sign—full or empty. They owned the motel free and clear and were not about to let business interfere with their lives. In the interest of economy and to help the light-sensitive Mrs. Jensen sleep, they also turned off all outdoor lights.

Jackpine had persuaded the Jensens to leave some lights on all night, and he and Paul patrolled the parking lot from time to time. The crime wave ended, much to the relief of Ernest Marshall, who would have been happier if they had caught someone. His report would have looked better, but the whole detachment was pleased that the pain-in-the-ass phone calls had stopped.

Jackpine knew that the lights and beefed-up surveillance had nothing to do with the cessation of the plate-switching episodes, but he did not tell that to the OPP. Jackpine had stopped Robby McLeod on the street for a very short theoretical chat. He had told Robby that the OPP was pissed off, which seemed to please Robby. Jackpine told him innocent folks were having their vacations ruined. That hit home. Robby had not realized the effect that plating had on people. Robby agreed, theoretically, that anyone involved in plating should find another diversion. There were no further incidents. Coincidentally, the first murder in front of the Falls View Restaurant occurred two days after the chat.

Jackpine told the Jensens they could now start turning their lights off at ten thirty again. Mrs. Jensen was relieved to hear she could get a proper night's sleep once again. Jackpine should not have waited so long to close the loop on the case. He had procrastinated because he knew that once he made this last call on the Jensens, he would have to do a report. He would fire off a one-pager to Marshall when he had time.

Jackpine went back to the station and parked his car. He decided to walk through the downtown to the town council meeting at the Rainbow Falls Hotel. He only walked fifty yards before the first group of people stopped him. He answered their questions politely, trying to be brief. The questions were always the same. Yes, he had managed to stay in pretty good shape; yes, it's too bad his career ended prematurely; Gretzky is the best ever, so far; yes, the guys made a lot more money today, good for them; he lives here because it's his home, and he's chief of police because he wants to be; he was a tall, skinny, ugly kid so they named him after a tall, skinny, ugly tree; and it's nice to meet them too. It was boring, and Jackpine was embarrassed at being treated like a celebrity.

Jackpine was happy his hockey career had ended when it did. He had played pro for five years: one in New Haven and four with the New York Rangers. He had been an NHL all-star defenseman his last three years. He had made Team Canada and played against Russia. During the exhibition season of his sixth year, he was hit in the left eye by a deflected puck. He lost vision in his left eye for a while; eventually it returned to ninety percent of what it had been. He could have returned to the Rangers, but instead he retired.

Jackpine had always loved the game of hockey; he grew to hate the business of hockey. He had a big problem with air travel: a desperate fear would grip him upon takeoff and stay with him until landing. Small bush planes did not bother him, because they looked like they could fly. Big jumbo jets looked like they should not be able to leave the ground. With all the flying a hockey team did, he thought he would get used to it—he never did.

New Haven wasn't bad. He had rented a small house in Madison near Long Island Sound. He used to enjoy running on the beach at Hammonasset. Best of all, he had met Janice there. She had been a nurse in emergency when he arrived needing stitching because of an errant high stick.

In Manhattan, with millions of people around him, Jackpine had been lonely. He and Janice had married after his first year with the Rangers. She had not liked Manhattan either. They had spent a lot of time with Boone, which helped. Boone knew where to go and when to go there. It was Boone's town, and he thrived on the hustle and the pace.

The game of hockey was even losing its thrill. Jackpine liked a freewheeling, fast-skating, wide-open game. Most teams in those days were playing a clutch-and-grab, grind-it-out style—with a lot of high sticks and dirty checks. As a kid and all the way through the junior league, he had played with winners. The teams played for sixty minutes, motivated by the thrill of victory. The Ranger teams he had played on had no chance of winning consistently. Jackpine found himself playing for his paycheck and nothing else.

After the eye injury, he adored long talks with Janice. He enjoyed a fat contract negotiated by Boone, and they lived frugally. He had saved a lot of money that grew substantially with conservative investment over the years. They decided Jackpine should retire. He did, and they moved to Rainbow Falls. Within two years of moving home, he became chief of police. They raised their family in the Falls. Both kids were now away at college and starting to spread their wings. Jackpine had never regretted his decision to retire in his prime. Neither had Janice. She loved the Falls as much as Jackpine did.

Jackpine encountered two more groups before he finished running the gauntlet and made it to the hotel. The Rainbow Falls town council worked well together. They were very compatible, all working together toward common goals. Each member was intelligent and efficient. Above all else, each one of them really cared about Rainbow Falls and its citizens. The elections were usually by acclamation. Five citizens ran for five council positions, and one person ran for reeve (the equivalent of mayor). Reeve Ron Evans had held his position as reeve for fifteen years. Ron was the town postmaster, and almost everyone thought it logical he should be reeve. Postmaster in a small town was not a very intense line of work. There was no mail delivery; everyone picked up their mail at the post office. Ron was always willing to stop sorting the mail to discuss concerns with citizens. The concerns were few and usually petty, but it was reassuring to have access to the reeve all the same.

In a bigger town, there might be outrage at potential conflicts of interest among the councilors, but not in Rainbow Falls. A councilor's business affairs were often interwoven with each other and the town's business, like family relationships after a hillbilly wedding. An investigative reporter could have a field day investigating the relationships, but in Rainbow Falls the reports were nothing more than innuendo. Abuse did not exist in Rainbow Falls.

Councilor Toivo Huhtela was a contractor of sorts. His company snowplowed the town streets and airport. Toy was also the manager of the airport. Toy's primary business was demolition, and his company did jobs throughout northwestern Ontario. He needed other ventures to keep busy, for as Toy put it, "Not many things need blowin' up anymore. When they do, I blow 'em up good." Detonating explosives by remote control had given Toy a real interest in electronics. His RadioShack store in town was more of a devotion to his hobby than a moneymaker. The town was too small for specialized retail. Local pundits called the store Toy's Toy. Toy had owned the school bus that the town hired to transport students back and forth to Blackwater Regional High

School. Toy sold the bus to Heinz Shultz, restaurateur and the newest councilor, because Heinz needed something to keep him busy in the winter.

Councilor Stew Larson was an independent insurance agent. He sold insurance to the town. Stew and Ron Evans owned a marina and rental-cabin business on Dead Horse Lake. Ten years ago, when the cabins were being built, Alistair Boone had encouraged them to name the operation Blue Water Cabins. They had taken Boone's advice over their choice of Dead Horse Cabins.

Councilor Andrew McLeod managed Rainbow Falls Lumber, the town's biggest source of tax revenue. The only councilor standing clear of the shadow of a potential conflict of interest was Janice Keating, unless marriage to the chief of police was deemed a semblance of a shadow.

Jackpine attended most council meetings as a town-father emeritus. They were in a private meeting room off the main dining room at the hotel where council, the Lions, or anyone else convened, requiring food and beverage while meeting. They chatted and ate lunch while waiting for Heinz. Apparently, a tour bus had arrived an hour late, so Heinz was occupied cooking them lunch.

When he appeared, Heinz apologized profusely for being late. Punctuality was inherent in his Germanic upbringing. No one minded. The reeve asked if he had eaten. Heinz had partaken of sole almondine that one of the "bustards" (Heinz's term of endearment for his tour clientele) had sent back to the kitchen. It was not clear with his accent whether he was paraphrasing bastard or had coined a new term "bus turd." It didn't really matter. "She said she thought sole almondine was French for fish and chips. She said she was allergic to nuts."

Andrew opened the meeting with a briefing on the grim situation at the mill and the glimmer of hope presented by Alistair Boone. All agreed to help any way they could, but none of them thought there was anything that he or she could do. The reeve brought a few minor items to the table and then wanted to adjourn. He wanted to get home and watch bowling on ABC.

Jackpine stood to address the council. For the second time that day, he outlined Dan Golias's drug-running operation, the conspiracy of William O'Toole, and the link to the deaths of four people. When he finished, he saw shocked expressions from everyone except Janice. Jackpine explained that he was going to go to the lodge and arrest the culprits when they received the next shipment. The councilors concurred with his logic of not going to O'Toole's superiors with the information. Stew added the wrinkle that with so much money involved perhaps O'Toole's superiors were involved. Jackpine doubted it. His faith in the integrity of the OPP was solid; he thought it was just one bad apple.

Toy Huhtela and Heinz Shultz offered to go with Jackpine. He politely refused their help. "May God be with you," intoned Reeve Ron Evans. "Any other business?" There may have been, but after hearing about the imminent closing of the mill and Jackpine's plan to arrest a vicious group of drug runners, any other town business was too mundane to hold anyone's interest.

On the way out, Jackpine asked Toy Huhtela to drop by the station. When they got there, Jackpine went to the fridge and got a beer for each of them.

"You know I'd go there with you, Yackpine," said Toivo in his hard-to-miss Finnish accent. Toivo Huhtela was in his early sixties. His rock-solid, wiry, one-hundred-seventy-pound body on a five-foot-ten-inch frame was the envy of many younger men. Toy had been a blaster in the gold mine when he first came to Rainbow Falls from Finland. When the mine closed, he combined his knowledge of explosives and detonation with his nerves of steel to start his own company. Rock cuts, gravel pits, beaver dams that threatened highways, old buildings, or anything that had to be demolished was Toy Huhtela's forte. The specialized nature of his work meant traveling far afield in this big, sparsely populated country. The necessity of travel led Toy, many years ago, to acquire a pilot's license and buy a plane. Since he had built the runway and maintained it, he kind of backed into managing the airport.

"I need your help for something else, Toy. When I go up there, I have to be able to disable their planes."

"When do you go?"

"A week or so."

"Good. It will be easy. The planes come to town all the time. I'll plant a charge in each engine and give you remote-control detonators. When the time comes, push the button, bang!"

"The pilots won't notice you?"

"Nope. They're used to me servicing the planes. Nobody would see the charges unless they were specifically looking for them and knew what to look for."

"Thanks, Toy. One other favor—can you fly us up there when the time comes?"

"No problem, Jackpine."

As Toy Huhtela was leaving, Big Paul Desroches lumbered in, chewing on a slice of pizza.

"Havin' lunch on the run, Paul?"

"No, sir. I had lunch earlier. Just a snack." One measly slice of pizza did not achieve meal status in the mind of Paul Desroches. "Saw a major-league badass in town, Wilf Boucher."

"He's outta jail?"

"Yup. I talked to Ernie Marshall. Been out two months now. Been in Thunder Bay. Ernie says he talked to someone on the force there; Wilf's been pushin' drugs. Some real high-quality cocaine. Haven't been able to nail him yet."

"Give 'em time. He'll do something stupid." Stupidity was a cornerstone of Wilfred Boucher's modus operandi. Spur-of-the-moment theft and robbery were his specialties. When he was broke, he would go to the nearest gas station or convenience store and rob it—in much the same manner as using an instant cash machine at a bank. Inevitably, he would get caught and be sent to jail. Occasionally, he would be busted for assault rather than robbery, but the result was the same.

"Usually he steals to buy drugs and booze." Jackpine added. Pushing drugs required some time and planning. "He must have fallen into the dope. He was out of the slammer when his brother Jimmy came back from Blackbear. Paul, I want you to find out where Wilf had been staying in Thunder Bay. Then check the pay phone outside Lawrence's office on the Reserve. If there's a call to Wilf, it would have been Jimmy. Then real low-key, check with Marshall and see if there was cocaine in Jimmy Boucher's blood."

"So, you figger Jimmy Boucher swiped some coke from Golias?"

"Desmond found out about it and planned to come in and blow the whistle. Jimmy found out and helped himself to some. Desmond must have given some to his no-good brother, and Wilf had a new line of work. Must have given him more than Wilf and his cronies could snort; otherwise, he wouldn't have dealt it."

Paul wrote down the assignment. He was thrilled to be given detective work; however routine, it beat a slow day in the radar trap.

"First, give me a lift. I want my goddamn cruiser back."

* * * * * *

Boone's first task on Tuesday morning was to call New York. Sid did not foresee any problems with the purchase of Rainbow Falls Lumber. Initially, they were eager, but now CMI had become weasels, trying to drive the price up. A meeting was scheduled for Thursday at eleven a.m. in New York to iron things out. Boone agreed to meet with Sid and the banker at seven a.m. to finalize strategy and review the dossier on CMI.

The bankers had good news for Boone. Two groups were interested in the project. Both groups thought the impending free trade between Canada and the United States would be a boon for the Canadian lumber industry, and they had faith in Alistair Boone.

Boone's second task proved easier than anticipated. He called Chip Carpenter's office. Chip returned the call minutes later. Boone was surprised to discover that the Carpenters were at the Riverview Motel.

Chip had taken advantage of the long weekend to bring his family to Rainbow Falls. He wanted to see the town before making any kind of commitment to Boone. They were staying over Tuesday morning to visit the school. Garth Carpenter was a sixth-grade student. Boone was even more convinced he had chosen the right man; he admired that kind of initiative. The trip to the Falls showed that Chip was cautious and prudent. Boone needed those qualities in his managers, lacking both himself. Boone arranged to meet for lunch.

The taxi driver from Blackwater arrived with the two-dozen roses Boone had ordered. Inez Mahoney was going to get his full-court press. He put the flowers in the back seat of his car and drove to Northland Crafts. He arranged for each of the Carpenters to get mukluks and gloves with his compliments. Boone then drove to Rainbow Falls Lumber for the meeting he had arranged.

Boone was shown into the meeting room. He shook hands with Andrew McLeod and was introduced to the human resource manager, the union president, and four members of the union executive committee. It was a very somber-looking group. Andrew had just told them that CMI was going to close the mill and that he was unable to find a buyer. He explained the problems in the lumber market and that there was no hope on the horizon for improvements in the market. As Boone walked in Andrew introduced him as the last hope to keep the mill operating. Andrew set the stage just as Boone had asked.

Boone addressed the group. He wanted to be homey and folksy but tough, simple, direct, and blunt, and he wanted to be brief. He would fail on the last count. "North American industry enjoyed a heyday in the post–World War II era. Demand outstripped manufacturing capacity in almost every industry. Today capacity exceeds demand and manufacturers are being squeezed." He spoke for an hour. He talked about the auto industry, electronics, and the steel industry. He discussed Japanese manufacturing techniques, digressing into a lecture on just-in-time, statistical process control and employee involvement. He talked about quality and how important quality was to consumers. He puffed his Monte Cristo, catching himself and deciding to end his tirade. "People can buy lumber from a lot of sources. How do they choose? By a combination of quality, service, and price." He puffed his cigar and looked intently at each person. "You guys have screwed up on one or all of these three things, and as a result you're going to lose your jobs." Both Andrew and the union president tried to speak. "Who? Management will blame labor, and labor will blame management, and you'll blame each other all the way to the unemployment office." They hung their heads. "I'm not here to try and break your union. But I can't afford to lose $200,000 a month just so you can keep your jobs. I'll buy this company, if you five"—Boone looked at the union executives—"promise me a dedication to work as a team to improve quality, improve service, and be the lowest-cost producer. If you guys can't make a two-by-four cheaper than someone else, then the bottom line is no one will buy your two-by-four."

The union president spoke: "We're between a rock and a hard place. Me and the executive committee and the full membership will work with you. We'll do anything we can to help save the mill and our jobs."

They talked for another hour. Boone listened to the union's complaints: some had merit, some did not. At the end, the air seemed to be cleared, and Boone felt he had a legitimate pledge of cooperation. He shook hands with everyone, thanked them, and then left for his meeting with Chip.

The Carpenters were waiting outside the Riverview Motel. Boone chatted a few minutes. He told Dee and Garth to go to Northland Crafts for their mukluks and gloves. He asked Dee to select some for Chip. They thanked him profusely. Boone took Chip to the Falls View Restaurant.

Boone had told Heinz he wanted privacy for an important meeting. Chip was pleased with the view of the Falls, noting that they could not see the river from the River View Motel. Boone noticed Heinz's Teutonic efficiency and love for signs. All of the tables around Boone's table displayed "RESERVED" signs, even though the restaurant was nearly empty.

Heinz and Olga had had a full house on Monday, attracting many locals for a Thanksgiving feast. Their first attempt at a themed dinner had been a resounding success. Heinz had thanked Boone many times for the idea. Heinz had balked at the pilgrim suit, but Boone had insisted. When Boone suggested something, it was difficult to take bits and pieces of the idea— Boone always pushed for full execution. Boone had attended with Inez and the Keatings, and he thought the stern countenances of Heinz and Olga were perfect for the pilgrim outfits. As expected, it was slow all day Tuesday. The weekend tourists had departed, and drawing locals two days in a row was too much to hope for.

No menus were offered. Boone had asked Heinz to prepare an authentic north-woods lunch. The New Yorker and the German had created the menu. For appetizers they offered smoked lake trout. The word appetizer may have been a misnomer, since Boone devoured two whole fish. Smoked trout was always featured at Falls View. Heinz drove halfway to Thunder Bay once a week to buy trout from the old Indian that Boone had told him about.

They discussed Chip's impression of Rainbow Falls over the main course: fresh walleye dusted in flour and pan fried in clarified butter, wild rice, sautéed wild mushrooms, and fiddleheads. The fiddleheads were frozen, not fresh, as the young ferns were only harvested in the spring. Fresh bread from Mrs. Riccio and a bottle of Riesling (too sweet for Boone, but he let Heinz pick) completed the repast. Chip did not like fish, preferred tame rice, thought the fiddleheads tasted like the hated spinach, and never ate any kind of fungus (wild or tame). He did the best he could, somewhat inspired by Boone's obvious enjoyment. Both Chip and Dee were raised in rural Manitoba, but they had grown to like city life very much. It would be difficult for Dee to get one of the few teaching jobs at the elementary school in Rainbow Falls, but if the compensation for Chip was right, she would retire. She was tired of teaching anyway, as it turned out. The opportunity for Chip's career advancement took precedence, and after long deliberations, they had decided that, if offered, Chip would accept. They were concerned about Garth's commute to Blackwater when he reached high school, but Garth was an enthusiastic supporter of the move. He had learned that Jackpine Keating would be his hockey coach.

Heinz, in addition to chef, was their personal waiter. As a town councilor, he was very interested in the conversation. Boone tolerated Heinz's eavesdropping. Boone was trying hard to adjust to small-town life where there were no secrets. Hearing mention of the school bus, Heinz piped up, guaranteeing Chip that the driver was safe and reliable and that the bus would be clean and in good working order. Heinz assured Chip that the commute would be quiet and school-like onboard, so students could do their homework. No one consulted the kids before Heinz took over the bus. Discipline may have been lacking in some of the classrooms, but not on a school bus with Heinz Shultz at the wheel.

Over fresh blueberry pie made that morning by Olga, they discussed the lumber business. Chip had done extensive research and had held discussions with many contactors in the industry. He knew he could deliver a big share of the Winnipeg market and talked to enough people in Toronto to feel confident they could compete, providing they could get their costs down. Chip's estimate of potential volume dovetailed with Boone's numbers on production levels at full capacity.

Over their second coffees, Boone offered a good salary with a generous profit-sharing bonus. Chip negotiated a few details, but not very tenaciously. They agreed and shook hands. Boone reiterated that the offer was contingent, of course, on the deal going through.

Boone planned to talk to Andrew McLeod after lunch, before Heinz had a chance to. Boone would install Chip as president and promote Andrew to vice president of operations. It was really a demotion from general manager, but he would not cut Andrew's pay, and the new title would make it easier to accept. Boone told Chip he would initiate a search for a cost accountant and an engineer, but the selections would be Chip's decision.

As Boone was signing his president, Jackpine drove home to meet Janice for lunch. Janice had tuna sandwiches and tomato soup ready when Jackpine came in. If left to his own devices, Jackpine would have tuna and tomato soup each and every workday. He was flexible enough to have a ham sandwich (occasionally), and he wouldn't complain if cream of mushroom replaced tomato soup now and then; but Jackpine Keating was a creature of habit, and his habit was tuna and tomato at 12:05. On Saturdays they had lunch out, and on Sundays they had a late bacon-and-egg brunch after church. Janice had halfheartedly fought these rituals early in their marriage but gave in years ago.

Janice asked Jackpine, "What's wrong with Boone?"

"Whattya mean, honey? Nuthin."

"He's sooo mellow. He came into the store this morning. He wasn't even in a hurry." She laughed and marched quickly across the kitchen, arms flailing, doing a very accurate Alistair Boone. "He didn't give me any advice on merchandising. He didn't extol the virtues of the mail-order business." She grabbed the carrot she had been eating and pretended to smoke a Monte Cristo, "Mail order, Janice, my dear. Can't be a shopkeeper all your life. This store is the anchor, the showplace, but mail order is the real business. You could do millions, my girl...millions." She was spreading her hands to visualize millions. She and Jackpine burst out laughing. Janice laughed so hard she had to sit down, ending her impression.

"What did he say?" asked Jackpine.

"He asked how business was. I told him real good and that I was going to hit $100,000 in sales. And you know what he says? He says, 'That's nice, atta girl.' Can you believe that? No lecture, no advice, just 'that's nice.' That is not Alistair Boone!"

"He's really trying to wind down—selling his businesses, talking about living in the Falls. This time he's serious, honey, at least so far, and he's head over heels for Inez." They gossiped for a few minutes about the courtship. Then Jackpine headed back to the station as Janice cleaned up.

* * * * * *

Boone walked into the station in midafternoon and found Inez alone. He swept her into his arms, leaned her over, and gave her a big kiss. Valentino would have been impressed. Inez was not overly impressed; this was rather typical of the man she loved, but she was shocked by the two dozen roses. No one had bought her flowers before. Her husband surely hadn't, and two dozen roses was so extravagant. She protested mildly, very mildly, because she loved the flowers and the thought behind them. She hurried

169

to put them in water as Boone asked, "So where are those stalwart bastions of law and order?"

"At the gravel pit east of town, as usual. They've been sneaking off there every chance they get. They're target shooting. This whole thing has me worried about all three of you, but especially you, Boone. This is not something you have experience in."

"Honey, I have to go with them. Those two Neanderthals tried to kill me, and that Hungarian goulash told them to. And that crooked bastard, O'Toole, has to get what's coming to him. Besides, Jackpine can use my help."

"I know. I just wish there was some other way."

"We've got the advantage, honey. We've got Jackpine Keating, and they don't." He smiled. He told Inez about his trip for the next day, said he would see her after work, and asked for directions to the gravel pit.

Jackpine and Paul were shooting clay pigeons when Boone arrived. Hitting a clay pigeon with a shotgun was something most experienced shooters were adept at. They were throwing up two at a time, which was much more difficult, requiring a fast aim. There were no unbroken discs on the ground; hence, neither one of them had missed. What Boone found remarkable was that they were using rifles, not shotguns. With a shotgun you just had to be close; a rifle required pinpoint accuracy. For about fifteen minutes, they continued taking turns shooting with neither one missing a shot. Then Paul chipped the edge of a pigeon, not completely shattering the disc. Both he and Jackpine counted it as a miss. They gave Boone a turn with a rifle. He was proud of his marksmanship, hitting four of the twenty discs. Paul had thrown one pigeon at a time instead of two; otherwise, Boone would have gotten four out of forty. He would never have gotten the second disc.

Boone noticed YIELD signs and STOP signs suspended by ropes over the side of the gravel pit. As he turned, he saw more of them. There were a dozen of them at distances varying between 100 to 200 yards. Jackpine put his binoculars to his eyes. Paul picked up his rifle. "Yield, ten o'clock," Jackpine yelled. Paul wheeled to his left, fired, and the yield sign spun wildly on the rope—a hit. Immediately following the sound of the shot, Jackpine yelled, "Stop, four o'clock." Paul turned to his right, then *BANG!* and the stop sign was spinning. Jackpine called two more signs, and Paul shot them both. As Paul turned and fired, Boone wondered when he had the time to aim. Then it was Paul's turn to call the signs. He put the binoculars to his eyes and called as Jackpine fired. To Boone's amazement, Jackpine fired faster than Paul and just as accurately. "Three of four, same as me," said Paul. They both looked disappointed.

"We should be better, Paul!"

Boone protested, "Wait a minute, both of you hit every sign you shot at."

"Paul was shooting at the *E* in YIELD and the *T* in STOP; I had the *D* and the *P*. We both missed a shot; that's why we used binoculars to score. Anybody could just hit the sign."

"We both missed the two-hundred-yard shot," offered Paul.

"No excuse, Paul. If those fellas end up throwin' some hot lead at us, our safety will be in bein' more accurate at longer ranges than they are."

The thought of people shooting at him (again) sent a chill down Boone's spine, but at the same time he felt secure knowing that Jackpine and Paul would be with him. "Why isn't Lawrence with you guys?" asked Boone.

"He says practice is a waste of bullets," Paul said.

"He's a good shot, Boone," Jackpine said, "He hunts moose with a single-shot rifle. He says anyone who needs more than one shot to kill a moose shouldn't be allowed to hunt. But it takes him time to sight in. Paul and I have been working on speed. That's where we need improvement."

Boone remembered when Jackpine was the fastest skater on the Ranger team, one of the fastest in the league. Every day at extra skating practice, Jackpine was there. Sometimes the Garden staff were starting the conversion of the building for a circus or the Knicks, as Jackpine got in his last few laps—the last guy left on the ice. "I must improve. I must prepare better for games," he would say.

Boone had heard kids in the Falls grumble about Coach Keating's optional practice in addition to the grueling regular practice. Any kid who failed to exercise the option or attended the regular practice without giving a hundred percent found himself riding the pines (sitting on the bench) for the next game. Superstar or journeyman—it did not matter. Jackpine coached one team, but attended and held optional practices for kids of all age-groups. Jackpine would skate with them at skating practice, and even after the third practice in a row, he was still flying around the rink long after many kids were winded. The Rainbow Falls kids' hockey teams competed against much larger towns with bigger talent pools to draw from, but they were always competitive. The teams from the Falls were renowned for third-period comebacks. They would play at full speed for the first two periods, and in the third, when the opposition was exhausted and spent, Jackpine's kids would pick the pace up a notch, scooting down the ice as fresh as if they were on their first shift of the game.

"Now, for the run, Paul," Jackpine announced.

"God, I hate this part," said Paul, as he took after Jackpine. In a few minutes they were out of sight. Boone stood and smoked his Monte Cristo thoughtfully. After what seemed to be a few minutes but was ten or twelve, Jackpine came into view, sprinting toward him. Jackpine was breathing heavily but didn't seem too winded. "Never know if we'll be called on to run a fast two miles up there. Preparation is the key."

"You run while I hold down the fort," Boone laughed. "Christ, it's getting cold!"

Big Paul Desroches came gasping to the finish line, sweating profusely. "I never thought I could run two miles!" Paul panted.

"We'll be runnin' marathons before you know it, Paul," Jackpine teased.

Jackpine went and got each of them a beer from his trunk. "Gonna be an early winter this year," said Jackpine prophetically.

"You can say that again, Chief," echoed Paul.

Boone wondered why no one ever did say it again and why people asked others to say it again when they really did not want them to. "You guys know that from studying flora and fauna, from watching squirrels frantically gathering nuts, from studying ducks and geese—you wilderness guys are amazing! How else do you know?"

Paul laughed. "I don't know about all that stuff. I was talkin' to a trapper. He told me beaver pelts are almost prime. When pelts prime early, it means an early winter."

"Oh," Boone sounded let down. "How about you, Jackpine?"

"I know by a more scientific approach—when it's only October and beer stays cold sittin' in the trunk."

* * * * * *

When they got back to the station, Inez handed Jackpine an envelope. "Ron Evans dropped this by." Jackpine opened the envelope and saw a letter on "Town of Rainbow Falls" letterhead. The letter was addressed to Chief of Police Oscar Keating and started "Dear Oscar." How formal, thought Jackpine. He smiled as he read the letter. "It has come to my attention that we have a problem with illegal drugs in our town and that the source of supply is a person or persons from the Blackbear Point Fishing Lodge. Even though the lodge is technically outside the town limits,

Rainbow Falls is the closest town to the lodge. I request that you and your staff travel to the lodge and perform a preliminary investigation. If your inquiries confirm my suspicions, we can turn the investigation over to the Ontario Provincial Police." It was signed Reeve Ron Evans. Ron was taking his share of responsibility, in case something went wrong. It was people like Ron Evans who made Jackpine proud to be a citizen of Rainbow Falls.

Paul Desroches left to meet Nelson Lesmontaignes. They were going to Blackwater to recondition the cooling system in Dan Golias's boat. Inez gathered her roses and left for the day. Toy Huhtela walked in carrying a paper bag. Toy asked to see Jackpine alone, but Jackpine assured him he could talk in front of Boone. Another formidable-looking recruit that Jackpine had enlisted, thought Boone.

Toivo pulled out four little black boxes. "Both planes have been in. They are taken care of. I did it with my own two hands, so I know it's done right. This one for the Cessna." He handed Jackpine a box with a *C* marked on it. The second had an *O* for the Otter. "Now, just in case they get another plane goin' there. If it refuels at my airport, I will fix it too." The third box had a *?* on it.

"What's the fourth one for?" asked Jackpine.

"We got lucky. You take out their planes, but they still have their radio to call for a new plane."

"I've been thinking about it, but I don't have a solution," said Jackpine.

"The pilot of the Cessna was in today. He brought in a broken part from their radio. He was going to my RadioShack to replace it. I said, 'You run your errands. I'm going to the store anyway; I will get it for you.' I got new part all right. It works yust fine. Little bit of powerful plastic explosive in the part." He pointed to the fourth box marked *R*. "As soon as you decide, you press, and *BOOM!* no more radio."

"Good thinking, Toy. Thank you!"

"Anytime, Yackpine, you know that. White Horse Parker was the first man I met when I came to the Falls. He was cooking at the dorm. I only knew a few words of bush-camp Finn, and he helped me out before I could speak English. He was a gentle man, wouldn't hurt a fly. Those sons of bitches at Blackbear Point deserve a dose of their own medicine, Yackpine!" Toivo smacked the table for emphasis before he got up and left.

"That's another guy I wouldn't want to be on the wrong side of," said Boone.

"No, you wouldn't. So, you're off to New York."

"Yeah. I'll try to finish up the lumber deal and get some poop on CMI."

"Only two things we're missing now, thanks to Toy. One, we need the link to CMI; and two, we have to determine when the drugs are comin' in without campin' in the bush for a week or ten days."

Lawrence Musgrove walked into the office while Jackpine was talking. "Maybe only one thing missing now."

"How was the powwow, Lawrence?"

"Good. I talked to all the chiefs from way up north. I told them some drug runners killed some of our people. Said I was going to punish them. Most knew nuthin', but the chief from Kashechewan told me a story. This summer some guys rented a house from some of our people. Stuff came in by helicopter. Stored it in this house. Guess the house was a long way from anything, very remote. Planes from a fishin' lodge flew in regular, took the stuff out piece by piece. Had Mexicans with machine guns guardin' the house."

"Are they renting the house again for this next shipment?" asked Jackpine.

"Chief didn't know. Doesn't see this guy very often."

"Can we talk to the man who rented his house?"

"Yup. Chief is going to go see him tomorrow. Going to get him to come back to his office to see me and you."

"Toy just left. We'll have to get him to fly us up there."

"Figgered as much. Toy was gettin' in his car when I was comin' in. He's gassin' up tonight. We'll meet him at seven thirty tomorrow mornin'."

"You can trust this chief?" Boone asked.

"He doesn't like guys killin' our people. I trust him. If we got along this good two hundred years ago, you guys wouldn't have taken our land so easy!"

Boone did not like the way the conversation was going. He tried to dig himself out of the hole by changing topics. "You missed a great Thanksgiving dinner yesterday."

"It's not my holiday. You white men invented it to thank the Indians for feeding you so you wouldn't starve as you took our land."

Boone plugged onward, determined to resolve this rapidly deteriorating dialogue. "Of course, it's not Thanksgiving back home. We celebrate Columbus Day on the same weekend."

"Because you think he discovered America?"

"Well, no. He is credited, traditionally, but it's clear that the Vikings discovered America much earlier."

"So, the Vikings were the people who discovered America. Are Indians not people? We were here long before the Vikings!"

"Well...yes...but...." Boone was seldom at a loss for words, but Lawrence had him tongue-tied.

Jackpine, the peacemaker, jumped in. "Now Lawrence, you get wound up like this after every one of your chief conferences. The point here is that we have to find out when the shipment is comin' in. We don't want to be campin' up there."

Boone wished he were as confident as these guys.

CHAPTER 10

Jackpine felt reasonably safe in the small plane. As safe as a man with a dreadful fear of flying could. He knew Toy Huhtela kept his plane in peak mechanical condition, and he had faith in Toy's skill and experience as a bush pilot. They were flying low in deference to Jackpine, who felt reassured looking out of the window of the floatplane, seeing thousands of lakes and rivers representing a security blanket of potential landing sites. They would retrace their route on the return trip.

The chief and Winston Wapiskateti were waiting for them in the chief's office in Kashechewan. Compared to this place, Rainbow Falls was like Manhattan, thought Jackpine. It took them longer than it should have to get Winston's story. Words were a luxury to Winston: he used them sparingly. A question would have to be directly on target to solicit more than one of Winston's three favorite words: "yeah," "no," and "mebbe." A small, wiry man with a weathered face, he looked as if he would be more comfortable riding a snow machine on a frozen wilderness lake than sitting in an office answering Jackpine's questions. Truth be known, he would have been.

Winston had never spent much time in a town of any kind. He did not feel comfortable in crowds. The two chiefs, Jackpine, and Toy constituted a crowd to Winston. He felt particularly uneasy around white men. He did not understand their odd and peculiar ways. He had only occasionally been in the company of white men as a fishing and hunting guide from time to time. A hunting client had once told Winston that he worked like a dog for fifty weeks to enjoy living two weeks up here in the wilderness. Why the man did not have the sense to live for fifty weeks and work for two, Winston could not understand.

As a young man, he left the bush—once. He had decided to go to Port Arthur for the winter. He was young then and did not know any better. On his first day in the city, he stood mesmerized on a busy street corner, watching the people and the traffic lights. He went home the next day. Imagine, he told his friends, they have lights to tell you when to cross the street. You cannot cross until the light tells you. Red, everyone stops. Green, everyone goes. He did not understand the concept of amber, so he left it out of his story. He would be damned if he would let any light tell him what to do.

He saw thousands of houses all built together. Imagine living so close to neighbors, he had thought. He had not gone into any houses, but he was sure they probably had lights to tell them when they were hungry and when to piss. He knew from guiding that white men looked at their watches. "It's twelve o'clock. Time for shore lunch," they would say. Winston always thought it made more sense to eat when you were hungry instead of when the clock told you to.

Winston was now hearing that many whites wanted to ban trapping, potentially destroying his livelihood. Winston had no comprehension of the issues involved, but he knew that once white men took a notion, that was that. He hoped it was just rumors. To Winston, the idea that trapping was cruel was as unfathomable as the white man's concept of a pet. In the days before the snow machine, dogs had been prevalent, not as pets, but as workers pulling sleds. Years ago, in particularly harsh winters when food was scarce, a dog provided a necessary addition to the meager dinner table. As a youth, Winston had partaken of filet de fido on more than one occasion. Eating a dog was certainly not appealing to Winston, but a hearty bowl of ragout de rover sure beat the alternative of possible starvation.

None of the crazy things white men did surprised Winston anymore. He had even guided for a group one time that wouldn't eat the moose steaks he fried. "We don't eat meat," they said. Then, they refused to eat the fish or potatoes because he fried them in lard, and they wouldn't eat the beans because there was one piece of pork in the can. The next day, he tried something different. He fried the fish in butter and opened cans of peaches. They wouldn't eat anything cooked in butter, and the peaches had too much sugar for them to eat. On the next two days, he did not bother making lunch for them. He knew he would never see them again. In his world, they would have starved to death long ago.

Just when he thought that all whites were crazy, he met a sensible one—Jackpine. The tall man looked like a jack pine. Even his name made sense. He asked Jackpine if they still had lights in Port Arthur, or Thunder Bay as they now called it. White men couldn't even make up their minds about what to call their towns, thought Winston. Jackpine reported that they had even more lights, and that's why he didn't go there either. Maybe if he ever went down south again, Winston thought, he would go to Rainbow Falls.

* * * * *

Jackpine finally drew the whole story from Winston. Three men came to him in July and rented his house. They gave him $2,000 to use his house for ten weeks. Winston had been happy to oblige. He really only needed his house in the winter anyway. Winston described them perfectly: Dan Golias, Bear Sawchuk, and one of the two pilots. Winston might have been unsophisticated and poorly educated, but Jackpine knew he certainly was not stupid. Golias's undoing would be that he underestimated the northerners, thought Jackpine grimly.

Golias's crew had brought in six loads in a small helicopter. Three Mexicans came up in a Blackbear Point Lodge plane to guard the stuff in Winston's house. A plane from the lodge came to Winston's house once a week, leaving with some bags. The Mexicans left with the last load in late September. Golias returned and rented Winston's home again for seven days beginning this coming Saturday. He offered $200. Winston said it was getting too cold to sleep in the bush. He asked for and received $2,000 for the week.

Golias's willingness to pay the exorbitant fee confirmed Winston's suspicions that they were doing something contrary to one of the white man's many laws. Winston went into town and told the local chief his story. The chief was planning to go to the OPP, but with the chief's conference coming up, he decided to wait a few days. Maybe he would find out something at the conference. The chief now agreed not to say anything to the OPP until he heard from Lawrence or Jackpine. Winston would report to the chief when the next helicopter arrived; then the chief would contact Lawrence. Jackpine had been willing to spend ten days in the bush waiting for the shipment. He was happy that he would not have to. Jackpine hoped they could find a way to involve Golias's backers. They were as guilty as if they had personally put the noose around Old White Horse's neck themselves. Jackpine Keating would make them pay for their crimes, or he would die trying. Dan Golias would be mortified if he saw the icy stare on the grim, granite-hard countenance of his enemy.

* * * * * *

Boone landed at La Guardia at eight o'clock Wednesday night. Poke Chop was there to greet him. Poke Chop was concerned about his future. Working for Alistair Boone was the best thing that had ever happened in his life, and he saw his job evaporating. "Boss don't need no driver if he ain't never in the city 'cept now and then." Boone had already given Poke Chop's future some thought. He told Poke Chop to drive to the Smith & Wollensky restaurant in midtown, where Boone had made a reservation for the two of them. Smith & Wollensky was known for jumbo lobsters and huge steaks. The quality and service were good, but Boone had selected it because he knew that quantity was Poke Chop's overriding concern in restaurant selection and that the place was not intimidating in formality. Poke Chop opted for a three-pound lobster and a big steak, while Boone confined himself to a three-pounder and a salad. Lobsters were available throughout North America these days, but Boone only ordered them on the East Coast. Lobsters existing in fish tanks in the Midwest with elastic bands around their claws, waiting to be selected as someone's dinner, did not appeal to Boone. Maybe he just felt sorry for them; however, he showed no remorse while devouring the three-pounder placed in front of him at Smith & Wollensky. The lobster he was served had come from a tank, but Boone allowed himself the fantasy that it had been caught hours earlier.

Boone told Poke Chop they were starting a limousine service. Poke Chop would be the driver-cum-manager, and he would have full access to Boone's limo. Poke Chop was guaranteed his current salary, and any profit after expenses would be split fifty-fifty. Boone said he would contact some people to drum up business. A well-appointed limo with a knowledgeable, courteous driver would be in demand, but the fact that Poke Chop was also a bodyguard would make the service particularly appealing to businesspeople from out of town. Living in the city, he had not noticed the gradual deterioration of the quality of life. It was a sad realization for Boone that a bodyguard would be so well received—that crime and senseless violence were choking the life from what he had always thought was the greatest city on earth. On the drive in, he forced himself to look at the great metropolis through the eyes of Inez Mahoney. Somewhere along the East River, he had quit trying, not liking what he saw.

Poke Chop was very pleased with Boone's largess and promised to bust his ass and to more than cover his monthly salary plus expenses.

When Boone returned home after dinner, he packed a large suitcase with winter clothes. If Paul and Jackpine were right about an early winter, he wanted to have warm clothing when they went to the lodge. He also packed a twenty-seven Magnum, an automatic twelve-gauge shotgun, and a bow with arrows.

* * * * * *

Boone was at Sid Rosenfeld's office at 6:45 Thursday morning. Sid was waiting when Boone arrived. Boone was always early. In a small, well-appointed meeting room, Sid had arranged for fresh hot coffee with real cream, fresh cold juices, bottles of Evian water on ice, fresh bagels with cream cheese, croissants still warm from the oven, and jars of imported jams. Sid knew who he was dealing with.

"Nice new furniture I bought for you, Sid," said Boone, attacking a croissant.

"Some deal," Sid laughed. "You pay my fees in pre-tax dollars; then you take it all back on the golf course in after-tax dollars. Besides the nerve of you, retiring before my kids are through college."

Both warriors laughed. Sid poured coffees. Boone started to read the dossier. CMI was owned by two brothers: Sandor and Julius Toth. Sandor, the elder brother, was in control. They were fifty-four and forty-four years old, and they had migrated to Cabbagetown in Toronto from Hungary in 1956. Sandor was suspected of being involved in a stolen-car ring—lots of innuendo, but no arrests. In the 1970s, they had started to develop a name for themselves in real estate. By the late 1980s, Toth Brothers Development was a major player. The Toths displayed an uncanny ability to put together major development sites. They were able to convince fifty or sixty, sometimes up to a hundred, small landowners and homeowners to sell to them. They would end up with a large package of land suitable for developing a shopping mall, an industrial park, office buildings, a housing projects, or condos. There were persistent rumors regarding their tactics in assembling parcels of land. Accusations of blackmail, arson, and assault were plentiful, along with whispered allegations of murder. No formal charges were ever brought against the Toths, but it was clear that the authors of the dossier considered them guilty on all counts.

With their burgeoning wealth, it looked as if the Toths had bought prestige, but they were never accepted by the traditional establishment. As their real-estate business prospered, their reputations, in direct correlation, became more tarnished. Their unethical and devious manner would never be accepted by the old-line bankers and developers to whom a handshake was binding.

They expanded into other businesses, but Toth Brothers Development remained the foundation of the conglomerate. A downturn in the real-estate market left the Toths with many half-completed projects. The inflated values of the projects gave the balance sheet an illusory robustness. If they had been forced to sell at low-market prices, the losses would have driven the corporation into bankruptcy.

The Toths bought a small chain of donut shops in the mid-1980s, which they expanded rapidly through franchising. Twenty company-owned shops were well established and profitable. The health of the company depended on how the lawsuits of the unhappy franchisees were resolved. Allegations of fraud had received sufficient publicity to curtail continued expansion.

Polarex had been a legitimate company engaged in mining exploration when the Toths bought it. Sandor Toth used the company as a tool in a shell game to manipulate the prices of penny mining stocks. Shortly after buying the company, Sandor Toth discovered opportunities in the exploration firm that meshed with his style of business. He found that he could start a mining company, send in his exploration crew, have some falsely optimistic preliminary reports written, start a few rumors, and presto—the stock of the company would fly. He would then sell the mining-company stock at the artificially driven zenith of its value, pocket the profits, pull out the Polarex team, and then send them on to the next scam. This was illegal, of course, and it was also very hard to prove. The dossier concluded that Polarex, as a company, was now virtually worthless. Investors had gotten wise to Toth's manipulations. Any involvement by Polarex was enough to cause a sell-off in a company. Legitimate mining ventures would no longer consider retaining Polarex.

The chain of budget motels seemed to be a bona fide extension for a land developer and builder. With solid occupancy rates and a positive cash flow, it seemed to Boone to be the healthiest of the Toth's enterprises. He wondered when they would initiate a franchise scam or convert the units into houses of ill repute. Sandor Toth had indeed considered both options. Were it not for legal complications, Toth thought a string of bordellos would be a great business. Instead, the dossier suggested that he planned to launch a franchise scam as soon as he had some ready cash. They also owned a brick-making company that was moderately profitable but highly leveraged.

The report was thorough. Boone did not want to think of what Sid's bill would be. The next venture detailed in the dossier confirmed Boone's suspicions. Neptune Shipping consisted of three tired, old cargo ships. Two of the three were the ships that Boone had identified in Mrs. Matthews's office in Toronto. Boone considered it to be conclusive evidence that the Toths were the kingpins behind Dan Golias's operation.

Boone looked up from the report. "Quite the pair of scoundrels, aren't they, Sid?"

"We were pretty mild in writing the dossier. If you were a little guy with land they wanted, they'd break your kneecaps, burn down your house, or have you shot if all else failed. But they're shrewd operators, I'll give them that. They keep their shenanigans at arm's length, so they've stayed out of jail."

Not this time you bastards, thought Boone. Jackpine Keating was more than either one of them had bargained for.

Boone's banker arrived. They started to review the information on Rainbow Falls Lumber. It was readily apparent to Boone why they decided to close up shop. The money they were losing every month was a drain on the cash-poor Toth Brothers empire. The Toths had already stripped the company out of every bit of available cash. The banker thought Boone's offer was fair but too generous, considering the plight of the Toths and the condition of the lumber company. Boone agreed with the vulture--like assessment, but he was willing to pay a little more than necessary to avoid protracted negotiations with these people. One, he did not like them; and two, he had more pressing concerns to attend to in Rainbow Falls.

Terry Timpano (the chief financial officer) and Rod Ballard (the head of the legal department) from CMI were feeling uneasy as they waited in the lobby of Sid's office. Sandor Toth had berated them: "I don't give a fuck what deal you made on the phone. These assholes are stupid, or they wouldn't be buying this piece-of-shit company. You figure a way to shake these fools down for a few hundred grand more."

Terry argued that anything they got was found money, but Sandor Toth did not see it that way. "When you get a chance to take a fool down, you don't leave nothing on the table." They agreed with Mr. Toth to avoid a longer tirade. They both enjoyed working for CMI, despite Sandor's caustic demeanor. It was their kind of company.

Four years ago, Timpano was in charge of the donut business. Before franchising, he had set up the flagship store. Half of the staff at the flagship store was on loan from two of their other stores, with the staff's wages paid for by the other stores. When supplies were delivered from the warehouse to the prized store, they were double shipped. If they ordered one hundred pounds of flour, they were invoiced for a hundred pounds but received two hundred pounds. The low labor cost and low cost of supplies gave the store a glowing profit-and-loss statement. The books from this store were then shown to prospective franchisees: purported to represent an average store. This sleight of hand enabled Terry Timpano to solicit much higher franchise fees. He focused on people with some hard-earned capital and get-rich-quick dreams but no business experience.

Rod Ballard's primary job was to prepare and execute the franchisee's contract. "No need to hire your own expensive lawyer. We're all partners, and I work for you," he would assure the franchisees. This lopsided agreement guaranteed a fat percentage of gross sales for advertising and administration. Franchisees quickly found that advertising programs were nonexistent. Each franchisee was supposed to benefit from in-depth market studies of demographics and traffic patterns. The studies were copies of a master with a few local names added for flavor. The contract stated that all supplies were to be bought from the company to ensure quality control and take advantage of the company's buying power. This meant that each franchisee paid substantially higher prices for flour, oil, napkins, and every other supply than retail supermarket prices. Two hundred franchises were sold before the bubble burst in a flood of negative publicity and lawsuits. Ballard's contract had proven to be an airtight defense so far.

Rather than getting fired for their fraudulent behavior, both men were promoted to their current positions by the jubilant Sandor Toth. "You guys are my kind of hustlers." And Sandor Toth was their kind of boss.

Timpano and Ballard were uneasy because the opulent furnishings did not exude an aura of a den of fools. Their suspicions were confirmed a few minutes after meeting Alistair Boone and his support team. These guys were obviously sophisticated pros. Rather than risk the wrath of Sandor Toth, they tried valiantly to add qualifiers to raise the price of the deal. After a few minutes, Alistair Boone stood up, puffing thoughtfully on a Monte Cristo. "I want you fellows to listen to me for a minute. We have made a generous offer for a company that you don't know how to run. If this deal doesn't go through, you know and I know"— Boone pointed his cigar for emphasis—"that you are going to close Rainbow Falls Lumber and walk away without one red cent. I've listened to your bullshit patiently, but the time has come to fish or cut bait. You're out of your league with this nonsense. You are going to agree to the deal in front of you within five minutes, or I am going to withdraw my offer."

"But, Mr. Boone..."

"No buts!" Boone yelled. "Discussion's over. You have five minutes. Let's go stretch our legs, fellas, and give these guys a few minutes to think." Boone and his group left the room.

The two budding young con men consulted. Mr. Toth would be furious at them for not getting a more lucrative deal, but they didn't want to envision the results if they blew the whole deal.

When Boone returned, they were feverishly signing documents. Board Foot Boone, Lumber Baron Boone, smiled.

* * * * * *

By noon Boone was back in his old office. There was nothing waiting for him. By divesting himself of his enterprises, he had become a forgotten man. It was bruising his ego that the businesses seemed to be running without him, but at the same time he felt relieved.

By five p.m. Boone was at Field Aviation, a private-plane hangar at the Toronto Airport, where Andrew McLeod and Chip

Carpenter were waiting for him. He was pleased to see they seemed to be hitting it off quite well. Over smoked trout and club sodas with lime, Boone explained the situation. Andrew seemed relieved. He was pleased to have the weight of responsibility taken from his shoulders. He knew he could handle operations. When Toth Brothers were their major customer, Andrew had managed well; abandoned by them, Andrew never grasped the sales and marketing end of the business. The vice president's title and the ten-percent raise were appreciated, but not really necessary.

Chip had taken time off to come to Toronto. The recruiter had lined up candidates for the engineering and cost-accounting jobs for Chip and Andrew to interview. Boone chartered a private plane for the return trip to Thunder Bay, so that they could discuss business.

"The deal is done, gentlemen!" Boone announced. "Rainbow Falls Lumber lives on." Chip looked happy, and Andrew looked relieved. Chip would give his notice and report for duty in two weeks. He would use the two weeks to do a thorough analysis of the capabilities, strengths, and weaknesses of the competition. Andrew would focus on getting a better handle on costs, and he would develop a plan to bring the mill to full capacity. They agreed on an engineer: both had picked the same candidate as the man for the job. They picked a progressive-thinking, well-trained young man who was feeling stymied after six years with a multinational and looking for this kind of opportunity. He was also an outdoorsman and enthralled with the idea of living in Rainbow Falls. To many people the remoteness and long, cold winters of the bush were a living hell; to a select few, it was utopia. It was important to find the few who wanted the lifestyle. The only solid cost-accountant candidate was a Toronto-born and -bred man. He was impressed with the opportunity but expressed reluctance about moving to the middle of nowhere, so they rejected him. They agreed on an offer for the engineer, and Boone instructed Chip to call the recruiter and give him hell. It was the headhunter's job to weed out candidates who were opposed to the lifestyle before wasting their time on an interview.

Boone had trouble keeping his mind on the discussions. Chip and Andrew were both in a gung-ho mood. Boone did not want to deflate them with his aloofness, but his mind was on the trip to the lodge. He felt vengeful, confident, and charged with adrenaline while at the same time petrified with belly-cramping fear.

* * * * * *

Jackpine started his workday on Thursday with an unpleasant but necessary duty. He authored a report on all the facts and suspicions concerning the drug-running operation and the related murders. The work went slowly. He was trying to be precise and concise but was experiencing great difficulty in communicating with clarity. He wanted to record a tape, but Inez cajoled him into the hated written format.

By noon the report was finally done. The report concluded that if something went awry with the plan to arrest the perpetrators at Blackbear Point, then Golias's boat, loaded with cocaine, would be found about thirty miles out on Lake Superior. Paul and Nelson had completed the work on the boat's cooling system without incident. Paul's role had been to stand guard. The report was formally signed by Chief of Police Oscar Keating and duly witnessed by Inez Mahoney and Constable Paul Desroches.

Jackpine went home to have tomato soup and a tuna fish sandwich with Janice. After lunch, he went to the post office to meet with Reeve Ron Evans. He thanked Ron again for his support, but Ron would not accept thanks. "Seems to me if you're going to risk your neck for this town then the town better back you up. It's the least we can do, Jackpine. I wish there was more." Jackpine gave Ron a copy of the report. Ron would give it to their local member of the provincial parliament if the need arose. The politician would be expected to help somehow. Ron Evans had helped the politician carry the Rainbow Falls vote in the last three provincial elections. With Ron Evans's persuasive endorsement, the electorate responded. A small town like the Falls was not the key to a provincial election, but a ninety-five-percent majority in any town certainly helped. Ron did not ask for much from the town. But when he did ask, he expected help and got it.

Jackpine left the post office and headed for Lac des Iles. It was nice to be driving his cruiser again. He preferred the Bronco for going to the Reserve. Paul Desroches, in releasing the cruiser, now took the Bronco hostage. The radar business had come to a standstill. The truckers were networking news about Paul's decoy, and it was no longer effective. The new plan called for Paul to park on the highway in the middle of town in the Bronco with his radar equipment on full alert. The cruiser was parked at the Esso on the east end of town. If a high-speed chase ensued, Paul would drive the Bronco to the Esso, hop into the cruiser, and give chase with sirens wailing. Jackpine had adamantly warned Paul not to get caught up in the heat of the moment and give chase in his Bronco. Jackpine was still uneasy. You cannot fight the force of nature, and having Paul give up precious seconds to change vehicles was going against the nature and instincts of Big Paul Desroches. Jackpine trusted Paul with his life, but he was reluctant to trust Paul with his Bronco.

When Jackpine entered Lawrence's office, Napoleon Martin and Esther were there. Esther's pretty face did not look pretty. Her upper lip was puffy and bleeding, her left eye was swollen shut, and her face was bruised. She looked like a ripe melon.

"What happened to you?" Jackpine asked Esther.

She said nothing, looking down.

"That goddamn, no good Wilfred Boucher beat her up," responded Napoleon.

"But why, Nap?" asked Jackpine.

Lawrence answered, "He was drunk or high or somethin'. Kept askin' her where the coke was. He figgered Desmond had a bag somewhere. He beat 'er up, and then he left. Said him an' his friends would find it."

"Desmond didn't tell me nuthin' bout no cocaine," said Esther quietly.

"When did this happen?" asked Jackpine.

"Just a while ago," said Napoleon. "She was walkin' down the road north of our house."

"Where are they now?" asked Jackpine.

"Disappeared. Got some guys out lookin' for them. Was a car full of rough-looking guys."

"You better get Esther home, Nap."

Napoleon helped Esther up. When they left, Jackpine said, "Bastards better not show up in the Falls tonight."

"I don't think so, Jackpine. They're not too smart, but they're smart enough to stay away from you. They'll be layin' low, like snakes in the grass."

"We'll keep lookin' for them, Lawrence."

"I'll help, if you need a hand."

They discussed the plans for Blackbear Point. Lawrence said he would have four guys on the river, one of whom would be Nap Martin. Jackpine knew the four men. Bear and Flip had raped one of the four men's daughters. He didn't know if the others had grudges against Bear and Flip or if they were just helping Lawrence. All four were trappers; one of them trapped on the west side of the river south of the lodge, and another trapped on the east side. They all knew the land like the back of their hands. They could glide through that brush like phantoms, and none of them needed a second bullet to shoot a moose.

"You couldn't run a rabbit through without them four knowing it," said Lawrence.

"And they know what to do?"

"Yup. Anyone tries comin' down the river, they stop him. They'll kill, but only if they have no choice. If it's Bear or Flip, I can't guarantee they'll try very hard to find a way other than shootin'. They're not afraid of gettin' caught. They know you're behind them. And no one knows they're there. No one will see them if they don't wanna be seen, and if they do shoot someone, no one will ever find a body."

"That's true," Jackpine laughed. "I wouldn't want to be in the bush with those four trackin' me."

"Me neither," said Lawrence. "I'm an Indian, but those guys are *real* Indians."

Preparation, thought Jackpine. He thought he should have the river blocked just in case Golias or one of his gang made a run for it or was sent for reinforcements. His plans were almost complete.

* * * * * *

Janice and Inez were in the kitchen making dinner, when Jackpine greeted Boone at the door. The ladies were in charge of making dinner, and Boone was under strict orders to stay away from the kitchen. The expression too many cooks spoil the broth was invented by an exasperated chef who had a Boone-like character looking over his shoulder offering helpful hints. Boone's only mission was to bring wine. He was a few minutes late because he had deemed it necessary to drive forty-five miles to the liquor store in Blackwater where the selection was much wider.

"Boone, c'mon in. How was Blackwater?"

"How did you know I went there?"

"If wine is your only contribution to dinner, I knew you wouldn't be satisfied with our store in the Falls."

"Good thing Constabull Desroches didn't see me. I was really hustling to be on time."

"Yeah, 130 kilometers an hour when you hit town."

"Paul?"

"Yeah. Did you see the Ontario Hydro pickup truck? Paul's new idea. You've created a monster, Boone. He called on the radio just now. It tore his heart out lettin' you go. He thought I'd be pissed off if he pinched you. I told him to go ahead next time. Would serve you right." Jackpine laughed. He took the wine out to the fridge and returned with a beer for himself and a gin and tonic for Boone.

Inez and Janice were putting the finishing touches on dinner. They had worked together on Caesar salad, veal piccata, and angel-hair pasta primavera. Mrs. Riccio had brought over a piping hot loaf of fresh broccoli bread. Inez was nervous. Both she and Janice were good cooks, but Inez had seen Boone berate too many maître d's to feel comfortable cooking for him. It was important to her that Boone enjoy the repast. Janice made her feel more at ease. "Anything Boone complains about—I made. Anything he likes—you made."

Boone seemed to enjoy everything. Either the meal met his exacting standards or his love for Inez Mahoney stifled his propensity for helpful hints. Jackpine also ate heartily, but he wondered why anyone would want to ruin a perfectly good loaf of bread by sticking broccoli in it.

After enjoying Janice's New York–style cheesecake, Boone and Jackpine went into Jackpine's study with coffees and Sambucas. Jackpine put some coffee beans in Boone's liqueur, but not in his own. They looked like rabbit shit to Jackpine. As D-day neared, Jackpine was bound and determined to find a way to lure the Toth brothers to the lodge. He pushed Boone to come up with some idea. Boone's common sense and instincts of self-preservation made him balk at the whole concept.

"Jackpine, have you heard the old story about the two guys who went to the Belgian Congo to make their fortune? Back in the fifties two guys were slaving in the garment district in New York. They thought there must be an easier way to make money, so they went to the Belgian Congo and hired on as mercenaries. Their pay was ten dollars for every enemy head they brought back. Two months roaming in the jungle with rifles and machetes, and they only had four heads. One morning one of them leaves the tent for a piss and sees five thousand hostile armed warriors surrounding them and preparing to attack. You know what he does, Jackpine?"

"No, I haven't got a clue."

"He yells to his partner. 'Grab your gun, Abe. This is our lucky day. We're rich!'"

Jackpine laughed. Boone continued, "You're just like those two assholes, Jackpine. We have enough to handle up there already; now you want the Toths and their gang of goons to join them. We have to be realistic."

"Those two are as guilty of murder as Bear and Flip. I won't let them get away with this. If they get away scot free, who's to stop them from doing the same thing again? Do you know how many lives will be ruined by a half a ton of cocaine? Think of it, Boone. That's probably how much is involved in these two shipments."

"OK, OK..." Boone was interrupted by the telephone. Jackpine spoke for a few minutes and hung up.

"Surprise. That was Toy Huhtela. The Cessna from Blackbear Point just came and left, flying at night. They picked up Appleton and O'Toole and took them back to the lodge."

"They all want to be there for the grand finale." The phone rang again. As Jackpine spoke, Boone began to write on a notepad.

Jackpine hung up. "That was Lawrence. Winston reported in. The Otter from Blackbear Point is at his place with the pilot, three Colombians, and Dan Golias. They seem to be expecting the helicopter tomorrow. Lawrence and Nelson will meet us at the station at five a.m."

"OK, Jackpine try this on for size. A crook like Sandor Toth survives because he always expects the worst from people. He anticipates deceit and chicanery because that's how he approaches life himself. What do you think of this fax? I'll read it to you. 'Mr. Toth, I'm faxing your office. It's late Friday night and I don't know how else to reach you. I suspect Golias has some plans of his own for our shipment of supplies. I have gone to the lodge to attempt to abort. You must come to the lodge as soon as possible. Sincerely, Steven Appleton.'"

"That's clever, Boone! A double cross is somethin' he would do himself, if he were Golias. Will it work?"

"Maybe. We'll have to get Toth's home number. Andrew McLeod should have it or know where to get it. We'll phone around midnight. A whoremonger like Toth will probably not be home with his wife and family. We tell his wife that it's Steve Appleton with an urgent message—tell her we'll fax the message to his office. Do you have Appleton's signature anywhere?"

"Sure. On a hundred letters in my office files."

"Good. We'll use Wite-Out on a letter and type our message over the signature. Then we have to break into Appleton's office and use his fax."

"Even easier, Boone. Ron Evans and Stew Larsen own the building where his office is. Ron will have a key."

"OK, when you call Toy to set up the flight, tell him to watch out for Appleton coming home unexpectedly. Ron Evans will be acting police chief?"

"Yeah."

"Tell Toy and Ron to arrest Appleton on some charge, if he comes back early. We have to be sure that Appleton is not able to get in touch with Toth. If this works, you'll have the Toths and probably a plane full of their goons to make your day."

CHAPTER 11

Jackpine heard the plane before he saw it. The drone of the engine grew louder; then he saw Toy Huhtela coming over the hill at the west end of the lake. It was dawn on Saturday morning. Roy Evans and Stew Larsen had dropped them off near a makeshift dock on Old Squaw Lake, thirty miles east of Rainbow Falls. Jackpine wanted to ensure that they were not seen leaving town. Word could not get back to Golias that Jackpine, Paul, Lawrence, Nelson, and Boone had flown off somewhere heavily armed and well supplied.

Jackpine moved out onto the rickety dock and caught the rope tossed by Toy. "Are you guys going to homestead up there, Yackpine? Look at all that stuff!"

"We have to feed Big Paul, ya know." Most of the supplies had been packed for a week. Jackpine had added the perishable food after he received Lawrence's call. Inez had typed their letter to Sandor Toth. They had sent the fax to Toth from Appleton's office, and there was no trace of the Wite-Out after it had been faxed. The call to Mrs. Toth had gone as Boone expected—she did not know when her husband would be home, and he always worked late on Friday nights.

"I've never seen canoes that big in my life," said Boone. There were two of them. They were twenty-foot-long, sturdy, heavy freighter canoes with square sterns. Alongside the canoes were two outboard motors and two gas cans.

It took Jackpine and his crew forty-five minutes to load all the gear and lash each canoe onto one of the pontoon's support struts. "Will you be able to get 'er up, Toy?" asked Jackpine, realizing the extent of the load.

"It'll take a long run, but she'll fly," said Toy confidently. It was awkward climbing into the plane over the canoes, but (with the exception of Paul Desroches) they all managed fairly easily. Once they pulled Paul up, there was some question where to seat him. When the manufacturer deemed this to be a six-man plane, a man the size of Paul Desroches was not factored into the equation. Jackpine took the copilot seat, ostensibly to help Toy navigate. His phobia would overwhelm him if he sat in the cramped rear quarters. The other four somehow managed to wedge in themselves in the back with all of the gear.

Old Squaw Lake was not large. Toy used the entire length of the lake to get airborne. They cleared the trees at the edge of the lake by only a few feet. They headed north, passing forty miles east of Blackbear Point Lodge. The visibility was poor due to rain and light fog. Flying low, Toy headed west; he and Jackpine were looking for the Blackwater River. When they found it, they headed north following the course of the river. When Jackpine noticed Two Sisters Rapids, he motioned to Toy. Above the rapids, the river widened into a lake. Toy landed smoothly on the lake.

The lake was fifteen miles north by northeast of the lodge. It was far enough from the lodge for Toy to get in and out of flying low and not be seen by anyone at the lodge. Jackpine had also picked this location knowing they could see a plane returning to the lodge from James Bay. They could quickly cover the fifteen miles downstream when the time came.

They deplaned in the middle of the lake: first putting the canoes into the water, then loading the gear into the canoes. Lawrence and Paul were in one canoe; Jackpine, Boone, and Nelson were in the second. They shoved off the pontoons, and Toy taxied to take off.

Jackpine selected a spot on the southwest shore of the lake, near the beginning of the rapids. After unloading, they carried the canoes a few yards into the woods. They turned the canoes over and put the motors underneath them; then they covered the canoes with branches and pine boughs, making them invisible from the air.

The rain had turned to sleet, the temperature was dropping, and Boone was chilled to the bone. Boone's heart sank after he asked Jackpine where they would set up the tent. No tent, Jackpine told him. It could be seen from the air.

They carried their supplies fifty yards back into the thick, dense forest. Boone watched as the other four took axes and busied themselves cutting down small sapling pines and pine boughs from some of the bigger trees. Boone realized they were building some type of shelter: weaving the saplings and branches among standing trees and then weaving in pine boughs. Soon, they had fashioned four walls about seven feet high on the high side and six feet on the low side with an opening of three feet as an entrance. Working from the inside, they laid saplings across the top, weaving pine boughs in through the saplings, and then from the outside they added more pine boughs in through the saplings to the top of the roof, leaving a small hole in the middle of the roof for smoke to escape. The three-foot opening was sealed, leaving a crawl space near the bottom as an entrance.

Paul and Nelson dug a trench around the shelter for drainage, while the other three took the supplies into the shelter. The finished structure was not completely rectangular, but it was roughly twelve feet by eight feet. Paul agreed to take the first watch looking for the plane. Their shelter was virtually invisible from the air. Jackpine went down to the lake and filled the collapsible plastic water tank. Once the four of them were inside, Lawrence put a few pine boughs across the entrance.

Boone was amazed that the structure seemed watertight. Jackpine fired up a small propane heater, and Lawrence heated water on a Coleman stove. By the time the coffee was ready, Boone had taken off his heavy jacket; he was warm, dry, and comfortable. Jackpine set out some ham, cheese, tuna salad, and bread. Boiled ham, processed cheese slices, and Wonder bread would not normally appeal to Boone's epicurean palate. It tasted so good that he built a second sandwich. Jackpine finished his tuna sandwich and put his jacket on. "I'm going to relieve Paul. If you want more to eat, get it now. It won't last long when Paul gets here." He grabbed a small 22-caliber rifle from one of the duffel bags. "While I'm watchin' for the plane, I'll see if I can find us some supper."

In a few minutes a cold, wet Paul Desroches came in. The weather had not dampened his spirits. "Welcome to the Ojibway Hilton." He took off his coat and poured himself some coffee. Paul attacked the luncheon buffet; the ham and cheese went quickly. He ran out of bread before he could turn his attention to the tuna, so he took his hunting knife and used it as a spoon to devour the last of the tuna. If the world were full of Paul Desroches, the word leftover would wither and die from disuse, having no purpose in the English language.

Jackpine returned in late afternoon. "North wind still blowin', but it's cleared up. Goin' to be real cold by mornin'." Lawrence put on his coat to go out and relieve Jackpine. "Come back as soon as it's dark, Lawrence. They won't be flyin' at night. We'll make a big fire to warm up."

"OK, get any supper, Jackpine?"

"I got ten partridge; see if you can find something else. Two partridge each isn't very much, especially for Paul."

At sundown, the four of them went to a clearing, and Jackpine started a small cooking fire. Lawrence came back with two grouse and two rabbits. He had already dressed them. Boone peeled potatoes, carrots, and onions, while Lawrence quartered the rabbits and tossed them into the stew pot. After the rabbit cooked awhile, they added the vegetables and the grouse.

When Boone deemed it ready, they all filled their plates and grabbed a few slices of bread from the new loaf Jackpine brought out. "This is the last of our bread; we'll be eatin' bannock tomorrow."

They ate quietly by the fire. Boone didn't care much for the rabbit, but he thought the grouse was good. When they finished eating, they washed their dishes in the lake. Jackpine said he would come down after the fire died out and the remains scattered. When they got back to the shelter, Lawrence built a small fire. "Won't the walls and roof catch fire?" asked Boone.

"If the fire's too big, yes. If it's too small, it won't keep us warm. I'm makin' it just right, so we keep warm and don't burn the house down."

Boone relaxed. If these guys could build a waterproof shelter in a few hours with no tools other than axes, then they could build a fire that wouldn't burn it down.

Jackpine woke up a few minutes before sunrise. The bright stars augured the arrival of a sunny morning. The wind was still blowing from the north, although not as hard. A few minutes later, Boone joined Jackpine outside the shelter. "Christ, it's cold out here." Boone was dressed warmly but was shivering.

"Mornin', Boone. Yeah, it'll keep gettin' colder, long as that north wind blows. Sun will feel nice when it comes up. What's the matter, Paul's snoring wake you up?" Paul snored all night. To Boone, the inhalations sounded like a giant, old, wooden roller coaster, and the exhalations like a room full of kids at their first tuba practice. The snoring was punctuated by the odd thunderous fart.

"I guess so. Bertha is destined for sainthood if she puts up with it," said Boone. He did not want to admit that it was the thought of someone shooting at him before the day ended rather than Paul's snoring and farting that had kept him awake most of the night.

"Do you think the plane will come today, Jackpine?"

"If that ship has off-loaded the coke, they'll come today. They could get grounded for a week if bad weather comes in, like it's apt to this time of year."

"Boone, why don't you wake up everyone? I'll start a fire. We don't have to worry about being seen for a while. They wouldn't leave until daybreak. We'll have a big breakfast. Don't know when we'll get a chance to eat again." Jackpine had a fire going in minutes. When the flames died down, Jackpine fried bacon and heated a pot of beans. Boone made coffee, and Lawrence made a batch of bannock. The simple meal tasted great to Boone, but he was troubled with thoughts of the last meal for a condemned man.

Boone understood why Jackpine and Lawrence were so calm. He knew that these two had been involved in similar plots on numerous situations attempting to arrest some evildoers. Jackpine had always kept a wall between himself and Boone when it came to his law-enforcement methods. He also understood Paul's casual demeanor. Paul was a Jackpine-in-training; he would pattern his mentor's attitude. But young Nelson was another matter. Diesel mechanics did not have shoot-outs with desperadoes in their job descriptions. Nelson was as serene as if he had been invited on a cookout and partridge hunt with friends. Boone hoped that his gnawing fear was not obvious to his companions.

After breakfast, they put the canoes in the water, loaded them, and departed. Jackpine determined that they had time to safely move closer to the lodge. Within a few minutes, they were on the Two Sisters Rapids. Boone did not understand the "sisters" part of the name but the "two" became evident when the river forked. The rapids were rugged but easily navigable. Jackpine and Lawrence were able to use the motors all the way. The land was a lot flatter here than the terrain between the lodge and Rainbow Falls. The river was winding, and the current much less intense.

Once they reached the lake, they stayed along the east shore. Jackpine did not want them to be seen by people on the west shore of the lodge. There were one-foot waves on the lake, and the canoe was not the most stable of crafts in rough water. At first, Boone was concerned. But after experiencing how well Jackpine and Lawrence handled the canoes, he stopped worrying about drowning and started worrying about being shot. A half mile out into the lake from the lodge was a small island, roughly circular in shape with a diameter of a half mile. A channel cut through the center of the island, meaning technically it was two islands. It was named Birch Island for the stands of birch that grew in contrast to the predominantly spruce and pine forests on the mainland. The long-forgotten namer of the island had either not known of the channel or had chosen to ignore it in selecting a name, forever deeming it to be one island.

Jackpine led the canoes to the far side of the island, coming in from the east where the island blocked their sight from the lodge. They took the canoes into the channel and unloaded. Each man checked his arsenal while waiting for the drug-laden plane. Boone was not surprised by any of the weaponry: Nelson and Lawrence each had single-shot 308 rifles, Paul had a rifle and a shotgun, and Jackpine had the same plus a twenty-two for hunting game. It was not until Jackpine brought out a box of grenades that Boone was surprised.

"Where the hell did you get those?" Boone asked.

"I confiscated them from old Sulo Maki. I went out to see him one day. I'd heard he was giving away pickerel to a lot of people. It's up to the Mines and Natural Resource folks to catch poachers, but I thought I'd check it out. He was in his garage when I got there, so I went in to talk to him. Saw these two boxes of grenades on the floor. Turns out his son in the army got them for him. He says to me he's too old to fish but likes to eat a lot of pickerel. So, he fishes with grenades."

"How does he do that?" queried Boone.

"He pulls the pin and tosses a grenade in the lake. When it explodes, all the fish within twenty feet or so come floatin' to the surface belly up. I told him I don't mind that so much, but if he's sellin' fish, I do mind. I said I was going to confiscate the grenades, and he says, 'Yackpine, don't take all my fissing lures,'" said Jackpine, in a Finnish accent. "So, I left him a dozen and told him he could eat pickerel 'til the cows came home with that many fissing lures. I confiscated forty of them. I've had them 'bout a year now. I tested a couple out in the bush, saved the rest for a rainy day—today might be a rainy day."

Jackpine started to worry when the plane had not been seen by two o'clock. Had someone let the cat out of the bag? Maybe the plane would go directly to Blackwater. Jackpine didn't think that Golias could have known their whereabouts, but if he did, he would want a showdown. Getting rid of Jackpine and his cohorts would tie up loose ends. With our bodies weighed down in the middle of the lake, Golias would get off scot free, thought Jackpine grimly. Boone came over to Jackpine; he was shivering. "I'm freezing, Jackpine," he complained.

"Me too," said Jackpine, but he wasn't showing effects of the cold. "It's uncommon to be this cold this time of year. Look at the ice." The wind had died down, and the temperature was around zero degrees. A thin crust of ice had formed on the lake. "If it gets much colder that plane will need skis to land," he said, half in jest.

At four o'clock they heard the faint but steady drone of an airplane engine, and a few seconds later an Otter came into view. Flying in from the north, it landed on the lake (breaking up the thin ice) and taxied to the front dock of Blackbear Point Lodge. A reception committee had gathered on the dock. Jackpine focused his binoculars on the dock. "There's fucking O'Toole out of uniform for once. I see Bear and Flip. There's Golias getting out of the plane. There's that weasel Appleton, six Colombians, might be more somewhere else, and two pilots. That's twelve if we don't count Appleton, thirteen if we do.

Let's go, guys!" They walked back to where their gear was stored. Jackpine put on his bulletproof jacket and was busy filling his pockets as he spoke. "Paul, you and I are going to try and arrest them. Put on your jacket. You three stay back here out of sight." Boone began to protest but stopped short. Jackpine was in charge here, and Boone could tell by looking at the stern countenance that nothing was up for discussion.

Paul and Jackpine loaded their rifles. Jackpine grabbed a bullhorn from one of the duffel bags. Boone wondered what else Jackpine had in those bags of his. The two of them got in the canoe: Jackpine in the bow and Paul in the stern. Paul started the motor. The ice was getting thick; Jackpine was breaking the ice with his paddle to save the bow of the canoe. They moved out of the channel and into the lake. Jackpine looked to the dock. The drug-smuggling bandits had set up a bucket brigade (in this case, a cocaine brigade) and were busy unloading the aircraft. To Jackpine, it looked like small cement bags were being handed from person to person.

Jackpine motioned Paul to stop. "Keep it idling in neutral; don't shut it off. We might have to get out of here in a hurry." Jackpine picked up the bullhorn. "This is Chief Keating. You are under arrest. Put your hands up."

There was a flurry of activity on the dock. Rifles and guns appeared quickly. The Colombians began firing bursts from machine guns. Bear and Flip grabbed rifles and were taking aim, and O'Toole was firing his revolver. Appleton was running for the lodge. A couple of bullets ricocheted off the ice and hit Jackpine in the chest. They were out of effective range, so the bullets stung but were ineffectual for the purpose intended. "Let's go!" shouted Jackpine.

Paul gunned the engine; they turned in a tight circle and headed back to the channel. Jackpine directed Paul to shore. Jackpine clambered up the rocks until he had a view of the dock. He saw Golias waving his arms wildly and yelling. It looked as if he was directing the drug smugglers to the planes. The two pilots came running down the dock. Jackpine activated the first remote-control device. There was a loud explosion, and the nose of the plane disappeared, with pieces of metal flying high into the air. Gaping holes appeared in the front of both pontoons, and the plane quickly began sinking front first into the lake. It tilted on its side as it sank; one side was supported by ropes anchoring the plane to the dock. Jackpine pressed the second button, and the other plane met a similar fate.

He could have waited until they were airborne, killing the pilots and drowning their passengers, but he wanted to give them another chance to surrender. He saw Golias running back to the lodge. He waited until Golias got to the lodge and then called him on the radio. "Golias, this is Keating. You have a last chance to surrender."

"Fuck you, Keating. You don't know who you're fucking with. We'll get you hick bastards."

"Come and get us, over and out." Jackpine put down his radio and activated the device to take out the radio. He wondered how much of the cocaine was unloaded and how much was still on the plane. He thought Flip and Bear were about to have a long night in the frigid water. As low men on the totem pole, they would be appointed as divers. Jackpine heard a rustling behind him and looked back. Boone was climbing up the rocks.

"Did you think they would surrender, Jackpine?"

"No, not really. But I wanted to give them every chance."

"What do we do now?"

"For now, we wait. If they try and attack us by boat, Paul and I will put a few bullets in their motors on the way over here. We'll strand them on the lake and see what they want to do: surrender or freeze to death." Jackpine picked up the radio and got Paul. "Start a big fire to warm us up and set up the tent. We'll sleep in comfort tonight."

Paul acknowledged, and Jackpine put the radio back in his pocket. "We'll take turns watchin' the lodge. Maybe they'll make a move tonight." The sun was going down, and Boone did not think it possible, but he was getting even colder.

"I think I'll go back to the fire," said Boone. They both heard the sound at the same time. "Another plane, Jackpine!"

A Twin Otter came into view, circled once and landed. The plane, one of the Sportsmen's Paradise fleet, taxied to the dock. Golias directed the pilot to the side of the dock, to avoid hitting the two sunken planes. Jackpine and Boone each looked through binoculars. Jackpine counted nine people (including the pilot) disembarking—all seemed heavily armed.

"The first six guys are from the Polarex crew. I wanted them for raping old Mabel Sanderson, but I'll take them for drug smuggling."

Boone couldn't believe his friend's confidence. The enemy now numbered twenty-two. While looking at two figures in brightly colored ski jackets, Boone announced, "The Toth brothers."

"Great, it worked! They look sleazy even from this distance." One of the men in a ski jacket walked toward Golias and, ignoring the outreached hand, punched him in the face. Steve Appleton was talking toward the other man wearing a ski jacket. As Appleton spoke, both men in ski jackets turned and looked out toward Birch Island, realizing their problem was on the island and not in camp. The two men in ski jackets then walked toward the lodge. The one who had punched Golias did not stop to apologize.

Jackpine pulled the last remote-control device from his pocket. He activated it and pressed the button. Nothing happened. He shook it and continued pressing, to no avail. "Damn, they must have stopped in the Falls to pick up the Polarex derelicts. I guess they never gave Toy a chance to get into the engine. This changes everything. They're gonna hit us tonight from the air with everythin' but Jesus Christ and his brother!"

Boone did not understand the brother part, but the thought of attack sent a chill down his already freezing spine. "What are we going to do, Jackpine?"

"We will prepare; then we will find a way to react. Stay here for a few minutes. I'll send Paul back to keep watch."

Boone stared through the binoculars. It was dark, but there were lights on in the lodge. A nice warm lodge with a big fire, thought Boone. Paul Desroches sat down beside him. Boone had not heard him coming. "Go back and get warm, Mr. Boone. It's going to be a long, cold night."

Boone walked back to the campsite. He found it hard to navigate without a flashlight. He stood with his hands out over the roaring flames, noticing the big tent a few yards away. The fire helped with his chill. "Where are Nelson and Lawrence?"

Jackpine handed him a welcomed cup of hot coffee. "They're up on the hill. I found a big rock overhang up there. There's room for all of us underneath it. They won't be able to get us from the air. Nelson and Lawrence are up there making a lean-to. The propane heater will keep us warm."

At one in the morning, Nelson was on watch, and the other four were in the lean-to. They all heard the sound of the Twin Otter roaring into life at the same time. "Now, everyone just sit tight," said Jackpine. "They have a big advantage; this is the time to lay low. Paul, are you sure Nelson will be OK?"

"Yeah. We found a place to hide in the rocks. He will be able to watch for boats, and they won't see him from the air. Findin' any of us is like looking for a needle in a haystack."

Boone wondered who would bother looking for a needle in a haystack. Why would someone be sitting on a haystack sewing in the first place? For that matter, there were no haystacks. Old-fashioned farmers made little square bales; progressive farmers made big round bales. Boone did not think he'd seen a haystack in North America in thirty years. Someone should change the saying to "like looking for a haystack!" His mind returned to the impending assault. He concentrated on controlling his anal sphincter.

CHAPTER 12

Nelson watched the shoreline until he was confident no boats were being launched to augment the aerial attack. Turning his attention back to the Twin Otter, he saw that it was completing a turn and coming toward Birch Island. The bright, full harvest moon, low in the sky just over the horizon, made visibility good. The plane was coming directly toward him; Nelson did not run and hide. He put a bullet into the chamber of his 308. He was sure he could shoot the pilot; it would be an easy shot. He supported his rifle on a low limb of a birch tree, took careful aim, and fired.

Nelson looked up, expecting to witness a plane crash. The bullet had gone through the front windshield, but it was six inches over the pilot's head. Nelson was still standing when the spotlight showered him in bright light. He put his hand up instinctively to shield his eyes.

He heard bullets pinging off of the rocks around him. Two machine guns opened fire on the illuminated target. Nelson died where he stood; he fell in a macabre death dance as both guns riddled the target at the same time.

Seconds later, the plane advanced upon the campsite. The blue tent reflected in the glare as both guns erupted in a staccato burst. The guns went silent as the plane, staying about a hundred feet over the frozen surface, roared out over the lake. The side door of the Twin Otter was open. The two gunners sat with their feet on the rung of the steps. The man with the spotlight stood behind them. The plane turned for another pass. They focused their attention on the campsite. Jackpine and his group lay huddled under the protective rock overhang, catching glimpses of the light but not exposing themselves for a closer look. Jackpine counted fifteen passes over the island by the Twin Otter. They were methodically strafing the entire island. Finally, Jackpine heard the plane landing back near the lodge. He ran out for a look. They were landing from the south, coming in exactly where they had broken up the ice on takeoff. He watched carefully, calculating as best he could where the ice was broken up.

Jackpine walked back to the campsite. The others were there inspecting the damage. The tent had collapsed under the hearty barrage, riddled with holes. Lawrence spoke first, "Give me a hand, Paul. We'll bring Nelson's body to the campsite."

"Maybe, he's OK. He had good cover," Paul protested.

"Why do you think he's dead?" asked Boone.

"Lawrence is right, I'm afraid," said Jackpine.

"We heard one shot from a 308, just before the machine guns opened up the first time. He had balls, that Nelson; he tried to take them out himself. Boone, why don't you and Paul go and get him." Boone and Paul walked off. "Let's check the canoes, Lawrence."

"That's what I thought. Son of a bitch," muttered Jackpine, as he and Lawrence looked at the remains of the two canoes. Both had been shattered beyond repair by the automatic-rifle fire. The canoes had been concealed, but the pine-bough camouflage was no help in the random strafing.

"We'll be sitting ducks tomorrow. Do they figger they got us sleepin' in the tent, Jackpine?"

"I don't think so. They don't know how many we are. They know they got Nelson, maybe they think they got a couple more. They wanted to soften us up, then come and finish us off tomorrow."

"What's that?" Jackpine noticed an orange plastic garbage bag on the beach. It hadn't been there before; it must have been thrown from the plane. He walked over and picked up the bag. A sudden chill went through his body as he picked it up. Jackpine dumped the contents onto the ground. The bag contained a few small rocks to give it weight and a cigar box taped shut. Jackpine opened the box. Giving in to the violent upheaval in his stomach, he vomited. He continued puking and sobbing, his empty stomach heaving violently long after there was nothing left to disgorge.

He reached into the bloody box and gently lifted out the finger. He recognized the wedding band on the swollen ring finger. It was Toy Huhtela's. They had either killed Toy or taken him hostage. Jackpine felt an overriding sensation of guilt and remorse for involving Toy in his scheme.

Lawrence looked on; his stoic mask hid his emotion— disgust, horror, and a swelling tide of vengeance.

Jackpine carefully put the finger back into the box. Nelson Lesmontaignes was dead and so (probably) was Toy Huhtela. Jackpine accepted the responsibility, knowing he would never overcome the feeling. He was no longer sobbing. His paleness was replaced by a surging crimson countenance; the veins in his neck were bulging. His eyes burned with raging fire as he stood and looked in the direction of the lodge. "You'll pay for this, you bastards!" he screamed.

Jackpine walked up toward the shelter. Lawrence walked over to the fire, hoping the roaring blaze would warm his chilled soul. Boone and Paul walked toward the fire. Paul was carrying Nelson's body in his arms. Boone was carrying Nelson's rifle. Lawrence told Boone and Paul about the box.

Chief Lawrence Musgrove felt two hundred years of civilization ebbing from his pores. The pencil-pushing bureaucrat was becoming wild and savage. By dawn the transformation would be complete, and the mild-mannered diplomat would be replaced by a ruthless, cunning Ojibway war chief, seeped in a ferocity for vengeance.

Paul Desroches felt his mortality and the tenuous hold he had on life. Paul's parents, his teachers, and now Jackpine constantly reminded him to keep his temper under control because of his ferocious strength. The leash had snapped. He might die, thought

Paul grimly, but not before they felt the full fury of his awesome physical power.

Boone stared into the fire. He was looking forward to dawn. He looked forward with iron-will resolve to the next encounter. There was no fear left in Alistair Boone. The boardroom warrior was a battle-ready paladin. Boone wondered what Jackpine's plan would entail. If the enemy was foolish enough to attack by boat, he knew that Jackpine and Paul would pick them off like flies.

Each of their silent reveries was interrupted by the appearance of the steel-jawed Jackpine Keating carrying a pair of ice skates.

"You brought ice skates?" asked Boone incredulously.

"Prepared for anything. That's the key," responded Jackpine.

"But the ice won't hold you!" protested Boone.

"We'll see. Watch."

Jackpine pried two equal-size stones loose from the frozen ground. He dropped the first rock on the ice. *Plunk!* The rock broke through, leaving a round hole. The second rock he threw sidearm onto the lake. It rolled across the ice, disappearing from view as it skimmed across the ice.

"It's not a question of weight. It's a question of speed." Jackpine took off his boots and put his skates on, lacing them tight. Lawrence walked over to Jackpine and handed him a ten-foot, birch sapling that he had cut and limbed while Jackpine was getting the skates on.

"What's that for?' asked Boone.

"Always carry a staff on thin ice. If you fall through, you use it to distribute your weight so you can climb out," offered Lawrence.

"The trick will be getting up to speed fast before I break through." Jackpine was on the ice, legs churning. Instant acceleration had been his big asset when he played hockey; now, he was putting that technique to good use. The ice was cracking, but his long legs at full stride kept the ice from breaking beneath him. Jackpine skated the length of the channel and disappeared out onto the lake. A few minutes later, they saw him coming back down the channel to the beach, running up onto the sand. He sat on the beach and began unlacing his skates. Paul brought Jackpine's boots over to him.

"Lawrence, you're better with an axe than any of us. I want you to make me a hockey stick." If this request was outlandish, one would not have known by the reaction from Lawrence Musgrove.

"OK," he said, and started walking up toward the shelter to get his axe as if it were perfectly normal and routine to be asked in the middle of the night to find a suitable tree and carve a hockey stick.

They sat by the fire quietly, sipping coffee and waiting for Lawrence. He was back in twenty minutes, having found a small spruce with a branch growing at the correct angle to approximate a hockey stick. The branch would become the handle, which needed very little work. There was a ten-inch-long piece of tree trunk attached to the branch. Lawrence carefully sawed off the tree trunk with a small bucksaw. He then trimmed the stick's blade with his knife and carved the body of the handle into a rough rectangular shape. It took an hour and a half, but he carved what was unquestionably a hockey stick.

Lawrence presented it to Jackpine. "Don't try any slap shots; blade will break." Lawrence had also cut a ten-foot sapling with a Y-shape at the top. He wove string back and forth across the Y-shaped appendage. When he was finished, there was a tight webbed pocket. It looked like a long lacrosse stick.

Boone glanced at Paul. He could tell that Paul did not know any more than he did. The two chiefs seemed to be on the same wavelength, understanding and anticipating without really talking.

"There'll be some light in an hour. You better head out. Make a wide circle south to avoid the open water where the plane took off. Remember, Lawrence, don't be a dead hero. Create a diversion and get the hell out."

"Right, Chief," said Lawrence. He and Jackpine started walking up to the shelter to get their gear. They were back in a few minutes. They all walked down to the beach. Jackpine showed Lawrence how to activate the grenades. Lawrence stuffed some into his small backpack. He cut a piece of rope and fashioned a sling for his rifle. He added his hatchet to the backpack and then closed the pack.

"There's a bear living on this little island. A big bear," said Lawrence.

"You saw his tracks. You could tell from the size and depth of the tracks that he was a big bear—right, Lawrence?" offered Boone.

"No, I didn't see no tracks. I stepped in fresh bear shit when I looked for the hockey stick. Wasn't frozen. It was a big pile of shit, so I figger a big bear."

Boone looked sheepish.

Lawrence checked his radio and then put it in his pocket. He laced on his skates. "I'll be there in an hour—on the hill behind the lodge." He grabbed the lacrosse-like staff. He took a running start on the beach, and then he was on the ice. It was cracking, but he picked up speed and was off down the channel. He was much slower than Jackpine but fast enough to keep from falling through the ice. He soon rounded the corner, turning left to make a wide circle to the south around the lodge.

"When did you two decide to bring skates?" asked Paul.

"I decided at the last minute. Weather gettin' colder, you never know. Lawrence decided the same thing on his own."

"I should have thought to bring some," said Paul dejectedly.

"Ice wouldn't hold a big guy like you. You do a lot of things well, Paul, but skating isn't one of 'em."

"Lawrence looks comfortable on skates," commented Boone.

"He played in the Canadian Junior Hockey League in Thunder Bay, rugged left-winger. He was tough in the corners. Couldn't skate well enough for pro, but he's not bad. 'Course that was twenty-five years and fifty pounds ago."

"He looked pretty comfortable to me," said Boone.

"Like ridin' a bike, Boone. Bet you could swim Long Island Sound again, if you wanted to."

"Maybe," laughed Boone. He was on the swim team in college. Swimming was almost the only exercise he got these days. He was still a strong swimmer but doubted if he had the stamina to swim the Sound again from Bridgeport to Port Jefferson.

* * * * * *

Lawrence was enjoying the skate. It was calm and peaceful but cold. The sweat was freezing on his forehead. The moonlight shimmered off the glass-like surface of the lake. He skated into the back bay behind the lodge. He was at least half a mile from the lodge, skating along the shoreline. The lodge was between him and the moon; there was no chance of being seen. He skated onto the shore. He removed his skates and replaced them with the pair of moccasins from his backpack. He thought of leaving his skates on the shore but decided against it. If he was in a hurry coming back, he would not have time to waste trying to find his skates. He climbed the big hill and then walked in the direction of the lodge. He walked to a flat plateau at the top of the hill, picking his way quietly through the dense forest. The sky was grey with pre-dawn light.

He turned on the radio. "OK, Chief," he said.

He heard Jackpine's response, "OK, chief, ten minutes." Lawrence looked at his watch.

Jackpine was ready to go. He had a canvas bag tied around his waist. His rifle on a sling was on his back. "Gonna even things out some. Paul, you and Boone watch from the point," Jackpine said grimly.

From the point, Boone watched Jackpine glide seemingly effortlessly across the lake toward the lodge. Boone was a sports fan. He enjoyed watching touchdown passes, three-run homers, three-point shots at the buzzer, and thirty-foot putts to win tournaments, but nothing matched the exhilaration he remembered like the intensity of Jackpine's performance on a hockey rink—circling his team's net with the puck, picking up speed, weaving in and out of defenders, splitting the defense, driving down the ice, and slamming a hard, fast wrist shot toward the opponent's net. He would raise his arms and coast if he scored; if he did not score and the opposition gained possession, he would streak back down the ice with elbows pumping. In the good seats, you could hear the swoosh from his long strides, and he would get to the other end to defend before the opposition arrived. Boone had that same feeling watching Jackpine skate toward Blackbear Point Lodge.

There was a Colombian sitting on the deck who had been on watch for three hours with another hour to go. He was not sure he would make it. He wondered how cold a person could get before he froze to death. He was sure he was on the brink of such calamity. Growing up on the coast of Colombia near Cartagena, he had never seen snow, never been exposed to weather like this. He had spent two months in this god-awful wilderness. They were supposed to leave today, but first they had to eliminate Jackpine and his gang. Maybe Jackpine and his gang were already dead. They should have been in the tent on a night like that. But Bear had said they would not be cold. "Ain't cold yet. Come here in January, you wanna see cold." He had told Bear he would take his word for it. He had enjoyed shooting from the Twin Otter. Strafing the stupid Indian had been good sport.

He had also really enjoyed toying with the black bear and watching it run confused and frightened. The bear took thirty bullets before it died. Yes, the bear had been better sport than the Indian. Flip had promised to get the bear paws for him. He planned to have a macho necklace made from the bear's claws. He was thinking about how he could embellish the story.

"Mother of God!" he shouted. The devil was coming to get him. Ice was something that came in drinks; he never really appreciated the concept of the lake freezing over. That a man could strap steel blades onto his feet and move at a speed of twenty-five miles per hour was incomprehensible. He realized what was happening; he was freezing to death, and the devil was running across the lake to claim his soul.

Jackpine could only see one guard. Jackpine reached into his bag for a grenade, pulled the pin, and gently placed it on the ice. He counted to ten as he stickhandled the grenade; after weaving back and forth, he fired a low wrist shot. The grenade hit one of the pontoons of the Twin Otter just as it exploded. The guard got to his feet, fumbling his gun with numb fingers. Jackpine unslung his rifle and was aiming as the guard got control of his weapon. Jackpine's single shot took the guard in the chest. The guard's machine gun sputtered ineffectively as he fell from the deck through the ice and to his frigid grave.

* * * * * *

Lawrence pulled the pin from a grenade and placed it in the webbing of his staff. Using leverage, he flung the grenade. It flew high into the air, much higher than Lawrence had anticipated, and finally came hurtling down end over end. Range seemed about right, thought Lawrence as it fell. The explosion only took out the small tractor used to ferry luggage. Lawrence's second attempt was better; it went through the big plate-glass window into the dining room of the lodge. Glass burst out of all the windows in the dining room. There was a gaping hole in the roof near the grenade's point of entry.

Lawrence pulled the pin on a third grenade and launched it. He did not stop to admire his handiwork. People were milling about like bees to a hive. Most of them had no idea where the attack was coming from. He saw someone point up toward the hill just before he fired the last catapult.

Lawrence raced toward the lake, not caring about making noise; he regretted his big belly slowing him down. Lawrence stopped in the thick forest to listen for just a second. A man was coming hard; he was alone. There were three other men in the woods; they were swinging farther north. If he could quietly stop the near enemy (without alerting the others), he would have time to get to the lake and put his skates on. Lawrence moved thirty feet to the right in complete silence. He was a pretty fair Indian warrior when his life depended on it, he thought to himself. He backtracked until he heard his quarry charging through the bush like a horny bull moose hearing a cow moose pissing. He moved to within ten feet of where his quarry would pass. He melted into the bush, still and silent, virtually invisible unless the enemy stepped on him.

A Polarex crewman rampaged by him. Lawrence quietly followed, stopping to listen for the sound of footsteps. Not hearing anything, Lawrence had the sudden thought that he had become the hunted. The Polarex soldier was an experienced woodsman. He too stopped to listen and intently stared forward, looking for any kind of movement. Thinking ability was not among his enemy's primary assets—it did not occur to him to look behind.

Chief Lawrence Musgrove had thrown hatchets as a kid, practicing hour after hour. He never knew why he did it; it was just something to do. Maybe it was because Daniel Boone's Indian sidekick had done it on TV. Anyone could throw a hatchet. Hitting the target on the blade's first sequence of its rotation was the hard part. Lawrence wished he had a couple of practice throws to zero in on the range.

Lawrence sneaked to within fifteen feet. As the idea to turn around was just beginning to traverse the vast, vacant expanse of the enemy's brain, Lawrence threw the hatchet. The blade of the hatchet caught the enemy high in the middle of his back. His hands flew into the air as he fell forward. He was dead before he hit the ground.

Lawrence stopped to remove the hatchet. It was deeply embedded and took a strong tug to remove. Lawrence wiped it clean and started running toward the shore.

He had his first skate on when he heard the sharp report of a rifle. One or all of the other three guys had found him, thought Lawrence, hoping it was only one and that he was a poor shot. He got the other skate on as quickly as he could. The skates were twenty-five years old, and his feet had grown like his belly over the years. He successfully shoved his fat, swollen feet into the skates and started lacing them up. Three more shots—he could hear them now—sounded like two men. When the skates were on, he wasted no time getting to the lake. He faked left, then a hard right, before reverse zigzagging out onto the lake. After a few hundred yards, he slowed the pace. His heart was thumping in his chest. He peeked over his shoulder. He saw two of them on the shore aiming at him; the third man was charging down the hill. Within a few seconds, he was safely out of range.

* * * * * *

With the guard dead, Jackpine knew he had a bit of time. He heard Lawrence's first grenade; he saw the effect of the second hit on the dining room. Lawrence must be right in front of the lodge to throw one into the dining room. He was supposed to stay under cover in the bush, thought Jackpine. He skated by the plane, tossing a grenade in the small hole in the door created by his first grenade. There were four men running out toward the dock. He skated south as they fired a few machine-gun bursts in his direction. He was around the corner in seconds, skating into the back bay. He wanted to get to the storage shed where the boat motors were kept. If he could destroy most of the motors, he would prevent a large-scale attack on the island. There was a big group running toward the back-bay dock (six or eight of them; he was not sure). He would have time for one grenade if he hurried. He pulled the pin, easing it onto the ice, and stickhandled it toward the dock and motor shed. He fired a hard wrist shot. The grenade bounced off the shed and veered left. It landed on the dock and exploded. Pieces of lumber flew through the air. Jackpine banged his stick on the ice with frustration. He had shot too hard. He skated out into the bay, out of effective rifle range. There was no use trying again. There were eight men; he counted them. One of them was O'Toole, who was a pretty good shot, and most of the others had automatic rifles. One of them would get him no matter how much he dipsy doodled, thought Jackpine. The plane was the biggest worry. The second biggest worry was the radio on the plane to call for reinforcements. He had taken care of both of them.

A big smile appeared on Jackpine's face as he looked down the bay. Lawrence was heading down to the end of the bay. He was alive and not injured, based on the way he was skating. Jackpine suddenly saw Lawrence's target. The gasoline storage tank was at the end of the bay. Gasoline was the lifeblood of a wilderness lodge, not only for the boats but also for the generators to supply power. Storage tanks were kept out of sight of the lodge for aesthetic purposes. Generators were kept far enough away to prevent the noisy hum from assaulting the pristine wilderness that the guests had paid so much to enjoy.

He saw four men getting motors from the shed. Jackpine knew that it would be hard going but possible for his enemy to break through the ice. If they broke through along the entrance of the bay, he and Lawrence would be trapped. He started skating toward and yelling at Lawrence. Lawrence turned and skated toward Jackpine.

"They're going to break the ice at the mouth of the bay!" yelled Jackpine. "I'm faster. I'll take out the gas tanks. You haul ass back to the island."

"I'll take out the motor in the lead boat as it passes by," Lawrence shouted as he skated toward the mouth of the bay.

Jackpine, skating like the wind and throwing off his parka and bulletproof jacket, headed toward the gas-storage tanks. Speed was now more important than warmth and protection. He took a grenade, pulled the pin, and gave it a light tap; then he did the same on a second and a third. As he came to the first grenade, he fired a wrist shot. As he came upon the second grenade, he fired another seething wrist shot. He shot the third grenade in an arching pattern; he hoped it would come down on top of the tank. The three missiles were in the air at the same time. He didn't stop to watch them land. He turned on a dime, his long legs churning and his elbows pumping. He heard the first grenade go *BOOM!* Then he felt the heat on his back and the ice tremble. He had done it.

He saw Lawrence shoot his rifle. He heard the sound of a bullet striking metal and saw the driver of the lead boat dive for cover. Lawrence had put the motor out of commission.

Jackpine was pumping his legs furiously and heading for the island. The other three boats were halfway across the bay. There was no time to launch a grenade, no time to fire a rifle. Jackpine put his head down, leaned forward, and skated as fast as he possibly could. He crouched down low to reduce wind resistance and to make a smaller target. As he reached the mouth of the bay, his lungs were burning (in a request for more air) and his legs were seething in pain as he pushed piston-like for greater speed. Rifle fire filled the air. The boats were still moving. To hit a fast-moving target with a rifle was a difficult shot, and from a moving boat almost impossible, but an automatic rifle was a great equalizer.

Jackpine skated past the boats, staying close to the far shore and as far from his assailants as possible. He felt a searing pain in his left thigh. He knew he was slowing down, so he pushed harder for more speed. His left leg was not cooperating. Thirty seconds, he thought, and he'd be out of range. The seconds seemed like hours. The rifle fire abated somewhat. He glanced over his shoulder; he was gaining an advantage—the boats weren't making very good time. Lawrence was skating toward him. Lawrence aimed carefully and fired. The driver of the boat closest to Jackpine fell over into the water. The welcomed sound of rifle fire came from the island. Boone and Paul could not hit anything from that range, but their shots had the desired effect. The boats ended their pursuit and headed back to the safety of the dock.

Jackpine skated just fast enough to keep from falling through the ice. He noticed a trail of blood behind him. His legs were throbbing; he could not distinguish the pain of the wound on his left leg.

Jackpine and Lawrence skated into the channel together. Paul and Boone were waiting at the beach, looking concerned. Jackpine had sent Paul for extensive first-aid courses as a condition of employment. Now he was glad that he had. Jackpine coasted to the shore and into the arms of Paul Desroches. Paul carried him to camp and laid him on a sleeping bag beside the newly rejuvenated fire.

"You'll have to get back on watch, Boone," said Jackpine. Boone lingered.

Paul slid Jackpine's pants off and examined the wound. The bullet had gone right through the back of his thigh. "Just little more than a flesh wound. I'll get the bleeding stopped, and you'll be just fine." That was what Boone was waiting to hear. He filled his coffee cup and headed over to the point to watch the lodge.

CHAPTER 13

"I come up here just checking out my investment. And what happens? I land in the middle of a fucking war!" Sandor Toth was furious, slamming his fist on the coffee table for emphasis.

"It's not a war, Sandy. Just that cowboy cop and..." Golias was interrupted by the irate Sandor Toth. Golias's protests fueled Sandor's ire.

"Not a fucking war he tells me, Julie," Sandor raged, looking over at his younger brother, Julius Toth. "Not a fucking war. I got three planes sunk in a fucking lake. I got fucking bombs blowing everything up. And now I got six dead bodies. You go, Danny, tell them fucking bodies it's no war—just a cowboy cop and some fucking Indians. What do you think? You're 'Kit Fucking Carson'!" Julius, Dan Golias, and Steve Appleton hung their heads. None of them wanted to attract Sandor's attention.

"One of our Colombian friends shot, and two blown up. I bring my Polarex crew here and already one guy blown up, one shot, and one killed with a fucking axe—for chrissakes! You tell me it's just some hick cop. He's smart enough to get me to come here. He made me think Danny was double-crossing me!"

"He tried to do the same thing to me, Sandy," offered a tentative Dan Golias. "Keating tried to make me think two of my men turned against me."

"Maybe they did." Sandor Toth trusted no one.

"Bear and Flip are too fucking dumb to try anything, Sandy. They figure they're retiring in the Caribbean next week." Golias laughed, trying to ease the tension in the room. "After the deal goes down, those two will be onboard when the boat sinks. They're going to retire at the bottom of Lake Superior. I get the insurance money. And I save all the money I promised those guys. Those dumb fucks did my hits for me this summer. When two of the guides and the cook saw the dope, Bear and Flip took them out. Didn't do it here at the lodge, either. When they disappear, there's no linking me to any of this shit."

"Shut up, Danny, for chrissakes. They could be standing at the door." Sandor Toth turned his attention to Steve Appleton. "So how does this cop get to use your fax machine and get your signature on the letter? That's what made me swallow the story."

"They must have forged my signature, Sandy. And I bet Jackpine's buddy the reeve let him in. He's my landlord, so he has a key to my office."

"You dumb fucking twerp. You knew they had a key all along. I don't believe it!"

"They entered my office illegally; I'll sue them." said Steve Appleton adamantly.

"OK, get in a boat and go over there and serve him with papers. You'll get a bullet in that wet-behind-the-ears head of yours. Serve you fucking right. Keating is after the dope, so he can sell it. And he's playing hardball." Toth turned from Appleton and focused on Golias again.

"And what do I tell Mr. Mendez? He says: 'Señor Toth, I will lend you some good men; your shipments getting through is critical to both of us. We both sleep better if you let me help.' So, I'm gonna tell him: 'Señor, here's your good men back. Minor problem, three of them are fucking dead,' or more? Who the fuck knows? Maybe Keating will kill the rest of them too."

"Don't worry, Sandy," Julius offered. "Danny and I got a plan. We'll go over to the island after dark. We'll come in from all sides. We'll get the bastards. Surround them—it'll be like shooting fish in a barrel."

Sandor got up and walked to the small window. They were in one of the guest cottages. It had two small bedrooms, a bathroom, and a small great room with a table, four chairs, a couple of sofas, and a small wood furnace. The main lodge was cold with some of the windows and part of the roof blown out.

Sandor looked out toward the island. He didn't see anything moving. He walked over to the door, opened it, and stepped outside. He wanted to cool off. Golias had been overzealous in loading the wood furnace; it must have been a hundred degrees inside. A strong wind had picked up from the southwest. Even though he did not know or care the direction, Toth was pleased that the wind was warm—at least warmer than the wind from earlier in the day. He wanted desperately to get this whole business over with. He had been nervous about it all summer. His concerns were not moral or ethical; he needed the money that this second shipment would generate.

He and Julius had come a long way in twenty years—from petty criminals in Cabbagetown to wealthy entrepreneurs. They had graduated from petty crime to running major stolen-car rings in Ontario, Quebec, and upstate New York. Cash had been coming in steadily, so they had diversified into real estate, partly to launder money and partly out of an old country belief in the prestige of owning land.

Fifteen years earlier, the Toronto real-estate market had been in the midst of a long boom, enabling them to disband the stolen-car ring and go legit. (Legitimate, of course, only under the expansive, encompassing use of the word as defined by the Toths.) One of the keys to their success as developers had been their uncanny ability to put together packages of land. Frequently, all of the homeowners in an entire neighborhood had been willing to sell to Toth Brothers, enabling them to convert older single-family dwellings into an attractive commercial development. They had been persuasive, acquiring numerous parcels of land this way.

They also had a good grasp of where the Toronto market was going to be hottest; in those years, it was almost impossible to be wrong. But the real secret to their success in acquiring parcels of land reached far beyond cunning tactics and good salesmanship. Their repertoire had also included blackmail, arson, hired muscle, bribery, forgery, and occasionally (but not frequently) murder. And they did not count deaths in fires caused by arson or overeager goons carrying their lessons too far as murder—those had been simply accidents.

Real-estate development proved so lucrative they had diversified and gone legit ten years ago. For the most part, the new acquisitions were very legitimate enterprises. Polarex was a small but highly respected (until after Sandor Toth had acquired it) exploration company.

The donut chain had been built store-by-store, donut-by-donut by a hardworking entrepreneurial immigrant. The founder had died of a heart attack, at least partially attributable to his expanding girth brought on by his enthusiastic approach to quality control—indulging in two or three dozen of his products every day for thirty years. The opportunistic Sandor Toth had convinced the widow to sell the company, paying her almost half of what it was worth. The founder would roll over in his grave if he knew what Sandor Toth had done to his name and reputation with the franchise scam.

The hotel chain, brickyard, and lumber company had been run by honest, hardworking management when the Toths had bought the companies. Sandor Toth had not yet devoted his personal energies to any of these three businesses. Sandor laughed to himself, thinking about the clown from Rainbow Falls Lumber that had come in to see him on bended knee, begging to keep the operation going. Some jobs and a one-horse town in the middle of nowhere were insignificant to Sandor Toth. He had gotten lucky when the fools from New York bought the loser lumber company. He initially bought Rainbow Falls Lumber thinking he would save money controlling the source of lumber for Toth Brothers Development. It had proven more lucrative to deal with other lumber suppliers, squeezing low prices out of them, then finding reasons to delay payment.

Sandor Toth considered himself a visionary. When Julius came to him last winter and said that his boyhood pal Danny Golias was an OPP sergeant who lived in the boondocks and could be bought, Sandor had not thought much of it. The downward spiral in the Toronto real-estate market was continuing, and the highly leveraged Toth Brothers had a lot of half-finished projects. Without a major infusion of cash, their whole empire would crumble. The idea came to him like a bolt of lightning: use boats to get a shipment of coke to Hudson Bay, and then use the crooked cop to cover his ass in getting the shipment through to the States. Julius came up with the idea of the fishing lodge and the charter airline.

Within a month, they had found a lodge for sale that was located in the jurisdiction of their cop. Through his own cocaine supplier, he had been able to network up to Mr. Mendez. Mr. Mendez had agreed to buy whatever quantity he could get into the States, and he had put Sandor in contact with people in Colombia to make the buy.

Sandor had put the Polarex crew, formerly involved in his mining swindles, at work near Rainbow Falls. He could run one of his scams from almost anywhere in the northern Canadian Shield, and he had thought that they would be good backup to have handy in case he needed them. To be prudent, he had also sent a lawyer to Rainbow Falls to open a practice and keep an eye on the town. He should have sent one with more street smarts, but it would still work out all right. They would take care of these hicks and be home free.

He'd had foresight to take out an insurance policy. After he had received the fax, he had called Mr. Mendez to arrange for more muscle to meet him in Rainbow Falls. His Polarex guys had told him that the local pain-in-the-ass cop had headed out of town, and two of his men had caught the old man trying to sabotage the engine of their plane. He put two and two together and then told the Colombians to snatch the cop's wife and hold her somewhere with the old man from the airport.

He wished he had a radio to confirm that his guys had found the broad. But it was a small town, and he was sure they had found her. Too bad he had no time to stick around town to confirm. One of her fingers would have been an effective visual aid in dealing with Keating, if it came down to it.

He had hired a guy in Miami to knock off O'Toole when he arrived. The extra cash he would save by double-crossing his partners would save his business until the market turned around. There would be no loose ends. Toth flicked his cigarette to the ground and went back into the cabin.

"I want you guys to get another plane up here. I don't want to waste any time after we take care of this business tonight," ordered Toth.

"But we don't have a radio, Sandy," whined Golias.

"I put you in charge of a simple operation. Julie tells me, 'You can trust him, Sandy.' Trust. my ass. You can't even manage to have a fucking radio that works."

"It worked all summer, Sandy. I don't know what happened to it all of a sudden."

Golias's defensive posture riled Toth. "You started this mess, Golias. I wanted to put a staff of guys up here we could trust. No, you tell me. It would be suspicious. We need some real guides. You tell me you gotta hire fucking Indians. You tell me: 'It's OK, Sandy. They're fucking stupid; they won't see anything.' Two of them find out what's goin' on. You know what really pisses me off? You waste these two guys, and you fuck it up even when you own the fucking cop."

"They didn't screw it up, Sandy. Both deaths were accidents. And the cook hung himself."

"Killing fucking cooks. No wonder that hick cop got wise to you, and it's your fucking fault." Toth thrashed his finger in front of the nose of the cowering Steve Appleton. Waking up to the sound of grenades had put Sandor Toth in a foul mood. He was not to be appeased. "I send you up here from Toronto. Easy job. Make life easy for Polarex and watch the town. So easy all I think I need is a two-bit lawyer. You're not even a two-bit lawyer—you weasel. I asked you one question. Just one. I asked you, 'Do you think we gotta get the Rainbow Falls cop on the team?' Simple fucking question. 'No way, Mr. Toth. He's just a hick cop, too stupid to see things under his nose, and O'Toole has jurisdiction.' That's what you told me, isn't it?" There was no response. "Isn't it?" he screamed.

"O'Toole does have jurisdiction, sir." Appleton quivered.

Appleton wondered how he had gotten himself into this mess. He had graduated from law school twenty-fourth in his class at Osgoode Hall. He had struggled for a few years, while becoming disillusioned that the pot of gold at the end of the rainbow he thought should be waiting never came. He had become bitter. He had become the type of person that the Toths recruited. How far he had fallen.

"And Keating couldn't be bought, sir."

This enraged Toth. "Everyone can be bought. And jurisdiction. I'll show you jurisdiction!" He grabbed Appleton by the collar and dragged him to the window. "He's out there with bombs and rifles, trying to steal my cocaine. That's fucking jurisdiction!" He slapped Appleton across the face with a full right-hand blow. The lawyer reeled to the floor, sending his glasses flying off.

"Danny, it's nine o'clock. You send one of your goons down the river with this shyster. Now! When you get to town,"—he pointed to Appleton—"you get us a plane, right away. Understand?"

"Yes, sir," Appleton squeaked.

"Danny, do you think they have someone guarding the river?" asked Julius Toth.

"I don't think so, Julie. Keating can't have that much support in this. At most, they'll have one guy. Probably just an Indian, if anyone at all." Golias reasoned.

Sandor jumped into the conversation. "OK, send one of your goons to lead the way. Shyster, you follow him. We'll have one of the Colombians follow on the trail a ways back. If there's any trouble, he'll save the shyster's ass. They'll get your goon if they get anyone, and he's expendable.

"I'll keep Bear Sawchuk here. He's a good shot, and he's tough. We'll send Flip Lafontaine."

"Go, now." Toth dismissed them. Golias and Appleton walked toward the main lodge.

"As soon as you get to town, Steve, call Sportsmen's Paradise and get one of these pilots." Golias scribbled two names on a piece of paper. "They're both on our team. Have the pilot fly directly from Thunder Bay to the lodge and then go down to Blackwater to check on our boat and make sure it's OK."

"Dan, things are going to work out OK? Aren't they?" Appleton implored.

"Guaranteed," said Golias. "We'll get those assholes tonight. We'll weigh them down, toss 'em in the middle of the lake. Nothing will trace them to us, and we'll be on easy street for the rest of our lives." They walked into the dining room. Everyone was busy nailing pieces of plywood over the apertures that were once windows. They completed makeshift repairs to the roof. They had planned to put the plywood up for the winter anyway; Lawrence Musgrove just accelerated the plan. Even the Colombians were busy; cold weather was their incentive to work. A fire was roaring in the huge stone fireplace; once the plywood was up, the room would warm quickly. Without the gas generator, the fireplace was the only source of heat.

Golias picked one of the Colombians to accompany Appleton and Flip. The three men left quickly to prepare for their trip. Golias walked out to the front dock where Bear Sawchuk was on guard. "Any sign of them, Bear?"

"No, it's quiet, Mr. Golias. It's startin' to rain. The ice will break up soon. I hope I'm the lucky one who gets to put a bullet into Keating tonight."

You're already lucky, thought Golias. If we had gotten out of here, you would be dead by now. Your luck was getting to live an extra couple of days. "Won't be long until you're down on your island in the Caribbean, drinking rum, and screwing your ass off. Here," he tossed Bear a small bag of cocaine. "Don't let anyone see you."

"Thanks, Mr. Golias," Bear grinned as he caught the bag.

Golias headed back to the lodge. He had helped Bear and Flip create their utopian island. Painting the fantasy had been useful in recruiting them and keeping them motivated all summer. The Toths had told him to keep drugs away from the hired help, but he found a bag of coke now and then helped keep Bear and Flip in line.

* * * * * *

Bear enjoyed a huge snort in each nostril before Golias had walked ten feet. Euphoria rushed through his body. He would have a hard time getting used to diluted street coke after enjoying the pure stuff all summer. It had been a great summer, and he was going to cap it off by killing his nemesis, Jackpine Keating. Mr. Golias was a great guy to work for. Golias had not minded committing murder; in fact, he had enjoyed it. He had never felt such exhilaration. Beating someone up, compared to killing them, was like comparing street dope to real dope. He had told Desmond that he was going to kill him before he started hitting him. Flip had held him and Bear had savored the look of terror before beating him unconscious. Bear had made sure that

Desmond was still breathing when they threw him and the canoe into the river.

Boucher and his broad had been fun sport. Boucher had been drunk when they found him. A few snorts, a few more drinks, and he had passed out. They had thrown him in the trunk and driven up Spruce Hill Road with the girl. She had been hot to trot, and Flip had fucked her in the back seat on the way there. She had been willing to take on Bear too. Dumb broad had called him a faggot and she hadn't known that he liked it rough. He had beaten her up to put some fright in her, before he screwed her up the ass. The fact that only rape sodomy appealed to Bear Sawchuk had not made him a sexual deviant by his own definition. When given a chance, he preferred women to men. Any fool knew a faggot preferred men. He had put Jimmy Boucher behind the wheel and had beaten the girl unconscious before pushing the car over the cliff. They had then walked overland to the river—another perfect crime.

Flip had been bothered by the hanging of White Horse Parker. Bear had maneuvered Old White Horse into a bear hug and then took him to the basement. Flip had tied the rope to the rafters and then put the noose around the old man's neck. They had watched for a while; then Bear had pulled on the old man's legs. Bear smiled when he thought about what he'd said: "Teach you to kill dumb animals, you old prick." He didn't know why Flip had not found it funny.

Yes, it had been a great summer, thought Bear as he heard the boat leaving. Poor Flip was going to miss the fun.

Boone also saw the boat leaving and quickly reported it to Jackpine. Jackpine relayed the message to Napoleon Martin.

Nap and the other three Ojibways had worked their way up to the first portage. Four small, scrawny, wrinkled old men (all between the ages of sixty and seventy) did not seem to be much of a match for the brawny Flip Lafontaine, a ruthless Colombian (both armed to the teeth), and a two-bit lawyer. The antiquated aboriginals had a few factors in their favor: they were not in Miami or in a northern Ontario beer parlor, and home field advantage was paramount. They were also the hunters; roles they had trained for all their lives. They also had time to plan and prepare.

Steve Appleton began leading the way. Flip thought he was going too slow, and once on the trail he took over the lead and picked up the pace considerably. He had been told there might be a couple of guys trying to stop them. He was ready for them; Flip wanted to kick some ass. He would enjoy teaching some Indian a lesson.

Steve Appleton was happy to be in the middle. It seemed like the safest place, and he was confident in the abilities of his protectors. The Colombian stayed well back. If there were trouble, he would have time to survey the situation before he acted. He could either save his traveling companions or turn and run back to the boat.

The bush was ominously quiet. They could hear the strong wind in the treetops, but the forest floor was calm. A heavy ground fog hung like a soft, white blanket. It was like walking on clouds. The rain was getting heavier, but the tree cover made it almost dry. All three of them heard the sound simultaneously from behind them, or ahead of them. They couldn't tell. Violin music! Haunting and melancholy at first, then louder, then erupting into a lively Andy de Jarlis tune, "Red River Jig." The jig was the celebratory music of the voyageurs during rendezvous in the fur-trading years of long ago.

The Colombian looked furtively in all directions. Why had he come to this crazy place: men ran like jaguars across the water, trees threw grenades, and now the forest played violin. He hoped that bullets would stop whatever demon it was.

Steve Appleton felt an eerie, supernatural terror envelop him. Fear made the hair stand up on the back of his neck. Flip

Lafontaine did not possess a complex emotional range. He felt simple raw fear. Flip reacted first. He ran as fast as his quaking knees allowed. Steve Appleton was hot on his heels.

A limbed spruce tree bent over in an arc was something a woodsman would notice. If Flip Lafontaine had not been spooked and running headlong through the woods, he certainly would have noticed it. *SLAM!* The steel jaws of the bear trap encased the left foot of Flip Lafontaine. The movement released the power of the spruce, and it sprang to attention. Flip Lafontaine was hanging upside down before he realized what had happened.

The trappers all knew how to set traps that catapulted their quarry into the air. It was not done that way very often. It was time consuming, and often the trap would be sprung by accident, resulting in an empty trap for all the hard work. It was sometimes necessary to trap this way, if the trap line was cursed by a particularly wily wolverine who would destroy all of the pelts in the traps before the trapper could get to them. None of them had ever set such a trap for a man before, but the principle was the same. It just took a bigger spruce.

Steve Appleton's instinct of self-preservation was much stronger than his concern for the welfare of Flip Lafontaine. He ducked under Flip's outstretched hands.

The music was growing louder, in eerie harmony with the screams of Flip Lafontaine. Appleton had gone thirty feet before he heard the snap, felt the searing pain in his ankle, and pitched face forward to the ground. He started to cry.

The Colombian stopped in his tracks at the sound of the first scream. He hesitated, not knowing whether to advance or retreat. He decided to strafe the woods with automatic rifle fire, hoping to hit whoever or whatever was playing the violin. He raised his rifle. It was a terrible mistake. It was the last one he would ever make. A single shot echoed in the woods. He clutched his chest as he died.

Sixty feet away, a weathered old Ojibway calmly put another round in his single-shot rifle. He melted into the background so well as to be almost invisible. He waited, watching the trail. There were only supposed to be three in the group. He would wait awhile, just in case there were four of them.

Another old Ojibway was chopping down the spruce that held one of the men who had beaten and raped his daughter.

Nap walked toward the sobbing Steve Appleton. He knelt down and gently removed the bear trap. "Please don't shoot me!" Appleton wailed.

"Well, I've trapped a few skunks by mistake in my day, but you're my first lawyer." Nap helped him to his feet. He put Appleton's arm over his shoulder and helped him the fifty yards into the bush where they had fashioned a wigwam.

* * * * * *

By eleven o'clock, the wind and rain began to break the ice's tenuous hold on the lake. Paul Desroches was on watch. Boone and Lawrence were perched on a driftwood log near the fire. Jackpine was in his sleeping bag, propped up against a big boulder. They had made a lean-to out of the remnants of the tent to keep them dry.

"Weather's turnin' against us; ice will be gone soon," said Jackpine to no one in particular.

"Yep. Gonna get worse too," agreed Lawrence. "'Nother hour and the ice will be gone; then the fog will get thick."

"So, they'll be on top of us before we see them," said Boone, confirming the obvious implication.

"Yep. We'll have to do the best we can. Assuming Nap and the guys got their men, we'll still be outnumbered; probably a dozen of them near as I can figure against our four. They have superior firepower from short range with their machine guns. We'll have to prepare ourselves and minimize their advantage."

"Fog cover can work two ways," said Boone pensively.

"There's half a mile of water, probably thirty-three degrees, maybe a bit warmer. Jackpine, I believe I could swim that. There's probably only one guard on the back bay. I just have to take him out and get us a boat and motor."

Jackpine was reluctant to let Boone accept such a risk. They discussed the pros and cons, and finally Jackpine agreed. Their situation was nearly hopeless, and Boone's plan gave them a chance to turn the dilemma into an advantage.

"Big Paul wouldn't have any trouble with the swim," offered Lawrence. Jackpine nodded. There was no doubt in his mind.

* * * * * *

When Paul Desroches was thirteen years old (just before he had crossed the two-hundred-pound milestone) he had been fishing in Lake Superior with his father. They had been four miles out in a twelve-foot aluminum boat, with a capacity for four adults, or the Desrocheses: father and son. Like many old-timers of the North, Paul Desroches Sr. could not swim a stroke, even though he had spent much of his life on the water. Paul Jr. was a strong swimmer. His awesome strength, his natural buoyancy, and the fact that he was virtually a man competing with children had made Paul a legend in swim-meet competitions against other towns in the northern shore region.

The Desrocheses should not have been that far out in the lake with such a small boat, but it was a calm day. The storm had come up suddenly; the big lake had lashed out in anger with choppy five-foot, white-capped waves, forcing much larger boats to run for cover to protected bays and coves. The old seven-and-a-half-horsepower motor had taken away the option of running from the squall. Paul Sr. had managed to get the boat turned. As they plodded for shore with Paul Jr. bailing furiously, the waves had come crashing over the front of the boat. Paul Sr. had motioned for his son to take his boots off. A renegade wave had slammed the boat from behind, capsizing it immediately. Paul Jr.

had come to the surface, but there was no sign of the boat or his father.

Paul had treaded water for an hour, waiting for his dad to appear. Paul Desroches Sr. and his boat would never be seen again, lost forever in the icy depths of Superior. Paul, crying and his teeth chattering from the cold, had managed to remove his heavy jacket. Although it had been summer, the water along the northern shore had been in the mid- to high thirties. So cold that most locals would have guffawed at the idea of wearing life jackets: "Might as well drown as freeze to death" was the common axiom. As advocates of this philosophy, the Desrocheses had been without life jackets.

Young Paul, realizing his dad was gone, had started to swim. He had been four miles from the lighthouse on the shoals outside Blackwater's natural harbor. Slowly and methodically, stroke after stroke, Paul Desroches Jr. (he had been Little Paul until it was no longer appropriate, then Paul Jr., and now suddenly he was simply Paul Desroches) swam for the lighthouse. He had seen the lighthouse clearly when he was at the top of a swell. He saw nothing but a wall of angry water at the bottom of each wave. He had continued on his course. It had been considered a miracle when young Paul washed up on shore and walked unsteadily toward the lighthouse.

There had been lighthouse keepers in those days, and the attendant had called for help. Suffering from hypothermia and vomiting the gallons of lake water he had swallowed, he had been taken to the hospital in Blackwater. He had been released in good health in time for his dad's funeral. The distance had been stretched to eight miles, the water temperature had dipped to thirty-two degrees, and Paul's arm had conveniently been broken, as the legend of Paul Desroches lived on and grew with zealous embellishment.

* * * * * *

Jackpine and Lawrence both knew that Paul Desroches could swim the half mile and arrive with the energy left to do what had to be done. Lawrence looked at Boone with skepticism. Jackpine saw the icy confidence in Boone's eyes and knew that there would be no use trying to discourage his friend.

The radio crackled into life. Nap Martin was calling. Lawrence answered and they spoke in Ojibway for a few minutes. Boone and Jackpine waited eagerly for the translation. "Nap and the boys stopped them." Lawrence chuckled. "They set bear traps on the trail, and Nap spooked them into running into the traps by playing an Andy de Jarlis jig on his fiddle."

"Are they alive?" asked Jackpine hopefully.

"Mexican needed killin'; he was goin' to shoot up the bush and maybe shoot someone. They got the lawyer. Busted ankle, but he's OK. Flip? I don't know."

"What do you mean you don't know?" asked Boone.

"Well, he's OK right now. Guess his ankle's busted and his leg must feel like it was almost pulled off in that trap, but old George's daughter was beat up bad and raped by Lafontaine. Now, old George is sittin' drinkin' tea and talking about hunting accidents. He told Nap he's old, that his eyes are playin' tricks on him, and sometimes a man looks like a moose. Nap's goin' to keep an eye on Lafontaine, but he says there's no guarantee that George won't have a huntin' mishap."

Boone was pensive. There was no guarantee that any of them would make it through this alive. If they did make it, there was a good chance there would not be many survivors among the enemy. This would be a good time to secure some collaborating testimony to try to support Jackpine's rather unorthodox approach to law enforcement. He pulled a miniature tape recorder from his pocket. He always carried it to retain the sudden inspirations and ideas that had been the lifeblood of his business for so many years. Boone explained his idea to Lawrence and Jackpine.

Lawrence called Nap and gave instructions in Ojibway. Nap chuckled and agreed to carry out his role with relish.

Nap went into the wigwam. A dejected Steve Appleton was sitting on pine boughs rubbing his ankle. Nap removed his skinning knife. "Don't figger a lawyer's pelt will be worth much. There's too many of you around. Jackpine told me he wants your pelt. I was going to kill you first. But Jackpine says you're a drug-peddling killer, so he told me to skin you alive. I'll start on your belly, so you won't have to put up with too much before you die." With a flick of his wrist Nap slit the buttons off Appleton's jacket. Appleton fainted.

Nap splashed him with water to revive him. Alistair Boone called, and Nap gave the radio to Appleton.

"Steve, this is Alistair Boone. I'm sorry about what these guys are going to do to you. Maybe if you make a full confession to me, I can stop them."

The trembling Appleton had not lost his sense of propriety. "I can't. I can't violate an attorney-client confidentiality."

"I understand and admire your respect for a sacred trust. OK, Nap, go ahead and skin him alive!"

Nap Martin grabbed Appleton's wrists. "First, I'm going to make a circular cut around your paws."

"Jesus Christ!" yelled Steve Appleton. "Mr. Boone, I'll tell you anything you want to know."

"I've turned on my tape recorder. I'm speaking with Steve Appleton. Mr. Appleton, do you agree that I am not coercing you in any way?"

"Y-y-yes, sir."

"This testimony is completely voluntary. Mr. Appleton is making it as a good-faith gesture in appealing for clemency. Now, Mr. Appleton, please begin by telling us how you became involved with the Toth brothers and Dan Golias and their cocaine-smuggling operation."

The floodgates were opened. Appleton spoke for half an hour. He spoke of corruption and coercion in land deals, intricacies of the donut-franchise scam, the murders of Jimmy Boucher and his girlfriend, White Horse Parker, and Desmond Lesmontaignes. He confirmed the involvement of O'Toole, who was personally responsible for delivering the envelopes of cash. He outlined the astounding fiscal scope of the cocaine-smuggling operation.

After the canary finished singing, Boone told Nap not to proceed with the skinning. Feigning a look of dejection, Nap replaced the skinning knife in its sheath. He went outside the wigwam. Flip Lafontaine was far more dangerous than Steve Appleton; consequently he was tied to a tree. Old George was guarding him. Lafontaine was completely motionless. Old George had said he would shoot if Lafontaine so much as blinked. Flip believed him. So did Nap Martin.

Nap addressed George and his other two cohorts in Ojibway. Within minutes the three of them had cut sticks and were roasting links of moose sausage over the fire. The pork fat, mixed with the moose meat, sizzled and crackled as it dripped into the fire. The radio barked to life, startling Flip Lafontaine.

"Flip, this is Chief Lawrence Musgrove, do you hear me?"

"Yeah, I fuckin' hear you."

"I'm going to get them to let you go, Flip. One thing first."

"I'm real sorry they don't have a pot with them, except their can for making tea. Nap won't let you boil your prick in his teapot. You're going to have to roast it on a stick before you eat it."

"What the fuck?" Flip Lafontaine's face was as white as fresh snow.

"Promise is a promise, Flip, and I keep mine. As soon as you've eaten your prick, you can go."

As Lawrence spoke, Nap Martin unzipped Flip's pants and pulled out his limp penis. The other three Indians were enthusiastically slicing off pieces of sausage and eating the slices from the tips of their knives.

"Flip, this is Alistair Boone, can you hear me?"

"Y-y-yeah."

"Flip, I don't like you much, but I can't let them do this. It's goddamn barbaric. Do you want my help?

"P-p-please, any th-th-thing."

The four old Indians were not professional thespians, but their performance was entirely credible, and it dripped with sincerity like pork fat into the hot fire. To retain his phallic resource, Flip Lafontaine babbled freely. He confessed to the murders of Jimmy Boucher, Jimmy's girlfriend, Desmond Lesmontaignes, and White Horse Parker. He confirmed that the unfortunate Reg Frenette was indeed interred in shaft number two of Spruce Hill Mine. He even confessed to the planned crimes of sexual deviancy that he and Bear had intended to perpetrate on their island in the sun.

When the testimony was complete, Nap Martin was kind enough to close Flip's zipper. Nap also offered Flip a piece of sausage. Flip declined.

Boone rewound the tape. But before he could play it, Jackpine said, "Good work, Boone. But before we listen to it, we have some work to do."

Lawrence stood, grabbing his knife, and said, "I'll do the north part of the island."

Boone wished he were on their wavelength. "You take the middle, Boone. I'll go and relieve Paul. He can do the south end." Jackpine got up slowly, using his hockey stick as a crutch.

"What the hell are we doing?" asked Boone.

"We're huntin' bear," said Lawrence, as if stating the obvious.

Boone was now completely puzzled. Rather than pursuing the logic behind the operation, he thought he would ask a far more practical question. "How do I find a bear?"

"Just think like a bear. The bear was scared last night, half out of his mind with the lights and the shooting. He knows we're here, but he's not sure what to think of us yet, so he'll keep his distance. With winter coming, he wants to eat. He'll be conscious of his safety, but he'll be looking for food," explained Jackpine.

"Now I understand," said Boone, not understanding at all. He did know why he was getting the middle of the island. They considered him incompetent, so Lawrence and Paul would gradually make their way to the middle of the island to compensate for Boone's lack of bush sense. Boone set out determined to be the one who found the bear. Once he was alone in the woods, he began to have a change of heart. His hands were sweating despite the cold. Now he hoped he would not be the one who stumbled across a big, angry bear. He found the bear on a rocky outcrop near the east shore—big it was, angry it wasn't. It was already dead. He fired a shot in the air to alert the others.

In ten minutes, Lawrence appeared silently from the forest to the north, followed minutes later by the not-so-silent Big Paul Desroches. "Nice shootin', Boone!" yelled Paul. Boone was glad he had dropped the "mister." His ego urged him to take credit for the kill, but he did not.

"I found him dead."

"Good thing you had this part of the island. We never would have thought to look in a place like this. If he'd been alive, he wouldn't be out in the open like this," said Paul. Boone absorbed the unintentional insult, not claiming to have any prowess in thinking like a bear.

"Those bastards shot the poor bear for fun." Lawrence was furious over the wanton slaughter. His expression never changed noticeably, but Boone was learning to read the little clues in his stoic, seemingly unchangeable countenance. Boone was confused. Here was a man who had been hunting the same bear. Given the opportunity, Lawrence would have shot it without remorse. It was unfathomable to Boone since the bear ended up dead either way. Killing for need versus killing for sport was a distinction Boone could not understand.

Boone was dispatched to build up the fire. Lawrence and Paul pulled out their knives to start whatever surgical procedures were in store for the unlucky bruin. Boone hoped that carving meat for dinner was not among the operations scheduled.

Boone built the fire up. He walked over to visit Jackpine: progress was slow over the rocks, carrying two cups of burning hot coffee. It splashed on his hands a few times. Boone's hands were so numb from the cold that it did not hurt very much. Jackpine was fishing from the shore. He stopped and took the welcomed cup of coffee.

"How's the leg, ol' buddy?"

"Fine, just a bit stiff. Paul's got it bandaged well, stopped bleeding."

"Any action from the lodge?"

"Quiet on the western front—I think, anyway." Visibility was only a few hundred feet; the lodge couldn't be seen. The wind had died down to a light breeze. The ice had completely broken up. The fog was blanketing the lake and getting denser. There was still a choppy wave, a final reminder of the high winds. "I'm listening more than watchin'. With the wind down but still blowing toward us, I could hear them if they were comin'. When you're on watch, Boone, listen for sounds that don't belong. Try to listen for the clank of an oar against an aluminum boat. Listen for any sound that is not right. These guys aren't good enough to bring the boats across quietly."

"OK, revered Bush Master," laughed Boone. "I always consider myself a woodsman 'til I'm around you guys. Do you and Lawrence have ESP?"

Jackpine laughed. "When you're in the bush a lot, you learn to be quiet. You learn to communicate without talking. I knew two old Finn lumberjacks: worked side by side in the bush for twenty years. Hated each other's guts. They never talked. You never saw two guys work so well together. One would finish limbing a tree, stand up, and the other one would fell another tree right in front of him. No wasted steps gettin' to the next tree. Other lumberjacks would come and watch these guys, amazed at how productive they were."

"Why did they work together so long?"

"No one else could keep up with them. They worked piecework, and any other partner would cut into their income. Plus they were both ornery bastards, and nobody else could get along with them. But they always knew what the other one was doing without looking. Lawrence and I both know the bush. We are aware of things around us. Some courses of action seem obvious and don't have to be discussed first. We sense things, but it's really not that cerebral.

"OK, why was it so obvious to you guys that we should kill a bear?"

"Well, we all knew there was a bear somewhere on this small island, because Lawrence saw fresh sign. So, if you're goin' swimmin' in cold water, bein' covered from head to toe in bear grease will help you retain body heat. When you have a need, you automatically consider what nature provides to fulfill it. In this case it was obvious."

"It makes perfect sense. I just never considered it."

"Sounded like your gun. Did you shoot the bear?"

Boone explained that he had found the bear. In its panic, the bear had run to a place where a bear should not have been.

"Got one!" Jackpine reeled in a protesting walleye. "They don't bite much in weather like this. You have to snag them when you feel a little nibble." The fish was hooked externally, near the gill plate.

"Got enough for lunch?" Lawrence asked. Boone jumped. Lawrence was standing directly behind him. "I'm surprised they're biting. Never get pickerel in weather like this. Pike are always hungry," he added. "I'll stand watch. You better take care of that leg, Jackpine. We better let Paul and Boone get some rest if they're goin' swimmin'."

Boone was a little put off. He was planning to swim a half mile in frigid water to attack armed cutthroats, and Lawrence was as nonchalant as if Boone was going for a dip in a warm pool.

CHAPTER 14

While Lawrence was cooking, Boone went down to the lake. He examined the pot of bear fat that was cooling in the shallow water. He found the strong, wild smell unbearable. He walked back toward the fire. "Have you guys got a plan about how to get this grease off me after Paul and I successfully complete the mission?"

"Look at it this way, Boone," offered Jackpine. "You'll go back to town smellin' like a bear—a big improvement over how you smelled the last time you came back from this lodge."

"Show some mercy for Aqua Warrior, won't you?" Boone laughed.

Boone ate voraciously: fried fish, fried potatoes with onions, pork and beans, bannock, and canned peaches for dessert. The last-meal complex was nagging him again. He drank some cold lake water with Tang orange drink mix, instead of coffee. He didn't want to be any jumpier with nervous energy than he already was. He knew he should sleep for a few hours.

Somehow Boone was able to sleep. Three hours later Jackpine poked Boone with his hockey-stick crutch. "Time to get goin', Aqua Warrior. Lawrence and I patched up one of the canoes best we could. The pine gum and waterproof tape from the first-aid kit should hold for a few minutes. I think you should make it halfway across before it sinks."

The slight breeze had subsided. Darkness was coming quickly with the overcast sky and fog. Paul and Boone removed their clothes. Jackpine slathered Boone with bear grease, while Lawrence did the same to Paul. The grease made their fingers slippery, so Boone and Paul donned disposable plastic gloves. The gloves from Paul's first-aid kit were far too large for Boone, so he put elastic bands over his wrists to secure the gloves. Boone checked the accessibility of his knife. The sheath was taped to his left leg above the ankle.

Finishing with Boone, Jackpine turned to help Lawrence. The greasing of Paul Desroches was a substantial task. Paul leaned over and Lawrence used the last of the grease on his huge head. "Good thing we have a fall bear with a lot of fat. It would take three spring bears to grease you," said Lawrence. Ashes had been mixed with the grease. Paul was almost invisible to Boone from ten feet away.

Boone could not stop shivering. The bear grease did not seem to be keeping him warm. It was intended to keep him alive, not comfortable. Boone hoped they wouldn't smell him coming. Arrows were taped to the bows. The bows were secured to their backs with heavy string. Paul and Boone talked quietly, finalizing their plans.

Lawrence had carried the canoe to the point facing the lodge. Paul grabbed a paddle, and the four of them walked to the point. Boone was not allowed a paddle. They thought he would hit the side of the canoe with it while paddling. They could not risk alerting the enemy. Surprise was their only advantage. Boone did not protest. He knew they were right, plus he would rather not waste precious energy paddling. The swim would require everything he had.

Let's kick some ass, Boone!" said Paul, displaying a confidence that Boone wished he could muster himself. They had made one miscalculation. With bows tied to their backs and hanging down past their butts, they could not sit in the canoe. They removed the bows.

As soon as Big Paul got in, the canoe started to leak. The big, wide canoe was propelled against the waves by the strong strokes of the stalwart Paul Desroches toward their Armageddon. Within a quarter mile, there were six inches of frigid water in the bottom of the canoe. Boone's feet were numb. Boone hoped they would respond when it was time for him to swim.

After another fifty yards, there was too much water in the canoe for Paul to make further progress paddling. Boone felt a tap with the paddle; he looked back. Paul motioned for him to grab his bow and fall toward the right into the water. The icy water shocked Boone. They helped each other secure the bows to their backs. Boone was surprised that his arms and legs responded as he began to swim. They swam side by side toward the lodge. With the exertion, Boone felt warmer than when he was sitting in the canoe, but it was a fine line of distinction. He was still numb and freezing.

When they got within fifty or sixty yards, they were able to make out the lodge. There was one man on guard. He was sitting on the end of the dock. Paul's big hand grabbed Boone's neck and pulled him close. Boone's head was pulled within an inch of Paul's. Boone thought Paul was going to kiss him. Paul whispered, "Only one. Swim in. Wait. I'll swim to the dock in the back bay. In half an hour, take the man out. I'll be doing the same on the back dock. OK?"

"OK." Boone swam to his right. He wanted to approach the dock outside of the guard's direct line of vision. He swam underwater, coming up carefully for air when necessary. He reached the side of the dock without being noticed. The water was low this time of year, so he was able to swim underneath the dock and stand up.

Boone clenched and opened his hands. They barely responded. He hoped he would be able to get off an arrow with some power. He took his knife and cut the strings that held the bow on his back. He cut the tape and removed his arrows. The bulky guard had to be Bear Sawchuk. If he was going to kill someone in cold blood, he hoped his conscience would take into account that the person was an enemy who had tried to murder him.

Gas lanterns were burning in the lodge, so they would not be able to see out to the dock. He considered swimming out from under the dock and shooting an arrow into Bear's back. The trouble with the plan was that Bear would fall into the water. He needed the rifle that was across Bear's lap, not to mention his nice warm jacket.

Boone considered swimming underwater to the front of the dock, surging out of the water and then letting an arrow fly. He wondered if he could propel himself out of the water with enough force to drive his upper body high enough to fire an arrow. He was not sure he could manage it, and he would only get one chance. The half hour was up. It was time to act.

He came out of the water on the dark side of the dock, away from the glow of the lanterns in the lodge. He stood in the shallow water. He notched an arrow. He laid the other arrows quietly on the dock.

Boone knew he would only get one good shot. If he missed with his arrow, he knew Bear Sawchuk would not miss with his rifle at this range. Boone drew back on the bowstring. In a voice loud enough to be heard by Bear, but not by anyone at the lodge, he said, "Hey Bear, Mr. Golias wants to see you in the lodge. He says on the double."

"Jesus Fucking Christ! Don't a man never get no peace and quiet 'round here," Bear grumbled. He got to his feet unsteadily. Bear Sawchuk was not a man to show restraint. He had snorted all of the coke that Golias had given him and smoked the two joints that were in his pocket. He had been sitting for hours staring out into the lake. Bear had an ability that few people possessed—he could sit for hours and not think about anything. His legs were asleep, so he used his rifle for support to get to his feet. It did not register in Bear's vacant mind that whoever had just spoken to him should be standing on the dock.

Bear was halfway down the dock. Boone rose from a crouch.

"Rot in hell, you murdering son of a bitch!" The bitch part did not come out very audibly because Boone was inhaling as he drew back on the bowstring. *Thwack!* The arrow was true, catching Bear in the middle of his chest. Bear looked dumbfounded as blood trickled from the corner of his mouth. The rifle slipped out of his hands and clattered on the dock. He clawed feebly at the arrow before falling backward onto the dock. Boone did not feel exhilaration from the kill, the conquest of a formidable foe. He felt nauseated. There was no joy or elation, like winning a contest in business, just the sickening realization that he had just taken the life of a human being. Bear's fate was well deserved and Boone's action would save future innocent lives. Boone's conscience was not buying any justifications. Boone moved toward Bear with his knife in his hand. Remorseful or not, he was still prepared to slit his throat if a breath of life remained. He was spared the grisly task. Bear Sawchuk was dead. The Duke of Earl would rise no more in lustful rape.

Boone broke the arrow off and removed Bear's parka. He quickly put it on. He cut the laces from Bear's boots to save time. He tugged the boots off and put them on his feet. He grabbed the rifle, checking quickly to verify that it was loaded. He ran to the end of the dock and through the woods to the back bay.

* * * * * *

Paul Desroches came up for air. He surveyed the dock in the back bay. Boats were lined up on either side of what remained of the dock. Two men were sitting side by side at the end of the pier, their legs dangling over the edge. They were talking in Spanish and smoking cigarettes. Paul was tired after the long swim. He had underestimated the distance around the point. He had to swim at full speed to make it to the dock in the half hour allotted. As it was, he was a few minutes late. Paul remembered the day—long ago—in Lake Superior. Although he was spent and physically exhausted, he knew there was a storehouse of energy hidden somewhere in his cavernous frame. It would be there when called upon. He discarded his bow and arrows. The bow was of no use with two armed men on the dock. Their automatic rifles were beside them. If he shot one guard with an arrow, the other guard would be on his feet shooting before Paul had time to notch a second arrow.

Paul swam underwater. He came up under the dock. He could make out the four feet of the two men at the end of the dock. He swam quietly toward their feet. He stopped and filled his lungs with air. He surged forward, grabbing the two middle legs in a vise-like embrace. He pumped his powerful legs and dove to the lake bottom, tightening his death grip. The two Colombians were jerked into the icy water without any idea of what just happened. They thrashed with their hands and each kicked to no avail with his free leg. Paul's huge legs kept churning, keeping the three of them submerged. The bodies quit resisting, but Paul Desroches did not release them. He went up for air when his lungs were burning. He gulped a breath of air and submerged again. A minute later, Paul came to the surface releasing his victims to the lake. He saw Boone's bare ass. Boone was leaning over untying a boat from its mooring. Boone had been watching from the edge of the woods. He had seen the two guards get the sudden inspiration to leap into the water for some underwater synchronized-swimming exercise. He had waited until he saw Paul's huge hippopotamus head rise for air before rushing to the dock to begin untying boats.

Paul put a leg up on the dock and pulled his big body out of the water with great effort. He picked up the two Uzis that were on the dock and walked toward Boone.

"Paul, we have a chance to take all of their boats. I'm tying them together in a train. You start with the ones on the other side." Paul put the Uzis down carefully and started to help.

Once they were finished, Boone said, "Let's each take one boat and a train."

"No, Boone." Paul had a long rope. He tied the lead boats in both trains together, making one long string of boats. "You take the boats out. I'll stay here. They will come running when you start the motor. I'll cover your ass."

"When I get out in the bay, I'll release the boats and come back for you."

"Right! Now hurry!" Paul took both Uzis and walked into the shallow water. The dock was between him and the lodge. He crouched to stay out of sight.

Boone prayed that the motor would start on the first pull of the rope. He unscrewed the air vent on the gas tank and then pumped the bubble, making sure the motor was in neutral. He pulled hard on the cord. The motor sputtered but did not catch. Again he pulled—nothing. Boone was beginning to panic. On the third pull, the outboard rumbled into life. He clicked the lever to forward gear and turned the throttle to full power as he pushed the choke in. The boat moved forward at a snail's pace. Boone leaned forward to become a less prominent target. A rifle barked as the last boat in the twenty-boat train departed from the dock.

Automatic rifle fire joined the din. The first two men who attacked were cut down from behind by Boone's overzealous comrade-in-arms. The pilot had never fired an automatic rifle before. As a eulogy to his downed compatriots, he muttered, "Fucking hair trigger."

Boone had released the extra boats and was making his way back toward the lodge when he saw Big Paul Desroches stand up. The assault contingent was only thirty feet from the dock. Paul had an Uzi in each hand as he stood, spitting lead directly in the path of the surging throng. He emptied both clips into them as they crumbled in front of him. Paul threw down both guns and ran to the end of the dock. Boone gunned the motor, speeding toward him. Boone turned at the last moment, crashing sideways into the dock. The huge nude cargo jumped into the boat. Boone was surprised the boat took the abuse, he half expected Paul to go right through. "Let's go!" boomed the excited Paul Desroches. Boone needed no coaxing; he turned hard left and charged out into the safety of the lake.

Paul grabbed the rope from the water, reassembling their convoy. He looked at Boone. "You sure have got style, Boone. You stopped and got dressed."

"Ordinary mortals have to be concerned about freezing to death. I was worried when I got to the dock that you might not recognize me."

"First thing I saw was a big bare ass covered with grease. I knew it was either you or a faggot out trollin'."

Boone laughed, not so much at what Paul said, but more at Paul's rumbling belly laugh that followed the remark. After they rounded the point and entered the open lake, Paul told Boone to stop. "I'll take a boat and go toward the front of the dock. I don't want anyone hitting us with wild potshots as we head to the island. Give me the rifle."

Boone handed Paul the rifle and the box of ammo he had found in the pocket of Bear's jacket.

Jackpine or Lawrence had started a big bonfire on the point, helping Boone to navigate. Boone heard the sharp retort of a rifle. Paul had been right. Somebody was on the dock firing Hail Mary shots into the fog in Boone's general direction. He leaned over in the boat and kept a steady course toward the fire.

Paul shut the motor off. He was sitting in the middle seat paddling, making progress toward the front dock.

William, not Bill, O'Toole was shooting from the dock—his dreams crumbling before his eyes. Maybe he could finally get some of the luck that he deserved, and one of his bullets would accidentally nail the perpetrator. Unfortunately, he was the perpetrator in this situation! He'd had visions of owning a charter-fishing operation in the Caribbean. Oh, how proud his mom and dad would have been, and how envious his brothers would have been. He would have shown those pompous brothers—a successful businessman living in paradise. When his bitch ex-wife heard about his success, she would have been sorry she had run out on him. He hadn't caused anyone any real harm; so what if some addicts got a bunch of coke? They would have gotten it from somewhere anyway. And who really gave a shit about a couple of dead Indians, especially young Boucher; he would have ended up that way anyway, sooner or later. And that senile old fool Parker, what did he have to live for? Nothing, that's what. Better off dead.

Why couldn't that fucking Keating just have let it alone? It was all Keating's fault. Keating had been a thorn in his side for years. Everyone looked up to him for one reason, thought O'Toole—because he had been a hockey star. Washed-up stupid jock, that's all Keating was. Kissing up to the fucking Indians like he cared about them—bullshit.

O'Toole's thoughts turned to Boone—big bag of wind Yankee bastard. O'Toole had coveted Inez Mahoney for a long time; only reason she had given him the cold shoulder when he tried to date her was because fucking Keating had lied to her and poisoned her against him. Then, adding insult to injury, she had dated that blowhard Boone the first time he had asked her out. None of it had been fair.

O'Toole's rifle barrel was hot now. To hell with it, he thought. As he fished in his pocket for ammo to fire a few more rounds, he heard an outboard motor. The boat was coming out of the fog from his right.

"This is Constable Paul Desroches. You're under arrest!" Paul waited until O'Toole needed to reload before starting the motor and moving in. O'Toole threw down his rifle and ran down the dock. Paul raised his rifle but could not bring himself to squeeze the trigger. It had been different somehow with the guards, maybe because he had not really seen them. He wasn't sure. The guards had been running toward him shooting. That had been an easy decision—kill or be killed. He couldn't bring himself to shoot O'Toole in the back. He lowered his rifle, nudged the outboard into forward gear, and headed toward the bonfire beacon.

* * * * * *

Reeve Ron Evans did not know what to do. Being unable to get a hold of Janice Keating or Inez Mahoney, he had become worried. He rummaged through the drawers of his desk until he found the key for the police station. He saw the note on Jackpine's desk and recognized Janice's writing. "Jackpine. They have taken Inez, Bertha, and I hostage. Love, Janice." Ron had tried to call Toy. Toy had also disappeared, and his wife was worried. Not knowing what else to do, he called an emergency meeting of council. Stew Larsen and Heinz Shultz, the available members, met him at his home.

Stew had worked himself into a dither. Stew avoided stress in his life. He crumbled under pressure. Stew's hand wringing was not helping Ron retain his composure. Heinz Shultz, restauranteur-cum-bus driver, was a different story. Heinz calmly listened to Ron, asking a few questions for clarification.

"Relax, gentlemen. I have some experience in matters such as this." Heinz was living undercover. He could not stand by in the role of a helpless cook and see tragedy befall Inez or Bertha or Janice. He and Olga were happier than they had dreamed they could be. They had been accepted in the Falls—this remote, dying little village was utopia to the Shultzes. Heinz Shultz was powerless—but Heinrich Bahr, East German Secret Police enforcer, KGB hit man, and CIA informer and double agent, was not. Heinrich Bahr took charge. It might mean they would have to abandon the Falls, but he would have been unable to live with himself if he had done nothing.

"The first priority is finding where they are being held.

Somebody in this town has seen them. Perhaps they thought nothing of it at the time. It's impossible to fart in this town without someone smelling it. Ron, tomorrow at the post office you will see most of our residents. Ask everyone when they last saw the three ladies. Stew, I want you there to help Ron. Find out where they were last seen and then come and get me immediately."

"What will you do, Heinz?" asked Ron Evans.

"I will fix this. The ladies will be returned unharmed. Please, not a word to anyone."

Looking into his German friend's face, Ron saw a person he did not know. It was a face that commanded respect and made the hair on the back of his hands tingle with fear. Heinz's face exuded an icy confidence that the situation was well in hand. Ron Evans saw nothing of the smiling host in the silly pilgrim suit. He was looking at the face of Heinrich Bahr. Most people who had seen Heinrich's steely countenance had not lived long enough to describe it.

Ron decided not to radio Jackpine. There was nothing Jackpine could do about it, and he was sure Jackpine had his hands full at the moment. For some reason he had a lot of faith in the ability of Heinz Shultz, and no one had a better opportunity to talk to everyone in town than the postmaster.

* * * * * *

Boone and Paul wiped off as much of the bear grease as they could before dressing warmly. Feeling somewhat revitalized, Boone wanted to return to the lodge and conclude the mission. Jackpine disagreed, "We're goin' to wait until morning. I'm not sure how much damage was done by the grenade that Lawrence threw into the lodge, but we can assume they have as few as three men left. At most, they have six, so we're evenly matched at worst. Daylight gives us the advantage; we are much better marksmen. It's also our advantage to have you and Paul rested and rarin' to go."

"They are gonna be up all night lookin' out for us. We'll be sleepin' like logs. Come mornin' we'll be in a lot better shape than them," added Lawrence.

Boone did not like the idea of another cold night in the lean-to under the rock overhang, but the logic of the argument made sense to him.

"And we should make sure they don't sleep," added Lawrence. "Jackpine, can you fix one of the boats so that it goes in a straight line with an outboard at full throttle with no one aboard?"

"Yeah, I can do that. Tie the motor down to lock it in position and tape the throttle. But why?"

Lawrence chuckled.

"I see. Put some of Sulo Maki's fishin' lures in the boat. Boat runs up on the shore near the lodge and *KABOOM!* That will keep them on their toes the rest of the night."

"Exactly!" confirmed Boone.

"Let's you and I do it now, Lawrence. Dinner will be served when we get back." Jackpine got to his feet. The wound was still painful, but he was able to get up without using his crutch. Before leaving, Jackpine tried to get his office on the radio. There was no response. He had tried numerous times during the day with the same result. He expected either Inez or Janice to be there, and it worried him that they were not.

* * * * * *

Janice Keating was sick with fear. She was trying not to let it show to Inez and Bertha. They had been abducted from the police station and taken to the Keatings' summer cottage on Tamarack Lake. The Polarex thug did not scare her, but the three Colombians certainly did. Her rudimentary knowledge of Spanish, garnered in high school, enabled her to comprehend their predicament. They had been kidnapped for insurance. Apparently, the rest of the group had flown to the lodge. She was worried about

Jackpine, but she had a lot of faith in his abilities. The women had been captives for almost twenty-four hours. The Colombians were concerned that they were unable to make radio contact with their cohorts. They planned to wait another twenty-four hours. If no contact was made, they were planning to abort the mission and flee. It was the rest of the plan that chilled Janice to the bone. They did not plan to leave any witnesses. They were going to kill the old man, Toy Huhtela, and Bertha Olesen. Then they planned to take turns bedding the two good-looking ones before killing them. The only points of discussion left were the sequence of the rapes and whether they should kill the Polarex man or take him with them when they fled. She was racking her brain to develop a way to thwart their plans. So far she had not thought of anything.

* * * * * *

Two boats raced toward the lodge, side by side. Two boats were tied together, bow and stern. Lawrence pulled the pins on two grenades and tossed them gently into the second boat. On the count of three, Lawrence cut the bow rope, and Jackpine cut the stern rope. The boats raced toward the lodge, side by side. The boats hit the shore twenty yards to the right of the main dock. In a few seconds there was an explosion, followed quickly by a second one. The lodge and dock were briefly illuminated.

"That's gonna keep them thinkin'," said Jackpine.

"Yeah, and we'll be having a roasted goose for dinner." While Paul and Boone were sleeping in the afternoon, a flock of Canadian geese had conveniently landed in the shallows at the east end of the channel. The geese anticipated a quiet night feeding on wild rice: one of their last quiet nights in the wilderness before running the gauntlet of hunters on the trek south. It was not to be. Their ranks were thinned by four during the unscheduled takeoff.

Lawrence had taken the second canoe out to retrieve the geese. The canoe had only lasted for five minutes before sinking.

Lawrence had enough time to retrieve the birds and make it close to shore. He had been forced to wade the last twenty feet. They had skinned the geese, avoiding the laborious plucking. The geese had been stuffed with wild rice, basted in a Tang and cranberry sauce, and wrapped in foil. The foil was covered with wet mud clay. The birds were placed in a shallow pit on a bed of hot coals and covered with hot rocks and gravel from the fire.

Boone had been wondering what his hosts had planned for dinner. He was getting tired of fish, and he had not noticed any grouse on the island. He was very pleased when he was presented with a goose. It looked like Beggar's Chicken from his favorite Chinese restaurant—a little dirtier and without the Chinese characters painted on the side. Boone presented the chefs with a bottle of wine he had stowed in his bag for a special occasion. The meat was so succulent and juicy that he was able to eat almost the entire bird.

Paul Desroches was presented with the biggest goose. He had met this match. He finished it, but he politely refused the remains of the other three birds.

* * * * * *

Sergeant William, not Bill, O'Toole spent a long night patrolling the grounds. He didn't mind. He was glad to get out of the lodge. The Toths were blustering about what they were going to do when their plane came in the morning. The Toths did not comprehend the severity of their predicament. O'Toole knew a plane would not be coming. No one asked for O'Toole's opinion before they sent the group down the river. O'Toole knew that Musgrove was with Keating. And Musgrove would have a band of Indians along the trail.

O'Toole knew that Keating and his gang would come in the morning. If the Toths and Golias were stupid enough to fight back, Keating would kill them all. All those years of busting his ass to get promoted—O'Toole should have been running the entire force. Instead, those political ass-kissers had kept him in the bush his whole career. Now he would be shot like a common criminal. The solution to his problems came to him like a flash. He had been too engrossed in self-pity to see the answer. It was almost dawn; he would have to hurry. He went back to his guest cottage to get his service revolver.

He would walk into the lodge, pull the revolver out from under his jacket, and arrest the Toths and Golias. When their hands were up, he would shoot them. When Keating took him back, he would say he had been working undercover, investigating the operation. He had been playing along until the drug shipment got to Blackwater. That's when he had planned to make the bust. He had decided to wait until he could get the Toth brothers along with Golias. His legitimate police work had been undermined by the kill-happy fool, Keating, and his gang of cutthroat klutzes.

Yes, he would turn the tables on Keating. He would retire in glory. If there was time, he would stash a few bales of coke near the lodge, just enough to replace the nest egg he would be losing. Maybe the Toths had a lot of cash with them. If they did, he would help himself to the money and hide it with the drugs. He would be a hero. Even his hotshot brothers, the Mountie and the car dealer, would look up to him. Maybe Inez Mahoney would too. Best of all, Keating would be ruined.

O'Toole tucked his service revolver into his pants. It was uncomfortable. He had never carried his gun this way before. He did up his jacket to hide the gun and walked toward the lodge. The sun was up. He would have to hurry.

* * * * * *

Boone and Lawrence rowed a boat from the island to the back bay. They were in the woods on a hill overlooking the lodge when they saw O'Toole hurrying toward the lodge. They ventured closer than the point where Lawrence had launched the grenade assault. Boone had given Jackpine his bulletproof jacket. Jackpine and Paul had rowed to a position on the shore near the back-bay dock. Boone got Jackpine on the radio and whispered, "Everyone seems to be in the main lodge."

"OK, we're coming in."

Boone and Lawrence were to cover Jackpine and Paul as they walked toward the lodge to make the arrests.

* * * * * *

O'Toole entered the lodge. His courage wavered for a moment. He hesitated, but there was no turning back. Golias and Julius Toth were sitting at one of the tables. There was an open bottle of vodka, a few glasses, and a couple of over-filled ashtrays on the table. Sandor Toth was pacing near the table.

"What the fuck do you want? Get back out there on watch," sneered Sandor.

"You are all under arrest!" exclaimed the nervous William, not Bill, O'Toole. He tugged at his revolver. He had never yanked the gun from his pants before, and he realized he should have practiced this seemingly easy maneuver. In his zest to remove the pistol, the sight got caught on his belt buckle. He tugged ferociously, freeing the gun but causing the buckle to unfasten. O'Toole had lost weight with the nervous anxiety experienced over the summer. The retaining properties of the belt were violated. The newly liberated pants fell quickly to the floor. Attempting to retain some measure of composure, he took tiny steps toward the table to prevent himself from falling face forward. "This is an Ontario Provincial Police undercover operation!"

"What the hell..."

"I said hands up, Toth!"

The three slowly obeyed, eyes glancing nervously at each other.

"Now, Bill," said Sandor Toth condescendingly.

"William, not Bill," said Golias, before O'Toole had a chance to.

O'Toole decided to enjoy a moment of superiority over the arrogant Sandor Toth. He allowed himself a leering smile as his confidence built.

"You are all under arrest. Including you, O'Toole. Drop the gun!" Jackpine Keating walked into the room, gun drawn. Big Paul Desroches filled the doorway.

O'Toole's bravado evaporated. He dropped his revolver to the floor and put his hands up. The gun fell near the feet of Sandor Toth. Jackpine turned slightly to address Paul, "Come in and cuff them, Paul."

The opportunistic Sandor Toth saw a chance and took it. He reached down and grabbed the gun. He was raising it as Paul Desroches and Jackpine both fired. Both bullets hit him in the chest. As he fell forward, the gun in his hand went off. The bullet went into the floor near O'Toole's foot. O'Toole screamed in agony, "My God, I've been shot!"

"Anybody else wants to try something, go ahead! I'll gladly shoot all of you bastards," said the grim Jackpine Keating. "And you quit bellyachin' and get to your feet, O'Toole—and pull up your pants."

Paul Desroches handcuffed them.

Julius Toth regained his composure first. "So you must be Jackpine Keating." The death of his only brother did not seem to affect him. "We better talk. We have your wife. We took her for an insurance policy. We also have the old man from the airport."

The veins on Jackpine's neck bulged, but he was outwardly remarkably calm. Boone and Lawrence had completed searching the grounds and had just entered the room before Julius Toth's pronouncement. Jackpine handed Boone his gun. He removed the handcuffs from Julius Toth. "Let's go outside and talk."

Julius Toth was pleased. He allowed himself a smile. Sandor had been right; every man has his price, thought Julius. Keating's price was his wife. It looked as if he would be a reasonable man. Julius would soon find out how wrong he was.

"Where is she?" demanded Jackpine, as soon as they got outside.

"We're going to have to arrange a little barter, Mr. Keating. Danny and O'Toole will be your fall guys; just give me half the dope and an airplane. You still get credit for a big bust, and you get your wife back."

Jackpine hit him in the face with a left-cross–right-hook combination. It was so fast, it was hard to determine which punch hit its mark first. The surprised Toth slumped forward. Jackpine grabbed him by the throat with his left hand and pushed him up against the building. Jackpine unclipped his chief's badge from his jacket and tossed it onto the ground. He punched Toth twice in the stomach. The surprise on Toth's face changed to terror.

"I'm acting as a private citizen. I'm going to do things to you that no law-enforcement officer would even dream of. The only thing you have to barter with is your life." Jackpine brought his knee up hard into Toth's groin. "Where is my wife?"

"I don't know!"

Jackpine slapped Toth's face hard a dozen times. He punched him again in the stomach. "I fully intend to beat you to death if you don't talk. Where is my wife?"

"Please, please, no more. Honest, I don't know. Mr. Mendez sent us three more Colombians. The Polarex guys said you weren't around town. Sandy figured you were here. He sent the Colombians and one Polarex guy who knows the town to snatch your wife. You blew up our plane before they reported where they took her. Somewhere near the town, for sure."

"Where's Toy Huhtela?"

"The old guy?"

"Yeah, from the airport."

"We caught him fuckin' around with our plane. One of the Colombians cut his finger off. It wasn't my idea, honest. He just up and cut it off. It was Sandy's idea to drop the finger in your camp. He said guys overcome with fear or anger make mistakes. That's why he did it. The old man is with your wife, wherever that is."

"Did they plan to take anyone else?"

"Your secretary too, if they could find her." Inez was probably easy to find, thought Jackpine. She would have been with Janice, probably at the police station. Jackpine hauled Toth back inside. "Cuff him, Paul. Lawrence, call Nap and tell him I'm comin' down the river. You can take me down to the first portage. Have Nap bring the prisoners there to meet you. Tell Nap he and the guys can go home. You bring the prisoners back here. Boone, they might have Inez too."

"I'm coming with you, Jackpine. Do you know where?"

"No, but I guarantee I'll find out. You have to stay here. It's important for you to get testimony from these guys. Let's go, Lawrence."

Jackpine drove the boat while Lawrence got Nap on the radio. When Lawrence was finished, Jackpine said: "Lawrence, if you don't hear from me by noon tomorrow, kill those bastards."

"I will."

CHAPTER 15

Jackpine took the first stretch of river at full throttle. He crunched the boat into the shore at the first portage, just above the big falls that Boone had miraculously survived. Jackpine leaped from the boat and started up the trail. He did not pace himself. His long legs churned at full stride. His wound began to bleed. It had been well bandaged, but the dressing could not survive such abuse. He felt warm blood running down his leg. Jackpine ignored the pain, refusing to acknowledge his body's complaints. His love for Janice and his anger at her abductors provided the fuel necessary to maintain the rapid pace for the entire two miles of the portage.

He did not stop to catch his breath at the end of the portage. Jackpine picked up the heavy boat and threw it in the water. He grabbed the outboard with one hand and the fuel tank with the other. He pushed the boat out into the current as he stepped in. The boat was already moving downstream as he attached the motor to the mount. He primed the bulb. The motor caught on the first powerful tug on the rope—as if it wouldn't dare to rebel.

Jackpine knew the river as well as he knew the back of his hand. At full throttle in the fast current, there was no time to react. Instinct was the only guide through the maze of jagged boulders and turbulent whirlpools at this speed. Jackpine opened the plug to drain the boat. He was taking on water, and there was no time to stop and bail. Jackpine Keating was looking and acting like a raging lunatic. A sane man would have stopped at the second portage. Jackpine sped past the landing and raced into the boiling, angry rapids. The boat went airborne over a six-foot falls; the motor whined with the sudden intake of air instead of familiar water. The boat smacked the surface of the seething whitewater, teetering dangerously on the brink of flipping over. The boat was half full of water.

As the river became calmer, the water in the boat drained; soon the bow was slapping the surface again at full power. The highlight of the third portage was a mile-long stretch of raging water where the river dropped a total of twenty feet. At the base of the rapids, the river hit an impenetrable granite cliff, protesting angrily into a reluctant L-turn. Perhaps in a few million years the persistent water would defeat the granite cliff; so far, there was no evidence that the river would someday win the battle. Jackpine kept the boat on the extreme right side of the river while he swept through the gut. He thought that if he stayed right he would avoid contact with the cliff. He had never been sufficiently motivated before to try this approach. At the last second, Jackpine was unable to prevent the bow from turning left. The boat was airborne when it hit the cliff head on. Jackpine was hurled forward on impact. His body left the boat and slammed into the cliff. His nose was broken, and a protruding rock created a jagged gash over his left eye. The boat did a 360 on impact, but remained upright upon hitting the water. Water rushed in through the rivet holes in the dented bow.

Jackpine was in the water, barely conscious. He had wrapped the rope tied to the bow around his right hand. He was underneath the boat, being keelhauled through the rapids. Fortunately, the motor had conked out on impact. The river quickly made peace with the terrain. Jackpine hauled himself to the surface. He found the strength to get his arm over the side of the boat, then a leg; he was able to haul himself into the boat. He got the motor started.

He fought to stay conscious. He ripped the torn sleeve from his wool shirt. He tried to tie a bandage around his head, but his hands were too numb to accomplish even a simple knot. He was blinded by the blood that was flowing freely from the gash over his left eye. He winced with pain as he used both hands to reform his nose to its accustomed shape. His nose was pliable, as broken noses of old hockey players often were.

The next sets of rapids were less severe. Jackpine had shot them by canoe many times. It was more difficult with a boat at full throttle and only one eye, but he managed. His speed was being tempered by the excessive influx of water into the boat. More water was rushing in through the damaged bow than could be drained by the small hole in the stern.

Jackpine stayed on the river as long as he could. Ten seconds before the river would have taken an irrevocable hold and swept him to certain death over Rainbow Falls, he pulled into shore. He tried to leap out of the boat, but his battered body would not cooperate. He stumbled face first into the shallow, frigid water. Jackpine fought to remain conscious.

His mind slipped away. He remembered the first night he had seen Janice. The beautiful face of the emergency-room nurse had mesmerized him, while the doctor was sewing the stitches in his face. She had brushed off the advances from the shy, gangly country boy. He had remembered her nameplate and tracked her down. She had relented to a date on his third phone call. He still didn't know how she had managed to fall in love with a rustic, awkward hockey player, but she had, and he'd been counting his blessings ever since.

The thought of Janice snapped him back. He would be damned if he would let anyone harm her. Jackpine dragged himself to his feet. He started to run into town. He fell face first. With his other pains screaming for attention, he had not realized the crash had also damaged his knee. It was badly swollen and wouldn't bend. He hauled himself to his feet and started running, stiff-legged, toward the police station.

* * * * * *

Boone built up the fire in the big stone fireplace. The warm air rekindled the noxious smell of rancid bear fat that still clung to his body and permeated his clothes. He tried to ignore the smell. It was the first time he had been truly warm in days. Boone was worried about Inez and Janice. Toth had said they would not be hurt, and Boone knew that Jackpine would find them. Boone was concerned about Jackpine's state of mind. Boone was as disturbed about the rescue mission as he was about the girls' captivity.

At Boone's request, Paul locked the three captives in separate rooms. Boone was planning his interrogation and hoped to be able to sow seeds of distrust, especially between Golias and Toth. He thought Julius Toth would be the most difficult to get talking, so he decided to start with him.

"Golias tells me that you and your brother masterminded this whole operation. Why don't you tell me about it?"

"Fuck off."

"Dan is willing to help us. He thinks that if he sets you up and helps to nail your ass to the wall, it will go easier on him."

"Fuck off. I'm not telling you anything."

Boone had not expecting this much resistance. He wondered how Jackpine would handle the situation. He decided to try a different tactic.

"Suit yourself." Boone walked back to the main dining room. He picked up one of the confiscated pistols and removed the bullets. He borrowed Paul's fully loaded service revolver. Boone walked back into the room where Julius Toth was being held. He threw the empty gun toward Toth. Toth's hands were cuffed in front of his body. With a surprised look on his face, he reached up and caught the gun.

"The gun is empty. Try it."

Toth aimed at Boone and pulled the trigger. *Click*.

"So, you are willing to shoot me. That makes this a whole lot easier. How does this sound? I walked into the room. Toth had gotten a gun somehow. He raised the gun to shoot me. So, I blew his fucking head off!" Boone fired Paul's gun a few inches to the left of Toth's head. He had fired much closer to Toth than he had intended. Toth dropped the gun. His face was chalky white. His lower lip quivered.

"You...you can't do this. You're crazy!"

"Your fucking right, I'm crazy!" Boone fired again, this time to the right of Toth's head. "You are going to talk, or I'll shoot you. Is that clear!"

"Yes." Partly because Julius spoke so meekly but also because his eardrums were still reverberating from the two gunshots, Boone had trouble hearing him. The look on Boone's face had apparently convinced Toth that Boone was serious. Was he? Would he have shot the man? Boone was not sure of the answer, and it scared him.

Toth's response was typical. The financial crisis in their real-estate empire completely justified the drug-running operation. Toth professed that he knew nothing of any murders. Responsibility for the death of Nelson Lesmontaignes was laid conveniently at the feet of his dead brother and his boyhood pal, Dan Golias.

He may have been intimidated into talking, but the amoral Julius Toth was not alarmed enough to tell the truth. Truth was a stranger to the Toth brothers. The idea of an honest confession had never crossed the devious mind of Julius Toth.

"So you're an innocent bystander, you lying son of a bitch!" Boone escorted Toth back to the dining room. Paul recuffed Toth's hands behind his back.

Boone walked in to see Dan Golias.

"What were the shots about?"

"None of your business, Golias." Boone turned on the tape. "Now talk." It was obvious that the gunfire had already loosened both forks of Dan Golias's tongue. Golias admitted his involvement in the cocaine-smuggling plot. There was no sense denying the obvious. He continued with a scathing report on the Toth brothers. He went all the way back to their days of the Toth's stolen-car ring, but he denied any personal involvement in the operation. The tides of friendship did not run strong with these types, thought Boone. Boone shut the tape off in mid-dialogue, as Golias was professing to be innocent—a bystander thrown into a den of murderous rogues.

Boone knew he lacked the intimidating aura of Jackpine Keating. He realized he would have to pistol whip Dan Golias to get any closer to the truth, but he didn't have the stomach for it. He took Golias back out to the dining room. He gave the revolver back to Paul. "Well, Paul, according to Golias, it's all Toth's fault. According to Toth, Golias is to blame."

The two former chums glared at each other as Boone turned and walked toward the kitchen to see Sergeant William, not Bill, O'Toole. Boone poured two cups of coffee, putting one down in front of O'Toole. Boone planned to be conciliatory. He knew instinctively that O'Toole was the type of man who genuinely believed others were to blame for his misfortune. A wise man accepted his flaws and weaknesses early in life but strived to correct the correctable and control the uncorrectable. O'Toole was not a wise man. O'Toole would blame Dan Golias for his own poor judgment. Boone pressed the appropriate button.

"These guys have sure gotten you into a mess, Sergeant O'Toole."

"My hot-shot brother, the stuck-up car dealer, sent me to Golias to buy a car. It's all Golias's fault. He got me into this situation. None of this was supposed to happen. All I had to do was look the other way for a few months while they moved some drugs through the lodge into the States. None of this is my fault. I wish I had never met Dan Golias."

"Tell me all about it." Boone punched the button to record.

O'Toole looked alarmed. "I'm not saying anything else."

"Suit yourself. Might go a bit easier on you, if you cooperate. Maybe you can avoid jail. You know what will happen to you in jail, don't you? Good-looking guy like you—and a cop." Boone had determined that O'Toole was a racist, based on some of his off-hand, derogatory comments about natives. Because a racist's hatred was usually based on fear, Boone developed this angle. "They'll probably throw you into a cell with a big black Rastafarian Jamaican: blacker than the ace of spades, long braided hair, and hung like a racehorse. Just imagine, the first night. Maybe he'll wait until the lights go out. Maybe he won't. He'll be over in your bunk lickety-split. Later he's going to swap you with his pals— trade your butt for a pack of gum or maybe a toke of ganja."

O'Toole was quickly losing his composure. Boone dabbed fresh paint on the grim canvas. "You'll be out in a few years, but you won't have to carry the burden of your shame very long. Sometimes AIDS can work very quickly. Just like that." Boone snapped his fingers. He had drawn the scenario too vividly. Sergeant O'Toole fainted.

Boone dragged him out to the dining room.

* * * * * *

Sometimes aboriginal skills were passed on genetically. In the case of Wilfred Boucher, a generation was skipped, and he must have cut every class in Outdoors 101 as a child. It had taken him a week to make the trip up the river to the lodge. The group included Boucher, the leader of the expedition, and his three pen pals from Thunder Bay. His buddies were not the type of pen pal that formed from writing letters (all four were functionary illiterate), but rather the type that developed from doing stretches behind bars. They had all partaken of the dynamite coke that Wilf's brother Jimmy had stolen from the lodge. Wilf maintained there was kilo upon kilo up there, waiting for the taking. All four had cheerfully agreed to the mission, not realizing the odyssey ahead of them.

Wilf got lost on the first portage. Planning was not Wilf Boucher's forte. They had not brought sleeping bags or food. After the third day of following Wilf aimlessly through the woods—starving and freezing—the first talk of mutiny started. They were so far from the river that they missed Nap Martin's reception committee. Nap did not foresee any group portaging eight miles from the river. Boucher was truly fortunate. A wilderness tribunal chaired by Judge Napoleon Martin would probably have enacted the death penalty for the senseless beating of Esther Martin, and there would be no liberal ears to hear the appeal. Sentencing would have been fast and final.

On day four, the gang stumbled across a warren of rabbits. Volleys of rifle fire erupted, reminiscent of a small war. Most of the rabbits escaped the onslaught, to be eaten some other day by some other predator. The unluckiest three of the rabbits were roasted over a fire. Using up all of the matches to roast the rabbits, it was a cold and bedraggled group that finally found the right lake on day six. They were too close to death to go through with the much talked about mutinous execution of their leader. It was on the afternoon of day seven that the war party circumnavigated the bay and came upon the lodge.

All four of them walked out of the woods and fired a few rounds into the lodge. "C'mon outta there an' bring the dope!" Wilf ordered. Wilf's carefully planned strategy was executed flawlessly.

Inside the lodge both captives and captors had hit the floor on the first sound of gunfire. Lawrence Musgrove peeked out of the window and saw Boucher barking orders. "It's that no-good Wilfred Boucher. Four of them, altogether, that I can see. I'll go out and talk to him."

"No, Lawrence, stay put. He knows you and Paul, so stay out of sight. From what you've told me about this guy, there's a better way. Golias, do you have any coke here?"

"There's a kilo in the top drawer of the filing cabinet in the office."

"Good. Stay put, everybody." Boone hurried to the office, crouching. He came out a few seconds later and moved toward the door. He yelled, "Hold your fire! I'll come out and talk. OK?"

"OK!" shouted Wilf Boucher.

Boone grabbed a bottle of beer from his pocket and took a drink. He motioned to Paul Desroches. Paul nodded and moved quickly toward the front door of the lodge, facing the lake. Boone moved toward the back door. He opened it slowly, giving Paul time to get in position. As he walked out, he glanced to the right out of the corner of his eye. He saw the end of a rifle barrel sticking out at the far corner of the lodge. He faced Boucher, confident that if any of them raised their rifles Paul Desroches would shoot them. He remembered the yield signs in the gravel pit and knew that he was safe. He took another gulp of beer, swaggered out to within ten feet of Boucher, and stopped. He moved a few feet to his left, ensuring that Paul had clear sight lines. By focusing their attention on himself, Boone lessened the chance that of any of them would look the other way and notice Paul's rifle.

"I'm surprised to see you guys. We could have used your help. It took us quite a while to take over the lodge and get the coke."

"Where's the lodge people?" asked Boucher.

"Feeding fish in the lake. What do you guys want?"

"We want the dope." Wilf Boucher had a one-track mind.

"And food," one of the other gang members piped up.

"And booze," added another.

"You guys are armed, and we're armed." Boone looked the part of the desperado he was playing: four days of beard growth, filthy clothes, and hair slick and matted from the bear grease. "We've got us a standoff. We can either fight or make a deal. I'm willing to deal. Why don't you guys rest up tonight? Come morning, we'll talk. If we fight, we fight then. If we deal, there's lots of dope for all of us. There's too much for my guys to carry anyway. You guys can stay up there. He pointed to the Colombian's house. I'll bring out some grub and booze."

"And some dope." Wilf Boucher was a tough negotiator.

"OK, I'll be right back." Boone went back into the lodge, then into the kitchen. He threw a random selection of canned goods into a box. He added matches and a can opener. He noticed an opened carton of cigarettes. He threw them in. He went to the bar and got a full case of rye whisky, two cases of beer, and a case of Pepsi. He stuffed the bag of cocaine into the pocket of his jacket. It took Boone three trips to take the supplies outside.

"Tomorrow we negotiate. Here's some coke." Boone removed the bag from his pocket. He reached in and put a pinch of coke on his left hand and then snorted it up his nose. He wanted to seem authentic. A few minutes later, his head exploded as a warm feeling of euphoric invincibility surged through his body. He felt fantastic. Boone quickly realized how the drug could become addictive. He tossed the bag to Boucher. Boucher and his gang each partook before continuing the dialogue.

"We need matches," someone said.

"In with the grub. Carton of smokes too."

"We'll go up to the house. You guys all stay inside. We'll be watchin' you, so no fucking monkey business."

"You need not anticipate any shenanigans from our quarters." Boone wandered out of the character he was portraying.

"Say what?" Wilf Boucher needed clarification.

"No monkey business."

"Better not be," reinforced Boucher.

"In the morning, we will apportion the contraband."

"What?"

"We'll split the fucking dope."

"OK."

Boone walked back toward the lodge. Boucher's gang had renewed faith in their leader. They walked up the hill toward the house with their supplies. Flexing the muscle of his exalted status, Wilfred Boucher did not carry anything.

Paul Desroches was beaming as he entered the lodge. "Great idea, Boone. How long before they're all passed out?"

Lawrence answered. "Just listen. When it's quiet, they'll be sleeping."

They heard someone sobbing and looked to the corner. It was Steve Appleton. They had run short of handcuffs, so two men were cuffed together using one pair. Appleton was the least dangerous of the captives, and Flip Lafontaine had a broken ankle and torn ligaments in his leg, slowing him down. One cuff was on Flip's right wrist, the other on Appleton's left. Flip tolerated the pain stoically. Appleton had a slightly sprained ankle. He was sobbing and rubbing his sore ankle with his free hand.

Flip Lafontaine had quickly established his physical superiority over Appleton in their mock-Siamese-twin incarceration. With his right hand, Flip was continually picking his nose, rubbing his head, and scratching his balls, keeping Appleton's left hand in perpetual motion. Occasionally, Flip brought his right hand up quickly, forcing Appleton to slap himself in the face. As a reaction to the sobbing, Flip reached across with his free left hand and slapped Appleton's face. "Quit whining or I'll give you something to whine about."

Appleton looked up. Seeing that no help was forthcoming, he quit sobbing to avoid another slap. He was humiliated from being treated like a common criminal. A constable was allowing a common thug to abuse him. He planned to inform the authorities about Constable Desroches' lack of concern.

With the diversion created by the arrival of Boucher, Paul had not yet recuffed O'Toole's hands behind his back. As Paul recuffed one hand, O'Toole reached out with his free hand and pulled Paul's service revolver from his holster. He stepped quickly away from Paul and ordered everyone to raise their hands, including the other prisoners.

Golias smiled. "Good man, William!"

"Stand back and keep your hands up." He waved the gun menacingly at Golias. "All I wanted was some money to buy a boat and a bit of respect from my family and my bitch ex-wife. You got me into this. It's all your fault!" he screamed at Golias.

O'Toole sincerely believed what he was saying. He should shoot Golias here and now for everything that had happened to him. He decided not to. He was not a murderer. O'Toole moved toward Golias and removed the keys to the fish-cleaning shack from his pocket. Then he removed the remaining cuff from his wrist and backed toward the door.

Everything was going to be all right. He would take as much cocaine as he could carry and head down river. He would go to Florida and sell the dope. Then, he would disappear on his boat. He smiled. Yes. He would escape this whole mess. As he stepped outside the door, two rifle shots echoed.

Wilf Boucher was sitting on the porch of the house. He had fired the shots. Wilf had been smart enough to stand guard or rather sit guard. How long he would last was another question. He had dumped out half of the contents of a liter bottle of Pepsi and refilled the bottle with Canadian Club rye whiskey. The bottle was one third finished. Not content to fly on one wing, Wilf had filled his jacket pocket with cocaine. While watching the lodge, he continuously reached into his pocket pulling out thumbnails of the potent nose candy. His gang was in no better shape. They were inside the house engaging in variations of the same behaviors.

O'Toole could easily have strolled down to the shack and made his getaway, but instead he dashed back into the lodge after he heard the two shots. Wilf Boucher was a terrible shot in the best of situations. In his impaired state, Wilf could not have put a bullet within ten feet of O'Toole. O'Toole's final escape was thwarted by his dogged bad luck; fate was not meant to smile upon him. As he re-entered the lodge, O'Toole saw Paul Desroches reaching for a rifle. O'Toole had time for one shot. If he shot Desroches, Musgrove, or Boone, there would be no place on earth he could hide. If the law-enforcement agencies failed to apprehend him, he knew that somehow, some way, Jackpine Keating surely would. O'Toole raised his gun and shot Dan Golias in the heart. Golias deserved it: not for drug smuggling, not for murder, but for ruining the life of William, not Bill, O'Toole. As Paul Desroches lifted his rifle, O'Toole raised the pistol and shot himself in the temple.

* * * * * *

Acting-detective Ron Evans questioned people all day at the post office. He sent Stew Larsen away at nine thirty because the flustered, nervous Stew was stuttering and shouting at people. Stew's questioning accomplished nothing except for making people jumpy. The unraveled Stew was pleased to take the backup role of waiting by the radio at the police station to hear from Jackpine.

Ron had no luck with his line of questioning either. He was beginning to think the mission was futile, until Slim Hiller came in just before closing to pick up his mail. "Nope. Can't say as I've seen them women folk. Did see Janice's car though, come to think of it. Out at Keating's cottage on Tamarack Lake. I wondered why they were out there this time of year and why they parked in behind the cottage instead of in the driveway. But I figgered the Keatings can do whatever they damn well please in this town. None of my business. Jackpine can fine a man for shootin' a fuckin' bird. Can do anything he takes a notion to 'round here. I was just out drivin' around lookin' for the boss. Mrs. Huhtela says Toy didn't come home last night, and that sure ain't like him."

Ron phoned Heinz immediately. Heinrich Bahr thanked him and told him to go to police headquarters and wait.

Heinrich dressed himself in black slacks, a black turtleneck sweater, and black rubber-soled shoes. He blackened his hands and face with charcoal and then pulled a black knit hat on his head, leaving his blackened ears uncovered. He attached the silencer to his pistol. It had been a long time, but the pistol felt like a familiar friend. He put the gun into the quick-release shoulder holster.

He checked the razor-sharp stiletto and replaced it in its sheath. He put binoculars, tape, wire, and wire cutters into his pockets. He checked through the window before going to his car. He did not want neighbors seeing him. He drove down Tamarack Lake Road with his parking lights on. He pulled into a vacant cottage's driveway, about half a mile before the Keating's cottage. Heinrich Bahr was pleased there was no moon.

From the woods, he looked toward the cottage. A screened-in veranda faced the lake. Behind the picture windows was the great room and kitchen: one room running the length of the cottage. Heinrich knew the hall from the great room led to two bedrooms on the left and to one bedroom and a bathroom on the right. He could see Janice, Inez, and Bertha. They were sitting at the kitchen table. Bertha was cracking and eating nuts.

As a concession to her betrothal, Bertha had committed to do what she could to avoid a weight gain that would propel her to two-chairs-at-bingo status. She thought mixed nuts in the shell were a step in the right direction. She believed that the work involved in removing the nutmeat from the shell was a form of exercise, slowing caloric intake. Bertha had become so adept at cracking nuts that she would have been an even-money bet in a nut-eating contest even against other contestants eating shelled nuts. While a nut was being chewed, another was being shelled; as the masticated nut was swallowed, a fresh replacement was popped in to repeat the process. Bertha was a nut-eating machine.

A big pile of shells littered the table. Her cavernous purse was bulging, indicating a healthy supply yet to be cracked. Bertha believed in a save-the-best-for-last philosophy. Consequently, most of her remaining inventory consisted of Brazil nuts, referred to by Bertha with a name akin to the pedal digits of African Americans. The shells of Brazil nuts were very hard and difficult to crack. It was easier to indulge in serious snacking by first attacking the wimpy nuts: walnuts, filberts, hazelnuts, and pecans.

There was an armed guard, a Colombian, in the kitchen, watching the three ladies. The guard seemed mesmerized by Bertha's prowess at cracking nuts. In the living-room section of the great room Heinrich saw two other armed guards. They also looked like Latinos to Heinrich. In the corner sat Toivo Huhtela; his hands and feet were bound. There was a big blood-stained bandage on his left hand. Three men for sure, possibly more in the bedrooms, thought Heinrich.

Heinrich circled around, well out of view to the back of the cottage. He quietly checked each bedroom window; they were locked. The bathroom window was open slightly. He did not think there were other guards sleeping in the bedrooms, but he would verify before making any move on the guards. He clipped away the screen from the bathroom window and quietly opened the window. He brought out his gun. If he were disturbed while climbing in, he would need to be prepared to act quickly. He pulled himself up through the window. There was a time when this would have been a routine maneuver. He strained to pull himself up. Once in, he reclosed the window to its original, slightly open position. He did not want them suddenly feeling a cold draft from down the hall.

He peeked around the corner from the bathroom. The hall was not visible to the guards. He quietly moved into the hall and down to the biggest bedroom. He had assumed that if someone wanted to sleep, they would have choose the queen-size bed in the master bedroom over a bunk in one of the other bedrooms.

Heinrich heard the regular breathing of someone sleeping. As he walked toward the bed, Heinrich detected a slight change in the breathing pattern—a subtle but detectable change, enough to forewarn a trained professional that the person was now awake, feigning sleep. As the form on the bed reached for his rifle, Heinrich lunged forward. Gripping the man's neck, Heinrich quickly rendered him unconscious. He tied the man's feet together and taped his hands together behind his back. Heinrich shone his light into the man's face and experienced a glimmer of vague recognition. Seconds later, he made the connection. It was one of those crude, obnoxious members of the worthless exploration crew that had been around town all summer. Heinrich did not understand the complexities of mining exploration, but he had doubted that these bums could find gold in Fort Knox. He taped the man's mouth. He listened carefully to determine if anyone had heard the activity. He decided it was safe to move.

He moved across the hall. The second bedroom was empty. He moved stealthily into the third bedroom. It too was empty. Three enemies to deal with. He would wait until one of them went to use the toilet. He would take him out, leaving two.

* * * * * *

Lawrence stepped outside and looked up toward the prefab house. It had been completely quiet for a little more than an hour. He went back into the lodge. "It's time, Paul."

"Good. You stay and watch these guys, Lawrence. Boone, you can back me up subduing Boucher and company. It looks like it will be simple." The arrest of Boucher was police work. Constable Paul Desroches, in the absence of Jackpine, had assumed command of the operation. Boone bristled but did not say anything. He was being appointed to a backup role on Paul's mission because in Paul's mind it was the easiest and least dangerous job.

Paul had found some lengths of chain and some padlocks. He used them to bind Lafontaine, Appleton, and Julius Toth. The four pairs of handcuffs were now needed in the capture of the Boucher band.

Boone grabbed his shotgun. He removed the plug and loaded it with five rounds of number-two shot. He clicked the safety off as he followed Paul up the hill toward the house. A gang member, the sentry, was sleeping on the front porch. Paul quietly walked up three steps to the porch; his service revolver was drawn and ready. He took the rifle from the hands of the sleeping desperado and handed it to Boone. Paul was able to cuff his hands behind his back without waking him.

Paul quietly opened the door, and he and Boone entered the house. Wilf Boucher and one other man were lying on the floor beside the fire. The third man was sleeping on the couch. Paul knelt beside Boucher. He rolled the sleeping thug over and cuffed his hands. Boucher didn't stir. Paul moved to the next man. As Paul rolled him over, he woke up. Startled, he tried to get to his feet. Paul moved quickly and sat on him. The man did not attempt to get up; trying to breathe was the man's only priority with the bulky Paul Desroches sitting on him. Boone watched Paul apply the cuffs.

Out of the corner of his eye, Boone detected movement to his right. The man on the couch had been awakened by the commotion of the one-sided wrestling match on the floor. As the man raised his 30-30, Boone tried to shout but no sound emanated from his throat.

Boone raised his shotgun, pointing toward the couch rather than aiming. There was no time to aim. The first blast blew a gaping hole in the wall above the couch. The second and third shots from his automatic shotgun ripped the torso of the would-be assassin. The body fell back onto the couch.

Paul Desroches looked up. "Thanks, Boone!" He turned his attention back to binding his prisoner's feet with rope. Boone wondered how Paul could be so nonchalant after coming so close to being shot. Boone's hands were trembling so actively that he had to put the shotgun down on the table. Paul moved across the floor to bind the feet of Wilfred Boucher.

The three blasts of the twelve gauge had been sufficient to revive the comatose Wilfred Boucher. He demanded clarification of the scenario leading up to this predicament. He said, "What the fuck?" Both Paul and Boone considered the question rhetorical and not worthy of a response.

They heard a noise on the porch. The sentry had also awakened and decided to dash for freedom. The freezing wilderness as a sanctuary for a man with his hands cuffed behind his back was dubious at best. Paul Desroches leaped to his feet, and in two cat-like strides he was on the porch. He raised his pistol. "Stop or I'll shoot."

The fleeing man paid no attention to the order. He was almost parallel to the back door of the lodge. *Thwack!* A hatchet whacked into the spruce tree, inches in front of the nose of the fugitive. He stopped immediately. He looked at the axe and then to his left. A calm Lawrence Musgrove was standing outside the door. "Stay right there." Lawrence did not even raise his voice; his command was obeyed.

Boone went back into the house and untied the feet of the two captives. Now that they were awake, Boone and Paul walked them back to the main lodge. It would be easier to watch the prisoners if they were all together.

* * * * * *

Jackpine Keating—his bloody nose smashed and bent, blood flowing freely over his left eye and down his face, his shirt bloody and torn with one sleeve gone—charged into the police station in a maniacal rage.

He went to his desk and got out his 45 Magnum. He loaded it.

"Where are they?"

The flustered Stew did not attempt an answer.

"Your cottage at Tamarack Lake, we think. Heinz Shultz has headed there," Ron replied.

"Stay here!" Jackpine grabbed the gun (not bothering with a holster) and his car keys.

Jackpine Keating was well past any form of subtlety. He was beyond any type of planning. He got in his cruiser and sped to Tamarack Lake. He pulled into the driveway of his cottage. With a mighty kick, the door exploded off its hinges, falling forward, narrowly missing Janice.

The ladies all jumped to their feet, backing toward the great room. The surprised Colombian in the kitchen looked at the blood-soaked monster, recoiling in horror. In close quarters, the sound of the 45 Magnum was deafening. The Colombian flew back, blood spewing from the gaping hole over his heart.

The other two guards recovered their composure. Grabbing their guns, they charged the kitchen. One guard grabbed Janice Keating by the neck, shielding himself from Jackpine. Jackpine shot over Janice's shoulder. *Poof!* The guard's head exploded as the bullet from the silenced gun found its mark.

The cool Heinrich Bahr stalked from the hall into the great room, trying to draw a bead on the remaining guard. Bertha Olesen, clutching her purse, effectively shielded the guard from Heinrich. Unfortunately, the size of the quaking Bertha in comparison to the diminutive guard also blocked Jackpine's sight line.

The guard reached around her with his left hand. His intent was to get an arm around her throat. His arm was not long enough to extend around her. Consequently, his left hand clutched her huge right breast. The unexpected fondling propelled big Bertha into action. Grabbing her purse straps with both hands, she swung the heavy projectile—with all the power her considerable torso could muster—at the groin of the unlucky guard. A plethora of rock-hard Brazil nuts struck his testicular Colombian nuts with the inevitable result. It sounded like a truck running over a large, overly ripe, rotting pumpkin. *Splat!*

The guard clutched his groin in agony. He fell forward, past the protective shield of Bertha Olesen. It may have been a time for mercy, but no sympathy would be doled out by the icy, professional Heinrich Bahr. An appeal for compassion was made by the doubled-over guard, but Jackpine Keating, the enraged bull, was stone-deaf to the request. The thundering *kaboom* of Heinrich's 45 obscured the *poof* of the equally lethal, silenced pistol. Both marksmen intently watched the body. A twitch would trigger another injection of hot lead. The body did not twitch.

"Any more, Heinz?"

"One in the master bedroom. He has been neutralized."

"Did they hurt you, darlin'?" asked Jackpine, looking toward his trembling wife. Jackpine's tone and demeanor suggested that he was fully prepared to mete out some punishment worse than death to the slain guards if she answered affirmatively. As Jackpine addressed Janice, Heinrich moved to the corner and used the stiletto to free Toivo Huhtela.

"No," she said quietly. Her high school Spanish had been sufficient for her to know that they were going to rape her and Inez soon. Not viewing Bertha as a sex object, they had planned to slit her throat. She decided not to tell Jackpine.

"What happened to you?" Janice hugged her husband, oblivious that she was being covered in blood.

"Janice, your first-aid kit, quickly," said Heinrich. He was unable to resume the persona of Heinz Shultz yet. Janice rushed to the bathroom.

Heinrich tended to Jackpine with the skill of someone

schooled in the field treatment of battle wounds. Janice, a nurse, did not interfere. She saw that she could do no better than the restaurateur. She turned to treat Toivo's hand.

Jackpine noticed Heinz's professionalism. As Jackpine reflected upon past partridge-hunting outings with Heinz, a mystery suddenly became clear. Jackpine had just solved the mystery behind Heinz's alertness, his ease and comfort in the woods, his lightning reflexes, and his deadly accuracy. Those kinds of instincts were not honed by putting icing and sugar roses on fancy cakes nor by cutting hair, thought Jackpine. There was a past that Heinz wanted buried. He had risked his privacy tonight to save Janice's life.

"Thank you, Heinz. Now everyone listen to me, carefully. Heinz was not here tonight. I take full responsibility. You must all remove from your memories, now and forever, that Heinz was here."

"Thank you, Jackpine. It means a lot to me," said Heinz Shultz. He turned to Bertha, "And I hope I never make you angry, Miss Olesen." She smiled sheepishly.

"If you were here, I would thank you," said Toivo. "And thank you, Yackpine."

"I'm taking you and Toy to the hospital. Right now!" said Janice forcefully.

"First things first, honey. I have to go to the station for a few minutes."

* * * * * *

Jackpine radioed the lodge while he was waiting for Ernest Marshall to arrive. Jackpine told Boone that Inez, Janice, and Toivo Huhtela were all safe and sound. Jackpine had decided not to tell Paul that Bertha was among the hostages until he was back in Rainbow Falls. Bertha was safe; but Julius Toth might not be, if Paul Desroches knew that Toth had kidnapped his betrothed.

Jackpine had been surprised to hear about the arrival of

Wilfred Boucher and company. He was relieved to hear that the gang of desperadoes had been subdued.

Jackpine talked to Constable Marshall for half an hour; afterwards, Marshall drove Jackpine and Toy to the hospital in Blackwater. There was another passenger in the cruiser. Stew Larsen was also going to the hospital for severe ulcer-like abdominal pains.

* * * * * *

Inez Mahoney was standing on the dock when she heard the plane coming. She had been pacing on the dock for two hours waiting to hear that sound. The OPP plane landed smoothly and taxied to the dock. Paul Desroches and Lawrence Musgrove were the first to get off. Boone, sitting in the copilot's seat, was the last to get off. The pilot was heading back to Blackbear Point Lodge. He had been happy to bring the passengers back to Rainbow Falls.

The lodge was a madhouse of activity. The flotilla of OPP at the lodge, combined with the half dozen Royal Canadian Mounted Police and the two Drug Enforcement Agency men from Minneapolis were tripping over each other in their eagerness to examine the drugs and question the prisoners. There weren't enough prisoners to go around. Flip Lafontaine and Steve Appleton were flown to the hospital in Thunder Bay. There was only Julius Toth and the Boucher gang left to entertain the inquisitors. Toth would not talk without benefit of counsel, and the Boucher group did not seem to know very much.

Inez ran toward Boone. There were tears in her eyes. She had promised herself not to cry. It was silly to cry from happiness. She yelled, "Yes I will!" as she ran to her man.

"Will what?" Boone was startled.

"I will marry you, if you still want me."

"Of course, I do!" Boone reached out to embrace Inez.

Inez felt nauseated. This was the happiest, most romantic

moment of her life, and she felt like she was going to be sick to her stomach. She fought the feeling and embraced her man. It was worse up close. He smelled like a dead animal. It was an overpowering, revolting odor.

The pilot stood on the dock as Boone and Inez walked away hand in hand. The plane's doors remained open. The pilot needed to air the plane before he left.

"Darling, you smell even worse than the last time you came back from that lodge."

"I know. I'm covered head to toe in rancid bear grease; it's a long story."

CHAPTER 16

Boone shivered as he looked out his office window. Halloween had just passed, and it was snowing. October had been filled with Icy blasts of arctic air, reminders that winter would soon have a stranglehold on the frozen north. Every time Boone was cold, he was reminded of his swim to Blackbear Point Lodge and the thought made him colder. The past year had been a triumph for Alistair Boone: he had survived his first winter in Rainbow Falls and was settling into the (once again) peaceful ebb and flow of life in the Falls. There had been times last winter (with short, cold days and long colder nights) that he had questioned his resolve. Inez Mahoney's bed had seemed like the warmest place on earth on the coldest nights, and that had made the difference.

Throughout last winter, Boone had spent one week a month at home in Manhattan. New York in January had never seemed warm and balmy before. Last winter had felt subtropical to Alistair Drayton Boone. Inez had accompanied him on the trips. By the fourth trip, the consummate salesmanship of Boone combined with the underlying allure of the great metropolis had begun to work its magic on Inez. The theater and restaurants had been important parts of the allure. Inez was now capable of stacking up a respectable number of dim-sum dishes. But it was the plethora of great museums and exhibitions that had closed the sale. At first, Inez would not go anywhere without Boone; then she had begun to make a few solo expeditions under the watchful eye of Poke Chop Miller. Now she was comfortable walking and taking cabs on her own. Inez and Susan Klein, Adam's wife, had become fast friends. Susan took Inez to museums that Boone had never heard of. Tina Rosenfeld, Sid's wife, had introduced Inez to the glory of Bloomingdale's shopping. The practical, conservative Inez rarely bought very much, but she enjoyed browsing. Bur she had become quite freewheeling about buying books at Barnes and Noble, her favorite store.

While Inez was indulging in the splendors of the big city, Boone was learning to enjoy the tranquility of Rainbow Falls. As the peace and harmony of the town worked its bucolic magic on Boone, so too was his influence felt on the town. At last count, Tony had added forty new SKUs to the shelves of his grocery store: canned escargot, straw mushrooms, hot Hungarian paprika, tofu, anchovies rolled on capers, couscous, and other such exotica. None of them were selling very well. Boone had purchased a year's supply of each of these new offerings, feeling guilty as they collected dust on the grocery store shelves.

Boone had badgered Phil into offering a free-encyclopedia promotion at his gas station. Phil's Esso was the only gas station in Rainbow Falls open during the winter months, so he already had what limited business there was. Phil doubted that people would drive more just to get a free encyclopedia, but Boone's tirade had eroded Phil's resistance. To cover the cost of the books, Phil had to raise his prices a few cents per liter of gas.

Members of the Blackwater Golf and Country Club governing board had elected their eager new member, Alistair Boone, to the position of secretary-treasurer. When they elected Boone, they had no idea of the impact that electing Boone would entail. The golf course had been built in the 1950s by Kenogami Paper; the corporation later gave the course to the town. The last two holes had never been finished, so technically it was a sixteen-hole golf course. To simulate an eighteen-hole golf experience, two holes had to be played twice. In the seventies, the sixteen-hole course had become a private country club. Until Boone arrived, no one had seemed to mind or had proposed that the other two holes be completed. As a member of the board of directors, Boone vowed to correct the abomination. Securing the treasure's job was critical to his mission; Boone knew that completion of the two additional holes would come down to savvy fiscal maneuvering.

Andrew McLeod had gladly relinquished his chairperson position at the chamber of commerce to Boone. In the spring, radio listeners heard radio ads sponsored by the chamber of commerce extolling the virtues of Rainbow Falls as a delightful vacation destination. The Falls was the only town in northwestern Ontario to enjoy the distinction of ads produced by the top creative team at one of the largest advertising agencies in the United States. Boone thought the ads could have been better, but he had not complained, since they had been produced free of charge as a favor to him.

Boone's big idea for the town had been the Winter Carnival. It would be an annual event, but it would start this winter. It took Boone a long time to convince the town's merchants of the carnival's feasibility. Now, they were all enthusiastically behind the project. Even seasonal restaurants and hotels had agreed to reopen for the carnival.

Rainbow Falls Lumber was donating lumber to the Lions Club. Over the summer, members of the Lions Club had build small ice-fishing shacks that were to be used on Dead Horse Lake. Lions members planned to offer a snowmobile shuttle service to take guests to and from the shacks. Ron Evans was in charge of working with the Ministry of Natural Resources for a fish-stocking program to make Dead Horse Lake more productive both for ice fishing and summer fishing. "We need a strong sport fishery handy to the town. That's what we're selling, and it has to be first rate for us to attract more tourist dollars." Boone had been adamant.

Boone had also pushed for a big dance, a concert, and a snowmobile race to complement the array of contests and events the townspeople had planned. The merchants had been relatively easy to convince since they stood to profit from a successful carnival. Most of the townspeople were behind it too, but some expressed concern that Alistair Boone, left unchecked, would turn Rainbow Falls into the type of town that some of them had moved a thousand miles to get away from.

No one felt the influence of Alistair Drayton Boone more than Tom at the Bamboo Garden Chinese Restaurant. The Chinese were flexible entrepreneurs. The restaurant's sign proclaimed "Cantonese and American food." If people were offended by the advertisement of "American" (instead of "Canadian") food, they never mentioned it to Tom. The sign proclaimed one feature dish: "Chop Suey." One could argue that the feature dish belonged on the American page of the menu rather than the Cantonese, but that had never been debated until the arrival of Alistair Boone.

Boone was Tom's best customer. With his penchant for entertaining, Boone had brought Tom a lot of plus business. If the sign were to accurately depict the offerings requested by Boone and prepared by Tom, the sign would have stated "Szechwan, Hunan, and select Thai dishes available upon request." Tom did not think highly of the Japanese: the food or the people. He had steadfastly refused to start a sushi bar. He had bought a small hot plate for shabu-shabu as a minor concession.

Heinrich Bahr was dead and buried. Heinz Shultz was alive and well. Event nights at the Falls View Restaurant had become an institution. They had proven to be a great way to draw the local citizens to the establishment. New Year's Day, Valentine's Day, St. Patrick's Day, Easter Sunday—they were all successful. Boone had also concocted a series of events that were not tied to holidays. Heinz no longer balked at Boone's insistence about wearing costumes. The football helmet had been hot and uncomfortable to wear, but both the Grey Cup and Super Bowl events had been well attended. Heinz had actually looked very distinguished as a sea captain on Lobster Day. He had achieved a silliness rivaled only by the pilgrim suit on Mexican Fiesta Night with his mariachi suit, big drooping black mustache, and huge sombrero. It had been a straw sombrero with little red pompoms. Otto, the butcher, had bought it on impulse during his recent Acapulco vacation. Otto had not lent the hat to Heinz; he had given it to him, with only the proviso that Heinz not admit to anyone where he had secured the sombrero.

Italian Night was a huge success, and Heinz looked quite dashing as a gondolier. The event had been repeated twice, and looked as if it might become a monthly occurrence. The only event approaching it in popularity was Oktoberfest Night. The fact that it had been held in March bothered no one. Otto was enjoying newfound business supplying meat for these extravaganzas, which was the only reason he had allowed himself to be cajoled into being a one-man oompah-pah band. Otto had looked uncomfortable in his Tyrolean mountain outfit, but Heinz looked quite at home in his.

* * * * * *

Boone's phone buzzed. His secretary, Bertha Desroches, nee Olesen, asked for an extension to her lunch hour. Boone approved it. He was not really busy enough to require a full-time secretary. He was used to having one, so he allowed himself the luxury. The newly mellow Alistair Drayton Boone was easy to work for. The only time he had really put his foot down was over Bertha's nut eating. The constant cracking of nuts annoyed him, and Bertha's desk always looked as if she was hosting a squirrels convention. Nuts were banned from the office.

Paul had been promoted to sergeant last February. To ease the financial burden on the town, Jackpine (who did not need the money) had taken a cut in pay equal to Paul's substantial raise. Jackpine considered it a bargain. Sergeant Desroches was now responsible for all the paperwork. Paul absorbed the extra workload readily. He did not like forms and reports any more than

Jackpine did, but he was pleased because the prestigious promotion and raise enabled Paul and Bertha Desroches to buy their first home.

Paul came to pick up Bertha for lunch. "Hi, Mr. Boone." Paul had reinstituted the "Mr." in addressing Boone after their return from Blackbear Point. "Could be a bit late gettin' the wife back. I've got a big appetite today. Been washing the police cruisers all mornin', thanks to you."

Boone laughed and told them to take their time. Boone knew that he was partially responsible for the sergeant having to personally wash the cruisers. The day before Paul had been lamenting that he would miss the great food at the Falls View Restaurant's Halloween dinner and not get to see Heinz as Dracula, so Boone presented Paul with a scheme to eliminate pranks. "Here's what you do, Paul. You round up the worst pranksters in town. Make all those kids special constables for one night. They'll be in charge of catching pranksters. They will patrol and have a ball. But, of course, they won't catch anyone. Any kid liable to do a prank will already be a constable. It'll work like a charm, Paul."

It was an ebullient Paul Desroches who reported for work the day after Halloween, beaming to the Chief that there had been no sign of any vandalism or shenanigans. Earlier that day, chief of the special constable brigade, Robby McLeod, had reported that no one in his group had discovered any perpetrators. A dead skunk had not been found in the visitors dressing room at the arena; no skull and crossbone flag was found flying at town hall. There had not been any switching of Stop and Yield signs, no false detours, no flat tires on the police cruisers, no "top prices for dead cats" sign on the Chinese restaurant, and no turning over the bleachers at the ball field. The trashcan in front of the fire hall had not even been set on fire. It had been the quietest Halloween in the history of Rainbow Falls.

Jackpine and Paul relied on Halloween to find "volunteers" to wash the police cruisers on Saturdays. Halloween usually supplied a staff for seven or eight months. The other months were filled in as the year progressed from an incident now and then. Robby McLeod spent so many Saturdays washing the cruisers that it was almost considered his job.

Paul Desroches, thanks to Alistair Boone's advice, was now responsible for washing both cruisers once a week. Jackpine looked forward to the day that Robby McLeod graduated from college. Once Robby had officially moved away from the Falls, Jackpine hoped Robby would tell him how he had managed to get a skunk into the visitors dressing room without stinking up his father's car. It had puzzled Jackpine for years.

* * * * * *

As Boone sat quietly in his office, he pondered his adventure at Blackbear Point Lodge. Sometimes it stirred in him a sense of macho virility, but those times were few and far between. Today he felt a deep, blue melancholy as he thought about O'Toole paying for his mistakes by putting the pistol to his head and about the shooting of Nelson Lesmontaignes in the prime of his life. Sometimes when he closed his eyes, he could see Bear Sawchuk clawing at the arrow with a blank, puzzled look on his face. He could still see the body on the couch, almost cut in half by the close blasts of the 12 gauge. Boone's bouts of depression were becoming less frequent. Time was a great healer.

There had been quite a furor when they returned from the lodge. The major drug bust had been big news, but the media had a short memory. With no further fuel to keep the story fired up, the story had quickly died. The OPP had not wanted to keep the story going. They had acknowledged the participation of William O'Toole in the operation, but naturally they wanted the whole fiasco forgotten.

Steve Appleton had cooperated fully with the investigation,

with all of the self-preservation instincts of a rat on a sinking ship: He was trying to avoid criminal prosecution. It looked as if he might avoid a jail sentence, but he was disbarred from practicing law for life. Boone considered it fair punishment.

Flip Lafontaine had confessed to murder and was facing life imprisonment. Boone considered the punishment just. Jackpine thought, hanging was too good for him.

Julius Toth had admitted to the charge of possession of cocaine for the purpose of trafficking. The charge carried a long prison sentence, but the crown attorney was pressing ahead with murder charges for the death of Special Constable Nelson Lesmontaignes. Toth had planned an expensive defense, but since CMI had fallen into bankruptcy he was unable to afford the prestigious lawyers he had initially engaged. There were many documents linking Julius Toth to the cocaine operation, but none linking the cleverer brother, Sandor Toth. Sandor might have avoided prosecution on the drug charges, had he lived.

Wilfred Boucher and the remnants of his gang were back home in prison. They could only be charged with attempted armed robbery. The charges of possession of cocaine for the purpose of trafficking were dropped when the crown attorney discovered that the drugs had been given to them by Special Constable Alistair Boone. Wilf would be free in a few years, but he would not be free long.

For Jackpine Keating, life returned to business as usual. He felt remorse over the death of Nelson Lesmontaignes, but Lawrence Musgrove had helped Jackpine absolve his soul of guilt. Lawrence said Nelson had acted rashly and would be alive today if he had done what he was told. Lawrence's consolation helped, but Jackpine's guilt would never completely dissolve. As far as Sandor Toth, Dan Golias, William (not Bill) O'Toole, Bear Sawchuk, the three pilots, the nine Colombians and the six Polarex crewmen were concerned, Jackpine rested well knowing that they all got what they deserved.

Jackpine had been chastised by the crown attorney, the OPP and the Royal Canadian Mounted Police for the methods he employed. The fact that Reeve Ron Evans had written a letter asking Jackpine to investigate Blackbear Point Lodge did not give him sufficient authority justifying his actions. Drug smuggling did not fall under the auspices of the chief of police of Rainbow Falls, and the lodge was located well beyond his jurisdiction. There were some serious threats of criminal prosecution, but Jackpine Keating stood his ground. His response to the allegations of impropriety was simply, "I didn't know how many bad apples were in the barrel. When I saw murders being covered up, I couldn't be sure it was just O'Toole involved." His statement was difficult to rebut. In the end, Jackpine was let off with a warning. And they all knew that if a similar set of circumstances were to arise in the future, Chief Keating would react exactly the same way.

* * * * * *

Boone returned his attention to business. He reviewed the third-quarter results of Rainbow Falls Lumber again. The business was running pretty much as Boone had expected, but he had made one serious miscalculation. If he had spent more time investigating the lumber business before buying Rainbow Falls Lumber, he would have anticipated the problem—but that was not Boone's style.

Chip Carpenter was delivering on his promises. Sales volume was up seventy-five percent versus the third quarter of the previous year. The groundwork was being laid to achieve record sales next spring, the upcoming peak construction season. Andrew McLeod was spending all of his time focused on improving operations, with gratifying results. The new engineer was a great help in innovating new production efficiencies. The new cost accountant had helped to identify major opportunities for cost reductions that the whole team was pursuing aggressively.

Boone's mistake had been to underestimate the reaction of the competition. He was competing with big multinational pulp and paper companies. They were not willing to sit back and watch Rainbow Falls Lumber take market share away. They were pricing their product aggressively in the markets Rainbow Falls Lumber targeted for penetration. Costs were low and sales were on forecast, but Boone was losing fifty thousand dollars a month. The large multinationals could last a lot longer in a price war than the upstart Alistair Boone. There was no end in sight to the downward spiral.

The solution to the dilemma had come from something Boone had seen at Blackbear Point Lodge and from a recent conversation with Lawrence Musgrove. Boone and Lawrence had been discussing Nelson Lesmontaignes. Boone had commented on what a fine man Nelson had been. Lawrence said there were a lot of young men like Nelson, and many of them would stay at Lac des Iles if there were jobs available. As it was, the industrious young men had to leave home to find work.

A few weeks after the conversation with Lawrence, Boone had been thinking about the Colombians' house at the lodge. The prefabricated house must have been easy to assemble, if Bear and Flip had been able to put it together. Boone had spent some time asking questions about the market for prefab homes. In boom-and-bust economies like logging, pulp and paper, and mining, prefab houses were a very viable form of housing. They were fast to put up during times of expansion, and in times of contraction, the relatively low investment made them easier to walk away from than traditional housing.

As Boone did more homework on the subject, he began to see potential for a company that constructed prefab homes. Vertical integration of a lumber company building homes was a natural fit. Without investing any additional capital, Boone had a strong connection to a captive market to supply lumber for prefab homes throughout northwest Ontario—Indian reservations.

Indian reservations were a huge potential market for prefab homes. And a construction company owned and operated by natives would naturally lock up most of that market. Boone presented the idea to Lawrence Musgrove as a way to provide employment on the Reserve. Lawrence embraced the idea enthusiastically.

Lawrence had secured financing from government agencies and the facility to produce prefab homes was under construction. Lac des Iles Homes already had orders for the first year's capacity to supply homes for other Indian reservations. In year one, the lumber requirements for Lac des Iles Homes would account for twenty-five percent of Rainbow Falls Lumber's capacity. Chip and Boone had priced the lumber to Lac des Iles Homes fairly, but profitably. The steady business from Lac des Iles Homes would enable Boone to break even on his whole operation. As Lac des Iles Homes grew, the future looked very promising for Rainbow Falls Lumber.

Boone knew that Lac des Iles Homes would grow; he would personally make sure. Lawrence had retained Boone as a management consultant. Lawrence was paying Boone the same rate that he had received as a special constable, a dollar per year. Boone did not have to spend much time at Rainbow Falls Lumber; he was enjoying giving business advice to Lac des Iles Homes two days a week.

Boone had given up his office at Rainbow Falls Lumber. He was confident that Andrew and Chip were fulfilling their obligations competently. The goals of the company were established, the strategies to achieve the goals were developed, and the systems to monitor progress were firmly in place. It was time for Boone to step back and let the managers manage. Timely, accurate feedback from sales to manufacturing, combined with the improved maintenance of equipment and the open lines of communication on the floor, had enabled them to eliminate or greatly reduce the huge inventory of finished goods and work in process. On most items, they were manufacturing to the orders they had in house.

The consistency of the quality of the product was much better. People reacted much faster to quality problems with a two-day inventory than they had with a six-month cushion of finished goods. Consequently, the service levels to their customers were vastly improved. It would take longer than six months to build a reputation for quality and service, but they were going in the right direction. It was difficult to compete with West Coast mills on quality. The huge trees they used were inherently superior lumber. But by paying attention to detail and running a tight ship, Andrew was confident they could overcome the disadvantage.

As Lac des Iles business developed, Boone was going to add a plywood-making operation to the mill. He was going to wait until the mill was profitable and able to fund the required equipment investment through operations.

After so many years of long days at full speed, Boone was not accustomed to so much free time. He would never fully adjust to the cadence of life in Rainbow Falls, but he had made great strides.

Mornings had been a difficult adjustment for Boone. There was a table in the corner of the hotel restaurant that was sacred ground. Everyone in town understood the ritual. Unaware tourists would be shooed away from the table, mildly rebuked for their impertinence. There were six chairs at the table. Every weekday morning sometime between eight and nine o'clock, each chair would be occupied by its heir. Members of the coffee klatch included Jackpine Keating, Toivo Huhtela, Stew Larsen, Ron Evans, Heinz Shultz, and Phil from Phil's Esso. Boone, not understanding ritual or tradition, had taken it upon himself to add a seventh chair. The other members had accepted the gesture.

The six-chair table had been permanently reset, probably the only one in North America, as a seven-person table. When Boone had first joined the coffee klatch, he would gulp down a few quick cups of coffee and rush off to his office; these days there was not much need to rush.

Boone's typical workday began over coffee with Andrew McLeod and Chip Carpenter at seven thirty at the mill. By eight, he was usually the first man at the table, and he was usually still there at nine when Heinz Shultz arrived. Heinz would park the school bus in a no-parking zone in front of the hotel. Understanding Heinz's reluctance to miss the morning ritual, Jackpine overlooked the misdemeanor. The diligent Sergeant Desroches was also asked to overlook the speeding yellow bus on its return trip from Blackwater High School.

Bertha Desroches returned to the office at 1:30, looking well fed. Of course, Bertha and Paul always looked well fed and in this case looks were not deceiving. Boone envied their copious lunch. He was dieting and had lost fifteen pounds. Wedding pictures tended to hang in prominent places forever. The wedding was scheduled for summer; Inez would be a June bride.

Inez was down in Blackwater at the municipal office. She was going to be back at 2:00 for a late lunch with Boone at the Bamboo Garden. Boone did not want to leave the office while Bertha was out, in case the phone rang. It hadn't.

Boone bundled up in his L.L.Bean down parka. He put on his tuque and pulled it down cover his ears. He wrapped his long, woolen scarf around his face and put on his moose-hide mittens. He thought he would walk over and talk to Jackpine, while he waited for Inez. It was a short walk. Boone had rented the office vacated by former attorney Steve Appleton. The locals teased him mercilessly about the way he dressed. Boone accepted the kidding good-naturedly. Because the cold chilled him to the bone, he was not prepared to alter his attire.

As he walked toward the police station, he noticed an airplane cavorting in the sky. He stopped to watch. The plane performed a loop-the-loop, flew straight up until the engine stalled, and then plummeted in a spiral toward the ground. Boone's heart was in his mouth. At the last possible second, the pilot started the engine and pulled the plane up. Boone watched dumbstruck as the plane began to dive-bomb Dead Horse Lake: Each time, the pilot came closer to impact with the frozen surface. Boone waited until the plane appeared to have landed before rushing into Jackpine's office to tell him.

Jackpine smiled when Boone told him. "I know, Boone; it was Toy Huhtela."

"Has the old Finn gone crazy?"

"Maybe. Any man who makes a livin' blowin' things up has to be a little crazy. But I asked him to take the joyride. Seems Robby McLeod is going to become a bush pilot when he graduates grade thirteen next June."

"I know. Andrew is very perturbed. He wants Robby to get an engineering degree. Then he can do whatever he pleases," said Boone.

"I agree with Andrew." The phone rang.

"It worked like a charm." It was Toivo Huhtela. "I didn't think I could scare a kid like Robby. I decided to do stuff that even scared me. Robby said he's going to college."

"Where is he now?"

"He's puking. Then he's going to tell his dad."

"Thanks for the help, Toy!" Jackpine hung up.

"You manipulative son of a bitch. You told Toy to take Robby for a ride and scare the shit out of him."

"I confess. I figured Toy could make it work."

Inez Mahoney walked in. Boone rushed over and gave her a big kiss. The moment was as exciting as the first time he had kissed her. While they were nuzzling, Jackpine redirected his attention to the report in front of him. He was not a geologist, but he understood the gist of the report.

Jackpine knew that the conglomerate that owned Spruce Hill Mine had lost interest in the property. The property satisfied some accountant somewhere, resting comfortably on the balance sheet as an asset. Jackpine had collected some random samples from the slag heaps at the mine and had sent the samples to a company in Thunder Bay for analysis. Slag was everything left over after the precious ounces of gold were extracted from the ore. The report was preliminary (more exhaustive studies would need to be carried out), but the initial conclusion indicated the ore contained enough zinc to sustain a functional zinc mine. There was also evidence of substantial copper deposits. Jackpine decided to keep the information to himself for the time being.

He wanted Boone to focus his energies on the lumber mill and on getting the prefab-home business up and running. When that was done, Jackpine knew that Boone would get antsy. Then all he had to do was show Boone the report, and nature would take its course. Alistair Drayton Boone, Hard Rock Miner, would look after it from there.

Jackpine Keating was quite pleased with himself. Rainbow Falls had survived a crisis. The town would live. Justice had been served at Blackbear Point Lodge. He thought Julius Toth and Flip Lafontaine should hang, but the world was not perfect. The DEA was close to nailing the elusive Mr. Mendez, probably the guiltiest of all the culprits in the mind of Jackpine Keating. When Inez Mahoney was off gallivanting with Boone, Boone always provided Bertha Desroches to fill in for Inez. As sergeant, Paul's responsibilities included all the paper. From Jackpine's perspective, things were working out just fine.

Jackpine closed the report and looked up. The union had taken years to accomplish, but Jackpine always knew that Inez Mahoney and Alistair Drayton Boone went together like blueberry pie and ice cream.

THE END

About The Author

 Keith Charles Koski (1950–2006) was the eldest son of Charles Koski and Dorothy (Mitchell) Koski. His father Charlie was a tall, handsome man, a proud Finn, and a respected war hero in the community. His mom was a smart, funny, resourceful woman who loathed the Canadian bush but dearly loved her family and family life while living in a small town surrounded by Canadian wilderness. Keith grew up in northern Ontario in the town of Terrace Bay, located on the north shore of Lake Superior, 125 miles east of Thunder Bay along Highway 17.

In the late 1940s, the Canadian government constructed a $10 million dam for the purpose of generating hydro-power to support a $53 million paper and pulp mill processing plant. So, instead of using Aguasabon Falls to shoot lumber to Lake Superior for an American company to convert into pulp, the Canadian government undertook a joint venture with Kimberly-Clark to convert pulp in Canada, generating $15 million in American business in pulp per year. In 1947, the town of Terrace Bay was established as a company town by Kimberly-Clark with the building of the pulp and paper mill.

Until completion of Highway 17 (part of the Trans-Continental Canadian Highway) in 1960, there was no road through Terrace Bay, so workers, residents, and supplies all arrived by rail. In addition to being the town's sole employer, Kimberly-Clark was also the lead developer of the community's basic infrastructure and social buildings. By the early 1950s, the town included a small hospital, a post office, a bank, schools, and churches. A recreation center was completed in 1953, consisting of an arena, a curling club, a restaurant, a bowling alley, and a library. Hundreds of homes were built by Kimberly-Clark and over the years these homes were sold to employees at affordable rates.

Keith and his family prospered in this booming bush town. His father worked in the mill, advancing to foreman, and his mother worked at the bank as the sole bank clerk (an unheard-of precedent for a woman at the time). If you acted up at the Legion, you could count on Charlie Koski to grab you by the scruff of your neck and the seat of your pants and throw you head first out of the Legion; and if you needed a loan, you would make an appointment with Dorothy Koski to discuss the details.

Much of Keith's childhood was spent in the bush learning the old ways of living off of the land. The bush was his childhood playground, and his father, his father's friends, and the native Indians were his playmates. He was a natural outdoorsman. He loved the adventures of portaging the waterways, building rafts and shelters in search of bountiful fishing. During these early years, he learned to think like the game he was sporting. From his elders and the native Indians who befriended him, he learned to think like a rabbit, a mink, a fish, and other wildlife that inhabited the bush.

Keith was a voracious reader and a precocious child. He devoured books and was known for reading the entire Encyclopedia Britannica by the age of twelve with remarkable comprehension. If asked what he wanted to be when he grew up, he would stand tall with his shoulders straight back and confidently proclaim "either president of General Motors or prime minister of Canada." For this small-town child who loved his Tom Sawyer–like childhood, the sky was the limit.

He spent his summers on a family farm branding cattle and baling hay for a penny a bale. He learned very early how to do a man's job. After skipping two grades in school and upon completion of grade thirteen, he headed off to university at the age of fifteen. Keith attended and graduated from the University of Manitoba in Winnipeg, Canada. During his summers, he worked as a fishing guide in the Northwest Territories of Canada. To Keith, guiding was heaven on earth.

Keith graduated with a degree in English and tried his hand at teaching and a few other jobs after college, but these opportunities did not suit him. He was an independent thinker and a man who did not need much direction. He also realized that politics and public service were not his calling.

Without any sales experience or understanding of the position, he interviewed for a sales position with the Bic Corporation. During the interview, he asked and cared about the answers to two questions: 1) how often would there be meetings; and 2) how often would he have to write reports. The answers were 1) there were no regularly scheduled meetings; and 2) reports could be communicated verbally. Keith was thrilled, and he was offered the sales territory of the province of Saskatchewan, Canada.

Keith found his calling in those early years with the Bic Corporation. He created marketing programs for gas stations, grocery stores, and hotel chains that resulted in record sales of Bic pens and lighters. Keith loved the game of business, and he quickly learned his way around a P&L and the boardroom. He was also notorious for combining his love for life with his love for business. In order to meet professionals whom he admired, he created ad campaigns around them—he hired Ken Follett to sign books with a Bic pen and Wayne Gretsky to promote Bic shavers. His fifteen-year career with the Bic Corporation culminated in him achieving the position of vice president of North American, with P&L responsibilities for operations and marketing in Canada, the US, and Mexico.

Over the next decade, Keith went on to run companies for investment bankers. He participated in leveraged buyouts in several consumer-goods industries. He would learn each industry, the players, and the competition better than the veterans in the industry, then train and mold his army to outperform the competition. Keith was a one-win-all-win leader, and as such his staff would attempt to move mountains on his orders. They called him "Chief," and he wore the moniker with a fierce sense of pride and responsibility.

I met Keith in 1992 at a lamb roast that my father was hosting at his country club. My brother Angelo was stopping by with his boss after a busy day of sales calls. I was making a surprise out-of-town visit. Keith and I were captivated by each other from the moment we met. We would share the next fourteen years of our journeys together.

It is with great honor that I publish his book in his memory. Our life together was a storybook tale, a love affair that never faded: I was Cinderella, and he was Prince Charming. Thank you, Keithie.

In loving memory,

Sandra Ferconio

www.ingramcontent.com/pod-product-compliance
Lightning Source LLC
Chambersburg PA
CBHW030531270626
47155CB00024B/2687